the Rising

I looked down to see the skin on my palms thickening, roughening. Hair had sprouted on the back of my hands. My cheeks itched, too, and when I reached up, I knew what I'd feel—the planes of my face changing, more hair sprouting. I barely had time to think "I'm shifting" when my knees gave way, like someone kicked them from behind. I fell to all fours, heaving, the air suddenly too thin, my chest too tight.

Not now. Please not now.

KELLEY ARMSTRONG

the Rising

KELLEY ARMSTRONG

www.atombooks.net

ATOM

First published in the United States in 2013 by HarperCollins
First published in Great Britain in 2013 by Atom

Copyright © 2013 by KLA Fricke Inc.

The moral right of the author has been asserted.

A CIP catalogue record for this book
is available from the British Library.

ISBN 978-1-907410-99-4

Printed and bound in Great Britain by
Clays Ltd, St Ives plc

Papers used by Atom are from well-managed forests
and other responsible sources.

MIX
Paper from
responsible sources
FSC® C104740

Atom
An imprint of
Little, Brown Book Group
100 Victoria Embankment
London EC4Y 0DY

An Hachette UK Company
www.hachette.co.uk

www.atombooks.net

For Julia

ONE

I WAS RUNNING THROUGH the forest. Running on all fours, huge tawny paws touching down so lightly they seemed to skim the ground. Yet somehow my pursuers were catching up. The pounding of their boots was so close I swore my tail switched against them as I ran.

I couldn't keep this up. Cougars are sprinters, not distance runners. I had to get into the brush, up a tree, someplace, anyplace where I could hunker down, invisible, until they passed, and then—

A dart hit my shoulder. I reared back, snarling, clawing—

"Maya!"

Hands gripped my front legs. No, not legs. Arms. I saw hands wrapped around my wrists, a familiar face in front of mine—wavy blond hair in need of a brush, blue eyes underscored with dark circles, wide mouth tight with worry and exhaustion.

"Daniel . . . ?"

He released my wrists.

Corey's voice sounded to my left. "Um, guys? Causing a bit of a scene here."

I looked around to see strangers staring. A man in a button-down shirt was making his way over, gaze fixed on us. Behind him was a counter stacked with books. In front of me was a computer, while Corey was seated at another beside me.

A library. We were in a library.

The man walked over. "Is there a problem here?" He was looking at me and I wasn't sure why, until he shot a glare at Daniel and I realized how it must have looked, him holding my wrists as I struggled.

"No," I said. "We were just . . . goofing around."

Not the right thing to say in a library. Even Corey—the king of goofing around—winced.

"I'm sorry," Daniel said. "It won't happen again."

As he spoke, he held the librarian's gaze and kept his voice low, calm. Using his powers of persuasion. With Daniel, it really is a power. I don't think the librarian needed it, though. He seemed content to leave us be. But the incident had caught the attention of people around us and, under the circumstances, we really couldn't afford to make ourselves memorable. So we left. Quickly.

"Well," Corey said as we tramped down the front steps. "It's not the first time we've had to leave a library. But it is the first time I wasn't responsible."

"I was having a vision," I said. "I can't control those."

"Uh, no, Maya. Unless you snore during your visions, you were asleep."

"I don't snore." I looked at Daniel. "Tell him I don't snore."

Daniel feigned great interest in the fountain. Corey didn't ask how Daniel would know if I snored. Daniel and I had been best friends since kindergarten. Though our parents had decided sleepovers required separate rooms years ago, we'd spent the last few days sleeping side-by-side as we trekked through the wilds of Vancouver Island. Not a voluntary hiking trip, either. A helicopter crash had stranded us with Corey and three other friends. That helicopter had been supposedly rescuing us from a forest fire that threatened our town, but it'd actually been kidnapping us. Now, less than a week later, we were in the city of Vancouver, only the three of us left, the others captured by the people we were still fleeing.

"You were exhausted," Daniel finally said. "Corey and I slept on the ferry. You didn't. I would have let you keep sleeping . . . but the snoring *was* getting kinda loud."

I aimed a kick at him. He grabbed my foot and held it, making me dance and curse. A passing security guard shot us a warning look.

"Holy hell," Corey said. "It's a sad day when I'm the responsible one. Speaking of responsibility, I'm going to take the reins of leadership and suggest food. It's nearly eight. Maya, use that cat nose and lead us to dinner."

Yes, my dream hadn't been pure fantasy. I was a shape-shifter. I'd discovered my secret identity about a week ago. Not surprisingly, it marked the point where life went to hell— for all of us.

I wasn't the only supernatural kid in our tiny town. In fact, Salmon Creek seemed to have been built as a petri dish to resurrect extinct supernatural types. Project Phoenix. I was a skin-walker, like Rafe and Annie, a brother and sister who'd come to Salmon Creek looking for answers. Daniel was a benandanti—a demon-hunter. As for Corey, we were pretty sure he had powers, too, but we didn't know what they were yet.

And as for the people chasing us, it was two groups, actually. The St. Clouds—who'd founded our town and Project Phoenix—and the Nasts, a rival supernatural corporation that thought we seemed like valuable commodities. Our friends were now divided between the groups, and we were on the run, trying to find someone to help us get them back. We wanted something else back, too: our parents. They'd been told we'd died in that helicopter crash. I'd been trying very hard not to think about that, what they were going through. I just kept telling myself it would all be fixed soon. It had to be.

We ate dinner in a chain restaurant. It wasn't one we knew, and we'd stood inside the door for five minutes, going over the menu, feeling like country mice in the city. That's nothing new. We grew up in a town of two hundred people. Put us in a metropolis of two million, and it didn't matter that we were private-school educated and wearing the same labels as every other kid—we still felt like hicks.

"This is what we need, guys," Daniel said after we ordered. "A huge city where we can just blend in and lie low for a few days."

"I know," Corey said. "But I feel . . ." He looked around at the other tables and scowled. "It's the St. Clouds' fault. All those years of stranger-danger classes, teaching us that no one outside Salmon Creek can be trusted. They did that on purpose."

"I know," I murmured.

"Teaching us to be afraid of the outside world so we'd never leave, when the real danger wasn't out here at all. It was right there. With everyone who was supposed to be looking out for us. Everyone we were taught to trust. Our teachers. Our doctors. Even some of our own parents might have been in on it. Hell, I'm not even sure my mom wasn't . . ."

He trailed off. I didn't rush to tell him I'm sure she hadn't been a willing participant. We'd already been through this. There were no guarantees.

In Corey's face, bitter and angry, I could find no trace of the guy I'd grown up with, the one who was always grinning, always up to something, never thinking any further ahead than the next party.

I cleared my throat. "So, what did you guys find out while I was sleeping on the job?"

We'd gone to the library to research a name that Rafe's mother had given him to contact as a last resort. We had no idea if this guy could—or would—help us, but it was our only shot.

"Cyril Mitchell is an unusual enough name. I narrowed it down to the most likely guy—the others were too young. I have a phone number, but that's it." Daniel unfolded two notes from his pocket. Scrap paper from the library. He ran his finger down his notes and let out a deep breath. If Corey looked bitter, Daniel looked defeated, and it was just as painful to see.

"It's okay," I said. "We call the number. We talk to whoever answers. That's all we can do."

One of the toughest parts about making that call was picking a pay phone. Not only are they rare these days, but we wanted one a fair distance from where we'd spend the night. Sure, the risk that someone was tapping this guy's phone—or that he was working for the people chasing us—was slight. But right now we only trusted one another.

6

We caught the SkyTrain and found a pay phone. Then I prepared to call the man we hoped was the right Cyril Mitchell.

While Rafe had been captured the first time, he'd found information about another experiment: Project Genesis. The kids who'd been guinea pigs in that one had supposedly escaped, along with their parents. Rafe was sure Mitchell would know more. If we could find those subjects, maybe they could help us.

I pumped five dollars in coins into the pay phone and dialed.

When a woman answered, I asked to speak to Cyril Mitchell.

"Sorry, wrong number," she said.

I read her back the number I'd dialed.

"That's right, but there's no one named Cyril here."

Before she could hang up, I said, "I really need to get in touch with Mr. Mitchell and this is the only number I have."

"I'm sorry. I can't help you."

My mind whirred, trying to think of something else to say before she hung up. But she stayed on the line. As if she was waiting.

"Do you know any way to get in touch with Mr. Mitchell?" I asked finally.

"No."

So why aren't you hanging up?

If Mitchell knew about Project Genesis and Project Phoenix, both top-secret supernatural experiments, maybe he was on the run, too. Maybe this woman was waiting for something—a name, a code word.

But if he's on the run, why would Daniel be able to find his number so easily?

Maybe it wasn't the right Cyril Mitchell. Or maybe it was and she could tell I was young and I was scared, and didn't want to hang up on me.

I took deep breaths and clenched the receiver.

This was our only lead. Our *only* lead. I couldn't let it slip away.

"I'm going to leave a message," I said. "Just in case." I chose my words carefully. "My name is Maya Delaney. I'm a Phoenix from Salmon Creek, British Columbia."

I paused. It took at least three seconds for her to say, "I'm sorry, but you really do have the wrong number." Which told me she'd been listening, maybe even writing it down.

"Just take the message. Please. Maya Delaney. Phoenix. Salmon Creek. He can contact me at . . ." I read off the email account Corey had set up at the library. "Do you need me to repeat any of that?"

A long pause. Then, "He can't help you, Maya."

My heart thudded. This *was* Mitchell's number. "Can I speak to him? Please?"

"Not without a—" She stopped herself. "He died six months ago. I'm his daughter."

I took a deep breath. Tried not to panic. "Okay. Can you help? Or can you give us the name of someone who can? Please?"

"No." A pause. "I'm sorry."

She hung up.

TWO

WE SPENT AN HOUR trying to call back. We even used different pay phones. She wasn't answering and she'd turned off the voice mail.

We took refuge in a half-constructed condo building. There were plenty of them around. Vancouver had been booming a few years ago, insanely priced condos popping up everywhere, eyes fixed on the Olympics. Then the economic crisis hit and developers fled.

We hadn't said much since our last attempt to call Mitchell's daughter. There was nothing to say except "What now?" and no one dared ask that. When the silence got too heavy, I snuck off to the highest level with a solid floor—seven floors up. I perched on the edge, letting my legs hang over as I stared toward the distant ocean. Toward my island.

I ran my fingers over the worn leather bracelet on my wrist, over the cat's eye stone. Rafe's bracelet, the one he'd given me.

A few minutes later I heard footsteps. Daniel.

He didn't come over and I didn't turn, in case he was just checking on me. I heard him settle behind me. Then silence, broken only by the soft sound of his breathing.

"You going to stay back there?"

His sneakers scuffed the floor as he rose. "I didn't want to disturb you."

I held my hand up behind me, and his fingers closed around mine. I clasped his hand, feeling the heat of it chase away the October chill. He sat beside me, his legs dangling, too.

"We need to find these other subjects," I said. "Project Genesis."

"I know, but . . . At the library, I searched on all kinds of words from those pages Rafe gave us. There's nothing. It's a dead end."

Silence thudded down again. I stared out at the city and tried to rouse myself. We had to move. We had to do something. The thoughts would skitter through my brain, only to be swallowed by a yawning black pit. Move where? Do what? Our only lead was gone and I felt lost. Too beat down to even look up for a spot of light.

"I think we should go to Skidegate and try to contact your grandma," Daniel said.

I looked at him. I wanted to shout for joy and throw my arms around his neck and thank him for giving me exactly what I wanted—contact with my family. But I only had to look at him, his eyes anxious, his face drawn, holding himself still as he awaited my response, and I knew this wasn't about choosing the right path. It was about making me happy. Or making one of us happy. Lifting the dark cloud for one so we could all breathe a little easier. He knew I wanted this more than anything. So he was giving it to me, caution be damned.

"I . . . don't think that would be safe," I said slowly.

"We could make it safe. We'd go over to the Queen Charlotte Islands and make contact with one of her friends, ask them to take her a note. She's a smart lady. If she knows what's going on, she'll find a way to meet us without being followed."

"You've thought this through."

"I've gone over all the options. There's my brothers, but they're too far away and I'm not sure how much help they'd be." His two older brothers were at university in Toronto and Montreal—clear across the country. "Corey's grandparents are in Alberta, but he said they wouldn't understand—they'd call his mom right away."

We couldn't let that happen—if our parents found out we were alive—and we weren't there to warn them—they'd confront the Cabals, not knowing how dangerous they were.

Daniel continued, "I've never met Corey's grandparents,

anyway. I've met your grandma. So has Corey. He's good with it."

I looked out over the city.

"It's not like we have a lot of choice, Maya," Daniel murmured. "Either we sit here waiting for divine intervention or we take a risk."

"It's not a short trip," I said. "We'd need to take the train to Prince Rupert and the ferry over. We wouldn't have much money left."

"We wouldn't need it once we made contact. Before we get on that train, we need to make sure she's there. Call again tomorrow and see if she answers—don't say anything, just confirm she's home. I don't know if she would be—she thinks you're dead, and the funerals . . ."

He trailed off. By now our parents might have buried us. Buried empty caskets, our remains lost at sea. We tried not to think about that, and sat there for a little longer, staring into the night.

"I know you're worried about Rafe," Daniel said at last. "You haven't said anything, but you must be."

I nodded. "He double-crossed the St. Clouds to protect us. I'm afraid they'll punish him. Not just him, though; I'm worried about everyone. Sam, Hayley, Kenjii, Nicole."

Did he notice I said my dog's name before Nicole's? I hadn't meant to, but the truth was that I wasn't at all worried about Nicole. She'd killed my best friend because Serena was dating Daniel. He didn't know that. Worse, at the time of Serena's death, he'd been ready to break up with her and if he'd just done it a little sooner, she'd still be alive. I hadn't told him because I didn't want to put that kind of burden on him. So I had to pretend I was still concerned about Nicole, too.

"It's not just worry," I said. "I feel responsible. Like they're waiting for us to rescue them and we have no idea how to do that."

He put his arm around my waist and pulled me, so I could lean against him. "We'll do our best."

I closed my eyes and tried to block the mechanical roar of the city and imagine my forest instead, the sigh of wind through redwoods, the buzz of thrush and the whistle of marmots, the soft drip of rain. It took awhile, but soon I was able to hear them, and when I did, exhaustion took over and I drifted off to sleep.

There was still no answer at my grandmother's place. She volunteered at the heritage center, most recently in project management. She was Haida, like my mom. Mom wasn't really active in the Native community, but Grandma was. I help her out with festivals and such, but I always feel a little out of place. I'm adopted and I am Native, but Navajo, not Haida. I don't know much about that part of my heritage, except that it doesn't usually come with the ability to shape-shift into a wildcat. I'm just special. Unfortunately.

There was a really good chance, then, that I knew the

woman who answered the phone at the heritage center, but not well enough to recognize her voice. And, thankfully, she didn't recognize mine.

"Hi," I said. "My name is Joy. I know this is going to sound weird, but I'm trying to get in touch with Maya Delaney's parents."

A sharp intake of breath on the other end.

"I know what happened," I said. "My mom saw it in the paper. We have a cottage near Salmon Creek, so I'd met most of the kids who died, and I wanted to let Maya's parents know how sorry I am about everything. But no one's answering the number I have. I remember she said her grandma worked at the heritage center in Skidegate, so I'm sorry to bother you, but this was the only thing I could think of."

"I'm afraid I can't help, either," the woman said. "Her parents are in Vancouver for the funeral."

"Vancouver?" I thought I'd misheard and she'd said Victoria.

"Maya's grandmother was hoping it would be on the island, but the people who ran the town are in charge, and I guess . . ." She trailed off. "I know they took the parents to Vancouver after the crash. Maybe they think going back to the island would be too much of a reminder. It's all such a horrible tragedy. I think everyone's just relieved someone else is handling the arrangements."

Yes, I was sure the St. Clouds were happy to make the arrangements. Get the families to Vancouver—farther from us—after the crash. Hold the service there so it would be smaller. Get this charade over with as fast as possible, then whisk them off to parts unknown.

"Have they had the funeral already?" I asked. "I was kind of hoping to go."

"It's the day after tomorrow. You should be able to find details in the Victoria newspaper. Maya's grandmother has a cell phone, but she's spending the day on Galiano at a friend's cabin. A retreat before the funeral. She'll be out of touch while she's there."

We'd spent time at my grandma's friend's place on Galiano. I could get us there, and it was a lot closer than Skidegate.

THREE

GALIANO IS THE SECOND largest of the Gulf Islands, between the mainland and Vancouver Island. It was an hour ferry ride, after catching a coach bus down to the terminal in Tsawwassen. From the ferry stop, we had a five-kilometer hike to the cabin, which was about as remote as you could get on the island.

By the time we arrived, it was after five. The cottage was a tiny artist's studio on a small windswept bluff overlooking the strait. There was an empty cabin about fifty meters away, and that's where we took refuge, hunkering down in its shadow to watch the studio and wait for my grandmother to come out.

Her car was in the drive, and a thin line of smoke rose from the wood-stove chimney, so I knew she was there. I expected her to come out at any moment. It's a tiny studio and Grandma hates being cooped up inside as much as I do. When we came here for weekends, I'd wake to find her already gone—walking the beach or gathering berries or just sitting on the deck, drinking tea and enjoying the morning. Yet today, despite the rare break of fall sunshine, the doors never opened.

"She's not coming out," I said.

This was stupid. Foolish. We should have stayed in Vancouver.

And done what?

That was the question, wasn't it? *And done what?* Hide forever? Give up dreams of a reunion with our families and reconcile ourselves to a life on the streets? None of us suggested that. We'd sooner take our chances with the St. Clouds and the Nasts. Corey and I would never surrender the hope of being with our families again. Daniel would—his father was an abusive alcoholic, his mother long gone—but he still wanted to return to some semblance of a normal life.

Corey scanned the quiet road. "There's no one around. Maya, why don't you go knock on the door. It's not like anyone's going to be watching the place."

"Are you sure?" Daniel said.

Corey shifted. "Look, I know we need to be careful, but"—he waved a hand around—"we're in the middle of nowhere. It's the cottage of her grandmother's friend. How would we even know she was here? No one's going to expect this."

"You're sure of that? Sure enough to bet Maya's freedom on it?"

Corey swore under his breath. "I didn't mean it like that."

"I know," I said. "You're right. We need to take a chance. But it's almost seven now. It'll be dark soon. Once it is, I can get to the cabin, get her attention, and get her to let me in."

Daniel shook his head. "If she sees you through a window, she might react loud enough for anyone watching to overhear. I should—"

"I'll do it," Corey said. "First, she knows me the least, so she'll have the least reaction to seeing me alive. Second, I'm the guy you can most afford to lose."

"We can't afford to lose anyone," I said.

"Let's not go through this again, okay? I don't need you guys to make me feel important. You and Daniel got us this far and you're the ones most likely to get us out. From now on, if someone needs to take a risk, it's me. Always me."

We finally agreed that it would be him *this time*. It was true that Daniel and I had done most of the planning so far. We'd all grown up together in a very small school, where Daniel and I were the class leaders, not because we were awesomely perfect, but because we tended to take charge naturally and the others were happy to kick back and let us shoulder that responsibility. In a crisis, they'd done the same.

Yet everyone had played their part in this ordeal. Often, that role had been the sacrificial lamb. Hayley, Sam, and Rafe had all let themselves be captured so the rest of us could escape. And with every sacrifice they made, the pressure to honor it by saving them grew greater, and I felt less worthy of it.

So we waited for dark. And as we waited, I became more and more anxious. It was already driving me crazy, being this close to my grandmother, with her in there grieving for me. I kept thinking Corey was right, we were being overly paranoid and maybe, in that paranoia, losing our best chance. Maybe it wasn't just paranoia, either. Maybe we'd become cowards. Unwilling to take a risk if it meant we might be captured, too.

"I need to move," I said finally as dusk fell.

We were sitting against the neighboring cottage, the long grass hiding us. Nobody had spoken in almost an hour and when I did, the guys both jumped.

"I just want to take a walk." I glanced down at my trembling hands and clenched them into fists. "I'll be careful."

Daniel looked at me, his head tilted, eyes dark, like he wanted to do something or say something. "Okay," he said finally. Then, voice lowered another notch, "It'll all be over soon."

You'll see her soon is what he meant. I nodded and said I wouldn't be long, then crawled through the long grass to a stand of forest. Only when I was deep enough in did I rise and begin to walk.

Being in the forest only reminded me of *my* forest, which reminded me of my parents and our lives there and made me wonder whether we'd ever be able to go back. Almost certainly we wouldn't go back. Salmon Creek was lost to us. My forest was lost to me.

And it was only then that I truly understood what I'd had—a damned near perfect life. Days spent tramping through the wilderness with my dog, with Daniel, endless idyllic days when we had nothing more to worry about than planning the next school fund-raiser. Even that was hardly stressful—we'd put on an event and the town would open its wallets. The St. Clouds would make a huge donation, and everyone would tell us what an amazing job we'd done. Now I wondered if we could have slapped together a bake sale with tables full of stale Rice Krispies Treats and gotten the same results.

The scientists had wanted us to grow up healthy and confident. Most of all, though, they wanted us to be happy, so that when we discovered the truth, we'd be okay with it.

Would we have been okay with it? No. We'd never have forgiven them for the lie. But could we have reconciled ourselves to a life as research subjects and future Cabal employees? I should say no. Emphatically no. Yet I can see a future where that might have happened. If they'd raised us knowing what had been done to us and why. And if they'd given us a choice. Accept what we're offering or you're free to leave.

I grieved for the loss of my old life, and I worried about my parents and my friends, and I couldn't even walk it off because the patch of forest was so narrow. So I had to circle, which started to feel like pacing, and only made me all the more anxious. When my palms began to itch, I rubbed them against my jeans, still pacing, until the faint rubbing sound turned into a harsh rasp. I looked down to see the skin on my palms thickening, roughening. Hair had sprouted on the back of my hands. My cheeks itched, too, and when I reached up, I knew what I'd feel—the planes of my face changing, more hair sprouting. I barely had time to think "I'm shifting" when my knees gave way, like someone kicked them from behind. I fell to all fours, heaving, the air suddenly too thin, my chest too tight.

Not now. Please not now.

I closed my eyes, fingers digging into the dry earth, willing the transformation to stop. Pain ripped through me and I gritted my teeth against a scream.

This hadn't happened before. It never hurt before.

Because you didn't fight it before.

But I had to stop it. I should be able to stop it.

Only I couldn't, and the harder I tried the more it hurt, the pain so strong I nearly passed out. If I did, then I'd finish the transformation in my sleep, as I had before. Either I let it happen or I passed out and it happened in spite of me. Either way, it *was* happening.

I pulled off my clothing. I'd barely thrown it aside before I crashed to the ground and everything went dark. A moment later, I woke up. There was that usual split second of "where am I? what am I?" grogginess before I remembered and leaped to all fours.

I peered around. It was nearly dark now, but my night vision was excellent. I took a moment to adjust to the other changes—four legs, whiskers, a tail. It all makes movement a little odd at first, even the whiskers, pinging as they brushed the long grass.

Sliding through that grass was a lot easier when I didn't need to crawl. And safer when I blended with the golden stalks. When I neared the neighboring cabin, I poked my head through the grass and let out a soft growl.

Corey peeked out first. He saw me and jumped back. Then Daniel appeared, hand on Corey's shoulder, murmuring, "It's Maya."

"I knew that," Corey whispered, looking abashed. "But why is she . . . ?"

"I'm guessing she didn't have a choice."

Daniel crawled over to me. As he did, I instinctively retreated. He'd never seen me in cat form—I'd only shifted twice so far. While I'd been around humans both times and hadn't felt any monstrous desire to devour them, I still scrambled away when Daniel approached.

But his scent filled my nostrils and I didn't smell a threat or—worse—dinner. I smelled Daniel, a scent I still didn't quite comprehend when I was in human form, but now it felt like a warm wave washing over me, relaxing me, telling me everything was all right, Daniel was here.

Even when I backed away, he kept crawling forward, as if I wasn't a hundred-and-twenty-pound big cat with two-inch claws and fangs.

"You okay?" he whispered.

I tried to say yes. It came out as a soft *chrr-up*, like my bobcat, Fitz, makes when he sees me.

Daniel smiled. "That sounds like yes, so I'm guessing you can understand me."

Another chirp.

"You've got some good camouflage there," he said. "A good nose. Good ears. And a good escape vehicle if you're spotted."

I realized what he was thinking. That I could scout the cabin before we sent Corey over. I chirped and tried motioning with my head that I'd circle the studio. I was sure there was no way he'd understand me, but he nodded.

"So you're okay with that? You'll take a look around before Corey goes in?"

I bobbed my head. He reached over to pat me, then stopped himself with a chagrined smile.

"Sorry, I probably shouldn't do that. But it's the only chance I'll get to pet a cougar."

I leaned against his hand and he buried his fingers in my fur, then he took a long look at me.

"It's pretty damned amazing," he murmured.

It was. Whatever else the St. Clouds had done to us, this was amazing. We sat there for a minute. Just sat together,

24

me leaning against him, feeling the warmth of his hand, listening to his breathing, slowly calming me down until I was relaxed enough to pull back and jerk my muzzle toward the cabin, telling Daniel I was ready. He gave me one last pat and returned to Corey.

FOUR

I SET OUT THROUGH the long grass. The wind was coming from the north, which was behind me. I couldn't pick up any traces of human scent on the breeze. That meant there wasn't anyone outdoors for at least a kilometer. No one directly upwind, that is. To the northeast or northwest? Possibly. So I covered a swath from the road to the water. A very faint scent came when I approached the beach—the smell of people mixed with that of burning wood. Someone with a bonfire up the beach. No one lurked nearby watching the studio—at least not in that direction.

I wanted to cross the road to check over there, but it was paved, meaning my tawny fur would shine like a beacon against the black. I paced along the edge, in the grass, thinking. Then I heard a car. I'd been too preoccupied to notice it until it zoomed around a curve, less than a hundred meters away. I dived deeper into the long brown grass.

The car slowed. I plastered myself against the ground, ears flat against my head, tail curled behind me. I could see the driver. Just a gray-haired guy scanning the roadside.

What if he'd spotted me? Were there cougars on Galiano? Even if there were, seeing one would be a big deal. Vancouver Island had more cougars than anyplace else in Canada, yet people lived their entire lives there and never spotted one of the elusive cats.

If this guy saw me and told someone, it could get back to the St. Clouds or the Nasts. They'd know I'd come to see my grandmother and even if I left now, they'd presume I'd made contact and they'd question her. At the very *least*, they'd question her. At worst? I started to shake.

It took a moment for me to realize the car had moved on. It had never even come to a full stop, just a mildly curious driver who'd noticed a movement by the roadside. I chuffed in relief, my flanks vibrating with the sound as I lowered my muzzle to my paws.

I had to be more careful. Damn it, I had to be a lot more careful.

When I'd composed myself, I decided I wasn't crossing that road. Instead, I would circle behind the studio to check the other side. The least exposed route was right along the top of the beach embankment, a narrow strip of long grass.

Again, I screwed up. I'd completely forgotten that there was a path with steps leading from the patio to the beach.

27

Every cottage had one. Luckily, this open strip was barely a meter wide, and I'd only be exposed for a few seconds as I crossed.

I glanced out at the water. No sign of a boat. I peered at the studio. The whole back side was glass, for the artist. The glare of the setting sun against the window made it impossible to see inside. Still, there didn't seem to be anyone there.

As I crouched to scamper across, a scent wafted past. One that made my legs freeze. My grandmother's scent, drifting from an open window. I glanced over and inhaled, feeling my sides shake.

So close. God, she was so close. All I had to do was—

No. Absolutely not. If this worked out, she'd know soon enough.

I took another step. A gasp. I turned and saw a figure silhouetted against the open patio door. It squealed open, and the sound jolted me back to life. I dived into the long grass on the other side.

"Maya!"

My grandmother's voice. I froze again.

Her feet thumped as she ran across the tiny lawn.

"Maya!"

No. This wasn't possible. I was imagining things. There was no way she could know—

I remembered the story she used to tell me when I was little. To explain my paw-print birthmark and the fact that my birth mother had abandoned me on the hospital steps.

She said my real mother was a cougar who'd had a late summer litter. She'd been an old cat and knew the signs that it would be a long, hard winter and her cubs wouldn't all survive. So she'd begged the sky god for mercy, and he turned her smallest cub into a human girl and told the cat to take her into the city. She'd left me at the hospital, but before she went, she'd pressed her paw to my hip, leaving me a mark to remember her by.

Had my grandmother known the truth? That I was a skinwalker? Was I wrong to think my parents hadn't been aware of the experiments?

My gut clenched. I turned to see her standing in the path, her hands to her mouth, her gaze locked on the dark patch of my birthmark.

"Maya."

She dropped to her knees. I slowly walked to her. When I was close enough, she reached out and grabbed me around the neck, pulling me to her.

"It is you, isn't it?" she whispered. Then she hiccupped a laugh. "I guess, if I'm hugging a cougar and it isn't ripping out my throat, that answers my question."

She hugged me again.

"I'm sorry," she said. "You must be so angry and so confused. Are the others with you? Daniel and the rest?"

I let out a chirp.

She squeezed me again. "As horrible as this must be, at least you have each other." She clutched my face between her hands. "If there's any way for you to visit your parents, please, please do that. Your mother might not believe in the spirit world, but when she sees you, she'll recognize her child. She'll know you took the form of the cougar to come and say good-bye."

Good-bye? Spirit world?

She didn't know I was a skin-walker. She thought the birthmark meant I had a link to the big cats and that my spirit had taken their form to return one last time. It was like seeing a ghost.

I pulled back and shook my head.

"You can't go to them?" she said, her voice cracking, tears streaming down her face. "Do you want me to tell them I saw you?"

I shook my head again. Then I pulled from her grasp and started to run to the guys, to get them over here to explain.

"Maya!"

As she shouted, I caught a scent on the breeze. One I recognized. Moreno—a man who worked with Calvin Antone, my biological father.

Footsteps pounded so hard I could feel the vibration. I caught other scents. A Nast Cabal team with Moreno, approaching from the south.

"Maya!" Grandma shouted.

I wheeled, growling, hoping she'd see or hear the team, but she just kept running after me, calling my name.

A dart whizzed past. I ran faster. Then I heard a gasp

behind me and saw my grandmother falling face-first to the ground, a dart lodged in her leg. I tore back to her.

Footsteps came from two directions. Daniel called for me. Corey shouted, too, telling me to stop, to come back.

Another dart zinged past, so close it cut right through the fur on my haunch. I reached my grandmother. She was out cold, in the grass. I grabbed her shirt in my teeth and yanked as hard as I could. The fabric gave way and I tumbled back, a chunk of cloth in my mouth.

Daniel grabbed me by the loose skin around my neck. "You can't help her! Come on!"

When he heaved on me, I caught another glimpse of my grandmother, lying in the grass. Rage and fear coursed through me and the world turned bloodred. Daniel heaved again and I spun, snarling, jaws opening, fangs slashing for his arm. Then I saw him and swung to the side, biting air instead.

"Maya! Daniel!"

Another voice I knew. One that filled my gut with ice water. Antone.

"Daniel!" Corey shouted. "Leave her! She'll be fine. Come on!"

Daniel's grip on my ruff didn't loosen. He whispered, "Please, Maya. Please."

I looked back at my grandmother. Then up at Antone. Then at Moreno and two others running behind him, all armed with tranquilizer guns. And it was like when they'd shot Kenjii. When they'd shot Daniel. I'd watched them fall and there was nothing I could do. Not against so many.

I tore my gaze from my grandmother and ran. When another dart whizzed by, I veered to the side. Daniel shouted, then realized I wasn't circling back—I was separating us, making us tougher to shoot.

We were already in the long grass. That made me nearly impossible to hit. I looked over at Daniel. A dart hit the flap of his sweatshirt and lodged there. As he batted it out, I circled, racing behind him and bumping the back of his legs. He understood and bent over, running as low as he could, zigzagging, his dark shirt making him nearly invisible in the night.

"Corey!" He shouted. "Go!"

We made it to the neighboring cabin. That blocked us from sight—and gunfire—and we could hear our pursuers cursing as we slipped under the porch. They cursed even louder when they got around the cabin and didn't find us there. As we hid under the porch, Daniel whipped a stone into the woods. Antone and Moreno took off, with Antone shouting for the others to go back for my grandmother.

Three days in the Vancouver Island wilderness hadn't made Moreno any better at moving quietly through the woods. When he wasn't thundering across hard earth or crashing through the undergrowth, he was cursing. As we waited there, listening and tracking them, I relaxed, and as soon as I did I lost consciousness.

FİVE

"**M**AYA?"

I looked at my paw. Not a paw. A human hand. I lifted my head, blinking, then remembered.

"Grandma!" I said.

Daniel clapped a hand to my mouth. "I heard them talking. They're going to put her in her studio. They figure she'll wake up and think she had a dream. She's fine."

"Oh."

My fingers dug into the ground as I struggled against the first prickle of tears.

"I know," he whispered. "But she'll know the truth as soon as we can manage it. Better for now if she thinks it was a dream."

He was right, of course. At least the Nast team didn't plan to haul her away and lock her up.

Corey whispered, "I think the other two are gone. Your, uh, father and that guy. Can you hear anything?"

I started to rise up on all fours and felt a chill. I glanced down. I was lying on my stomach. Without clothing.

"Yep, you're naked," Corey said, with a ghost of his usual grin. "Don't worry, I'm saving all my skeevy comments for later."

"Thanks."

I realized then that there was something on my back, covering me down to my butt. Daniel's sweatshirt. It was too tight under the porch to put it on me, but he'd stretched it over my back.

I let out a soft sigh of relief and looked over at him. "Thank you."

A quirk of a smile. "Anytime. Corey? Keep your eyes on the forest while she puts that on."

"Seriously? You're going to rob me of the one ray of light in— Oww."

I crawled from under the porch and pulled on the shirt. Everything was silent. The scents I detected were very faint. Moreno and Antone had passed through the woods and carried on. We had to get moving before they came back.

I found my clothing and got my jeans and shoes on, saving the rest until we were farther away. Antone might be my father, but he wasn't on my side, no matter what he said. My biological mother had run away from the experiment before I was born, along with my twin brother. I didn't remember either—she'd abandoned me shortly after my birth and had kept my brother. I was still dealing with that. I was still dealing with a lot.

We carefully made our way back to the ferry docks. The last one had departed. Corey suggested stealing a boat. We could do it—he was an excellent boater. But it was too risky—they'd be watching for a small craft making a hasty exit. Through otherwise empty waters. Better to hole up in a stretch of woods and wait for the morning ferry.

First we found a park with a washroom. We *did* break into that—we had to. Then we cleaned up as best we could and found a safe place to spend the night.

We waited for the second ferry the next morning. We'd bottle-necked ourselves on the island. There was only one way off. Antone would know that. So he'd expect us to be on that first ferry.

When the time came, we sent Daniel to get the tickets. He had a sixth sense for danger. It wasn't perfect, but benandanti were mainly demon-hunters and Moreno *was* a half-demon. Meanwhile I'd be downwind, on full alert.

After Daniel got the tickets, we stayed hidden in the forest waiting for the departure time. The ferry dock was basically slabs of cement plunked down in the wilderness. A couple of buildings. A parking lot. A long pier. Not the ideal location for anyone trying to sneak on board. Just as we were thinking we might need to just make a run for it, a school bus pulled

35

in and disgorged a couple dozen students.

"Please tell me they're walk-ons," Corey said.

"Even if they're taking the bus, we might be able to sneak on with them," I said.

Daniel made a noise deep in his throat. Disagreeing. He was right. Kids on Galiano Island would be a lot like kids from Salmon Creek, where you'd known your classmates forever.

When the first group headed for the pier, we breathed a collective sigh of relief. They were indeed walking on.

"We'll split up," I said. "Daniel, you go first. Corey, you're next. I'll bring up the rear and keep my ears open for trouble."

We joined them in the parking lot. Merging with the group wasn't easy. When Daniel cut in, they noticed. The girls did, anyway. They always do. It's the blond wavy hair, the friendly smile . . . the wrestling and boxing champion physique.

When Corey joined, he took some of the attention, but that hardly helped us pass unnoticed. And when I slid in, they all noticed, because I was the only brown face in the group.

"Hey," one of the guys said to me. "You going to the mainland?"

"I am."

He started telling me about their trip and I struggled to pretend I was listening while my attention was attuned to the parking lot behind us. I hoped an overly polite nod or two would stop him, but he continued chattering away.

I glanced back. All the cars were on the ferry now, the gate closing.

"Looking for someone?" he said.

"No, I—"

"Right here." Corey appeared and slung his arm around my shoulders. "I thought you were already on board, baby."

The guy grumbled and walked faster as we reached the pier.

"Baby?" I said.

"You can thank me later." He glanced back. "I don't see anyone, but other than Antone and Moreno, I don't know who I'm looking for."

Daniel overheard, having slowed to let us catch up. "Just watch for anyone acting like they're looking for somebody."

"Like that woman running toward the gate?"

Corey didn't wait for an answer, just tightened his grip on my shoulders and started propelling me through the crowd.

"Slow down," I hissed. "Running will only make it worse."

Damn it, we shouldn't have attempted this. As soon as we set foot on the ferry, we were trapped. I looked up and down the pier, but there was no place to hide. We were being funneled toward the boat and—

"Jimmy!" the woman shouted. "Jimmy! You forgot your EpiPen!"

A few of the kids laughed. A red-faced boy grumbled something and stomped back.

"Bullet dodged," Corey said. "Now let's get on the boat."

We stayed with the school group until we were on. The ferry was the *Queen of Nanaimo*. It wasn't a little ship. It had room for a couple hundred cars and close to a thousand passengers.

We headed straight upstairs to the top deck. Some of the kids were already there for the best vantage point. We stayed behind them as we strained to look out. My night vision is better than average, but my regular sight is about the same. There were a few people on the pier as the ship prepared to depart, but no sign—

Daniel gripped my arm and whispered. "Don't move. It's Antone." He didn't say "your father." He knew how I felt— my father was Rick Delaney. "To the left. Back at the ticket counter."

He was right. Even from so far away I recognized Antone, and if I had any doubts, they evaporated when Moreno walked up beside him.

Antone was showing something to the cashier.

"Oh no," I whispered. "Photos. He's showing her . . ."

But Antone turned away and headed back toward a truck.

"What?" I looked at Daniel. "Why didn't the cashier recognize you?"

"Because I didn't buy the tickets."

I glanced at him.

"I persuaded a guy to buy them for me. Putting my mystical powers to good use. The extra five I gave him probably didn't hurt. He looked like he could use it."

"You are a genius."

A genuine smile. "Thank you. Now, as soon as we're in motion—"

The ferry's engines revved and we started pulling from the dock.

"Wow," I said. "Your powers work on inanimate objects, too."

He laughed. "I wish."

He waved me back from the rail, then led us to a tiny room off the main deck. It was a sitting room, with seats, windows, and a private bathroom.

"Um, I think these are reserved for paying customers," Corey said as Daniel walked in.

Daniel waved the receipt.

"Big spender," I said.

"It wasn't much extra." He closed the door. "I figured we could splurge for a few minutes of peace and quiet. And a real bathroom."

I collapsed onto the nearest seat. "Again, you are a genius."

"Not done yet. I got you a treat."

He reached into his pocket and pulled something out.

"Oh my God. Is that an apple? Two apples?" I leaped up, snatched them, then fell back on the seat. "I think Grandma was right. I really have died and gone to heaven." I took a huge bite of the apple and groaned.

"Normally, I'd say you're weird," Corey said. "But after days of eating junk food, those do look good." He turned to Daniel. "That's really sexist, you know, buying the chick a—"

Daniel took another one from his backpack.

"Oh my God. I think I love you." Corey threw open his arms. The apple bounced off his forehead. "Oww."

I shook my head, closed my eyes, and smiled.

SIX

IT WAS LESS THAN an hour to the mainland, but by the time we got there, we'd rested, cleaned up, and were feeling better. Most importantly, we'd come up with a plan. A desperate plan, but no worse than anything we'd tried so far. We were going to our funeral.

Crazy? Yes. And when Corey had suggested it, Daniel and I rattled off a list of reasons why we couldn't try it. Yet the idea took root and the more we thought about it, the more we realized it might be really our only chance to make contact with our parents.

Once we were back in Vancouver, we went to another library and found an obituary website hosted by the *Victoria Times-Colonist* newspaper. How strange was it, typing my own name into the search box? Not nearly as strange as seeing the details of my passing fill the screen, along with pages of condolences. Summer kids and their parents. Guys I'd dated. Coaches and fellow athletes I'd met at track meets. Employees at the Victoria Refuge Centre. People who knew my mom, my dad, my grandmother. People recollecting moments with me that, sometimes, I didn't even remember myself.

As I read, Daniel wheeled his chair over behind me.

"Everyone will know the truth soon enough," he whispered.

I nodded. As I printed the funeral details, Corey turned from the computer beside mine.

"Uh, guys? You know that email address I set up? We've got a message."

I slid my chair over. Corey had the message displayed on the screen.

It was from Cyril Mitchell's daughter. She'd decided to talk to us, but what she had to say was too important for a phone conversation. She'd looked up the area code from our phone call and knew we were in Vancouver, so she was on her way here and would arrive late morning.

"She sent it yesterday," Corey said. "Meaning she's already here. She says she'll be checking email and wants us to give a time and place to meet."

"Reply and say we'll meet at the aquarium at"—I checked Daniel's watch—"four. We'll be in the lobby."

He sent the message. We were still looking up maps for the funeral location when the reply came back. Four o'clock, yes. At the aquarium, yes. But not in the lobby. Someplace

42

more private. Fortunately, the aquarium was deep in Granville Park, meaning privacy was only a short walk away. We chose a spot, then sent a message back. Ten minutes later, she accepted.

We'd been planning to visit the site of the memorial service, to check it out, but if Mitchell's daughter was coming, then it seemed we wouldn't need that anymore. So we got a late lunch and tried to relax. Then we caught a cab to the aquarium. We'd just crossed the bridge onto Granville Island when Corey gasped. The three of us were wedged in the backseat, me between the guys, and I looked over to see Corey's face pale, his mouth open, his eyes filled with pain. Before I could say anything, he let out a strangled yowl and doubled over, his head in his hands.

"What is wrong with him?" the driver asked, his voice rising as he slowed.

I leaned past Corey to get the window down.

"It's just a headache," Daniel said.

It wasn't just a headache. It was one of Corey's raging migraines, which had been getting steadily worse. As he moaned, his head nearly in his lap, I managed to get the pill bottle from his pocket. I was shaking one out when he heaved and dry-retched.

The cabbie pulled over so fast we nearly got whiplash.

"Out!" he said. "No drunk kids in my cab!"

"He's not drunk," Daniel said. "It's just a—"

"Out! Out!"

Daniel started to argue. I stopped him. His powers only worked when someone was willing to be persuaded. This guy was not. We managed to get Corey—still coughing and sputtering—from the cab. Daniel turned to pay, but the guy was already speeding off.

"Should try that more often," Corey mumbled as we led him to the side of the road. "Save some cash."

Cars streaming into the park—which is a thoroughfare to downtown Vancouver—began slowing to watch us. For three days now we'd been moving through Vancouver and Galiano with only some thought to remaining hidden. Now, having seen our obituaries, I began to wonder if it was only blind luck that no one had yet recognized us from a newspaper article. The way we'd died—escaping a forest fire only to perish ironically in the helicopter taking us to safety—might have made us newsworthy. Slipping through the city, we'd probably go unnoticed. But standing by a busy road, helping a "drunk" friend after being kicked from a cab? We were calling too much attention to ourselves.

"Get him in the woods," I said, motioning to the forest that flanked the road.

As we did that, Corey had recovered enough to dry-swallow the pill and walk on his own.

"At least I didn't actually puke this time," he said. "That's a bonus." He winced and rubbed the back of his neck.

"Sit down," I said. "We're early and it's only a short walk."

He seemed ready to argue, then took another step and looked like he was going to throw up. He made a face and lowered himself onto a tree stump. We said nothing, just waited.

After a moment, he waved to head out. We did, but Daniel and I kept shooting glances at Corey. The St. Clouds had been keeping his headaches under control. They knew what was going on. We didn't. We couldn't. No one could, not even other supernaturals, because there was no one like Corey out there. If we never went back to the St. Clouds, never had contact with them again, how could we help—

We'd figure it out. We had to.

SEVEN

AS WE NEARED THE aquarium, Corey stopped suddenly.

"It's a trap," he said.

"What?"

"I—" He took a deep breath. "I think it's a trap. I mean, are we sure this chick is who she says she is? All we know is that someone emailed us."

"Using an address you just set up and we only gave to Mitchell's daughter," I said.

"What's wrong?" Daniel said.

Corey shook his head. "Nothing. I just . . . I think we should reconsider." He glanced toward the aquarium. "I think we need to be really, really sure that the person showing up is a woman. We should scout first."

Which made absolute sense. Except that Corey was never

the guy advising caution; he was the one *we* had to caution.

"It's not a woman waiting for us, is it?" Daniel said.

"I don't know. I'm just saying—"

"No, you're not."

Daniel instinctively took on his persuasive tone, then seemed to catch himself. He cleared his throat. Earlier we'd talked about this, how he didn't want to use his powers on us. Now, without thinking, he was doing it and he looked abashed, but I wasn't sure he had a reason to. It was a skill as much as a talent. Something he'd always done, except with me. Maybe because he knew I was too damned stubborn to be persuaded of anything.

He cleared his throat again. "You're not 'just saying,' Corey. You saw who's waiting for us. You had a vision with the headache."

"What?" Corey said. "Um, no. You're confusing me with Maya. She gets the visions."

"This is different," Daniel said. "You see images of things that don't make any sense. Like Maya with Rafe when we thought he was dead. You saw him with Maya in her backyard. Exactly the way they looked when we found them, right?"

Corey glanced at me.

"I didn't tell him." I said. "You know I wouldn't do that."

"I overheard," Daniel said. "You're never as quiet as you think you are, Corey. It didn't make sense at the time, but after, I started wondering. Then when we were in that van,

47

you knew it was Maya rescuing us before she got the door open."

He was right. Both about Rafe and the van. I just hadn't made the connection.

"What did you see?" Daniel asked before Corey could deny it.

Corey stood there, cracking his knuckles.

"You see visions of the future," I said. "That's your power. What's wrong with that?"

"Seriously?" He looked over at me. "Daniel is a demon-hunter. You're a shape-shifter. Apparently, I'm a fortune-teller. On a cool scale, that ranks about a five. Add in the headaches and puking, and I'd knock it down to a two."

"So, because you've decided your power isn't cool enough, you're going to let us walk into a trap?"

"No. I warned you, didn't I?" He caught Daniel's look and shuffled his feet. "Fine. But if anyone starts buying me crystal balls and Tarot cards . . ."

"Of course not," I said. "We can't afford it."

He grumbled, then shoved his hands in his pockets. "There's not much else to tell and I don't know whether it's real or not, so I don't want you guys relying on what I say. Deal?"

"Deal."

"There's a guy waiting for us. A kid, I think. Maybe our age. Brown hair. Wearing a T-shirt and jeans. Tanned. I didn't see much of his face. I'm not even sure about the—"

"We understand," I said. "Don't second-guess."

48

"He's in the woods. In a tree."

"A tree?"

"Don't ask me. I just get flashes. Images. I saw Maya in the woods right over there"—he pointed—"and there was a guy in a tree." He jammed his hands into his pockets again. "Hell, now that I'm saying it, I don't even know if he's waiting for us. It could just be a kid goofing off."

"Okay, well, let's just keep that all in mind, then." Daniel turned to me. "Are you ready?"

I nodded.

No one was waiting for us.

After ten minutes, I said, "Maybe this isn't the right spot. We said just inside the forest, but . . ." I peered deeper into the woods. "I'd say we should split up, but considering what Corey saw—"

I stopped and looked at them. "That's what Corey saw. We'd split up. I was in the forest alone."

"Okay," Daniel said. "So we don't split . . ." He trailed off and scowled at me. "That's not what you're going to suggest, is it?"

"Corey didn't see me getting attacked by some guy in a tree—"

"Hey, no," Corey said. "I see still pictures. No action. A snapshot. You were under a tree with a guy in it. For all I know, he jumped you two seconds later."

"But now I'm ready, so *we'll* get the jump on him."

We had to at least pretend that we'd split up to search for our contact. That meant I couldn't exactly walk around gaping at the treetops. I kept glancing up, but with the dense trees and shadows, every nest looked like someone crouching on a branch. Then, as I passed under a tree, I heard a limb creak.

I looked up. Sure enough, there was someone at least ten meters up, almost hidden by the thick needle-laden branches.

"Guys?" I said.

I waved Daniel and Corey over, and I looked up again.

"I can see you," I said. "Come on down."

The figure didn't move. I walked over and grabbed the trunk. That brought Daniel at a jog, but he didn't try to stop me, just watched as I shimmied up.

I made it almost as far as the first thick branch when the guy jumped onto the limb below him, then onto a neighboring tree and shuffled down a limb, gripping the one above for balance.

I grabbed the nearest branch and swung onto it. I caught a glimpse of the guy—just enough to see that he was young with brown hair, as Corey had seen. He didn't look back, just leaped down a branch, then along it, moving faster now. He swung to the next tree and almost missed. He righted himself, crouched, and jumped to the ground.

Daniel caught him in a running tackle and took him down. Corey raced over behind and bounced there, fists up, like he was standing outside the boxing ring, waiting his turn. As the guy struggled, Corey tensed, ready to leap in, but Daniel got him pinned facedown on the ground.

"What the hell is this?" the guy snarled. "A mugging? I knew I shouldn't have cut through the park."

"You always cut through using the sky route?" I said as I bent down and patted his pockets. "Huh. Nothing to rob, I guess, because you aren't carrying a wallet. That's a little odd, don't you think?"

He snarled profanities now. Daniel tensed, like he was waiting for the guy to aim those profanities at me. He didn't, though. Just general cursing. I double-checked inside his pockets.

"No ID. That *is* weird. So where do you have it?"

I tugged up his pant leg. He tried to kick, but Corey dropped and held his feet still while I pulled a thin billfold from his sock. It was held on with an elastic for safekeeping.

Inside the wallet were a few hundred dollars and three credit cards. I fanned the cards.

"So are you Jason or Drake or Todd?"

The guy didn't answer. He just kept staring at the ground.

"You don't look eighteen," I said. "So they're fake. Or stolen."

No answer.

Corey pulled up the guy's other pant leg. "There's something here, too."

It was a blue passport, attached with another elastic.

"An American passport," I said. "I'm pretty sure *these*

are hard to fake. So let's see who you really are."

I opened it. My gaze headed for the name, but the photo snagged it instead. I stared at the picture for a moment. Then I looked down at the guy on the ground. At his bare arm. Corey said he'd seemed tanned in the vision. He wasn't. He was Native.

I lifted the passport to get a better look at the photo. His eyes were hazel and his hair was light brown, but he still *looked* Native. As I stared at the picture, I could swear I recognized the face. I didn't, though. Not his name, either.

"Ashton Gray," I said.

He didn't respond. I looked at the birth date. It was a couple of months before mine. What was a sixteen-year-old kid doing climbing trees in Stanley Park with fake credit cards and an American passport?

He seemed like a street kid. The soles of his running shoes were almost worn through, his jeans were frayed, and his black T-shirt had been washed so often it was a dirty gray. But his nails were trimmed and his hair was poorly cut but clean.

I looked around. "Where are the others?"

"What others?" His first actual response. He didn't try to look at me, though.

"Someone contacted us and set up this meeting through an email address, which we only gave to one person. That person wasn't you."

"I don't know what you're talking about."

Daniel backed off the guy, staying poised to pounce if he bolted. "Get up."

"Well, since you're asking so nicely . . ."

The guy—Ashton—rolled over and pulled himself to a sitting position. He moved slowly, getting to his feet as if taking his time meant he really wasn't doing as he'd been told. His hair reached his collar at the sides as well as in back, and hung in his face. Only after he was standing did he bother to push it back. He fixed Daniel with a hard stare. Challenging. Pissed off that he'd been taken down so easily.

"Better?" he said.

Daniel looked at him. Stared, actually. He looked at me. Looked back at the guy. Then he swore under his breath.

I stared at Ashton Gray, too, and again I had this vague sense of *I know you*. Something about his face. Something familiar.

"Maya?" Daniel said.

Ashton flinched when Daniel said my name.

"Hmm?" I said.

"Rafe has a birthmark like yours, right? Where is it?"

"On his . . ." I trailed off. Daniel thought this guy was a skin-walker? Why? Because he was looking for us and happened to be Native? No, Daniel didn't jump to conclusions like that.

"On the back of his shoulder," I said. "A paw print like the one on my hip."

"Turn around," Daniel said to Ashton.

The kid's lip curled in a sneer and he seemed ready to snarl at us all, but when Daniel snapped, "Turn around" again, he obeyed. He was only a couple of inches taller than my five-five, which made him shorter than both of the other guys. Smaller, too—slight and wiry.

He yanked up his shirt to his shoulders.

The paw-print birthmark was there.

"What's the birth date on his passport, Maya?"

"Birth date? Um . . ." I double-checked. "August fifth."

"Fake, then. It's more like October, isn't it?" Daniel said, walking around to meet Ashton's gaze. "Early October. I don't know the exact date, because Maya's isn't exactly right, either, but the doctors had a pretty good idea how old she was when she was found, and they wouldn't have been two months off."

I tried to follow what he was saying. How would that have anything to do with . . . ?

I stared at Ashton Gray. No. It couldn't be.

"Is your real birthday in early October?" Daniel asked.

"Yeah."

"And you just turned sixteen?"

"Yeah."

"And you know why I'm asking?"

A pause. But only a brief one. His gaze started my way, then stopped, and he stared at the forest instead.

"Yeah."

"Holy hell," Corey murmured. "You're Maya's brother."

EİGHT

IS THERE A PROPER reaction for meeting your twin for the first time? A twin you never even realized you had until a week ago?

I'd seen long-lost-relative reunions in movies. I'd even read a couple of real-life stories where siblings were reunited. Judging by those examples, I should race over and throw my arms around his neck. Only I didn't.

I stood there, staring at this stranger, thinking, *My brother, my twin brother* over and over. I couldn't process it. We'd shared a womb for nine months. We'd been babies together, probably in the same cradle, his face the first thing I saw every morning and the last I saw at night. And yet he was a stranger. A complete and total stranger.

His reaction didn't help. He wouldn't even look at me. Just stood there, hands in his pockets, gaze defiant, as if . . .

As if he couldn't bear to look at me.

"It's true?" I said.

"Yeah." His voice was gruff, emotionless.

"Hi," I said, which was a dumb thing to say, but all I could manage. "I'm Maya."

"No shit."

Daniel rocked forward, like he wanted to cut in. He didn't, though. Not until Ashton yanked his hands from his pockets, the sudden move startling me. Daniel caught me and yanked me behind his back, then faced off with Ashton.

"I wasn't going to hurt your girlfriend." A sneer. "Damn benandanti."

"She's my *friend*."

"Good for you."

"Just my luck," I said. "Finally meet my twin brother and, turns out, he's an ass."

Corey laughed. Ashton looked at me for the first time, staring, as if he'd misheard.

"Oh yeah," Corey said with a chuckle. "She said that. You may have inherited the jerk genes, but Maya got the brutal honesty ones."

"Enough," Daniel said, stepping forward. "Is anyone else here? Or were you the one who sent the email?"

"It was me."

We all struggled not to look disappointed.

"So how did you get the email address?" I asked.

He turned and looked at me. Just looked.

"Great," I muttered. "Do I need to relay my questions through an interpreter?"

"That depends. Are you going to call me an ass again?"

"That depends. Are you going to act like one?"

I expected Daniel to intercede. He just stood there, arms crossed, face impassive, as Corey struggled not to laugh.

"Look," I said. "We're in trouble. Serious trouble. We reached out to the only contact name we had. You show up instead, spy on us, try to run, and now act like we're keeping you from a hot date. Somehow you got that message, knew it was your twin sister, and replied. That would make perfect sense if you wanted to help your sister. But that's obviously not the case."

"Oh, that's obvious, is it?"

"If I'm wrong, then let's start over. I'm Maya. That's Daniel and that's Corey. Is Ashton your real name?"

"Ash. Nobody calls me Ashton."

Guy couldn't even answer a benign question without attitude. This was going to be fun.

"How about we sit down somewhere and talk. Maybe grab something to eat," Daniel said.

"Umm, correct me if I'm wrong, but aren't you guys supposed to be dead? Currently being chased by two Cabals? You're waltzing around Vancouver, eating in restaurants?"

"Hell, no," Corey said. "I never waltz. I do the fox-trot sometimes, though."

"There's a café just a little walk away," I said as calmly as

I could. "We'll get something there and find a private place to sit. It's been hours since we've had any food, and I don't know about you, but these guys eat like they're in permanent training."

"So what's *your* excuse?" Corey said to me as we started out.

"It's the cougar shifts," Daniel said. "They take a lot out of her."

"Absolutely," I said, grinning at him.

Ash snorted. "It'll be awhile before you need to worry about that."

"Um, no," Corey said. "She's already shifting."

Ash's look darkened—telling me he wasn't shifting yet—and I quickly said, "It's only been a few times."

He glowered at me, as if I was bragging, then he fell back beside Corey and walked in silence behind me.

Great. Just great.

I inadvertently screwed up again at the café. Daniel, Corey, and I had pooled our money so we were taking turns grabbing stuff. Since it was my turn to buy, I naturally asked Ash what he wanted.

"I pay my own way," he said, with a scowl that I was beginning to think was as much a part of his normal expression as Daniel's smile or Corey's grin.

"Do you want me to grab it for you?" I asked.

"No."

As he stalked off, we watched him go, making sure he didn't bolt.

"Don't let him get to you," Daniel murmured. "Whatever his problem is, it's not you. He just met you."

"I know."

He leaned closer, squeezing my hand, and whispered, "I'm sorry. I know this isn't how you'd pictured it."

I could say that I *hadn't* pictured it—there'd been too much going on for me to even think about my newly discovered brother. Yet that was a lie. I *had* thought about meeting him. I'd thought about what it might be like to have a twin. Everyone said they shared a bond beyond mere blood.

I looked at Ash, standing in line, glowering.

Nope. No bond there.

I joined the line behind Ash. He must have known I was there but didn't turn, not even when I cleared my throat and said, "Ash?"

I tried again. "Can I, uh, ask you something?"

He glanced back. "What?"

"You are by yourself, right?"

"Said that, didn't I?"

Actually, no. He'd never answered the question. But I didn't point that out.

"So she's not with you," I said. "Our, uh, mother?"

"Nope."

"You left her behind?"

A look. One I couldn't decipher. "Not exactly," he said, and turned away.

"Is she . . . dead?"

He paused so long I thought he wasn't going to answer. Then he said, "No idea," and stepped up to the counter to place his order.

NINE

MY BROTHER HAD NO idea if our mother was alive or dead? That made no sense. I'd been told she'd kept him. He'd grown up with her. Had he run away? Or was "no idea" just his way of saying "piss off"?

At the table, Ash ate his wrap, but not without complaint. Wraps? Seriously? In a *park*? Where were the burgers and fries? Damned West Coast.

"So where are you from, then?" I asked.

From the look he gave me, you'd think I was asking for his home address so I could send a death squad.

"Around," he said.

"So where did you get the email address?" I asked.

"From the person you gave it to, obviously."

I shot a look at Daniel.

"We called the number for Cyril Mitchell," Daniel said.

"That was the emergency contact another skin-walker gave Maya. The woman who answered said he was dead. She claimed to be his daughter. Is that true?"

"Yeah, he's dead. Yeah, she's his daughter. But if you expected any help from that dumb bitch, you're even more clueless than I thought."

"So tell us what we're missing," Daniel said, his voice low, calm. "Clue us in."

Ash shrugged. "Later. Maybe. Point is, she's not going to help. She didn't want her dad mixed up with the St. Clouds or their genetic projects. Blames them for his death."

"They killed him?" I asked.

He looked ready to shoot back a sarcastic response, then checked himself. "No. It was a heart attack. She blames them because he was working for them. Working both sides—employed by the Cabal, but helping some of the Project Phoenix parents. So she blames us, too, which is why she isn't going to help. But she did decide it was her duty to pass on your email to me and tell me you phoned from a Vancouver number. She knew you were my sister. Acted like she was doing us a huge favor. She shouldn't have been passing out your contact info without asking you. Like I said, dumb bitch."

"So she told you I called, gave you the email address, and you decided to come meet me?"

"Yeah."

He was sitting there, barely able to look at me, barely able to speak without snapping at me, yet he'd dropped everything, paid God knows how much for a plane ticket, and crossed an international border to track me down. I didn't know how to reconcile that. I would have been sure it was a trap except, if it was, he wouldn't be nearly so pissy about the whole thing. He'd be all, "Hey, I'm your brother and I'm here to help."

"You know Daniel's a benandanti, and you know we're supposed to be dead, and you know there are two Cabals after us. Did Mitchell's daughter tell you that?"

He snorted. "She didn't tell me nothing. I already knew about the crash and the escape. There are a few parents out there who left Project Phoenix, like our mother. They've kept in contact with me. One of them contacted me after the crash. She had a Google alert on Salmon Creek. She told me—" The briefest hesitation. "She told me you were dead."

"Oh."

"Then I get this call from Sylvia Mitchell. So I made another call, to another parent, and found out you survived. This guy knew how to contact me, knew that I thought you were dead, and never even bothered to phone when he found out otherwise. Said it wouldn't do any good. That I was better off thinking you were dead."

"Nice," Corey murmured. "So I'm guessing these parents aren't going to be helping us anytime soon."

"You guess right. The one who told me you were dead is okay but useless. Just wants to protect her daughter." He paused. "Can't blame her, I guess. The other guy is even less helpful, though he knows more. He has contacts. Won't share them, though. Might endanger his kid. Cyril was in charge of this little network, but when he died, it just fell apart. He's the only one who would have helped—or made them help."

"Okay," Daniel said. "So who *can* we get help from? Your mother?"

Ash snorted. "You know where to find her?"

"Um, no, I thought you . . ." Daniel looked my way again.

I cleared my throat. "I was told our mother separated us because the St. Clouds would be looking for twins. She left me at a hospital in Portland, but she kept you. Raised you."

"You heard wrong."

"Oh." I paused. "So she aban— Left both of us?"

"Abandoned. She abandoned both of us. You at the hospital as a baby, me with some so-called friends when I was five."

"Oh."

"Yeah, *oh*. I haven't seen her since and I don't want to now. If you're going after her, count me out. I'll suggest you save yourself the trip, though. She doesn't give a damn about either of us. Dumped us on strangers to save herself."

I sat there, stunned. Then I said, "Is there anyone we can go to?"

He stared at me, then laughed. "You guys really are spoiled rich kids, aren't you? When things go wrong, you don't have a clue how to save yourselves. Just run in circles looking for a grown-up to do it for you."

"Does it look like we can't save ourselves? We're free, aren't we? But our parents think we're dead."

"Good. Makes it easier to disappear. No one to come looking for you."

"I don't want to disappear. I want my parents back."

"Why? They sold you out."

"I don't believe that."

"Then you're not just a sheltered rich kid. You're a stupid one, too."

Daniel cut in. "We also need help because the Cabals have our friends."

"Then wish them well and start making new ones. They'll be fine. The St. Clouds and Nasts will take care of them. They're valuable future employees." Ash eased back on the bench. "Look. I came for my sister. I know how you guys grew up and I figure she's not going to last ten minutes on the street. I'm going to take her someplace safe. I didn't expect"—he waved at Daniel and Corey—"an entourage, but I suppose it's a package deal."

"It is," I said. "But we're not running and hiding. We can't."

"*Maya* can't," Daniel said. "There's a problem with skin-walkers after they start shifting."

"What?"

"One of the first subjects is the sister of the guy who gave me Cyril Mitchell's number," I said. "She's been shifting for a few years now and she's . . . brain damaged."

65

"From the shifts?"

"Maybe brain damaged isn't the right term. It's like she's becoming more . . . animal. All she cares about is eating and sleeping and running around the woods. Now I'm starting to shift, and . . ."

"You've noticed changes?"

"No," Daniel said. "But it's only been a week and Rafe told her it took awhile with Annie. If Maya starts reverting like that, we can't exactly take her to a hospital and ask them to fix it. We need help from the people who did this to us."

"And how the hell are you going to get that? Ask nicely?"

Silence. This was the part we hadn't worked out. Hadn't dared discuss.

I spoke first. "Ideally, we'd find someone who worked for the project—a scientist or a doctor—who has either left the St. Clouds or is willing to work against them. Which sounds like Cyril Mitchell."

"Yeah, it does. Which means you're shit outta luck. I'm not even sure he could have helped. This is . . ." A look crossed Ash's face. Something like fear. "Big."

"It's huge," Daniel said. "And I'm not letting it happen to Maya."

"So how are you going to stop it, benandanti? Put all their scientists in choke holds and use your power to persuade them to help?"

"If I have to. The better option, though . . ." He took a deep breath. "Is a truce."

"What?" Ash laughed and shook his head. "You really don't know anything about Cabals, do you?"

"No, but I'm hoping you'll fill us in. I do believe, however, that under the right circumstances, a truce is possible. For that, though, we need our parents—not because we want Mommy and Daddy to hold our hands, but because these people won't take our demands seriously. We're just kids. We need to get to our parents and let them know what's happened. Yes, maybe some joined the project voluntarily, but they didn't sign up so their kids could be taken away. If they know the truth, they can use it. Threats. Blackmail. Whatever it takes. Get the Cabals to help us on our terms."

Ash looked me in the eye. "This stuff about the girl. Annie. You've met her?"

"I have."

"Could she have been faking it? Maybe her and her brother set this up so you'd think you need a Cabal's help?"

I shook my head. "It was real. She's regressing, and it's . . ." I swallowed. "I can't imagine it."

"Fine," he said. "We'll try it your way. It won't work, but I can tell you're not going to believe that until you've given it a shot."

TEN

ASH DIDN'T GET A whole lot more pleasant after that. He insisted he'd come to rescue me, but acted like I'd found him—against his will—and now I was clinging like a burr, tenacious and irritating.

When we finished eating, he wanted to find a spot to hole up for the night.

"We need to stake out a good place now," he said. "Before it's dark. Otherwise, all the good spots will be taken."

"We found one the night before last," I said. "We can just go back—"

"Never use the same spot twice. Not when you're running."

He seemed to have some experience with this. A lot of experience? I looked down at his tattered sneakers. I had a feeling he didn't live with those "so-called friends" of our mother anymore.

"So where do street people live in this city?" he said. He shook his head. "Why am I asking you? Hell, this is Canada. The great socialist nation to the north. You guys don't even have homeless people, I bet."

"We have them, unfortunately," I said as calmly as I could.

"Guess socialism isn't really working out for you, huh?"

"Canada is a democracy. That means we're not a socialist country or a communist country or a—"

"We have homelessness and we have gangs," Daniel cut in. "Both of which could be an issue in finding a place to spend the night. You're right, though. We have no idea where to look for a spot. We're going to need to rely on you for that."

I cleared my throat. "Actually, there are a few dozen homeless living here in the park. Long-term campers deep in the woods. When Vancouver had that big windstorm in 2006, they had to go looking for the homeless people, make sure they were all accounted for. Dad came over to help with some other rangers."

"Make sure they were accounted for?" Ash said. "What? They keep a roster, check in on them from time to time?"

"The park management knows they're there. They aren't hurting anyone, so no one bothers them."

Ash shook his head as if this, too, was clearly the sign of a backward nation.

I said, "As long as we get deep enough in the woods and don't bother them, we can stay here for the night."

And I'd really like to stay in the forest, if I can. But I didn't say that. I had a feeling it would make him decide to stay anyplace but here.

"We should," Daniel said. "It makes sense. We're not going to need to worry about gangs in here."

"All right," Ash said. "Find a spot."

As we headed into the woods, Ash just followed along, glancing from side to side, as if he expected wolves to leap out.

Earlier, he'd seemed perfectly comfortable climbing trees. Adept at it. And as long as we'd kept to the edge of the forest, he'd been fine. But Stanley Park is bigger than New York's Central Park. As we got in deeper, leaving the sounds of the city behind, he grew even more tense and quiet.

"You okay?" I said when he jumped at a sparrow hopping through a bed of needles.

"'Course," he snapped. "Just paying attention. Someone has to."

Corey nodded. "You never know. That sparrow could have had an Uzi hidden—"

Daniel elbowed him to silence. Ash fell back, scuffling along, until we got far enough in. He caught up then. He didn't join our conversation, but did stay close as we continued moving through the woods.

We found a decent place. As Daniel and I cleared twigs and brush for sleeping spots, Corey and Ash stood off to the side. Ash watched us, as if daring us to ask him to help. We didn't. Corey seemed not to have noticed what we were doing. He was staring out into the forest, lost in thought.

I leaned over to Daniel as we both bent for the same rock. "You should probably talk to Corey about the vision thing."

"I was just going to say the same to you." Daniel took the rock and motioned for me to follow him a few steps away. "You're the one he told about them in the first place."

"Only because—"

"He didn't want to worry me. I know. But while I think that might have been part of it, it's partly just . . . It's not about boxing or girls or cars. Not something he wants to talk to a guy about. Having visions? Way outside his comfort zone. Too . . ."

"Touchy-feely mystical?"

"Exactly. For that, he'd rather talk to you. Like I'd tease him or something." He rolled his eyes.

"*I'm* more likely to tease him. But okay. Let me give it a shot."

"Thanks." He glanced over at Ash. "Speaking of comfort zones, I think your brother finds it easier talking to me. Is

71

there anything I can ask him for you?"

I shook my head. "There's plenty I want to know, but I need to ask myself. When I think he might actually answer. Which could be never."

"Don't let it get to you."

"I'm not."

"Liar."

I smiled, shook my head, and walked over to Corey.

Daniel was partly right. Corey was really uncomfortable with his newfound powers. But I'm not sure talking to me helped. Everyone else seemed to have physical powers. His was mental. Corey was really better with the physical. It didn't help that his came with the most serious side-effect of all—debilitating headaches. He felt ripped off.

"I think it's just a transition period," I said. "You're coming into your powers, and the headaches are a sign of that. Once it develops properly, they'll go away."

"Or not."

"Maybe if we do get you a crystal ball, that would help."

"Thanks."

"You know I'm teasing."

"Yeah, and I also know I'm being a brat. I just . . . I don't . . . I don't understand it. What's happening. It doesn't feel . . ." He glanced over. "It doesn't feel like me. Changing into a cougar fits you—you're a nature freak. Being an evil-hunting warrior fits Daniel. Sam, too. Being mermaids or whatever fits Hayley and Nicole. But this . . . it doesn't fit me."

"There may be more to it," I said. "Parts we don't know about. No one else just has one power. We need to find out exactly what you are."

He was quiet for a moment, then said, "I think I might know more. I . . ." He glanced over to where Daniel was trying to engage Ash in small talk. "He should hear this. Daniel, I mean. I guess there's no way of doing that without *him* overhearing." A pointed look at Ash. "But if he makes a crack—any crack—I'll deck him. Brother or not."

"No argument here. He's not exactly Mr. Congeniality."

"No kidding. I think we're going to need a DNA test to prove you two are related."

"I'll take that as a compliment."

ELEVEN

WE WERE BACK AT the "campsite," which was just a sheltered clearing with an empty spot that should have held a campfire, except that we had nothing to start one.

When Corey announced he had something to tell Daniel and me, Ash decided to take a walk. I would like to think he was being polite, but he probably just didn't want to sit through a boring personal conversation.

"I know what I am," Corey said. "I looked up those two words you guys saw on that paper with skin-walker and benandanti. I had to guess at spellings, but I eventually got a hit."

Daniel caught my look and gave an abashed nod. We hadn't even thought of that. The words had been blocked when we looked them up in Salmon Creek. That should have been the first thing we researched at the library.

"I'm sorry," I said. "We should have done that."

Corey looked confused. "Why? Finding the right term for what I am is hardly a priority. It's not like looking up something that's supposed to be real. Whatever we find on the web is just stories. Like with you guys. I looked up you both, too. Daniel's supposed to be fighting for the olive crops. I bet you don't even know where the nearest olive crop is."

"No idea," Daniel said.

"And Maya? You're supposed to be an evil witch." He paused. "Well, they got that part right."

I pitched a pebble at him.

"Hey, I was nice to you earlier. Gotta balance it out. Point is, I looked up *sileni* and *xana*. Hayley and Nicole are xana, which is a really obscure kind of Spanish mermaid-siren cross. A blond water spirit that sings. I couldn't find much on them. But apparently, they have some kind of evil-fighting skills themselves. You know how sirens are supposed to drive guys crazy with their singing? Well, xana can do that, too, but only to folks who deserve it." He paused. "Which means I really gotta be a lot nicer to Hayley."

"Good idea," I said. "So that makes you a sileni, then. Which is . . . ?"

He poked a stick at the dirt, like he was prodding an imaginary campfire. It took a moment before he said, "You know what a satyr is?"

"Um, a guy who's half goat?"

He glowered at me.

"What?" I said. "It is, isn't it? Centaur is part horse. Faun is part deer. Satyr is—"

"It's a lie. They were confused with some Roman monsters when the Romans and Greeks started hanging out together. The real Greek satyrs were followers of Dionysus. They looked human."

"Dionysus," I said. "God of wine, women, and song. You know, when you said you didn't fit your type—"

"Yeah, yeah. So okay, these satyrs liked to run around, drinking and chasing women and playing some kind of harmonica. Their leader was a guy named Silenus, who had visions of the future."

"Ah . . ."

"He was a minor god," Corey said. "He taught Dionysus."

"Like Chiron and Achilles."

"Huh?"

"Oh, right. You slept through Greek and Roman mythology. You said you didn't need to know it because it wasn't applicable to your life. Guess you were wrong, huh?"

Daniel chuckled.

"So Silenus was a minor deity," I said. "What's the connection to you?"

"It's complicated. You remember those long stories we had to write in English last year? Mr. Parks accused me of having constancy errors?"

"Continuity errors," I said.

"Whatever. It wasn't a big deal."

"Your characters changed names. More than once."

"Only by a few letters," he said. "Anyway, obviously Parks never read myths. Those guys were zinging out continuity errors all the time. Sometimes Silenus was one guy and sometimes sileni was a word used for all his followers."

"It's the influence of other cultures. Plus regional difference and the impact of oral storytelling."

"Was that an exam answer you memorized?" He shook his head. "No one likes a keener, Maya. Stuff the commentary or I'll call your brother back."

"I heard that," said a voice from the woods.

"Yeah?" Corey called back. "You know how to avoid hearing things you don't want to? Don't eavesdrop."

"Hard to do when you have super hearing," Ash said as he stepped into the clearing.

"Also hard to do when you won't go very far, in case that Uzi-toting sparrow finds you."

Ash flipped him off and strolled back to the "campfire," taking his time, so we wouldn't make the mistake of thinking he wanted to join us.

"Yeah, you're a sileni," Ash said as he lowered himself onto a log.

"You knew?" Corey said. "Thanks for the 411."

"You never asked."

"I'm asking now, then. What else can you tell me?"

Ash shrugged. "Nothing, really. I know what benandanti, xana, and sileni are, but it doesn't have anything to do with me, so I didn't see the point in studying up. You're supposed to see visions, which I guess you do. That's your main power. That and charm."

"Charm?"

Another shrug. "Like benandanti have the power of persuasion, sileni have the power of charm. People like them. Doesn't seem as if that one kicked in yet. Maybe someday."

"Hey, I've got charm. It just works better on chicks." He glanced at me. "Right?"

I arched my brows.

"Not you," he said. "I mean chicks I actually like."

Daniel sputtered as my brows went higher.

Corey glared at both of us. "You know what I mean."

"Yes," I said. "Speaking purely from an observational standpoint, you have your charms. Particularly with girls who've been drinking or whose sense of judgment is otherwise impaired. Which probably comes from the satyr angle."

"Very funny. What happened to wanting to make me feel better about this whole vision thing?"

"That was before I discovered you're a Greek god. I don't think you get to feel bad about that."

"Greek god?" He smiled. "I kinda am, aren't I?"

"Great," Daniel muttered. "His ego really needed that."

"A minor Greek god," I said. "Very minor. Possibly with a horse tail. Or goat legs."

Corey reached over to thump me in the arm and I ducked away, laughing.

I could see Ash getting ready to leave again, so I turned to him. "Is there anything else you can tell us? About any of the types?"

He shrugged. "Probably not. Depends on what you already know."

I could just ask him to tell us everything he did, but I had a feeling that the more specific our questions were, the more likely he was to answer. Lengthy discourses weren't his style. Yet another reason to wonder if we really were related after all.

"Can we tell you what we know and you can help us fill in the blanks?" I asked.

"Guess so."

His tone suggested he'd really rather not, but he'd agreed, so I plowed forward before he changed his mind.

According to Ash, Project Phoenix hadn't attempted to resurrect four extinct supernatural types. It had tried for six. Two had been a complete bust, though, as far as anyone could tell, which is why they weren't on Mina Lee's list. As for what those two types were, Ash didn't know. It didn't concern him.

That seemed like a selfish way to look at things. But living in Salmon Creek, I could afford to pursue anything that interested me. I had parents who gave me everything I needed. I didn't even have to take a part-time job. No Salmon Creek kid did. Our "job" was school. If we wanted to do more, we were encouraged to volunteer in our community.

If you lived on the streets, though, your job was survival. You couldn't afford to take an interest in much that didn't directly affect you. Obviously, Ash had focused on the skin-walker aspects of Project Phoenix. Anything else, he'd learned incidentally. I couldn't imagine not wanting to know more. Not being curious. But so far, he hadn't shown much curiosity about anything—our situation, our experiences, our lives. Maybe even that—basic personal curiosity—is a luxury for some.

Given his lack of interest, I suppose it was surprising how much he remembered of things he'd heard in passing. He knew what the four successful types were even before meeting us. He also knew that every kid between the ages of fifteen and seventeen in Salmon Creek had been a Project Phoenix subject.

Every kid between fifteen and seventeen. Every kid in our grade, most in the grade below us, and a few in the grade above. That didn't even cover all the subjects, though. There'd been a lot of attrition at the beginning—parents realizing they didn't want their kids being brought up in a lab after all, however utopian that lab might be. All four skin-walker parents went on the run, as Rafe already told me. Which is why they'd fought so hard to get me back into the fold.

There'd been six subjects in each of the six groups. Thirty-six altogether, excluding the preliminary subjects like Annie. Of the eight in Salmon Creek showing powers—me and Rafe, Daniel and Sam, Serena, Nicole and Hayley, and

Corey—seven had been on that helicopter. The eighth—Serena—was already dead. Was that a coincidence? No. We were the only ones for whom the modifications seemed to work.

While it was still possible there would be late bloomers, we were the guarantees. That's why we'd been on the same helicopter. That's why the mayor went with us. We were the most precious cargo. The Nasts knew that, which is why they'd targeted our helicopter. Hell, it's probably why they started the fire to force the evacuation.

That was really all Ash knew. I'm not sure how much it helped our situation, but at least we understood it a little better.

TWELVE

OUR MEMORIAL SERVICE WAS set for three thirty the next afternoon. That seemed like an odd hour, but maybe it was the only time they could get the park. Or maybe it was like holding it in Vancouver—a way to minimize the turnout. I'm sure they would have liked to skip the memorial altogether, but that was impossible, as long as they were pretending they gave a damn.

As soon as we realized the St. Clouds had declared us dead, we'd understood that they'd washed their hands of us. Traded us to the Nasts. Ash had a little more insight into the deal from his contacts, who knew supernaturals in both Cabals.

Cabals were, as we'd figured out, corporations run and staffed by supernaturals. Huge corporations. For regular supernaturals—like witches and half-demons—it gave them a job and a community where they didn't need to hide their powers. Kind of like what they apparently had in mind for us. You work for us; we'll look after you. Wage slaves provided with a decent job and good benefits.

The St. Clouds were the second smallest Cabal, more heavily invested in science than industry. The Nasts were the biggest. They'd let the St. Clouds do all the hard labor of creating and raising us, then they'd swooped in to steal the finished product. After the fire and crash, the two Cabals had negotiated a deal. The Nasts got all the kids on the helicopter . . . if they could catch them. The St. Clouds got paid for us and kept the "rejects" in hopes that some would be late bloomers.

So we'd been sold. Did that mean Rafe and Sam were with the Nasts now? What about Annie? We had no idea.

Not surprisingly, Ash hated the idea of showing up at the memorial. Also not surprisingly, he didn't keep his objections to himself.

"This is the stupidest idea ever," he grumbled as we lay on adjacent tree limbs a hundred meters from the memorial site.

"Is it any more stupid than it was the last fifty times you said that?" I asked.

"Maybe."

I sighed, shook my head, and looked around. Our ceremony was being held in a park. Outdoors, at the request of the parents. I knew whose parents had initiated that. Mine. An outdoor ceremony for the daughter who loved the wilderness. If I had any doubt who'd selected the location, it vanished when we'd arrived and I realized we'd been there before, my parents and me, for "breaks" when we'd come to Vancouver and the city got to be too much for me.

"I still don't get what you hope to accomplish here," Ash said.

I twisted to look at him. "We're going to try to make contact with one of our parents. Hopefully mine."

"Yeah, I get that part. What I don't get is how in hell they're supposed to help you." He put up a hand against my protest. "Your dad's a forest ranger. Your mom's an architect. You're sure they don't know about Project Phoenix, but hell, we'd be better off if they *did*, so at least they'd have some idea what's going on."

"Which is why they'll talk to Corey's mom. She's the police chief. Corey doesn't think she knows about the project, but she might. If she doesn't, they'll talk to Daniel's dad, who does know."

"So why not target him?"

I couldn't tell Ash about Daniel's father. Not without breaking a trust. So all I said was, "He isn't a good choice."

"Great. So we have a guy you don't trust, a small-town cop, and your parents, who know zip about the experiment, zip about fighting bad guys, and probably zip about supernaturals in general. Can I ask again what exactly it is you hope they can do?"

He already knew the answer. We'd told him the first time he asked. He was just making a point now. We really didn't know what our parents could do. We held on to the hope that someone would know about the experiment and the Cabals, and if they didn't, then they'd know someone who did, someone from Salmon Creek who could help us.

Help us do what? Free the others. But we couldn't take Annie on the run if the Cabals knew how to fix her. We couldn't take Corey on the run either if they could fix his headaches. And what if I started regressing?

The trouble was that the source of care was also the source of the threat. How were we supposed to reconcile that? I had no idea. All we could do was focus on making contact. On getting help and answers, and as nebulous as that plan was, it was all we had. Even Ash himself had admitted he didn't have another.

Ash wasn't the only one who didn't think I should be here. Daniel and I had a bit of a dustup about it this morning, when I'd declared my intention to watch the proceedings.

"I don't think you should do that, Maya," he'd said.

"Um, that's the plan, isn't it?"

He'd gone quiet then, shoving his hands in his pockets before saying, "The plan is for us to go and try to talk to someone. Not for you to watch the service. I think it's going to be too much for you."

I'd stared at him, unable to believe what he'd just said. Daniel might have a mile-wide protective streak, but he's never treated me like "a girl." If he had, our friendship would have ended years ago.

"What? I'm going to start sobbing and run to Mommy and Daddy? Seriously? You think—"

"I worded that wrong. I think it'll be too much for you *and* Corey. Watching your families grieving . . . It's going to be tough."

"I know that."

"Good. That's why I'm asking you both to hang back. Ash and I will watch. If my dad is mourning, the most I'm going to feel is shock."

"That's not true."

He shrugged. "Okay, maybe, but it's not going to hit me as hard. You know it won't. We haven't gotten along in years and I'm past the point of wishing it was otherwise. It'll upset me to see my brothers, but we're not really that close, either." He looked at me. "The point is that I'll be okay."

"And I won't?"

"I'm not saying—"

"Then don't say it. The more eyes on the service, the more likely we are to spot someone we can approach."

That hadn't ended it. We'd fought. Really fought. Enough to bring Corey running, and when I told him what Daniel wanted, Corey lit into him, too. Yes, this would be hard, but we could handle it and we weren't happy with Daniel for implying otherwise.

"What are the chances one of your parents is going to

wander off anyway?" Ash said, bringing me back to the present. "We're taking a huge risk here, you know."

"If you're worried, you can go wait—"

"I'm not worried." His chin shot up, eyes flashing, and I recognized the look. Probably the exact same one I'd given Daniel when he suggested I couldn't handle this. At least we had something in common.

I looked over to where Daniel and Corey were hidden in the long grass, just inside a patch of woods. I couldn't see either of them. Which meant they were well hidden. Except that I'd feel better if we had visual contact.

Ash had a cell phone. We probably should have bought a cheap prepaid ourselves. I hadn't thought of it until now. Hindsight . . .

At the rumble of tires on gravel, I looked over to see a black car pulling in to the parking lot. It had been roped off, but a man in a dark suit now held the rope as a line of black cars rolled in. They parked. Doors opened. I inched forward, wriggling to see better. My branch creaked.

"Careful," Ash said.

I stopped moving.

Mrs. Tillson climbed out of the first car, leaning heavily on the arm of a white-haired man I recognized from corporate literature as the head of St. Cloud corporation. Head of the St. Cloud Cabal, I should say. A sorcerer. Ash said all the Cabals were led by families of sorcerers. Did Mrs. Tillson know what he was? Did she care? Not right now. She'd suffered the greatest loss. Her husband—the mayor—really had died in the crash, and she believed that both her daughter, Nicole, and her niece, Sam, had perished, too.

Corey's mom was next. Chief Carling. Only she didn't seem like the Chief Carling I remembered, a petite blonde who could make her son quail with a single look and make him laugh just as easily. She looked tiny now, fragile and overwhelmed, clutching the hand of Corey's brother, Travis. He was all she had left—her husband had died a few years ago from an epileptic seizure. Was that seizure caused by sileni blood? One more thing to worry about for Corey.

Mr. Bianchi and Daniel's older brothers were in the next car. His brothers walked stiffly, side by side, gazes straight ahead. They hadn't helped their father from the vehicle. Hadn't even waited for him to get out. Just walked away, as if they blamed him for this. He followed, head bowed, like he accepted that blame, shambling along in a daze. I glanced toward the thicket where Daniel was hiding. I couldn't see him. I wished I could. I wished I wasn't up in this tree. My idea. A stupid idea. We should have been together for—

My parents stepped out of the last car. Dad first, then reaching in and helping Mom, and when I saw them, my heart stopped. I just lay there, frozen, clutching the tree so hard I dimly registered pain in my fingers, but only clutched it harder.

"Those them?"

Ash's voice brought me back again. I tore my gaze away

just long enough to nod. When I looked back, Mom and Dad were at the front of the car, helping Grandma from the passenger seat.

"They Navajo?" Ash asked. "The women?"

"My mom and grandmother. They're Haida."

"What the hell's that? Some Canadian tribe?"

"Yes."

He snorted. "Figures. Got a spare Indian baby? Give it to any Indian who'll take her. They're all the same anyway." He waved at my parents. "Hell, doesn't even matter if the new dad is Indian or not. He's a forest ranger? That's close enough. At one with nature and all that—"

"Shut up," I snarled. "Just shut the hell—" I choked on the rest and turned back to my family. They were making their way forward. Dad had his arm around Mom, gripping so close he seemed to be holding her upright. Grandma was on her other side, clasping her hand.

Someone met them and gestured to chairs in front of a giant photo. It was from this past spring, of me crouched, hugging Kenjii, and grinning. We were both splattered with mud after Dad let Daniel and me take his Jeep off-roading after a heavy rain. We'd come back and Mom made us stay outside—not because of the mud, but because she wanted pictures. In the real photo Daniel was there, too, standing behind me, and I could see his hand in the blown-up version. A disembodied hand resting on my shoulder. I wished they'd left him in it, maybe even let us have a joint photo, but his dad had picked one of Daniel in a suit, looking somber and uncomfortable and not like Daniel at all.

When the man directed them to their spot, Mom seemed to notice the photo for the first time. She stopped, making Dad falter and Grandma stumble. Then she . . . she made this noise. This horrible noise. A keening wail as she dropped. Just dropped, like someone had cut her legs out from under her, and Dad grabbed her before she hit the ground, and he crouched there, bent on one knee, with Mom collapsed against him, and I could hear her crying. Even from here, I could hear her crying.

"I can't do this," I said, scrambling onto all fours. "I have to go tell—"

"No!" Ash swung up. He poised there, ready to pounce on me. "You can't, Maya."

I looked back at my parents, buried against each other, my dad's back rising and falling hard, and I knew he was crying, too. I should have listened to Daniel. Why the hell hadn't I listened to Daniel? Because I'd been stubborn. Stubborn and proud, as always, and now I saw exactly what he'd meant and how right he'd been. This was cruel—unbelievably cruel—watching my parents suffer when all I had to do was leap from this tree and run over—

I let out a shuddering breath and looked over to where Daniel was hiding and saw him there, half rising from the grass, his gaze fixed on me. He raised his hand, not quite a wave, more just . . . something. Some attempt at contact, at comfort, and I wished I was there. Damn it, why wasn't I with him? What the hell had possessed me to be up here, to go through this alone?

I lifted my hand, reaching out. Then Corey pulled him down.

"Good," Ash grunted.

I glanced over and reminded myself I wasn't alone. Not really. But in some ways, I wished I was, because I got nothing from Ash. Not a smile. Not a kind word. Not even a sympathetic look. He just scowled, like I was going to blow our cover over nothing.

I turned back to my parents.

"Don't."

I looked over again. Now I saw some glimmer in his eyes, though he held his face tight, lips still compressed.

"Don't look," he said. "Just . . . don't look."

I hesitated, and I wanted to say I could handle it. But I couldn't. Not this. So I dropped my cheek to the rough bark, closed my eyes, and listened to the ceremony.

Listening wasn't easy, either. It was surreal when you knew that the kids they were reminiscing about were still alive. It was like hearing speeches at a wedding or a graduation, talking about someone's life, the best of their life, but instead of joy and laughter, each new recollection brought a sob or cry of grief.

When my dad got up to speak, I plugged my ears. I knew I had to. One crack in his voice and I'd have leaped from that tree, running to the stage, shouting, "I'm here, Daddy. I'm still here." So I plugged my ears and I squeezed my eyes shut until Ash reached over and tapped my arm.

When I took my fingers from my ears, he caught my hand and I looked over to tell him not to worry, that I wasn't going to do anything stupid, but he only gave my hand a squeeze— a quick one—before letting it fall.

THIRTEEN

THE SERVICE ENDED AFTER that. It wasn't until it did, and people started filing back to the cars, that I realized what had happened. Nothing. Not a single parent had wandered from the service for a few minutes of solace. How could they? They were all trapped in the front row. They couldn't have slipped away even if they had wanted to.

When the service ended, ushers surrounded our parents and escorted them directly to their vehicles, just as they'd escorted them in.

"They're not letting them stop for nothing," Ash said. "Not even a piss break. They have to hold it until they get them someplace safe."

I kept watching. Kept hoping. But Chief Carling and Travis climbed in their car. So did Daniel's family and Mrs. Tillson and the Morrises. My parents and Grandma lingered.

They didn't get up and talk to anyone, just sat in their seats as if they hadn't realized it was over. Two more ushers came over and finally got them into the car.

"No one left," I whispered. "No one at all."

"Could have told you that," Ash said.

I glared over at him.

"What? I could have. Cabals are geniuses at this kind of thing. They've been around since the Inquisition. That's hundreds of years of experience acting like good corporate citizens while they do stuff that would make the Mafia take notes. They'll cover up your deaths and they'll hold your parents prisoner until they've rounded you all up. And the beauty of it? Your parents won't even realize they were prisoners. They'll just think the St. Clouds were being really, really helpful."

He eased back on his branch. "I knew they'd never let you near them."

"Then why didn't you say so?"

"You wouldn't have listened."

There was no response to that, so I lay on the branch, staring down, sifting through the remaining friends and families for someone left that we could contact. Maybe. If we were careful. And desperate. When I saw Brendan Hajek over by the washrooms I turned my attention to him. He started heading in the opposite direction—away from the service area. I glanced back to see his mother, the local veterinarian, helping remove the posters from the stage.

So Dr. Hajek had volunteered for clean-up duty and Brendan was using the break to wander off for a bit. Alone.

"I need to talk to Daniel," I said. "I'm going down. Can you cover me?"

"What?"

Ash had been peering at something and jumped when I spoke. I had to repeat myself.

"No, we need to stay here."

"There's no one around. I can dash—"

"You need to stay here, Maya, until those guys are gone." He pointed to a cluster of strangers beside the stage.

"You know them?" I said.

"No, but they're obviously Cabal goons."

They looked like normal mourners to me. The two guys in suits could be security—they were certainly big enough—but everyone else just looked ordinary. Until one of them took a two-way radio from his pocket and stepped away from the group, and I followed his gaze to see another "ordinary-looking guy" across the park, also on a radio.

"Why are they still here?" I said. "Almost everyone's gone."

"You're not." He swore under his breath. "They knew you'd come. They must have. They're searching the park now."

"Okay, we knew that might happen. We'll lie low until everyone's gone."

We continued watching. Another car arrived and a woman got out. She looked as ordinary as the rest of them.

Older, maybe in her fifties, with short graying hair. She wore a stylish jacket and slacks.

Ash cursed and scrambled up.

"What?" I said.

"Witch."

I peered at the woman, who looked more like a prep school teacher. "How can you tell?"

"By the long black hair and pointed nose." He shot me a look. "I recognize her, obviously. The St. Clouds only have one witch, as far as I know, and that's her."

"One witch? Are they rare?"

"No, it's just that sorcerers don't like working with them and vice versa."

"Okay, so . . ."

"Cabals have witches so they can use high-powered witch magic, like sensing spells."

I remembered a memo I'd seen about our escape. Calvin Antone had been asking for a werewolf and the Enwright witches to help track us.

"And sensing spells do what exactly?" I said, pretty sure I didn't want to hear the answer.

"They . . . sense." He waved his hand and made a face, like this was a stupid question. "Like radar or heat detectors. The St. Clouds are going to wait until the park is clear of mourners, then have her start casting. When she does, we're toast. The Nasts are probably here, too, with their witch. A joint effort to get you guys off the street."

"We need to get—"

I looked down. The second guy with the radio was heading our way. To our left a man and a woman pretending to be a couple strolled along, but I could see the radio stuffed in the guy's pocket.

"Yeah," Ash said. "Coming to your own memorial service? Really not a bright idea. We're trapped in this tree, Maya. The guys can get away through those woods. Except they have no way to know what's going on because we're the ones who can see and we have no way of telling them."

"We need to—"

"We're trapped, don't you get that? We can't get down there without being spotted, and if we can't get down, we're going to get caught as soon as that witch casts her spell."

"Are you supposed to be helping? Because I thought that's why you came. To help."

He answered with a scowl.

"I'll take that as a yes, though it's hard to interpret, because glowering seems to be your all-purpose response. Telling me what *won't* work doesn't help." I looked up. "We can climb higher. What's the range on her spell?"

"How the hell would I know?"

"Higher, then, if that's the only option we have. But it doesn't help the guys."

"You can't worry about the—"

"Yes, I can."

I leaned out as far as I dared, with the patrolling

employees getting ever closer. I waved. No response from the thicket. I pulled a penny from my pocket and turned to Ash.

"How's your aim?"

"I'm the pitcher on my varsity baseball team and archery champ at my country club."

I threw the penny. It didn't come close.

Ash sighed and zinged one from behind me. It hit the right spot. So did a second. But the guys didn't pop up.

"They're gone," Ash said. "Either that or they didn't notice. Nothing else you can do."

"I can—"

"Have you been holding their hands since the crash? Single-handedly fighting off the bears and wildcats and rattlesnakes?"

"We don't have rattlesnakes."

"They're big boys, Maya. They can take care of themselves. And your benandanti boyfriend seems to know you can take care of yourself."

"He's my *friend*."

"Why do you keep saying that? I don't care if you're going out with the guy, which you obviously are."

"How is it obvious? Because we talk? Because we're close?"

"Um, no. Because you're *always* talking. Except when you're whispering or giggling. And if by 'close' you mean 'can't keep your hands off each other'—"

"Excuse me?"

"Maybe you guys are trying to hide your relationship, but he can't get near you without finding an excuse to touch your hand or your arm, and you're just as bad."

I glowered at him. "We've been through hell. It's called compassion. Maybe you should try it."

"Yeah, that's not compassion, Maya." He lifted a hand against my protest. "Fine. You're just friends. Point is, Daniel will trust you're okay and get Corey to safety."

Ash surveyed the ground. The three people we'd spotted earlier were still close by. Over at the nearly dismantled stage, the witch looked as if she was getting last-minute instructions.

"Shit," Ash muttered. "I'm going to need to save you."

"Excuse me? No one needs—"

"I'm saving you, so shut up and be grateful." He moved to a crouch. "I'll get to the next tree and jump down. That'll create a distraction. When they take the bait, you run."

He crouched and reached for the limb above his head.

I pushed up. "I'm not letting you—"

He wheeled so fast I nearly lost my balance. "If I'm putting my ass on the line, you'd damned well better stay right there, Maya. You think I'm a jerk now? This is me being nice. You come after me? I won't be nice. Now sit down and wait. They don't know me. They won't do more than chase me a bit and it'll give you time to get away. I'll find you later."

He was right—they wouldn't recognize him. If he could create a distraction, I should use it.

I watched him cross to the next tree. I tensed, ready to leap down and race into the woods. It was the safest place for me. I'd also run past where Daniel and Corey were hiding, so I could warn them if they were still there.

Ash didn't jump down from that tree, though. Once he got to it, he must have realized it was closer to the next one than he thought, and I watched his dark figure make another leap. Then I heard something. A voice I recognized. I swiveled fast, following the sound, hoping I was wrong—

Antone and Moreno walked from an SUV over to where the St. Cloud witch and two men were heading out to begin scouting.

Ash was right. Both Cabals were here. They might be rivals, but it would be in everyone's best interests to work together on some issues. Like rounding us up before we caused trouble.

But if Antone was here . . . I glanced up at the dark shape that was Ash, moving through the third tree.

I got to my feet, grabbed the next branch and went after him. Adrenaline slammed through my veins and I moved so fast that when I was leaping to the third tree, I never even paused to check the distance, noticing only after I jumped that the next branch was too far. A brief flash of terror as I realized my mistake too late. A grunt of surprise from Ash as he saw me jump.

Somehow I landed on the next branch easily, as if it'd been a mere step away. I looked back, wondering how I'd done that. Another power?

Ash let out a stream of hissed profanity as he made his way toward me. "I told you—*told you*—to stay there. Are you trying to get us both—?"

"You can't jump down," I said, crouched and holding the limb tight as I caught my breath. "He'll recognize you."

"Who'll recognize me?"

"Our . . ." I gulped breath. "Our father."

"What?" His face screwed up. "You mean your dad?" He peered down. "Did he come back?"

"No, *our* father. Our biological one." I pointed across the park. "Calvin Antone."

He squinted. "That guy over there? In the jean jacket? That's . . ." He was looking away, so I couldn't see his expression.

"It's our father," I said. "We've met. He used to work for the St. Clouds, then he switched sides. He's the one who tipped the Nasts off and started this whole mess."

He continued watching Antone, then gave his head a sharp shake and turned on the branch to face me. "Doesn't matter. No way in hell he'll recognize me. You look like him. I don't."

That wasn't true. When I first saw Ash, I'd thought he looked familiar. Now I knew why. Antone and I might share the same eyes and cheekbones, but Ash was nearly the spitting image of him. What had thrown me was his hazel eyes and brown hair. That's what he meant, I'm sure—that he didn't have our father's coloring. It didn't matter.

"He'll recognize you," I said.

"He's never met—"

"Doesn't matter. Do you know why he quit the St. Clouds? Because they wouldn't give me to him. That's why he turned us in to the Nasts. Because they promised to give me to him."

"That's you. That's not—"

"He wants me because I'm the one he found. He's still looking for you. If anyone has ever taken a picture of you, you can be sure he has it. Probably in his wallet. Which would be very sweet—if he wasn't willing to mow down anyone who gets between us and him. He'll know you, Ash. I can guarantee he'll know you."

"Fine." One last glance at Antone, then he pulled his gaze away and looked out over the park. "Now what?"

"We go back to where we were and make a dash to the woods—"

"They'll see us."

"We can—"

"You're only thinking of doing that because of your friends." He inched along the tree. "I get that you're worried about them. You guys have grown up together and you've been through a lot and Daniel is obviously . . . important to you."

"All my friends are."

Ash rolled his eyes but didn't pursue it. "That's great, I'm sure. Except when you're so concerned that you'll make a bone-headed move to reach them. You need to trust that they can look after themselves, Maya. You need to look after yourself."

His gaze jerked left and I saw Antone, the witch, and the others less than a hundred meters away.

Ash swore. "Great. Pep talk over." He met my gaze. "Either you come with me or I leave. I didn't come to have my ass hauled into a cage."

"I'm with you."

I scanned our surroundings. The tiny building housing the washrooms was right under the next tree. I pointed to it.

Ash shook his head. "Already scoped it. Can't jump onto the roof without being exposed and the branches over it don't go far enough to get us to the other side, where we could jump down and be hidden."

"Then we'll have to jump farther."

"Too much risk. I can't see how thick the branches are, and—"

"Has anyone ever told you you're hopelessly pessimistic?"

"Has anyone ever told you you're recklessly optimistic?"

"It's not reckless if you don't have a choice." I started out. "Follow my lead. Try not to fall."

He muttered something under his breath, but he stayed behind me.

FOURTEEN

ASH WAS RIGHT. THE branch over the washrooms didn't extend all the way—not before it tapered off too much for us to balance on. We'd have to get close enough, try to jump over the building and hope we didn't thump down on the roof instead. I went first. The hard part of this was, well, the hard part—namely the ground at the end of the four-meter leap. I managed it, but pain still stabbed through my legs. I was safe, though, hidden on the other side of the small building.

Ash wasn't quite so lucky. He wouldn't go as far out on the branch as I had. I'm sure he'd say it's because he was heavier, but I wasn't wrong when I said he could be overly cautious. His jump was a few inches short, which meant he didn't land on the roof, but his back did bump the edge. He hit the ground harder, too, and crouched there, teeth clenched as he inhaled and exhaled.

"You okay?" I whispered.

He glowered up at me.

"Hey, we're where we wanted to be, right?" I tilted my head to listen. "No cries of alarm."

He grumbled.

"Yeah, yeah. Now turn around and give me your shirt."

"What?"

"We're trading shirts. I was wearing this one the last time Antone saw me. Then we're going to walk. From this far away, I'm hoping, if we are spotted, they won't recognize me if I'm with you. You're too small to be Daniel or Corey."

He scowled. "Thanks."

"It's a fact, not an insult. Stop being so damned sensitive and take off your shirt."

We switched tops with a remarkable lack of further muttering on his part. I tucked my long hair under it, so from a distance, it would look short. There were more trees in front of us—too widely spaced for us to climb through, but they cast plenty of shadowy shade. On the other side was a playground, then another parking lot. Lots of obstacles in both. My plan was for us to just walk out of the park, as casually as possible, using what cover we could.

It wasn't a great plan, but if our sensitive hearing picked up a cry or approaching footfalls, we should have time to run. They wouldn't use a tranq gun in a public park. Not with a scattering of parents and little kids over in the playground. Or so I hoped.

"Okay, now hold my hand," I said.

Ash looked at me like I'd asked him to swallow live bugs.

"I'm your sister," I said. "If I have cooties, they're the same as yours."

When he stuck out his hand, he looked like he was getting ready to arm wrestle. I took it, and he tensed, biceps flexing, stance widening.

I sighed. "I'm not going to throw you over my shoulder."

He snorted, as if such a thing was beyond the realm of possibility. I was briefly tempted to show him otherwise. Instead, I wrapped my hand around his fist and we set out, a teenage couple strolling through the park.

We wandered, talking. Or I talked, to the point where another couple of guys passing by shot him sympathetic looks.

As we approached the playground, I whispered, "We'll get behind that big slide structure, then hurry to the parking lot."

He let out what sounded like a sigh of relief. We stepped into the park. A little girl stopped swinging to watch us. I smiled at her and she grinned back. When Ash looked over, the girl stopped smiling and jumped off to run to her mother.

"Can you try not to frighten small children?" I whispered.

He grunted and kicked up wood chips as we walked alongside the play structure, moving into the shade behind it. Only a quick dash to the parking lot, and—

I caught a movement to my left and looked to see someone

106

standing about fifty meters away, by the edge of the woods. A teenage guy in a suit. Staring at us.

Brendan.

I'd forgotten about Brendan.

Could I make it to him? Just long enough to pass on a message?

What message? What could I possibly tell him in thirty seconds or less that wouldn't just make matters worse?

Not even thirty seconds—two of the searchers were heading straight for him. Walking fast, as if they'd just realized they had a Salmon Creek kid on the loose.

I ripped my gaze from Brendan. He hadn't recognized me. Couldn't. Not from this distance. Not with Ash. Not when I was supposed to be—

"Maya?" Brendan called.

I didn't look over. Ash did, then swore. He pulled his fist from my hand and grabbed my wrist instead, yanking me along as he broke into a jog.

"Maya!" Brendan yelled.

"What the hell are you doing?" I said, tripping as I tried to pull free from Ash's grip.

"He can't help you and I'm not letting you do something stupid—"

"Like breaking into a run and letting him know it really is me?"

He cursed as he realized his mistake and slowed.

"Too late now," I muttered, grabbing his elbow. "Run!"

We raced into the parking lot as shouts and cries rang out behind us.

I didn't hear Brendan's voice again. I think they must have gotten to him, bustling him off before he was absolutely sure of what he'd seen. *Who* he'd seen. I hoped so. Really hoped so. I didn't want to think what they'd do if he insisted that he'd spotted me.

We should have thought of that—what would happen if someone saw us and we couldn't warn them to keep quiet? We were so desperate that I think Ash was right—we were being reckless, however hard we tried not to be.

We escaped the park. If you have enough of these encounters, eventually that's all it comes down to. Was anyone captured? Anyone hurt? No and no. Then it's not worthy of comment. We'd had a good enough lead on our pursuers, and by the time they got vehicles to come after us, we were gone.

We returned to Stanley Park. We'd left our bag of extra clothes and supplies hidden there. The guys would come back.

We returned around seven, after two hours on buses, transferring and retransferring just in case we were being followed. I expected the guys to be at our campsite when we returned. When they weren't, we settled in to wait.

We'd been there for about thirty minutes in silence, which only added to the hours of silence since we'd escaped at the park. I'd tried several times on the bus to strike up conversation with Ash. It was met either with suspicion—what does it matter where I've lived?—or sarcasm—hobbies? sports? yeah, did I mention the varsity baseball and country club? By this point, I began to suspect "what's your favorite color" would be seen as intrusive. So I stopped trying.

"What's it like?" Ash said finally as we sat on the logs around our nonexistent campfire.

"Hmm?"

"Shifting into a mountain lion. What's it feel like? Hurts like hell, I bet."

When I didn't answer in the next two seconds, his face darkened. "I was just curious. Skin-walkers are supposed to be extinct. Not a lot of people I can ask."

"I was trying to decide how to describe it. I know you're not happy to be here, Ash. I don't know what you expected. Not me, that's obvious. Maybe you're pissed because you came all this way and I don't seem grateful. I am. I really am. But I can't figure out a way to show that without pissing you off all the more. You've got your back up and there's no way I'm getting it down."

"Do I?" His eyes narrowed. "Huh. Let me ask you this, Maya. In all these years, when you were growing up in your perfect town, with your perfect friends and your perfect parents, did you even think about me? Wonder where I was? Worry about me? Or were you just happy you didn't need to share all that? Because I've been thinking about you for as long as I can remember. Asking our mother about you.

Wondering what happened to you. So, yeah, I dropped every-thing to come up here. And you really don't seem to give a shit."

I took a deep breath and considered my words before speaking.

"I'm sorry," I said.

He tensed, waiting for more, waiting for the snap, the growl, the snarl. When I said he had his back up, I hadn't meant that as a skin-walker jab. But now, when I looked at him, it was an apt description. His back was up, at least met-aphorically. Fur bristling. Eyes glittering. Lip curled. Ready to bite my head off. When I didn't respond in kind, he just sat there, tense and waiting.

"I didn't know about you." I spoke the words carefully, trying not to sound defensive. "I should have explained that better. I only found out a week ago that I had a brother. Rafe's the one who told me, when he told me about being a skin-walker."

Silence. Then, "Right." More silence. He shifted on the log. "Makes sense. It's not like she left a note with you."

"No. She didn't. But . . . after Rafe told me, I felt . . . guilty, I think. That I didn't know about you. Like I should have remembered you."

"We were only a few months old."

I shrugged. "It feels as if I should have known. Like in stories where someone grows up feeling like something's missing, then they discover they had a twin."

Silence.

"When I found out, I *did* think of you. Maybe not as much as I should have. When I thought of you, I felt . . ." I searched for the right words. "I won't say jealous, because I don't remember our mother and mine is great—I wouldn't trade her for anything. But it hurt, growing up knowing I'd been abandoned. Finding out there'd been two of us and I wasn't the one she'd chosen? That really hurt."

I sighed and stretched my legs. "I'm sorry. That was all I wanted to say. I didn't want to make excuses, which is what I'm doing." I looked over at him. "I am glad you came."

He mumbled something and got to his feet. He walked away, and I wanted to go after him, but I knew it wasn't that easy. One little discussion wasn't going to make everything better. It wasn't just about him feeling hurt and me feeling hurt. We were brother and sister—twins—and yet we were strangers. If it wasn't for that blood tie, we'd probably have chosen to remain strangers. That hurt, too, but again, it couldn't be fixed with a few words.

"You want dinner?" he said.

I shook my head. "I should stay for the guys. If you could pick me up something, though, I'd appreciate that."

I was quick to pull out a twenty, so he wouldn't think I was asking him to pay, but he still grumbled.

"Or I can run out for something after you get back," I said.

"I'm not bitching because you asked me to grab you food,

Maya. 'Course I will. But you shouldn't stay here alone, not when it looks like they've nabbed your friends."

That's what I'd been thinking, of course. What I'd been trying very, very hard not to think, because if I did, I'd slide into a full-blown panic. When Ash put that fear into words, I stiffened.

He sighed. "Yeah, you don't want to hear that. I'm not trying to make you feel bad. But if the Cabals have your friends, they might have gotten them to tell where they could find you."

"They wouldn't—"

"Let me try that again. They might have gotten Corey to tell them. Daniel wouldn't rat you out unless they stuck red hot pins under his nails, and probably not even then."

I glanced up at his face to see if he was being sarcastic. He wasn't.

"You guys are tight," he said. "Friends or whatever. But while Corey might be a good and loyal friend, he's not made of the same stuff as you two. I'm not saying he's a coward or anything. He's just . . . They could talk him into it. Tell him lies and shit until he really thinks he's saving your life by helping them find you."

Corey wouldn't be so quick to cave, but if they separated him from Daniel, he'd be uncertain, lost. He'd try hard to do the right thing, but eventually, they might be able to convince him that turning me in *was* the right thing. Especially if they knew I was with Ash. Corey hadn't trusted him. It wouldn't take much to convince him Ash was a traitor sent to turn me over to some even worse fate.

"I can leave a note," I said. "We have a pen and paper in our bag."

"Good. Just don't tell them where we're going."

"Can I draw a map?"

Now it was his turn to look over, to see if I was serious. I smiled and he shook his head, but I caught a hint of a return smile there before he told me to hurry it up.

FIFTEEN

THE CITY OF VANCOUVER is on a peninsula, bounded on three sides by water, so you usually need to cross a bridge to get from the suburbs to downtown. If you take the Lions Gate bridge—preferably not at rush hour—you drive through Stanley Park. That meant we had a pleasant evening stroll through the park to get downtown. Or I did. Ash seemed a lot more comfortable in the city proper.

By the time we arrived downtown, night had fallen. That made Ash anxious, but it didn't bother me. It was downtown Vancouver. As long as we didn't stray into a few bad pockets, we were fine.

I was wise enough to avoid suggesting sushi, but I did mention a falafel stand a few blocks away. From the look Ash gave me, that was just as bad. He wanted a burger. I knew a couple places that served amazing gourmet versions, including one just a block over that Daniel loved. But ten-dollar burgers were not on the budget, and even if I would have liked to treat Ash, he would have taken it the wrong way. So we settled for A&W.

Afterward, as we walked, Ash said, "You mentioned buying a prepaid cell earlier."

"Right."

"We should do that. In case you and I get separated." He paused. "Or for your friends. Uh, when they get back."

"You really think they were—" My chest tightened and I couldn't get the rest out.

"If they were, we'll deal. For now, you need that phone."

I peered down a street of closed shops and scattered bars. "It's a little late . . ."

"Corner stores sell them these days. Just gotta find one."

I wasn't sure that applied in Canada. We didn't have nearly as many cell providers as they did in the States. But I nodded and let him lead the way down the next street.

We'd gone down four blocks and into two corner stores with no luck. I wanted to ask the clerks if they knew where to buy a phone, but Ash wouldn't let me near the counter. I suggested *he* ask. He just rolled his eyes, as if I was naive to think they'd be helpful.

At the third store, a guy was outside talking to himself. Harmless, I was sure, but Ash insisted I go inside with him, though I had to wait by the door.

I heard the drunk guys before I saw them. They were loud

enough that feline hearing was not required. They stopped outside the store and peered in. I stepped out of their line of sight, but not before I got a look at them. College guys, wearing sports jerseys and sloppy grins. They slammed the door open hard enough to make the clerk wince.

"Hey!" one yelled as he walked in—though the clerk wasn't more than a couple meters away. "We want beer. You got beer?"

"We do not sell alcohol in these shops. You must go to a liquor store."

In unison, two of them repeated the guy's words, exaggerating his accent. I shook my head. Tourists. There were a couple of provinces that sold alcohol in corner stores, but I was guessing these were Americans. Our lower drinking age is a draw. Which was not to say that all drunken louts are obviously American—only the ones who didn't realize they couldn't buy beer in any store.

I'd moved back as far as I could without hiding, but when they took another step, they could see me.

"I bet *she* knows where we can find beer," said the redhead in front. "Hey, cutie, make you a deal. Tell us where to find some and you can come drinking with us."

"No, thank you," I said, straightening, so it wouldn't look like I was shrinking against the shelves.

"What makes you think she'd know where to find booze?" Ash came around the counter, gaze fixed on the guys as he moved between me and them.

I whispered for him to let it go, keeping my voice low enough that only he'd hear. He knew exactly why these guys thought I'd know where to find alcohol, but this really wasn't the time for a lesson in racial stereotyping.

Ash kept moving forward. *Stalking* forward, like a cat, eyes on his prey, muscles tight, almost gliding across the floor, smooth and silent. The guys just snickered and jostled each other.

"Do you want a chocolate bar before we go?" I said to Ash. "I'm going to grab one."

His head whipped my way, eyes narrowed in a "What the hell?" look. I was trying to diffuse the situation. Of course, he didn't see that. He probably thought I was standing there, being insulted, and honestly thinking, *You know, I'd like some chocolate.*

"You go do that, cutie," the redhead said. "We'll get rid of your boyfriend for you."

"I'm her brother," Ash said.

"Oh? Good. So then you won't mind if I . . ." He suggested something we could do together. It wasn't "go see a movie." He got about halfway through before Ash took a swing at him. I was already mid-pounce and grabbed Ash's arm before it made contact. When I wrenched it back, he wheeled on me, lips curled in a snarl.

"You want to fight?" I whispered under my breath. "Fine. But if you do, I'll need to run before the cops show up."

He blinked and removed my hand from his arm. Then he

nodded and rolled his shoulders. I could feel the rage pulsing off him. The drunk guys just stood there, snickering and lobbing insults. I zeroed in on the fourth guy, a blond who was hanging back, looking uncomfortable. I propelled Ash toward him, saying, "Excuse me," and he moved aside. I bustled Ash past before the others could block our escape.

"Morons," Ash muttered as we reached the sidewalk.

"Agreed," I said. "But picking a fight with them won't help."

"So you just put up with that crap?"

"No, I usually have a comeback, unless they're too drunk to get it, which those guys were. Now, let's put off buying a phone until morning and—"

"Hey!" The corner store door banged behind us. "Did we say you two rez rats could leave?"

"Keep walking," I murmured.

"I am," he said, with a growl that told me it wasn't easy.

"Hey, you. Half-breed. I'm talking to you."

Ash slowed, tensing fast, and when I gripped his arm, I could feel the muscles bunching.

"Keep walking, Ash," I whispered. "Please keep walking."

"That's what I'm doing, isn't it?"

"Yo! Half-breed. Bring your sister back here. We're not done with her yet. Hell, we haven't even started with her yet."

Laughter from the others. I had Ash's arm in a vise grip now, practically dragging him along, his sneakers scraping the sidewalk, as if he was two seconds from wheeling and charging.

"You shouldn't have to put up with that," he muttered as they called out suggestions behind us.

"Every girl has to put up with that. It doesn't matter what color her skin is."

Shoes clomped behind us, coming fast.

"Yo, half-breed. Tell you what. You show us where we can get some beer, and we'll give you a whole case for your sister. That's a good trade, isn't it, *kemosabe*? I know you guys like to trade, and she's such a pretty little—"

Ash spun and hit the redhead with an uppercut that sent him reeling. I grabbed his arm, but he shook me off. The other three thundered down the sidewalk as their leader recovered and swung at Ash. Ash ducked the blow and came back with a right hook that sent the guy spinning.

"Run," he snarled over his shoulder at me. "Get out of here."

That's what I'd threatened to do. That's what I should do. Even now, cars were slowing and a group of barhoppers were crossing the road to watch the entertainment.

If it had been one guy, I'd have run. Clearly Ash could take care of himself against one guy. Maybe even two. But the other three were moving in and I knew no one had planned on a fair fight.

As the redhead recovered, I leaped between him and Ash.

"That's enough," I said. "You aren't going to find beer at this hour unless you go to a bar. There are plenty around. Now go find one."

He shoved me out of the way. I lunged to grab him, but one of his friends caught me, yanked me off my feet, and threw me aside. I heard Ash snarl as I hit the ground. When I turned to scramble up, they were all piling on him. Rage filled me. I grabbed the back of the nearest one's jacket and heaved. He spun to backhand me, then stopped.

"What the hell?"

He knocked my hands off his jacket and stumbled from the heap, still staring. When he backed away, one of his friends glanced our way. He stared at me. Just stared. My hands flew to my face and I felt it shifting. I lowered my hands. Fur was sprouting on the backs.

SIXTEEN

"WHAT THE HELL?" THE guy said again, his voice rising.

The others had stopped hitting Ash. He caught a glimpse of me and let out a curse. He pushed his attackers off, ran over, grabbed my wrist, and started hauling me along the sidewalk. The guys just stood there, staring.

We nearly crashed into a couple stepping out of a restaurant. The man started to snap at us, then saw my face and yanked his wife aside.

"You need to stop," Ash hissed. "Reverse it."

"I'm trying." My voice was harsh, guttural as my vocal cords began to change. "But once it starts . . ."

He swore and looked around. I saw a parking garage across the road.

"There," I said, pointing, my fingers curving under.

I moved as fast as I could, but my hips were changing, too, legs bowing. Ash hauled me into the parking garage. I made it around the first corner, then staggered to a shadowy gap between two SUVs.

"Good," he said. "Get in there. I'll stand guard."

He pushed me. My legs gave way and I crashed down.

"Shit!" He swooped down to grab me. "I didn't mean to do that."

I waved for him to move away.

"Do you need anything? Can I do anything?"

Just get out of the way so I can get my clothing off before I pass out. That was too much for my vocal cords to manage, so I just shook my head and waved him back again.

Thankfully, I seemed to be getting more lead time before the passing-out part, and I managed to get mostly undressed before I hit the ground.

I recovered better, too, not lying there, dazed and wondering what hit me. I stood and stretched, letting out a snarling yawn. Ash spun from his spot guarding the gap. He stared at me.

"Maya?"

Who else? I would have said, if I could, but I knew he wasn't questioning whether it was me, but whether it was really "me" or was I subsumed by the cat, which might lunge and sink its fangs into his neck at any moment.

I chuffed.

"Okay," he said, still gaping. "So that's . . . you look like a mountain lion. I mean, obviously, but I wasn't sure if we'd look like real mountain lions or some kind of monster. Definitely a cat."

I stretched, head down, front paws out, hindquarters in the air. My tail flicked against one of the SUVs with a thump.

"You're bigger than I expected," he said.

I shot out the claws on my extended front paws.

He chuckled. "Nice."

I retracted my claws and settled on the pavement, head on my front paws.

"Yeah, I guess that's about all we can do." He lowered himself. "Sit and wait for you to shift back."

I chuffed. And so we waited. It could take awhile, but we were tucked back deep enough that cars passed without their drivers catching sight of us.

Then, "You! What're you doing there?"

Loafers slapped the pavement, the daintier click of high heels hurrying to catch up. Ash got to his feet and leaned out.

"Yes, you," the man's voice said. "Between the cars. What the hell are you doing?"

"Parking," Ash said.

"Right. Your car? Or one you jacked?"

"Bill," a woman's voice murmured, cutting him off. "Don't."

The man grumbled. "You just better hope it wasn't my truck you were breaking into, boy."

"This yours here?"

Ash thumped the SUV on the right. It was a light thump, just enough to let me know that I needed to get under the other vehicle. But the guy shouted, as if Ash had bashed it with a sledgehammer.

"Bill!"

There was no time to crawl under either SUV. The man was right there. Ash blocked, but he wasn't nearly large enough to hide the tawny big cat crouched on the dark pavement.

"Jesus!" the man said. "It's a cougar."

"It's okay," Ash said quickly. "She's just scared. I was getting a better look—making sure she wasn't hurt. She's fine, and if we all just leave her alone, she'll find her way out."

"Find her way out?" the woman exclaimed. "That's—that's a cougar. In the city. Bill! Get back from there." She pulled out her phone. "I'm calling 911."

"No, wait," her husband cut in before Ash could. "Get a picture first. Hold on. I'll get closer. I want to be in it."

"Bill! It's a cougar!"

"Stop shrieking. It's an overgrown cat."

Ash froze, torn between stopping him and stopping the woman from calling the police. The man brushed past him. I swallowed a growl and forced myself to stay perfectly still. If he wanted an overgrown cat, that's what I'd be. Let him get his photo. Convince his wife I wasn't a threat. I hoped Ash could persuade them to leave afterward.

"See, Sue? Just a big kitty. You're a pretty kitty, aren't

you? A big, pretty kitty cat." He kept inching forward. "Get the camera ready, Sue."

Every instinct told me to run. Cat instincts. Wild animal instincts. But I was still human. I didn't need to surrender to those. So I slitted my eyes and forced myself to stay still while this idiot approached a 120-pound cougar with his hand out, ready to scratch it behind the ears.

Wild animal attacks on humans are rare, but of all the predators in Canada, the cougar may be the one most likely to do it. Obviously, this guy never got the memo. After this, he'd probably be going to zoos, climbing the enclosure, saying, "Here, watch this. . . ." Famous last words, as yet another unfit human is removed from the gene pool.

His wife had gone silent, clutching her phone as she watched. Ash's chin bobbed, nodding encouragement to me. Just get through this. Let him pat me. Let him get his damned photo and leave.

"Nice kitty," he said. "Such a nice kitty. Sue? Are you ready?"

His wife hesitated, then lifted the phone for a picture. He glanced back at her.

"Good. We're going to get the photo of a lifetime. Bill Wilson taking down a cougar bare-handed."

"Wh-what?" Ash said.

The man lunged. He tried to grab me in a choke hold. I twisted out of his grip. Panic shot through me like wildfire, consuming all thought.

I was cornered. I had to fight back. Attack the threat. End the threat. Eliminate the threat.

When he came at me again, I felt my back legs bunching. Heard myself snarl. Felt my lips curl back, fangs flashing. It was like I was outside my body, watching it prepare for attack. Prepare for the kill.

"Bill, stop!" The woman's shrill voice knifed through my skull.

"No way. I'll teach this mangy cat to respect humans—"

Ash grabbed the guy by the jacket and yanked him so hard he stumbled. But he wrenched free and came at me again. That split-second interruption was all it took for my human brain to snap back to life and when he rushed me, I took a swipe at him. It was a good swipe—with a paw the size of a lunch plate—but my claws were retracted and I didn't plan to make contact. Still, it was enough. He saw that swat coming and he jumped back. Ash caught him by the collar and heaved him out of the way as I squeezed under the SUV.

"I'm calling 911," the woman babbled. "I don't care what you say. I'm calling."

I lay under the big vehicle. It was a tight fit and I was flattened against the pavement, ears smashed against my head. The woman reached the dispatcher before Ash could get to her.

"There," she said. "The police will come and shoot it."

"Hell, no," her husband said. "I've got my rifle from last

weekend. I should have remembered that earlier. Forget a photo. I'll get a real trophy."

The man opened the hatch of his SUV—the one right over my head.

"You're going to shoot her?" Ash said, his voice wavering, as if he was struggling to stay calm and reasonable. "Do you know how much trouble you'll get in? They're an endangered species."

"Not in BC they're not." He rummaged through the back of his truck. "I'm a hunter, boy. I know what's what, and this beast just attacked me—I hope you got a picture of that, Sue. I'm within my rights to shoot it."

"In a parking garage? After your wife called 911?"

"Couldn't be helped." A rifle case clicked. "It went after her, too. Right, Sue?"

His wife said nothing.

"Huh," the man said. "Looks like I forgot to unload it. We're all set, then. I'll just—"

I heard Ash let out a snarl and watched his running feet disappear as he jumped the guy. The man fell back. Ash took him down as the woman screamed. Ash leaped to his feet first. He kicked the man, hard enough to make him wail. Then he kicked him again.

"Run, Maya!" Ash shouted.

I was already squeezing out the other side of the SUV. I raced into the lane and heard a rumble. I looked over to see headlights, so bright they blinded me. Tires squealed.

Someone shouted. I saw the man lying on the ground, his wife running to the car, shrieking and sobbing. There was no sign of Ash.

"Run!"

Ash tore from between the SUVs, my clothes bundled under his arm. "Run!" he yelled again.

I roared up the ramp, Ash behind me. As I rounded the corner to the exit, headlights blinded me again and I dived to the side. The wrong side. I was pinned against a wall near the exit, trapped between it and a car. A police car.

SEVENTEEN

"OH, YEAH," SAID THE officer in the passenger seat as he lowered his window. "That's a cougar."

His partner swore and stopped the car. I could see Ash on the other side, tucked behind a pillar, his gaze darting from the cruiser to me.

The passenger door opened.

"Hey!" his partner called. "Don't do that!"

Ash stepped from his hiding spot and waved for me to get out of the building. I tore through the exit and nearly mowed down two girls in miniskirts. The police siren echoed their screams as the officers shouted at Ash and the girls to take cover.

I barreled past the girls and raced along the sidewalk, only to see a whole crowd of college kids pouring from a bar. I veered onto the road. I didn't stop to look. I didn't think to.

I saw all those people and my brain sent me flying the other way—right into traffic.

Brakes squealed. Horns honked. People shouted. A crash behind me as cars collided. I kept running, swerving around them, tearing down the middle of the street as drivers stopped and gaped and pulled out cell phones.

Another siren joined the first. Then a third. The sounds snapped me back and I raced to the opposite sidewalk, pedestrians flying like bowling pins as they scattered out of my way.

"Maya!" Ash shouted behind me. "You need to get—"

I veered down the first gap between buildings. An alleyway. I raced along it until I passed a row of recycling bins outside a doorway. I tucked myself between the bins and was standing there, flanks heaving, when Ash caught up.

I looked up at him.

"Yeah, that's what I meant. Take cover." He peered up and down the alley. "This looks good. Just stay where you are." Another look. "And tuck in your tail."

I pulled it in and sat, my sides still heaving as my heart rate slowed.

Ash crouched beside me. "You okay?"

I dipped my muzzle in a nod.

"Scary, huh?" He said the words awkwardly, like it wasn't something he was accustomed to admitting.

I dipped my head again.

He hunkered down, getting more comfortable. "I think we

did okay. Best we could, under the circumstances. Just . . . a string of bad luck."

I chuffed.

"I shouldn't have gone after that kid," he said. "I should have listened to you. Ignored it. But . . ." He rolled his shoulders. "Sometimes I can't." He looked down the alley. "Most times I can't."

It's not easy. There are all kinds of racism—from that frat-boy ugliness down to the kind of stereotyping and misconceptions where people don't even seem to realize they're doing or saying anything offensive. I had been lucky growing up in Salmon Creek. The way we were raised, I didn't even feel different. I was just one of the kids. My parents were just a normal couple. I think I was ten before I even heard the term *interracial marriage*.

Even when I encountered racism outside Salmon Creek, it usually rolled off me. The worst of it often came from rednecks whipping past in rusted pickups. I looked at them and I looked at me—class leader, track star, straight-A student— and their slurs about dirty Indians and drunk Indians and dumb Indians were laughable.

Mom says crap like that comes from people who've accomplished so little in life that they feel the need to lift themselves above someone, anyone. So they pick skin color or religion or sexual orientation and say, "Well, I might not be much, but at least I'm not a . . ." I'd look at those guys, and see the truth of her words. Even with the frat boys, I knew

131

I was their equal. In a couple of years, I could be sitting in class beside them.

But it was different for Ash. He certainly seemed smart, but from the way he talked, he hadn't spent much time in school. If I asked about college, I'm sure he'd make some crack about having to decide between Harvard and Yale. That wasn't in his future. Nor were athletic trophies and community awards and academic scholarships. He'd look at the rednecks in the rust-bucket pickups and say, "At least they have a truck."

I wished I could talk to him about that. I couldn't. Not now, obviously, and probably not even when I'd shifted back to human form. It wouldn't be a topic he'd discuss. Not with me. Probably not with anyone.

We waited. I could still hear sirens and shouting. At one point, a couple of cops looked down our alley, but it was only a cursory glance.

"When you're ready, we'll get in farther."

I chuffed. I was hoping it wouldn't come to that—all I needed was to shift back and we could walk out.

When a familiar scent wafted down the alley, I bristled. Ash noticed and looked over.

"You hear something?"

I shook my head and lifted my nose to make a show of sniffing the air.

"You smell someone. Daniel?" A split-second pause.

"No, you'd be a lot more excited if it was him. So it must be . . ." He cursed. "Someone from the Cabals?"

I nodded.

"I'd ask who, but I don't think you can manage charades. Doesn't matter anyway. If they're here—"

Words drifted in from the street, seeming to rise above the others. "—dark patch on her flank."

We both heard it and went still, straining to pick that one voice from the chaos.

"Yes, that's her," the voice said. "Juvenile female with that distinctive dark patch. She escaped earlier today. I notified animal control. They said they'd pass on the message to the city."

"We never got it," a woman's voice said.

"My apologies, then. We aren't local, and we were uncertain of proper protocol. We'll deal with that later. She needs to be found promptly and handled with care. She's a very valuable research subject. It's critical that we get her back safe and sound."

"I'm a lot more concerned about the safety of our citizens."

"You needn't be. That man said she attacked him, but you don't escape a cougar attack without a bite. You usually don't escape alive. She's accustomed to people and poses no danger to anyone except herself. My men have tranquilizer guns, as do the animal control officers. We need help locating her, but we can take it from there."

Ash looked over at me. "Is that . . . him?"

I nodded. It was Antone. I thought of how fast they must have heard the news of a loose cougar and how fast they'd mobilized. Not to mention how easily they seem to have convinced the authorities to let them take point on this operation. They were insanely organized. Insanely experienced. Insanely well funded. How could teenagers hope to outwit them?

I closed my eyes and slowed my pounding heart. We'd done it so far.

At what cost? How many are left? Maybe just you and your brother.

I kept breathing, struggling for calm. I could do this. I had to do this.

"We need to head out," Ash said. "Down the back way."

I nodded and took one last sniff. Antone's scent was gone. I must have caught it as he'd walked near the alley mouth, but he'd passed now, and even his voice had faded.

As I crept out, Ash stayed by the recycling bins, watching down the way we'd come. Guarding me again. I appreciated that. I'd have to tell him so when I could—and once I could figure out how to say it in a way that wouldn't embarrass him.

"All clear," he whispered. "Now go, go, go!"

He jogged along behind me and nearly smashed into my hindquarters as I leaned to peer around the corner. When I backed up, he said, "What?" then looked for himself.

There was nowhere to go. The alley was really just a

walkway for the adjoining businesses. It went around to a rear door, then stopped at a fence. Beyond the fence were more walls.

I considered. Then I rounded the corner and hunkered down. The alley was bounded by two buildings and a two-meter solid fence. While I didn't like the feeling of being cornered, if anyone approached, I'd have time to get over that wall. It was wood and I had sixteen razor-sharp climbing spikes permanently attached to my feet. Ash, however . . .

When he followed, I nudged him back. I used my head and then my paw to gesture around the corner. He didn't get it.

I head-gestured for him to go back to the street, then I pantomimed climbing the wall. He understood then. I think. But he refused to leave. Just told me to lie down and be quiet and no one was going to come back here. Wait until I shifted and we'd sneak out together.

So we waited. After about ten minutes, I heard a woman's voice say, "I'm picking up a presence back there."

"Probably homeless guy number four." Moreno. "Look, we know she's with her brother, so you need to detect two bodies. She's probably shifted back by now and they're long gone."

I waited, tensed, hoping they'd decide Moreno was right. I was guessing the witch only detected one form because we were huddled together. I inched closer to Ash.

Footsteps started down the alley.

"Does anyone listen to me?" Moreno said.

"Do you really want me to answer that?" Antone replied.

I leaped up. Ash started jogging toward the voices, his footfalls silent. I froze, panic filling me. But he only went a couple of meters, then turned around and ran at the wall.

I twisted, unsheathed my claws, and grabbed hold. As I scaled it, he took a running leap, grabbed the top and swung onto it with a gymnast's ease. Instead of going over, though, he crouched on the top, looking around. I scrambled up and perched awkwardly beside him.

On the other side of the fence was a tiny courtyard with a picnic table, a bicycle stand, and a tin half-filled with cigarette butts. A place for employees from a neighboring store to have a smoke and store their bikes. The only way out of there was a door into the shop. A solid metal door with no handle.

Ash wasn't looking at that, though. His gaze was turned upward, to a window on the building beside us.

"If we hide down there, she'll find us," he whispered. "We gotta go through the window. Can you make it?"

I nodded and cast an anxious glance at the alley. I could hear them coming slowly, checking behind every box and bin.

"I know," he whispered. "We need to move fast, especially since I have to bust that window to get in. They'll hear it."

I motioned for him to go. He jumped. He landed on the ledge easily enough, but it was only about ten centimeters of concrete, and he nearly lost his balance. He caught himself, turned his face away, and rammed his elbow into window, shattering the glass so expertly that I knew it wasn't his first break-in.

He looked back at me, still on the fence. I jerked my muzzle, telling him to go inside. He hesitated, but he didn't have a choice—I couldn't leap through with him blocking the hole. He quickly cleared the broken glass with his sleeve, then hopped down. It must have been a long jump because I heard him hit hard and let out an *oomph*. I listened for any sound of real pain. None came. When I was sure he was fine, I jumped off the fence—in the other direction.

As I tore down the alley, I thought I heard his voice. I flattened my ears and kept going. This was the only way. Otherwise, the moment they came around that corner, they'd know we were inside the shop and they'd surround the building. The witch only picked up one presence. If they saw me, they wouldn't go after him.

If I ran, he'd be safe. They'd never know he was there, and once I'd led them out of the alley, he could run. Maybe he'd try to find me afterward. Or maybe he'd finally realize the danger and decide it wasn't worth it—I wasn't worth it. I almost hoped he did, for his sake.

I whipped around the corner. I heard the witch cry out. I saw legs ahead of me, but I didn't look up, just kept running, ears down, eyes slitted, gaze fixed on the end of the alley. Get to the end. Barrel past them. *Through* them if I had to. Get to the road and let them chase me . . . while Ash escaped.

Antone leaped in front of me. I didn't look up to see his face, but his smell filled my nostrils. I hit him in the legs and he flipped up over my back. A dart whizzed past me. I hunkered lower, putting all my power into one last sprint. Behind me, I heard the witch say something. Words in another language. A spell? It didn't matter. I was almost to the street. Whatever she hit me with, however much it hurt, I'd just keep—

I stopped.

I just . . . stopped. My legs froze, like someone had disconnected the link to my brain. I skidded muzzle-first to the ground.

"Tranq her," the witch said. "I can't hold the binding spell for long."

My brain shouted orders. *Jump up. Fight. Run.* But my body just lay there, as if paralyzed, my eyes fixed open, staring at nothing. I felt a dart hit my flank. Then another. Antone said, "That's enough!" and the world went dark.

EIGHTEEN

I DREAMED I WAS sick with fever, my stomach cramping, sweat pouring off me. I was home in my own bed and Dad was sitting beside me, wiping my face with a cold cloth, saying nothing, just looking after me, as he'd done all of the rare times I was sick. Mom took care of me, too, but she did it by making soup and herbal tea and keeping my bedding fresh and dry and getting my medicine on time. She needed to keep busy. Dad was the one who'd just sit with me.

I wallowed in the dream even after I realized that's all it was. Slowly, though, I started waking and I felt the real burn of fever and the roil of nausea. Someone really was at my bedside, wiping my face. My first thought was "Daniel," and I opened my eyes, smiling, then saw Calvin Antone beside me. I scrambled back, hissing before I realized I was in human form. My stomach lurched and I retched. Antone grabbed a bowl from the floor and pushed it at me, but I shoved it away and sat up, clutching the sheets and looking around.

I was in a bed, dressed in a T-shirt and pajama pants. A man I didn't recognize stood just inside the door. He was wearing a suit, but he didn't look like security. He was too old, for one thing—at least fifty. And he held himself with an air that said he didn't take orders from anyone. He was tall—over six feet—with blond hair and bright blue eyes.

"Finally," he said. "Tell her I need her to answer some questions."

Antone glowered at him. "She speaks English."

"I'm sure she does. But she doesn't know me and I don't know her. I'm sure you can impress upon her the importance of answering."

"Is that a threat?" I said.

The man's blue eyes cooled. "I would suggest you modulate your tone with me, young lady."

"Because you're some important Cabal guy?"

"His name is Mattias Nast," Antone said. "He's the CEO's nephew."

Ash had told us that each Cabal was run by a family. The CEO and his sons were at the top, but a nephew would still have clout. Significant clout, judging by Antone's tone.

"I don't care who he is," I muttered. "I've got a good idea what he wants to know and the answer is 'go to hell.'"

The man's eyes chilled more. "Antone, you will tell your daughter—"

140

"I'm not his daughter. He's a sperm donor. My father is Rick Delaney."

Antone leaned closer. "I know you're angry, Maya, but you aren't making this easy."

"I don't want to make it easy. I know what you want to ask me—how to find Ash. I have no idea where he is or how to contact him. You don't believe me? Use magic or truth serum or whatever else you've got. The answer won't change."

I could tell by their expression that I'd been right about the question, and I breathed a sigh of relief. Ash had escaped. Good.

So where was he? Long gone. I was sure of that. Once I was captured, he'd run and keep running. It hurt, knowing I'd found him only to lose him again, but at least he'd be safe.

"We'll discuss this again later, Maya," Antone said. "For now—"

"Later?" Nast said. "I have three Cabal security teams waiting for her answer. Do you realize how much this operation is costing?"

"No more than it's worth," Antone said. "Or you wouldn't still be here. If your teams are so valuable, they should be competent enough to find my son without Maya's help."

"Your daughter isn't the only one who needs to modulate her tone. Don't forget who you're speaking to, Calvin."

Antone turned to me. "We'll discuss this later. Right now, there's someone waiting to see you." He smiled.

"Someone I know you'll want to see."

"Daniel," I said, sitting up. "Is he okay? And Corey?"

Silence. I looked from Antone to Nast, and I realized Daniel wasn't here. I felt a flicker of disappointment, but it vanished when I realized what that meant.

"They're still out there," I said. "You don't have them."

"No, but we're looking for them," Antone said. "Even harder than we're looking for your brother. For a very good reason. There was . . . an accident."

Nast spoke up. "Your Daniel got himself hit by a car running from the park."

"Wh-what?"

Antone glowered at Nast again. "Could I please speak to my daughter in private, sir?"

"No, because you'll sugarcoat it for her so she doesn't get sad and cry. We have got a very valuable asset out there—"

"Asset?" I said. "Daniel is not an asset. *We're* not assets. We're kids. Living, thinking, feeling—"

"That's enough, Maya," Antone murmured. Then to Nast, "This isn't your area of expertise, sir. I'm sorry if I'm not being properly grateful that the Cabal sent you, but I requested Sean Nast. He—"

"Sean is a boy, whatever his grandfather thinks, and he knows nothing of this project. Even Thomas realizes there are things his so-called heir can't stomach. This operation would be one of them."

I sat on the edge of the bed. "So this Sean guy would

have a problem with hunting teens like animals? Huh. Can't imagine why."

"Your concern for your friend seems to have faded very quickly, young lady," Nast said.

"Because I believed you for about five seconds before I realized you were full of crap. Daniel's not careless enough to run in front of a car. You picked the person I'm closest to and told me he was hurt. Terribly hurt, I'm sure, which is why I need to help you find him."

"Daniel *was* hit, Maya," Antone said, his voice low. "It wasn't his fault. He was running across an intersection to escape security officers and a car full of teens ignored a stop sign."

I shook my head. "Don't waste your breath. I know—"

Nast walked over and slapped a photo on the bed.

Antone grabbed for it. "She doesn't need to see—"

Nast stopped him. "I think she does. These are photos taken by a traffic camera, Maya."

I stared at the photos and my gut twisted, until I had to close my eyes and force the nausea back. Then I opened them for another look.

The first photo was taken at the moment when Daniel saw the car coming. The moment when he realized they wouldn't get out of the way in time. He was lunging to knock Corey aside. Terror on both their faces.

The second photo. The car stopped. Teenage driver getting out. Corey running back from the curb. His expression.

Oh God, his expression. Daniel. Lying on the road. Sprawled like a rag doll.

Nast slapped down a third. Daniel was on his feet now. Corey holding him up. Daniel's face was bloodied, his clothes ripped. One leg dragged. A bystander raced toward them, gesturing. The car full of kids was gone.

"Someone called an ambulance," Antone said, his tone still hushed. "But they got a ride with that woman"—he pointed to the bystander—"instead. The security officers thought they were just resting in her car. Then it drove off. They got the license number and we've tracked down the woman. She drove them to the hospital, but they vanished while she was speaking to an emergency room nurse."

Antone moved closer. "I know you don't want to believe us, but we are extremely concerned about Daniel. We have no idea how badly he was injured. There's a strong likelihood of internal injury. We need to find him."

I shook my head. Dazed. Numb.

"What proof do you need, Maya? Tell me and I'll get it. I can take you to the woman who picked them up. To the hospital where a nurse spotted them before they ran away."

"It-it's not that. I-I don't know where to find them. We got separated at the memorial and we didn't have any contingency plan for that. Ash and I were just waiting until it was late so we could go back to the memorial site, in case they returned."

Not completely true. Yes, we had no plan. Yes, I couldn't

contact them. But I did know where they'd go if they could—our spot in Stanley Park.

I would not tell Antone that. I didn't trust him; I did trust Daniel. And maybe even more important, I trusted Corey. If Daniel was too badly injured to make decisions on his own, Corey would get him to a hospital, whatever the risk. He wouldn't let Daniel—

I doubled over, stomach clenching again. When Antone passed me the bowl, I clutched the cool metal and leaned over it.

"That's called stress, young lady," Nast said. "And guilt."

"No," I said. "It's called a double-dose of tranquilizers. You made me sick."

"You made yourself sick by forcing us to tranquilize you. Just like your friend Daniel may have gotten himself killed—"

I flew at Nast. Just flew at him, howling, nails slashing like claws, raking down his cheek as he fell back, me on top of him. I dimly heard Antone shouting. Dimly felt him pulling at me. Dimly felt a surge of panic, something deep within me telling me to stop, stop now. But rage filled me, the smell of Nast's blood filled me, feeding the rage—

Antone pinned me to the floor and it was like a switch snapped off. I lay there, dazed.

"Maya?" he said.

"Wh-what . . . ?"

I looked up to see Nast swiping a handkerchief across his cheek. Deep furrows oozed blood. I looked down at my hand to see skin under my nails. I knew I'd scratched him. I remembered doing it. But I still stared at that skin, unbelieving, and then . . .

Shame. I felt shame.

As Antone released me, I pushed him away, ran to the bowl on the bed, and threw up. As I retched, he patted my back and told me it would be okay.

"No," Nast said. "It will not be okay. It's starting. She's had her first shift and now she's beginning to revert. Just like Annabella."

Annabella?

Annie. He meant Annie.

I clutched the bowl and retched again.

"This isn't like Annabella," Antone said. "Maya's still woozy and confused from the drugs. You just showed her photos of her best friend being hit by a car. You suggested he's dead. Combine that with everything she's gone through and she overreacted. That's all."

"No, she's reverting. This isn't like Annabella because your daughter isn't like Annabella. Those scientists predicted that the effects of the reversion would depend on the base personality. According to Annabella's brother, she was a sweet, quiet girl. Your daughter is not."

Before Antone could answer, Nast started out the door. "You need to control her, Calvin. We have two other skinwalkers in custody and another nearby. We don't need four of them."

NINETEEN

ANTONE TRIED TO CALM me down after that, to convince me Nast's threat was empty. But that threat was the last thing on my mind. I *was* freaked out about what I'd just done—that rage-blind attack on Nast. Was it a sign that I was reverting? Of course Nast would say that—another reason for me to need his Cabal. I couldn't put too much stock in his diagnosis.

My real worry was the guys. For now, I had to trust Ash was long gone, out of danger. I had to trust Daniel could look after himself. I had to believe he was fine, just battered and bruised and holed up somewhere with Corey. The alternative? I couldn't even think of the alternative.

When Antone finally left, I didn't really notice. The next thing I knew, I was being bowled over by a furry cannonball.

I looked up to see a German shepherd looming over me.

"Kenjii!"

I hugged her so tight she wriggled until I let go, then she bathed my face with her tongue, shoving me back on the bed every time I tried to get up. Finally I pushed her away, laughing.

"Now that's a sound I like to hear," said a voice. "I just hope I get the same reception as the dog."

I looked up to see a guy my age, with straight dark hair down to his collar, amber eyes dancing with a grin that turned an ordinary face gorgeous. Nast had said they had two other skin-walkers in custody, but I'd been too shocked over Daniel to process what that meant.

I launched myself at Rafe. He caught me and hugged me as tightly as I'd hugged Kenjii.

"You okay?" he whispered as he let me go.

I thought of Daniel and could only nod, gaze dropping. He lifted my chin and I knew he was going to kiss me but I backed off, still holding his hands, struggling to smile.

"Maya?"

Rafe stepped toward me. I retreated to the bed and collapsed there. Kenjii lay down with her head on my lap. Rafe reached to move the papers on the bed aside. Then he saw what they were. The photos. He leafed through them, once quickly, then slower, before he sucked in breath and swore.

"That's . . ."

I nodded.

"He was . . ."

I nodded again.

"When?"

"Yesterday."

"Is he . . . okay?"

"I don't know," I said. "They haven't found him."

Rafe sat on the edge of the bed with me.

Rafe set the photos aside, facedown. "They're lying. They doctored photos to spook you."

"I don't think so."

"Well, I do." He straightened. "I'm sure of it."

I shook my head. "We were separated. Daniel didn't meet up with us. The only reason he'd do that is if he . . . couldn't."

"Temporarily. He'd have found you as soon as he could."

Rafe drew my gaze up to the vent. A microphone or camera, I was guessing. Rafe was warning me not to say anything that could lead them to Daniel. I nodded and leaned against his shoulder.

He put his arm around me. "Daniel's fine. You know he is."

I nodded, closed my eyes, and tried to believe it.

When I felt a little better, I looked around. I'd known I was in a bedroom. Now I noticed the double bed, closet, desk, and dresser. It looked—

I fought back a chill.

It looked like my room. Not exactly—there were no photos or mementos. The furniture was different. But it was the same kind of pieces in the same configuration. I hadn't recognized it because the most important part of my bed-room had not been duplicated. I had huge windows along two walls that opened onto the wraparound second-story balcony. Mom's design, one that let me feel like I was outdoors even when I wasn't.

There was, to my surprise, a window here. Just a normal-sized one. It looked out onto what seemed like an empty blue sky, but when I walked over to it, I could see the glass was opaque. It let in light, but wouldn't let me look out. I rapped the pane.

"Shatterproof," Rafe said. "Believe me, I've tried. Broke my desk chair throwing it at mine."

"What'd they do?"

"Gave me a stern talking-to about damaging property, while letting me know that they understood the urge to act out." He rolled his eyes. "It's like being in a group home. No one ever gets mad about anything. They take away privileges, but they don't get angry—they just want to talk about it."

"They don't want us feeling like we're in a prison."

"Sometimes I'd prefer a prison. This is just creepy." He walked over to stand beside me at the window. "They say that when we accept the situation, they'll replace these with glass we can actually see through."

"Really? And they'll make them breakable, too?"

He laughed and put his arm around my waist. "Not a chance. But we will get field trips. To the mall and stuff. Because I know you love going to the mall."

I shuddered. He laughed again and pulled me against him, our hips bumping, his fingers warm, his smell washing over me, a familiar musky scent, skin-walker scent. I relaxed a little, then stiffened.

"Field trips? So we're . . . stuck indoors. All the time?"

He rubbed down the goose bumps rising on my arm. "There's a yard. With a twelve-foot wood fence and guards with tranq guns. There's a rooftop exercise area, too. More walls that we can't see past or climb over. Like a big kitty playground, with huge balls of yarn and wind-up mice to chase."

I stared at him.

"I'm kidding. Kind of. They have a boxing ring and weights for the benandanti and balance beams and hurdles for us. It sounds awful, and I've been really tempted to ignore it, but the fresh air and the exercise . . . ?" He shrugged. "It helps keep me from going nuts while I figure out a way . . ."

He glanced at the vent and didn't finish.

"Any luck with that?" I murmured.

"Not really. Scoping the situation for now."

"So we're in . . . a lab? A compound of some sort?"

He shook his head. "A house. Huge mansion of a place. It doesn't smell like city, so I think we're outside Vancouver. They're still working on the house, but it was pretty much ready to go when we arrived, which makes me think the St. Clouds had been working on it for a while."

"A contingency plan in case we decided we didn't want

to stay in Salmon Creek after we found out about the experiments. The Nasts must have bought it along with us. The lab rats and their habitat."

"Yeah. So for now I'm just taking stock and—"

A rap at the door. I waited for someone to enter, but Rafe had to call a "Come in" before it opened. He rolled his eyes at me.

In walked a woman I'd known for almost my entire life. Dr. Inglis. Head of the lab in Salmon Creek. She'd been in charge of our medical care since I moved there. She hadn't always been our personal doctor, but she'd been a fixture in town and in our lives. Last time she'd seen me, I'd been in cat form—pinning her to the ground.

When she stepped in, her gaze went straight to me, and she started to smile. She caught herself and turned to Rafe instead.

"Is it time?" he asked.

"Yes."

"It went well?"

She nodded. Again she looked at me. Her lips parted, as if she wanted to say something. Whatever it was, she just murmured it under her breath, gaze dropping, and withdrew.

"What's she doing here?" I asked.

"The Nasts hired her," Rafe said. "Seems she wanted to stay and 'help' us. Which I've suggested she could do a lot better by opening a door and letting us out. But apparently, that's not the plan." He shook his head. "Enough of that. There's someone I want you to meet."

He walked to the door and turned the knob. I expected a security escort on the other side. The hall was empty.

I peered out.

"Yeah, we pretty much have the run of the place. Not much damage we can do. Shatterproof glass. Cameras everywhere. Only two exits—both with alarms and guarded by multiple guys with tranq guns. Patrolling guards, too, both on foot and in cars."

He really had done his research. Not that I expected any less.

I started to step out, Kenjii at my heels, but Rafe waved her back.

"Better leave her here," he said. "She doesn't like some of our jailers, not surprisingly. They've threatened to kennel her."

I nodded and urged her back inside. She obeyed with a sigh, as if she was expecting it.

As he closed my bedroom door, I said, "So that wasn't locked?"

He shook his head. "They never are. *This isn't a jail, kiddies. Any security is for your own good. We all care about you. We all want you to be comfortable. We know you won't be happy—yet—but that is our goal, someday.*"

I made gagging noises.

He grinned. "Exactly. Prepare to be treated like a rebellious twelve-year-old."

There were stairs right outside my door. Behind us, the hall stretched for at least twenty meters, flanked by a half-dozen doors.

"My room's the third down from yours. Just in case you were interested. Did I mention they don't lock the doors?"

"I believe you did."

He grinned. "Good. And we don't have roommates."

"Duly noted."

I looked at those bedroom doors. Who else was here? I wanted to ask, but part of me was afraid of the answer. Was anyone still with the St. Clouds? Had anyone . . . not made it? At any other time, those questions would have been the first words out of my mouth, but I was feeling . . . not myself. Still off from the drugs, I guess. Dazed and bruised, physically and emotionally.

As we walked down the steps, voices downstairs broke the hush. I strained to hear familiar ones, but they all sounded like adults and no one I knew.

We passed at least a half-dozen people, a few obviously security, a couple who looked like medical personnel, and some who might have been house staff. Some stopped what they were doing, as if expecting Rafe to introduce us.

"Kitchen's through there," he said, gesturing down a hall. "We've got free run of it. There's a list on the fridge where you can add anything you want. Meals are cooked and we eat"— he motioned right past someone—"in the dining room there."

He continued on, giving me the tour as if no one else was

154

there. Treating them like furniture. It worked for me.

Finally, he led me down another flight of stairs. "All the rec stuff is down here. An indoor gym for bad weather. Home theater. Game room." He glanced over as we reached the bottom step. "Yeah, it's like they consulted a stack of teen life magazines, trying to build the ultimate hangout."

"Ignoring the fact that our idea of playtime involves kayaks, rock-climbing, dirt bikes . . ."

"Exactly." He opened the first door. "Here's the game room, complete with every console known to man, plus a prototype of a new kinetic one, just for us, 'cause we're so special."

"Special enough to get internet access on those consoles?"

"Not a chance."

TWENTY

WE WALKED INSIDE. AS we did, I stopped short. There was a girl sitting at a table across the room. She was bent over a piece of paper and seemed to be writing.

Rafe tugged me forward. "Maya, I'd like to introduce you to someone."

The girl at the table turned. When she did, I smiled.

"Annie." I started forward, then shot a glance back at Rafe. "I believe we've met."

"Not exactly," Annie said, and her voice was different, lower. Her smile was different, too. Not the exuberant grin I remembered, but something more tentative, almost shy.

She stood and came toward me. Not flying at me, arms wide, the way she usually did, but just walking, her steps as tentative as her smile. I looked at the table and saw what she'd been doing. Drawing.

I glanced at Rafe. He grinned and nodded, his face glowing again.

"They've . . ." I began, struggling for the words.

"Fixed me," Annie said. "For very brief periods so far. But it's a start." She walked over and hugged me, and even if it wasn't her usual rib-crushing embrace, it was still a real hug, tight and sincere.

"So you . . . remember everything?" I said.

She waved us to the sofa and patted the spot beside her. I took it, and Rafe perched on the arm, still grinning.

"There are bits and pieces I don't remember, probably when I shifted. The rest is . . . odd. Like I was watching myself." She shook her head. "No, watching someone that looked like me and felt a bit like me, but wasn't, not really. It was like being . . ." She blushed. "Like being high unexpectedly. Which wouldn't be a new experience for me. When you're trying to break in as an artist, you can't always be sure that the wine is just wine. I felt high and happy and carefree, but inside, part of me was banging at the walls to get out. To come down. To be myself."

"And now you are."

"For short periods. They'll continue with the doses and they expect I should be back to myself in a few months." She paused. "Rafe tells me you've shifted."

"I have."

"No . . . problems?"

I tried not to think about what Nast said. "Not yet. But I feel a lot better knowing there's a cure. They worked fast finding it."

"Not really," Rafe said. "They already knew there were possible side effects. They had something ready in case this happened. Untested but—" He shrugged. "Obviously working."

Annie clasped my hands. "I'm glad you're okay, Maya. I know you don't want to be here, but I'm glad you're safe, and I'm looking forward to getting to know you. Really know you." She smiled at Rafe. "You've made my brother happier than I've seen him in a very long time."

Rafe rolled his eyes, but he still hadn't completely wiped the smile from his face. I knew I wasn't the only reason he was happy. This was what he wanted—to help Annie. It was why he'd come to Salmon Creek. The reason for everything he'd done since he arrived.

"And with that, I'm going to take my leave and let you two catch up," Annie said as she stood. "I'm sure Rafael doesn't want his big sister around for that."

"You don't have to—" I began.

"My time's running out," she said. "I only get about twenty good minutes every treatment."

"That doesn't matter," I said. "You were fine before—"

"I appreciate you saying that, Maya. I really do. I remember how kind you were to me. But if you're going to get to know the real me, I'd rather . . ." She shrugged, looking uncomfortable. "I'd rather stick to that. With you and with Rafe. We'll get our twenty minutes a few times a day, and that's it for now."

"Believe me, I've argued," Rafe muttered. "But she's almost as stubborn as you."

As Annie walked by, she reached out and ruffled his hair, as I'd seen her do before, but gentler now, only laughing when he grumbled, then patting his shoulder, waving to me and leaving us alone.

Rafe waited until Annie closed the door behind her, then he slid onto the couch beside me. "So, any ideas how we should spend our time alone?"

I hesitated. I didn't want to. I wanted to just grab him and kiss him and forget everything else. That's how it used to be. See Rafe; forget the rest of the world. But now that world was thundering in my head, with those photos of Daniel front and center.

I turned away, trying to make it look casual, teasing even. But I needed that moment to clear my mind. Worrying about Daniel wouldn't help. I wanted to forget. Just for a minute. When I was ready, I glanced back at him and smiled. "I might have a few ideas. You?"

He grinned. "Maybe."

I inched closer. "I bet I can guess yours."

"I bet you can."

"Does it involve . . . ?" I crossed the gap and leaned

toward him. "This?" I thrust a game controller up between us. "I play a mean game of Mario Kart."

He laughed and pushed the controller aside. "I'm sure you do. However, that's not quite what I had in mind."

I waited until he bent for a kiss, then jumped up and grabbed a handful of cases from the coffee table.

"Call of Duty?" I said, lifting one.

He stood and stepped toward me. "No."

I backed up. "Left 4 Dead?"

Another step forward. "No."

I continued moving back, waggling the cases in front of me. "So you don't want to play games?"

"Mmm, never said that. Just not those. I prefer something more . . . physical."

"Got it!" I shoved a case forward. "Wii Fit."

He laughed and plucked it from my hand. We did another two-step—me back, him forward, his gaze on mine, his grin sending heat rushing through me.

"Do you like chasing?" I said.

His grin sparked. "You know I do."

"Wrestling?"

"Definitely."

I held up Grand Theft Auto and WWE. He lunged. I dodged, dropping the games and racing across the room. He gave chase and I felt his fingers brush the back of my shirt. I veered and vaulted over the sofa. He tried to do an end-run around it, but I quick-stepped the other way, then back again when he reversed course.

We paced along our sides of the couch a few times. Then he sprinted. I raced around the other side. He lunged over the back, fingers grabbing my shirt and yanking me to him when I tried to run.

"Gotcha," he said.

I rolled my eyes and let him pull me close. When we were almost touching, he relaxed his grip. I broke away. He managed to snag my leg with his foot. I stumbled. He caught my arm and redirected my fall, and the next thing I knew, I was lying on the couch, with Rafe over me, my arms around his neck.

"You are remarkably good at that," I said.

"It's all instinct."

"Uh-huh." I smiled and pulled him down into a kiss.

We were still down there, a few minutes later, when a voice over our heads said, "Jesus. I know you guys have been separated for an entire forty-eight hours. But really?"

I looked up to see Sam—Samantha Russo—standing there, arms crossed, looking remarkably like the teacher who'd caught Rafe and me making out behind the school. A crutch was propped under one arm.

"Yes," said another voice. "Get a room. Please."

When I looked at Hayley, Sam said, "Don't suggest that or he will. And Maya's too gaga to resist."

Rafe shot her the finger, but it was a cheerful gesture, as if even she couldn't spoil his mood. I got up and gave Hayley a hug. It was awkward—we've never been friends—and she seemed surprised, but not displeased. Sam just scowled, arms crossing tighter, as if I might try the same thing on her. I didn't.

"So you're both okay?" I said. "You look okay."

Sam shrugged. "We're good."

"I wouldn't say 'good,'" Hayley said. "We're lab rats in a secured facility under twenty-four-hour surveillance."

Sam shrugged again. "They haven't hurt us. They've helped Annie. They've fixed up my leg. It's not so bad, really."

"Not so bad?" I said. "We—"

Rafe caught my hand and squeezed. "We're having a difference of opinion that I'm sure we'll get into later. For now, let's just take a breather and get caught up."

Hayley nodded. "What's happening with Corey and Daniel? They're okay, right? Still running? Still safe?"

The room seemed to freeze. My breath jammed in my throat and I could hear my blood pounding.

Rafe led me back to the sofa. "They're okay, but that's something Maya needs to talk about. If everyone can just—"

"Maya?" Sam said. "I know you can be insufferably bossy, and I never thought I'd say this, but can you please take back the reins of leadership here? Your loser boyfriend—"

"Sam!" Hayley hissed.

Rafe only rolled his eyes. "As you can tell, Sam and I have not miraculously become BFFs in the last couple of days. I'm sure Maya will have lots of ideas and plans,

Samantha. But she just got here and—"

"Hey," said a quiet voice from the doorway.

I turned. There stood Nicole. For a moment I thought I was seeing things. Hoped I was seeing things.

"Hey, Nic," Rafe said. "Look who's here."

He pulled me up and smiled at us, and I had to stare at him for a moment before remembering. He didn't know. No one knew except . . .

I glanced at Sam.

She flushed and mouthed, "Sorry," then whispered under her breath, "I didn't know what to do."

"Do about what?" Hayley asked.

Nicole stood there, looking confused. Looking like the same Nicole I'd known for ten years. Sweet and shy and uncertain. The girl Serena took under her wing, trying to boost her confidence. The girl I'd pushed Daniel toward after Serena's death, thinking she was just the thing to help him get over her. The girl I'd struggled to befriend, even if we didn't have much in common, feeling guilty that we couldn't get closer when she seemed to need a friend so much after Serena died.

Now I looked at Nicole and I saw that girl, and I started wondering if I'd misjudged. If Sam and I had drawn the wrong conclusion. There was no way this girl could have done what we thought.

Except I'd seen another girl in Nicole a few days ago. The one who'd lashed out at the campsite when I'd refused to rescue her. The one who'd tried to get me captured, too. Who'd shouted at Moreno to shoot me. To kill me.

What mattered more to me was who we thought Nicole *had* killed. Serena.

"Get out of here," I said, barely able to open my jaw enough to get the words out.

Rafe looked surprised at first but seeing my face, that melted away and his own face hardened. He turned to Nicole.

"What'd you do?" he said.

"Wh-what did I do?" she squeaked. Her blue eyes rounded and she flinched, like a whipped puppy seeing a raised hand. "I-I don't understand."

"What's going on here?" Hayley said.

"She . . ." I clenched my fists tighter and my face started to throb, as if I was about to shift. I took a deep breath and tried to find calm so I could explain.

"I-I don't understand," Nicole said again, tears welling up.

"Oh, stuff the theatrics," Sam said. She turned to the others. "Nicole killed Serena."

TWENTY-ONE

ILENCE.

Hayley stared at Sam. Then at me. Nicole's mouth opened and closed as she made a strangled noise deep in her throat.

"Did you say . . . ?" Hayley began.

"Nicole drowned Serena. She dragged Maya under, too, probably as a warning. Then she tried to kill her after the crash."

"No," Hayley said. "Nicole was pulled under herself after the crash. I was there."

Sam shook her head. "She faked it. She dragged Maya down and wrapped her foot in some weeds. She hoped in the commotion, no one would realize Maya was missing until it was too late. But Maya got free."

"Th-that's crazy," Nicole said. "Y-you've always hated

me, Sam. You hated coming to live with us and you were jealous of me and—"

"Um, no, you're the one who was jealous. Spiking my orange juice with vodka so I'd go to school drunk. Planting drugs in my bedroom. Drugs you got from volunteering at the clinic. Like the drugs you got to dope Maya at her party."

"That was *Hayley*. Everyone knows it was. She worked at the clinic, too, and she hates Maya."

"I did *not* roofie Maya," Hayley said. "I didn't have access to the drug closet." She turned to us. "Dr. Blair caught me sneaking Ritalin this summer. She took away my key. I couldn't tell you guys that without admitting I got caught stealing drugs. I asked Nicole to vouch for me, but—"

Nicole crumpled—just let her legs give way and fell to the floor, hunched and sobbing. Hayley looked at me. Even Rafe did. Uncertain looks from both of them. I had to admit, Nicole was a good actor. If I hadn't seen her switch from "sweet Nicole" to "raving lunatic Nicole" in a heartbeat at the campsite, I might have believed her myself. Even now I felt that niggle of doubt.

Had I been wrong about people before? Oh, yeah. Repeatedly in the last couple of weeks. Starting with Rafe, which is why he stood here now, looking hesitant, studying my expression. He'd been the target of my snap judgments. So had Hayley.

"Maya?" Rafe said. "Is that what you think? She killed Serena?"

Before I could answer, Nicole leaped to her feet with astonishing speed for someone who'd been in a puddle of misery a moment ago.

"Maya hasn't said that," Nicole insisted. "Sam's the one doing all the talking. Maya's smart. She thinks things through and she knows there's no way I could have drowned Serena. How could I do that and escape without being spotted?"

"By swimming under the water," Sam said.

"Seriously? How long would I have had to stay under water? Ten minutes? That's impossible."

I glanced at Hayley, who'd gone quiet. "It's not, is it? At least, not for the members of Salmon Creek's championship swim team. Serena could hold her breath for at least five minutes. I'm guessing you could do the same, Hayley?"

Hayley nodded. "We all could. Me and Nicole and Serena. We used to have competitions when the coach wasn't watching. The winner was always . . ." She looked at Nicole. "Almost fifteen minutes one time, until Serena freaked out, worrying Nic would hurt herself. None of us could stay under nearly that long."

"No!" Nicole said. "That's a lie. No one can hold her breath that long."

"No normal person," I said. "But you're not normal, as I'm sure they've told you here already. You're a xana. Your talents are singing and swimming, which I'm sure includes holding your breath."

"No!" Nicole spun on Hayley. "You're lying about the competitions and you're lying about the drugs. If you can hold your breath so long, then you killed Serena. Killed her and drugged Maya."

"Why? What possible reason—?"

"Jealousy. You hated Serena because she was better than you in swimming and singing. You hated Maya because everyone thinks she's special."

"Yep, we're all jealous," Sam said. "All except you. Right, Nic? Which is good, or else you really wouldn't want to hear about Daniel and Maya."

"What?"

"Daniel and Maya," Sam walked toward her. "Who do you think comforted Maya when she thought Rafe was dead? Who do you think got *really* close to her on that long walk through the woods?"

"What?" I said. "If you mean—"

"Oh, Nicole knows what I mean. Gotta hand it to you, Maya, you played the grief card perfectly. Completely blind-sided poor Daniel."

"What?" I stared at Sam. I could see Rafe hesitating, looking confused. Confused and hurt.

"Don't lie, Maya," Sam said. "I saw you and Daniel together that night. Awfully chilly to have all those clothes off, but you seemed to be keeping warm just fine."

Nicole flew at me then, her face twisted with rage. She knocked me flying. Rafe and Sam jumped in to pull her off, but she grabbed my hair and wrapped it around her fingers, yanking, hitting and clawing with her free hand. I managed to grab her by the hair and yanked her off me. She yowled and kept coming, clawing and hitting, not caring that hanks of her own hair were ripping free as they held her back. Finally, I pinned her. I could feel the shift coming, my skin pulsing, my face changing. She could see that and still she kept fighting. I got my hand around her throat. Then the door slammed open and two guards raced in.

I backed off Nicole fast. They hit her with a needle, but she wouldn't stop trying to get me and they had to haul her out.

"You bitch!" she shrieked back at me. "You think what I did to Serena was bad? Just wait until I get ahold of you." They dragged her away, still spewing threats.

I stood there, doubled over, catching my breath. Hayley helped me straighten and led me to the sofa, then sat beside me.

"Are you okay?" she asked.

I gulped in breaths as the shift slowly reversed.

Hayley looked up at Rafe. "I don't know what Sam was talking about, because I never saw *anything* happen between Maya and Daniel."

"Because nothing did." I pushed up and advanced on Sam. "I don't know what game you're playing, but nothing—"

"Oh, of course, nothing happened," Sam said. "Like you'd watch your boyfriend die and jump the next available guy." She turned to Rafe. "And if your boyfriend thinks for a *second* that was possible, he doesn't know you at all."

"You caught me off guard," Rafe said. "I just didn't know what the hell you were playing at. I didn't think Maya did it."

Only he had thought I did. Or at least, he'd entertained the possibility. I'd seen it on his face.

"I think it's clear what I was *playing at*," Sam said. "Setting off Nicole. It worked, didn't it? When it comes to Daniel, she's got a few screws loose. More than a few. Now everyone's seen it, and she confessed to killing Serena, so it's all good."

"All good?" Hayley said, standing. "Not only did you just accuse Maya of messing around with Daniel, but you've convinced Nicole that she did. *Nicole*. The girl who murdered Serena because she was dating Daniel. The girl who tried to murder Maya because she's friends with him. And that's *all good*?"

Sam sputtered and spewed excuses, but I could tell she hadn't thought it through. Now I was trapped in a house with someone who truly wanted me dead.

The door opened again. In walked Nast, followed by Moreno, a guard, and a woman I didn't recognize. Moreno was talking, as usual. "Look, I know you're in charge, sir, but Calvin asked—"

"I don't give a damn what Calvin asked for. I told him to control his daughter."

Nast headed for me. Rafe moved closer.

"Get out of here, boy," Nast said. "Playtime's over. Take them"—a dismissive wave at Sam and Hayley—"with you."

They made no move to leave. Nast didn't seem to notice,

just continued bearing down on me.

"One hour," he said. "You haven't even been conscious for one hour and already you're attacking—"

"She didn't attack anyone," Rafe said. "Nicole jumped her."

Nast looked at Rafe. He didn't even seem to focus on him, just curled his lip, like Rafe was beneath his notice, before waving at the guard and saying, "Get them out of here."

"It was self-defense," Sam said. "Nicole attacked her."

"Get them out."

Nast didn't raise his voice, but the guard jumped as if he'd shouted. He took both Hayley and Sam by the arm and propelled them to the door.

"Moreno? Take the boy. Now."

Moreno wasn't so quick to obey. He sauntered forward, waving at Rafe. "Come on, kid. Your girlfriend needs to go with the doc for a checkup."

I caught Rafe's eye and mouthed, "Go on."

A second guard appeared as Moreno and Rafe left. Nast pointed to me.

"Take her to the lab for Dr. Wiley. And be careful." He met my gaze. "Her wild streak is showing."

TWENTY-TWO

DR. WILEY WAS THE woman who'd been standing there, silently observing. She followed as the guard led me away. We headed upstairs and into another hall. As Rafe said, the house was huge. This seemed like a wing, with doors lining the corridor. A few were open and I could see what looked like work areas. An office. A computer lab. A staff lounge.

Dr. Wiley opened the next door. Inside was a medical office, complete with paper-covered examining table and gown.

I hesitated.

"It's a physical, Maya," Dr. Wiley said without looking back. "On the table, please. Sitting."

The guard backed out of the room. As he was closing the door, a hand grabbed it. Moreno walked in. When he did, I felt a weird flutter of relief at seeing a familiar face. Which was stupid, really, because Moreno was no friend of ours. But at least he was a threat I knew. One I understood.

"Hey, Doc," he said.

"I'm busy."

"Yeah, I see that. Only . . . wasn't Inglis supposed to do the examination on Maya? Pretty sure she was. Pretty sure Cal insisted on it."

"Mr. Antone and Dr. Inglis are unavailable. Mr. Nast wants the examination done immediately. He's concerned about Maya's behavior."

Moreno gave a derisive snort. "Only because he wasn't the one chasing her though the forest for three days. Otherwise he'd know that misbehavior is pretty much par for the course with Miss Maya." He turned to me. "Isn't it?"

I gave him a look.

He laughed. "The killer glare. You inherited that from your daddy." He lifted a hand. "Yeah, yeah. Rick Delaney is your daddy. Spare me the protest." Back to Dr. Wiley. "If Mr. Nast thinks Maya's bad now, he should just be glad her partner in crime isn't here. First time I met those two? Maya tried to question me while her benandanti buddy knocked me around. It was kinda cute, actually."

"Beating and interrogation?" Dr. Wiley said. "We have a very different definition of cute, Mr. Moreno."

"Maybe. But the point is, she isn't acting out of character. Which means this examination isn't necessary. I'm sure you have other things to do. You go do them. I'll take Miss Maya back to the others, and Dr. Inglis can examine her later."

"My orders are to conduct a physical. I take my orders from Mr. Nast." She looked his way. "As do you."

Moreno blustered some more, but when Dr. Wiley picked up the phone to call security, he shut up and took a seat. The doctor settled for compressing her lips in a thin line of disapproval as she turned her attention to me.

I've been having physicals all my life. I always figured they were just the normal kind everyone talks about. Now I suspect mine were a little different. They were certainly thorough. At home, we all dreaded the twice-annual two-hour appointment.

This one started exactly as I remembered. Height, weight, blood pressure, eyes, ears, throat, chest. She drew blood. Ten vials. Nothing more than I was used to, but I could see Moreno's eyes widen a little as she passed number five and kept going.

When she was done with the blood, she sent it out immediately. I got juice and cookies while she waited for the lab tech. It was the same kinds of juice and cookies I'd been getting since I was five, which was creepy. The Nasts hadn't just bought us, they'd bought everything about us, replicating each detail to ease the transition.

I shivered.

"Cold?" Dr. Wiley asked.

I shook my head.

She frowned. "Have you been shivering a lot recently?"

"No."

"Anything more serious? Shaking? Convulsions?"

"The girl shivered, Doc."

"Mr. Moreno, I'm going to ask you to leave now."

"Ah, hell." Moreno leaned back in his seat. "Fine. I'll be quiet."

"I'm afraid that won't be sufficient. I need to conduct a thorough examination, which requires . . ." She picked up the robe and waggled it at him.

Still he hesitated.

"Mr. Moreno."

"Yeah, yeah." He stood and walked over to me. "Your dad will be here soon, kiddo."

Dr. Wiley sniffed and waved him out. I watched him go.

Okay, what was that about? I'd sensed the tension between Antone and Nast earlier, but I hadn't given it much thought. Antone was more accustomed to giving orders than taking them. But Moreno's hovering? That was weird, as was his insistence on waiting for Antone and Dr. Inglis.

Something was going on here. Serious tension, and not just between Antone and Nast. I could see Dr. Inglis being uncomfortable having someone else work on me. I was "hers," and there was bound to be conflict between the Nast camp and the former St. Cloud employees. But Antone and Moreno had been with the Nasts since this had begun.

The rest of the physical was exactly what I'd had since I turned twelve, right down to the order of the steps. Physical exam. Pap smear. Breast examination. Cheek swab. Vitamin injection. And, finally, the sour apple lollipop.

I stared at the green sucker. "Seriously?"

"We were told you liked green apple." She opened the drawer and pulled out a bag. "We have cherry, raspberry. Even . . ." She picked up a brown one. "Root beer? Oh, yes, that'd be for Daniel."

I stared at that brown sucker. My stomach twisted. She set it on the counter where I could see it.

"Do you know what happens when a car strikes the human body, Maya? Yes, Daniel got up and walked away. I'm sure he just felt battered and bruised. But the force of that impact must have done damage. Internal damage. He could go to sleep feeling fine and then . . . never wake up."

I clenched my fists to keep from shaking as panic whipped through me.

They're exaggerating. You know they are. Corey will take care of him. Trust Corey and trust Daniel. Worry won't help you get out of here. You need to focus on escape.

"I don't know where he is," I said.

"I think you do."

"I don't. We got separated—"

"Then he'll find a place you all stayed before that and go there to wait. You need to tell us—"

"There's nothing to tell." I hopped off the exam table, scooped up my clothes, and retreated behind the curtain to dress.

TWENTY-THREE

I LEFT THE EXAMINATION room to discover we were all on lockdown pending an investigation of my allegations against Nicole. That didn't explain why all the others would be confined. I suspect Nast was just happy for the excuse.

At least they let me keep Kenji. Antone's orders, apparently. They'd brought in her dishes and bedding. I supposed he thought I'd be grateful. I wasn't. Or, at least, I didn't want to be.

I'd only been in my room for a few minutes when Antone himself arrived with lunch. I considered rejecting it, on principle, but if I was stuck here I needed allies, and at this point Antone seemed my most promising option.

"I want to talk to you about your brother," he said as he pulled a chair over to where I sat cross-legged on the bed.

"I don't know where Ash—"

"I just want to talk about him." He popped open an energy drink and took a few slugs.

"You know that stuff is all marketing," I said. "You're better off having a Coke and some vitamins. Cheaper, too."

He smiled. "I'll remember that."

I squirmed, as if giving him advice was an olive branch I hadn't meant to extend.

"I'm not the enemy, Maya."

"Yeah, you keep saying that. Funny, because I could swear it was you I saw during the forest fire, pointing a gun at me."

"A tranquilizer gun. Because you were about to run back into a burning forest."

I took a bite of my sandwich.

"About Ashton," he said.

"Ash. He hates Ashton."

"Ash." He pondered. "All right, then. Ash."

Again he smiled and I realized he took this as another sign I was opening up. Helping him get to know us better.

"How much has Ash told you about his life, Maya?"

I shrugged.

"In other words, he's told you some, but you aren't going to share it with me in case you'd be telling me things I don't know. I can assure you that's very unlikely, and not why I was asking. I just don't want to tell *you* anything you already know."

Still I said nothing. He waited a moment, then nodded. "All right. From the top then. Your mother kept him when she gave you up. It seems she thought she'd call less attention to herself with him."

I bristled. "Why? Did I cry too much? Was I causing trouble already? I was only a few months old."

"That's not it, Maya. I'm sure you wonder what you did to make her choose him. The answer, as far as I can tell, is nothing. But your mother is only half Navajo and she doesn't look it. She can pass for Caucasian easily. You can't. Your brother?" He shrugged. "He can't pass for white, but he could clearly be her son. With you . . . ? People would have noticed. They can pretend they don't, but they do. If the St. Clouds went looking for a white woman with a Native American baby, they'd have had a lot easier time finding you. She knew that. So when she made her choice . . ."

"She kept Ash." I turned the pop can around in my hands. "But that only made it easier for you to find me, didn't it? An abandoned Native baby."

He nodded.

"So she basically tossed me to you and the St. Clouds so she could escape."

Antone rubbed the back of his neck. "I don't want to malign your mother. What she did to you was wrong. But I have to admit it was for the best. At least compared to what she did to Ash."

"She dumped him."

He sucked in breath and seemed to be struggling to put a better slant on it. Finally, he said, "Yes, she dumped him," and in his voice I heard all the bitterness I'd seen on Ash's face.

It took him a moment to continue. "I would like to think she did it for him. That she believed the St. Clouds were closing in and this was his best chance. The couple she gave him to were decent people. Not as good as your adoptive parents, but they did try. Then, when Ash was ten, his foster father was involved in a serious accident. He lost his job. They had three other children. They couldn't contact your mother, so . . . Ash entered the system."

"The foster care system."

Antone nodded. "In some cases it works well. There are wonderful, loving parents who sign up. And then there are . . . the rest. Those who do it for money. It's never easy for children of any minority. But in the area where Ash was living there wasn't a strong Native community. No Native community, really. That was hard on him. Really hard. He acted out. By thirteen—after a dozen placements—he ended up in a group home. He stayed two weeks. Then he was gone. He's been on the streets ever since."

I shook my head. "But he's been in contact with—" I snapped my mouth shut hard.

"In contact with other parents who left? Yes, I know. That's how I've gotten my information. Let's just say one of those parents isn't nearly as trustworthy as Ash believes." He paused. "No, I shouldn't say that. I suspect Ash knows they

180

aren't trustworthy. Otherwise, I'd have found him by now. He doesn't give away anything, even to them. But when Ash ran, he went searching online for answers and, at that time, he hadn't yet learned to be quite so careful. Someone found him. A man who used to work for the Edison Group."

Cyril Mitchell. I didn't say that, of course. I just waited for him to go on.

"From all accounts, Mr. Mitchell was a decent man. If I could have gotten in touch with him, this would have gone much better, but my contact was playing both sides and wasn't about to do anything to jeopardize that. Mitchell tracked down Ash and tried to give him a place to stay, but Ash had had enough of that with his foster parents. Eventually Mitchell realized he had a choice—help Ash from a distance or lose him completely. He went with the former. He seems to have tried to give him money, but the only thing Ash would accept was information."

"On the experiment."

Antone nodded. "So your brother has been on the streets for three years. You can try to understand that, but I don't think you can, Maya. I can't, either. Like you, I was raised by a wonderful family. Not wealthy, but certainly comfortable. If I needed clothing, I got it. If I asked for name brands, my parents would talk to me about peer pressure, but if I wanted it badly enough, I got it. Outgrow my bicycle? Get a new one. Eighteenth birthday? Get a car. Not new, but still a car. College? Sure. Ivy League? If I could get in, which I did.

I wasn't spoiled, but I was loved and, yes, indulged. Does that all sound familiar?"

I said nothing.

"Your brother has never had that. Never. Not with your mother. Not with the family she gave him to. Certainly not with his foster parents. But compared to what he has now? He was as pampered as a prince." Antone leaned forward. "He has nothing, Maya. Nothing."

"He has me." I didn't mean to say it. I could hear Ash's voice in my ear, scoffing, *Yeah, thanks. That and five bucks will buy me lunch.* But as I said it, I meant it. When I got out of here, I'd find him. I'd be whatever he needed me to be, and it had nothing to do with hearing the story of his life.

When I said that, Antone pulled back. I thought he was offended—I'd just met my brother and I was presuming so much. But his eyes glimmered.

"I'm glad to hear that, Maya. I don't think I can tell you how much it means to me, seeing the two of you together, looking out for each other." A deep breath. "But he has me, too. I can give him everything he needs. Everything you and I had growing up." He met my gaze. "Don't you think that's what he'd want?"

"If he does, then he knows where to find it. He knows you're here."

"He won't come to me."

"Then you'll need to find him and ask him what he wants. Because I won't help you."

TWENTY-FOUR

ANTONE HAD TO LEAVE it at that, as I was soon taken away for yet another medical appointment. A psych exam. Apparently Nast was a little concerned about my mental health.

I didn't cooperate nearly as well with that one. I mean, seriously? I'd just discovered I was a skin-walker and part of a secret science experiment, then I had been chased, nearly killed in a helicopter crash, nearly drowned by a friend, chased some more, discovered my town empty, realized my parents thought I was dead, got chased some more . . . The way I saw it, I was lucky I was still psychologically functioning at all. Of course, if I pointed that out, they'd take full credit for having "made" me strong enough to withstand this.

So I was not the most cooperative subject. Unfortunately, I couldn't outright refuse, because that would only give them further proof of my "damaged" psychological state. So I answered the questions with the minimum required response until the psychologist got frustrated and gave up. I hoped to return to my room then. No such luck. When the shrink left, the boss came in, accompanied by Dr. Inglis.

Now it was time for "the talk." I could have skipped it. I knew what Nast would say. The same message I'd heard at every encounter with the Cabals. Resistance is futile.

Yes, he admitted, things had gone wrong. Mina Lee shouldn't have come poking around, arousing our suspicions. The whole forest fire and helicopter kidnapping scheme? A bureaucratic mix-up. Yes, Nast actually blamed it on confusion at the corporate level, as if some misdirected memo had killed Mayor Tillson.

"I know you're still children—" Nast began.

Dr. Inglis cleared her throat and he amended that to "young adults." I'm not sure which was more condescending—calling us kids or thinking we'd respond better if they humored our delusions of maturity.

"At your age, you don't have to think about your future," Nast continued.

"Sure, we do," I said. "I've been thinking about my future a lot. Everything I'm missing. Like my hot date with Rafe for Friday or the big beer bash we had planned for Saturday night."

His lips tightened.

"We have plans," I said. "I want to be a veterinarian.

184

Daniel wants to be a lawyer. Serena wanted to swim on the Olympic team and study sports psychology. You've heard of Serena, right? My best friend? Murdered by one of your subjects gone psycho."

"We don't know that for certain," Nast said.

"She *admitted* it."

Dr. Inglis inched forward. "We do agree that Nicole appears to be responsible for Serena's death, Maya. We just don't know if the experiment had anything to do with that. Mental illness can have many causes."

"Whatever. We do have dreams. All of us. And none include being prisoners—or Cabal slaves—for the rest of our lives."

"Cabal slaves?" Nast laughed. "Do my employees look that miserable? Yes, we expect a return on our investment. We expect you to work for us, in the same way that the army expects military service after paying for a college degree."

"But people join the army knowing that. It's a willing exchange of services."

He waved off the distinction. "Think of it as being a very privileged young woman, which you are. You will get the best care and the best education, and when you graduate, you will have a guaranteed job waiting. A job that will pay you a six figure starting salary, in addition to covering all living expenses. How many young people dream of such an opportunity?"

"They dream of that as an *option*. A choice."

Another wave as if to say, *Such a petty distinction, really.* "You'll have choices, Maya. You all will. Daniel can certainly become a lawyer. The Cabal can always use more. He'd attend the Ivy League school of his choosing." A smug smile. "We can guarantee it whatever his grades. As for you, while we don't have much call for veterinarians, I happen to know you weren't as set on that career as you're pretending now. I'm sure we could find something that matched your interests."

"You didn't resurrect extinct species to become lawyers," I said. "You'll want more from us."

"We'll have other tasks, yes. But there's no need to worry about that now. The point is that you will be taken care of. Very well taken care of."

"In a gilded cage," I said, waving at the house.

Dr. Inglis stepped forward. "No, Maya. This is just temporary. Do you remember what I said about finding you another Salmon Creek? We have. That's where you'll live until you go away to college. After that, you'd be free to live on your own, as any other young person would."

Nast leaned forward. "Except you won't be living in a dingy one-room apartment in a questionable part of town. You would get a condo your average college grad can't afford unless she comes from a very wealthy family." He smiled. "Which, in a way, you do."

"What if I just want to come from the family I have now? My parents?"

Silence.

I turned to Dr. Inglis. "You said you're setting up Salmon Creek Two. I assume it'll be just like the first, right?"

"As close as we can get."

"So my parents will be there?"

She looked momentarily stricken, as if she'd thought they'd come close to selling me the deal, and the decision now rested on a response she couldn't give. I knew she couldn't give it. But I sat there, looking expectant.

"Your father will be there," Nast said.

I gave him a look that said I wasn't dignifying that with a response. Then I turned back to Dr. Inglis.

"My parents will know soon, right? They'll come live with me. Just like before?"

"I . . ."

"You remember my parents?" I said. "You've known them for eleven years. You've been to our house. You've gone to lunch with my mom."

"Your adoptive parents can't join you, Maya," Nast said.

I kept my gaze on Dr. Inglis. "I saw you at the memorial service. And you saw them, right? My parents? They seemed okay with me being dead, didn't they?"

She looked away fast.

"This is for the best," Nast said. "Perhaps, if you kids hadn't run like that, we could have avoided the ruse of your deaths."

"Like hell!" I said, wheeling on him. "When we crashed, we were being *kidnapped*. Of course we ran. You never

187

intended to return us to our parents. The crash just gave you a really good, really permanent way to do that."

"Permanent," he said, drawing the word out. "Yes, it is permanent, Maya, because there's no way we can reverse it without endangering the project. Your parents are human. They know nothing of the experiment or of supernaturals in general. If they found out, they would go to the authorities, which would be catastrophic. Catastrophic for us if the authorities believed them, but more so for your parents, when they didn't. And that's presuming they don't reject you outright. A girl who can change into a mountain lion?" He shook his head. "You're not theirs. Not really. For once, I suspect they'd be glad of it."

"My parents would never—"

"Of course they wouldn't," Dr. Inglis cut in. "They will mourn you. Deeply mourn you. But, after a time, they will move on. In fact, we're pulling in the full medical resources of both the Nast and St. Cloud corporations. When your mother is ready, we're going to offer to help her conceive."

"Help her . . . ?"

"Many advances have been made in the years since they adopted you. We firmly believe that, with the right treatments, your parents could have a child of their own."

"Wow," I said. "That's like . . . it's like losing your dog-pound mutt and getting a purebred puppy in its place. They're so lucky."

My hands started to pulse. I looked down at them, certain

188

I was imagining things. But I wasn't. The skin had begun to ripple.

Why was I shifting? It only seemed to happen when I got stressed. Sure, I wasn't happy with this conversation, but they'd said nothing I didn't expect. I was annoyed and frustrated, but my heart was chugging along at a normal—

Almost as soon as I thought that, it sped up so fast I had to gasp for breath. What was happening to me?

"Maya?" Dr. Inglis said.

I turned to her and when I saw her face, rage filled me. Blind rage, like in my room, with Nast. But I wasn't enraged with her. I was annoyed and frustrated and hurt. Yet as that untethered rage shot through me, it brought a wave of memories, of all the times I'd trusted her, all the times my parents had trusted her. As if my brain was finding reasons for the anger.

I gripped the arms of the chair and closed my eyes.

"Maya?"

Dr. Inglis touched my shoulder and I had to clench the chair harder to keep from smacking her hand away.

"She's shifting," Nast murmured as if I couldn't hear.

No, as if I don't matter. As if I'm nothing more than—

The rage surged and I clamped down as hard as I could.

"Maya?" Dr. Inglis said. "Can you tell us what you're feeling? What you're thinking?"

I'm thinking of launching out of this chair and taking you down. I'm thinking of putting my hands around your throat—

I jerked forward, a whimper escaping.

What the hell was happening to me? It was like I was outside myself, watching a stranger—

Annie's words came back. *It was like watching myself. No, watching someone who looked like me and felt a bit like me, but wasn't, not really.*

No. I wasn't reverting. I was stressed out, and they were making it worse by telling me to forget my parents. *They'll certainly forget you . . . after we give them a real daughter.*

My arms started to throb.

Don't think about that. Think about anything except your parents and Ash and Daniel . . . Daniel out there, injured, maybe even—

Do not *think about that!*

I took a deep breath and struggled to think of something innocent and meaningless. Think back to what I'd been doing before all this happened. Back in Salmon Creek before everything started with Rafe and Mina Lee.

Biology. I'd had a midterm coming up and I'd really wanted to ace it. I was always in competition with Brendan in bio and we'd laid a wager on who would do better this time. Winner got lunch at the Blender, which meant I needed to win, because Brendan could really pack away—

"Maya?" Dr. Inglis shook my shoulder.

Damn it, no. Leave me—

"She's stopped it," Dr. Inglis said.

I opened my eyes and saw her staring at me. When I

190

looked down at my hands, they'd gone back to normal. The rage had evaporated.

Dr. Inglis bent in front of me. "That was excellent, Maya. Can you tell me how you reversed the process?"

Nast brushed her aside. "That's not important. Tell us what happened, Maya. You got angry, didn't you? I could see it."

I looked at him, then turned to Dr. Inglis. "I'd like to leave now."

"You'll leave when—" Nast began.

"Yes, I think that's a good idea," said a voice behind us.

I turned to see Antone in the doorway, his hand still on the knob, his breath coming fast, like he'd been running. Moreno stood behind him.

Nast rose. "If you want to watch this discussion, Calvin, the video feed is active."

"I've *been* watching." He walked in. "Under the terms of our agreement, sir, I am allowed to veto any treatment of my daughter. I'm going to ask that you allow me to cut this interview short. It's been too much for her and the strain is clearly showing."

"That isn't strain," Nast said. "She's reverting. You know it and I know it, and coddling the girl isn't going to change that."

As they argued, Dr. Inglis tried to reassure Antone, verbally tripping over herself. Behind him, Moreno rolled his eyes and shot a smirk my way, as if we were sharing some secret.

Finally, Nast agreed they were done with the interview anyway, so Antone could take me. He led me out as Moreno stayed behind to talk to Nast.

"You started to shift, didn't you?" Antone whispered as we walked down the hall.

I considered ignoring him, but that seemed petty. Not just petty but unwise. What's that saying about the fire and the frying pan? Antone was my frying pan. It wasn't a comfortable place to be, but it was safe, at least compared to the fire.

"I did."

"I know what they were saying wasn't easy to hear, but you didn't seem that angry."

"I wasn't. Not until . . ."

"Until what? Did they say something to trigger it?"

"I . . . I don't think so. I was okay. And then . . . and then I wasn't. I don't know how to explain—"

"Calvin!"

Pumps clicked on the hardwood as Dr. Inglis jogged toward us. Antone looked back, then turned away and kept walking.

"Calvin, please."

He slowed until she caught up.

"I'm so sorry about—" she began.

He stopped so abruptly she fell back. "You were supposed to be in there for me. In my stead. Watching out for my daughter's interests."

"I—"

"I trusted you, Maggie, and when things went wrong, you were right in there, pushing Maya as hard as he was."

Her mouth opened and closed, and she stared up at him with . . . Oh God. I recognized that look. Any teenage girl did.

Dr. Inglis had a crush on my biological father. A serious, starry-eyed, "OMG, I'd do anything for you" kind of crush.

Ick.

I suppose I shouldn't say that. I'm not the kind of kid who freaks out when I catch my parents kissing. I don't think romance is reserved for those under the age of twenty. And yet, seeing Dr. Inglis making goo-goo eyes at Antone just seemed creepy. She was an attractive, smart, accomplished woman. She shouldn't be simpering over any man.

I suspect it didn't seem as creepy to Antone. But he didn't exactly return her moonstruck gaze. Just stood there, looking pissed.

"I'm sorry, Calvin. I thought I was helping. It won't happen again."

He hesitated, as if considering. "Have you gotten the results of Maya's physical yet?"

"No, but I'll do that right away."

He didn't exactly smile, but his face relaxed and she breathed an audible sigh of relief. I looked at him. *You're using her. You know how she feels and you're using her. And . . . and I don't care. Part of me feels bad for her, but mostly, I'm beyond that. Whatever works. Whatever helps.*

TWENTY-FIVE

D R. INGLIS LEFT AND Antone led me to my room. He didn't say a word until the door was closed. I walked to the bed and sat. Kenjii hopped up and laid down with her head on my lap.

"So they told you the grand plan," Antone said.

"Yep. I get a brand-new life. Everything I could ever want . . . except my parents, but that's okay, because they'll get a new puppy—I mean, baby."

He sat beside me on the bed. "If you think that means the Delaneys will forget you, they won't."

"You really think I'm worried about that?" I shook my head. "I'm not pissed off at being replaced. I'm pissed off at the basic lack of respect for my parents. They lost a daughter? Let's give them a new one. A real one. Then everyone will be happy."

"Except you."

"Oh, I'm sure I'll be happy. I get a new puppy, too. A brand-new daddy. Lucky me."

He flinched at my sarcasm, and I reminded myself that I couldn't do this anymore. I didn't have to suck up to him—I couldn't—but nor could I afford to antagonize him.

"This isn't what I wanted either, Maya," he said after a moment.

"What did you want?"

He took a moment before answering. "Contact. That's all I've wanted for years, since you got too old to be taken from the Delaneys. I just wanted to be part of your life. I won't make excuses. I allowed the Nasts to commandeer that rescue helicopter. They promised it would be temporary. They'd tell you kids what you were and, they hoped, woo you from the St. Clouds."

"Like head-hunting new employees? Seriously?"

"That's what you are to them, Maya. Very valuable future employees. The Cabals . . . I can't get into it now, but this isn't unusual, fighting for rare supernatural types. The Nasts would have laid out the situation. Positioned themselves, not as the people who kidnapped you, but as the people who were honest with you. Told you the truth. Let you make your own choices."

"And let me go back to my parents?"

"Yes. I know you don't believe that, but I'm really not the enemy here, Maya. I'm the guy trying to make the best of a lousy situation. An impossible situation." He looked at me. "You understand that, don't you? The situation. You can't escape it. There's no place to go. You need the Cabals."

"Good."

He hesitated. Then said, slowly, "Good?"

"Yes, good, because that means we can negotiate."

"Negotiate?"

I paused. Daniel and I had discussed this, but only briefly. Negotiate with our captors? We'd rather fight and we'd win.

Win what? Our freedom? No, because even if we got our friends and our families back, we were still held prisoner by our conditions. Corey's headaches would get worse, Annie would stop progressing, and I'd continue regressing.

I took a deep breath. "They want happy little future employees? Let's back up a step. Back to what they planned before the crash. They can pitch us their packages. We'll make our own decisions, including the decision to be reunited with our parents."

He went quiet. Very quiet. When he tried to speak, his breath hitched and he had to take another moment. Then he looked me in the eyes. "That's a very mature solution, Maya. Remarkably mature, and you have no idea how proud I am of you right now, for even thinking of it."

"So we can, right?" I knew the answer. I'd seen it in his face as soon as I suggested it. Pride and pain. Mostly pain.

"The Cabals would never allow that, Maya. The risk of

telling your parents, after they've buried you . . ." He shook his head.

"And after they paid good money for us."

"It wasn't money. It was a trade of resources and intelligence."

I gave him a look. "Do you really think that matters? We're bought and paid for, whatever the currency. They say they want us happy, but they really just want us compliant." I looked at him. "I don't do compliant."

TWENTY-SIX

I F IT WASN'T FOR the light coming through my window, I'd have been certain it was night by now. It had to be, after everything that had happened.

I'd been in my room for about an hour, just lying on the bed, thinking. No, not thinking. Worrying. About Daniel. I couldn't see a way out of this prison, so there was nothing to think about except a very general, incredibly unhelpful *I need to get out and find him*. And, while I was getting out, I needed to take Rafe and Annie and Sam and Hayley and Kenjii and how the hell was I going to manage that, short of having an armored minivan break through the gates and rescue us?

A staccato rap at the door broke my reverie.

The door cracked open. "Decent?" Rafe asked.

"Yep."

"Damn." He pushed it open.

"If you're hoping to see something, the trick is to not knock first."

"That would be wrong," he said as he walked in. "The trick is to hope you say 'no, but come in anyway.'"

"Ah."

I patted the bed. He waggled his brows. I shook my head and he murmured another "Damn." I laughed and watched him cross the room and I felt . . . lighter. Like the weight lifted, not completely but enough for me to function again.

He didn't sit, but just reached over to pet Kenjii. "I was hoping to talk you into coming up on the roof with me."

"Lockdown is lifted?"

"My door was open. Your door was open. I take it that means we can wander and, if it doesn't, we'll just get on the roof fast, before they notice."

"Good plan."

I glanced at Kenjii and was about to ask if she could come when he patted his leg, and she jumped up and followed us to the door. When he motioned for her to wait, she sat.

"I do believe you've stolen my dog," I said.

"Not quite. But we have been roomies for the last couple of days. They wanted to kennel her. I said 'like hell.' She's a smart dog. She knew her choices were to behave or sleep on a cement floor."

"Thank you."

He shrugged and opened the door.

I caught it in my hand. "No, really. Thank you." I leaned over and kissed him.

When I pulled back, he was grinning. "See, I'm not as dumb as I look. Most girls like flowers, candy, walks on the beach. But the way to your heart is through your pets." He paused. "And your friends, but I'm not doing so well with that part of my master plan."

We walked into the hall, Kenjii trailing.

"Are Sam and Hayley giving you a hard time?" I asked as he led me the other way down the hall.

"Sam, always. Hayley's not exactly chatty. I can't blame her. I was a real jerk to her, leading her on. I was trying to make inroads with Nicole and that seemed to be going better, until . . ."

"I'm sorry I didn't tell you."

"No way you could have. I'm just . . . shocked. Disgusted. I keep telling myself she must be mentally ill or something, but that doesn't make it better, you know? I don't see how anyone could do that, crazy or not." He looked over. "I'm sorry you had to go through this. Finding out. It must have been hell." He paused. "At least you had Daniel."

"He doesn't know."

We'd reached the door at the hall's end. He stopped and looked over, frowning.

"How can I tell him?" I said. "She killed Serena over him."

And, worse, he'd been about to break it off, and if he'd

only done that a little faster . . .

"Then she went after you," he murmured.

I nodded. "I don't get that. There's never been anything between Daniel and me. I guess it's only proof she's crazy."

He hit the buzzer for someone to open the door. It clicked open. On the other side were stairs heading up to another door.

He waved me forward. "You're right about Daniel. That's a shitty thing to pile on anyone. He doesn't deserve it. He's a good guy."

"He is." I glanced back. "And thank you for saying that. I know he hasn't always been a 'good guy' to you."

"Hey, like I said, the way to your heart is through your friends—furred and otherwise. He's had reason to be wary of me. I'm hoping I'll get the chance to change his mind."

"You will."

We climbed the steps, Kenjii following. At the top, I opened the door and we found ourselves walking onto a roof.

If I'd hoped for a huge flat roof with plenty of room to roam, I was disappointed. I suppose, being the daughter of an architect, I should have known better. Putting a flat roof on a house is not only problematic, but would give it an odd, industrial look. So we only had one flat section, maybe five meters by seven. And with high walls on all sides, the patch of late-day sun was barely enough to bask in.

"Looks like a prison exercise yard, doesn't it?" He waved at the basketball net and weight deck. "Even got the cameras.

There and there." He pointed them out. "Not quite what you were hoping for, I'm sure," he said. "But these are cool." He walked to a set of balance beams and swung up.

I took a running leap and landed in a crouch. Then I sat straddling the beam.

"Show-off."

I grinned. "If I was showing off, I'd have landed standing up."

"If you could, I'm sure you would have."

"Is that a challenge?"

I swung my leg over to jump off, but he caught a handful of my shirt.

"Not yet. Up first."

He let go of my shirt and rose, one foot in front of the other, standing as easily as if he was on solid ground. I joined him and when I did, I let out a gasp.

I could see over the wall. Not much, but enough to catch a glimpse of our surroundings. We were on a mountainside, high enough that I could see distant treetops and roofs of other houses. The surge of happiness didn't last long, though. While it was wonderful seeing trees, it only reminded me that I was stuck in a walled compound, unable to get to them, touch them, climb them. I could barely even smell them through the overwhelming stink of new construction.

"Yeah, it's not much," Rafe said. "Just enough of a peek to make us feel like we're doing something we shouldn't. Can't get a real sense of the place."

Of our surroundings, he meant. Where we were and how we could escape it.

I stood there, on tiptoe, staring out, wondering where Daniel was, how he was, how I'd get to him.

"Worrying about Daniel?" There was something in Rafe's tone that made me look over sharply.

"Of course you are," he said quickly. "Dumb question, huh?" He tried for a smile, but didn't quite find it and settled for lowering himself to the beam again, breaking eye contact.

He's jealous.

Please no. Not Rafe.

I've been dealing with jealous boyfriends since I first started dating. A lot of guys don't like their girlfriend having a male best friend. Considering I'd only dated summer boys—and dated casually at that—it wasn't usually a big problem. A couple times, though, I'd gotten an ultimatum by the second or third date—"You want to go out with me? You stop hanging out with him." The answer was always simple. "You don't want me hanging out with him? I don't go out with you." No exceptions.

With Rafe, though, I'd never gotten any flack over Daniel. He seemed to accept my friendship for what it was. Now I remembered his expression when Sam accused me of fooling around with Daniel.

I looked at him, sitting on the beam, gazing around as if the blank walls were fascinating. *Don't do this, Rafe. Please, please, please don't do this.*

Kenjii moved closer, whining softly.

Rafe looked up. "You want to talk about it?"

My throat seized. Finally I forced out, "Talk about what?"

"Daniel. You're worried and I don't blame you. Maybe if we hash it out, you'll feel better."

I exhaled and slid down to sit, straddling the beam, facing him. "Thanks, but I think talking will only make it worse. I'd rather be distracted."

"Ah." A flicker of a smile. "Like maybe . . ." He waved at the hoops. "A little one-on-one?"

"Exactly." I slid closer. "Just not with a basketball."

He inched back, hands going up as he struggled not to grin. "Hold on. I object to being used like that, you know."

"Really?"

"I do. It's . . ."

He met my gaze and his sentence trailed off. I thought about kissing him, about what it felt like, the feel of him, the smell of him. Usually, that was all it took. But now, that quickening pulse took a moment longer. It did come, though, when I concentrated. I looked over and saw the answering spark in his eyes, the amber glowing, pupils dilating.

"You were saying?" I murmured.

He crossed the short space between us so fast I didn't even notice him moving, and then he was there. When we kissed, I waited for those doubts to vanish, for that feeling to return. It was there, but different. I was too distracted. I had to stop worrying about—

The roof door crashed open.

"Good God," Sam said as she hobbled out. "Is that all you two do? No wonder she's still with you, Rafe. You're too busy making out to actually have a conversation so she can see what an idiot you are."

Rafe stiffened. I squeezed his leg and looked over my shoulder.

"I've been sent to invite you to join us for dinner." Sam hooked her thumb back toward the door and I saw a guard there. "He's been sent to hustle your asses if you don't move them."

We jumped off the bar.

TWENTY-SEVEN

THEY LOCKED ME IN my room that night. Locked all of us in. For our own good, until they could move Nicole to a secured area. Really, it seemed like more of an excuse to keep us all in our rooms. With Hayley, Sam, and Rafe, they'd had three kids who wouldn't trust one another to guard the bathroom door. They sure as hell weren't going to plan an escape together. But now I was here, and Rafe and I were already whispering in corners. Time for a lockdown.

I think they added an extra layer of security in my bed-time hot chocolate. Sleeping pills. Otherwise there was no way I would have zonked out so fast.

My dreams came in fits and starts, as if they were being stifled by the pills. I'll admit I was glad of that. What I saw was enough—images of Daniel being struck by a car, then Ash running into traffic while being pursued, then me chasing them, trying to warn them, but falling ever farther behind, unable to hear them, smell them, see them, my muscles seizing, reflexes slowing.

Then some cosmic force hit the rewind button, and I was in the lake with Serena again, seeing her pulled under the water, being pulled under myself. I tried to fight my way to her, but I couldn't see her, couldn't hear her, couldn't breathe. I was drowning. Really drowning. I couldn't get up. Couldn't get free. The water was everywhere, blocking my nose, my mouth, the smell of chemical lemon, the taste of cotton—

Lemon? Cotton?

My sleeping brain was alert enough to know neither of those scents fit the scenario and started pulling me up from sleep. But it was like pushing up through the water. Something held me down and the more I struggled, the more I choked and sputtered. I kicked and punched until my fist made contact and I heard a gasp. The water receded just enough for me to catch half a breath. It was enough. I pushed through the thick, sticky water of sleep and surfaced.

My eyes opened to darkness. Something was pressed against my face—lemon-scented fabric, the smell and the cotton filling my mouth and blocking my nose and covering my eyes.

A pillow. There's a pillow over my face.

I tried to claw the pillow away, but someone was on my chest, holding me down. I clawed at my attacker instead, convulsing and bucking and kicking. I grabbed fabric. Dug my nails into flesh beneath. Heard another gasp. The pillow loosened just enough for a breath. When it clamped down again, I stopped blindly flailing. I wedged my hands between my chest and my attacker, pulled up my knees and heaved.

My assailant flew off so fast I lay there another moment, frozen in surprise. Then I scrambled up, whipping the pillow to the floor and taking deep, shuddering breaths.

I looked around. Empty. My room was empty. I was alone.

Had I been imagining things? A weird waking dream from the drugs? I—

A figure leaped from the side, a blur in my peripheral vision. Hands grabbed for me. I rolled to the side, clear off the bed, landing on my feet.

I spun to my attacker, and I saw blond hair tangled around a thin face. Nicole.

She was crouched on the bed, her eyes so wide and wild they sent a chill through me. Not just crazy. Inhuman. She snarled and gnashed her teeth. Then she leaped.

I swung out of the way easily. She plowed into the wall with a thump that I swore I felt, but she only recovered and came at me again. Again I dodged. Again she missed, this time stumbling and hitting the floor, then she bounced back and charged.

I hit her this time. Part of me didn't want to. She wasn't a threat now—lumbering as blind and awkward as a newborn rhinoceros. And one look at her face told me that any trace of the Nicole I'd known was gone. She'd completely snapped, and as much as I hated her for what she'd done to Serena, when I looked at her now, I saw madness, not evil.

But I had to stop her. So I hit her. Hard. My fist plowed into her chest. As she stumbled back, a follow-up kick knocked her to the floor. The fact that I was able to do it so easily told me I wasn't exactly fighting a worthy opponent.

When Nicole went down, I pinned her. That was harder. She might not know how to throw a punch, but whatever madness infected her was pumping adrenaline through her veins. She'd been strong enough to almost suffocate me. Now she was strong enough to fight like a wild animal, writhing and bucking and hissing and biting.

As I struggled to hold her down—and stay away from her teeth and nails—I felt the first licks of rage. Again, it confused me at first. I wasn't truly angry, so why was my skin heating, the burn of rage building?

Then the rationalization came. Thoughts, images, whispers, swirling around me.

She killed Serena. Murdered your best friend. Tried to drown you twice. Almost suffocated you now. Of course you should be furious.

And how had this even happened? Wasn't she supposed to be locked up? Wasn't I supposed to be locked in?

And where the hell was Kenjii? My dog was gone. That

couldn't be a coincidence. Someone set this up. Someone here was trying to kill me.

They'd sworn to protect me. They hadn't. They didn't want to. It was up to me. Protect myself.

My hands started to pulse. The room tinged with red as my blood pounded in my ears.

Nicole was the enemy. To protect myself—to protect my friends—I had to eliminate the enemy. It was that simple.

My hands went to her throat. My nails had thickened to claws now and as my fingers wrapped around her throat the claws dug in. Droplets of blood popped up, bright red against her pale skin, the smell of it filling my nostrils, filling my head. Another smell, too. The stink of fear as I squeezed her neck.

She tried to fight harder. But she was already giving it everything she had and as my body started to shift, adrenaline pumped through me, too, and I held her easily. I kept squeezing. Blood dribbled down her neck. Her eyes bugged. She clawed at my hands, and I felt her nails dig in, but I just kept squeezing.

You're dying, I thought. *Strangling. Fighting for air that isn't there. How does it feel? Are you thinking of Serena? Wondering if this was what she felt when you drowned her? What I felt when you put the pillow over my face? Do you regret it?*

Nicole's hands stopped clawing mine. Her eyes closed. Her body went limp. Still I kept squeezing.

She's unconscious. You can stop. She's not a threat now.

No, as long as she's alive she's a threat.

You're killing her, Maya!

Good. It's the same thing she tried to do to me. She deserves to die. I want her—

My fingers froze. I stared down at Nicole, lying beneath me, face turning blue, and I leaped off her so fast I stumbled back onto the bed. I furiously rubbed my face, the thick pads of my hands rasping against my skin.

This isn't me. I'm not a killer.

Of course you are. You're a cougar. A wild animal. A predator. That's what they created. That's what you are.

No, I'm not.

I looked down at Nicole and squeezed my hands into fists. As I did, I felt the rage subside, the shift reverse, like a tide ebbing, slow but steady.

I looked around. My bedroom door was ajar. I walked over, cracked it open, looked and listened. The hall was silent.

I could escape.

Escape where? The house is secured.

But Nicole had gotten out of her so-called secured room and into mine. We'd fought and no one had come running. No one even seemed to notice.

Nicole didn't just wander into your room on her own. You know that. Someone let her in and took Kenjii and probably drugged Nicole to make her flip out like that.

Which meant that the "trap" had already sprung. I'd outwitted it and now the way was clear—or clear enough.

Was I sure of that? Of course not. But the alternative was to sit on my bed and wait for someone to come and find out I'd nearly killed Nicole.

I had to take a chance.

TWENTY-EIGHT

I SLIPPED INTO THE hall. I looked both ways and listened. I even inhaled, although I wasn't sure how much good that would do. There was nothing. A still and silent house.

I didn't do more than glance at the stairs. Yes, that was the way out, but I wasn't running off and leaving everyone else. Rafe said his door was the third down from mine. I crept to it and tried the handle. It was locked, of course.

When I twisted the knob, I heard a thump inside. Then the scratch of nails against the wood floor.

"Kenjii?" I whispered.

An answering scramble as she ran to the door. She leaped up, nails raking down it as she whimpered.

A sleepy grunt from inside. Then, "Kenjii? How'd you get in here, girl?"

"Rafe?"

A pause. His light footfalls hurrying to the door.

"Maya?" he whispered through it.

"Something's wrong," I said. "The security system seems to be down." I tried his door. Still locked. "Try it from your side."

He did. The knob turned but it didn't budge. He yanked at it. Still nothing.

"It's just yours," he said.

I tried his door again, pulling harder.

"It's locked, Maya. If you can get out, go."

"Not without—"

"Go. We're fine."

I tried again, but the door wasn't opening and every second I hesitated was another second to get caught. They were fine. Not happy. Not free. But safe enough. Safer than Daniel. And weren't they all better off if I was free and looking for a way to get them out?

"Go, Maya. I'm fine and I'll take care of Kenjii."

I hesitated only another moment. Then I tiptoed to the top of the stairs. As soon as I reached it, I picked up voices below. I strained to hear what they were saying, but it was too far. I took one careful step down. If no one knew the system had malfunctioned, I might be able to get past—

I caught the words "Nicole" and "security," and stopped. The voices grew more urgent, one man whispering harshly to the other to find Nicole before anyone discovered she was missing or their asses would be on the line.

I backed up and looked around.

The roof. I jogged barefoot down the hall. It was only when I reached the door that I remembered Rafe had to buzz down to be allowed out. I turned the knob. It twisted, the door opening.

It's a trap.

Or the system is malfunctioning.

What if Nast is watching me right now, rubbing his hands as he gathers evidence of how uncontrollable I am? How I need to be in a secure cell where I can't escape, can't collaborate with Rafe, can't cause any trouble? And can't be subject to any "deal" they'd made with Antone. . . .

I was so lost in my confusion that I didn't hear footsteps until I caught a flicker of movement and turned to see a security guard cresting the landing. He saw me and stopped dead. A split second of shock crossed his face, then both hands sailed to his belt, one grabbing his gun, the other hitting a button on his radio.

The wail of a siren jolted me to life. I yanked open the door and raced up the steps. I kept my gaze fixed on the door at the top.

Please be open. Please be open. Don't trap me here in this—

I turned the handle and almost fell through as it opened. Behind me, the guard barked into his radio.

I flew through the door and onto the roof. I blinked against the darkness. The sky was overcast, pitch black. After a moment, my night vision kicked in, fueled by lights below. When I could see, I realized why the guard wasn't racing up the stairs after me. Because there was no place for me to go.

Logically, I'd already known that. In my race to escape, I hadn't stopped to be logical, though.

Boots clomped up the steps. I looked around. There was nothing higher than the balance beams. I took a running leap and vaulted up. I was crouched on the beam when the door banged open. I turned to see the guard, gun raised.

"There's no place to run," he said. "Just come back down—"

I ran along the beam. He swore and fired. The dart zoomed past me. I saw the end of the beam coming and realized there was no way I could jump onto the wall. It was too high.

A second dart snagged in the folds of my shirt. As I measured the distance to the wall, the guard shouted that I was just going to hurt myself, halt now before—

I backed up and took a running leap. I didn't try to jump onto the wall. Too dangerous. Instead, I caught it with both hands, the stone scraping my bare forearms, shoulders wrenching before I swung my legs up and scrambled onto the wall.

The guard lifted his gun. A figure shot from the doorway and knocked him aside. I saw dark hair and thought "Rafe," but that hope lasted only a moment, while the two skidded across the roof. Then Antone scrambled up, gun in hand.

"Are you mad or just incompetent?" he snarled at the guard, who was pushing to his feet. "You're going to shoot a tranquilizer dart at a girl on a seventy-foot-high wall?"

I looked down and when I did, my breath caught. As I'd seen earlier, the house was built on a mountainside, and they'd put the rooftop courtyard at the front of it, meaning I was looking down at a drop of at least twenty meters.

"You can't jump that, Maya." Antone advanced on me, gun lowered. "You know you can't."

I looked over at the roof. It rose steeply beyond the wall.

"That won't work, either," he said. "They were very careful when they gave you this exercise yard."

I looked down again. I flexed my knees.

"Maya!"

He lunged toward me. I staggered back and pretended to nearly lose my balance. That stopped him.

"You cannot jump," he said. "You know that. At the very least, you'll break your leg. How far do you expect to get with a broken leg? Even without one, there's no place to go. Look around you."

Below the wall was a driveway. Solid pavement. Beyond that? A huge yard with a steep lane running down to a massive fence that wrapped around the property. Two guards already stood at the gate, flashlights and guns in hand.

I looked behind me.

"There's a gate that way, too," Calvin said. "Every guard—every staff member—heard the alarm and they're out there. If you jump, someone will grab you within seconds."

I continued looking around, assessing, measuring. There was grass to the side. I could jump there. Trees started just beyond it. If I got to the trees, I could make my way through the wooded mountainside behind the house . . .

A light flickered in the woods. Guards heading out. Blocking off my escape routes.

Still, I should give it a shot. Yes, the chances of me making it to safety were minuscule. But minuscule was above zero, and that's how much chance I had otherwise.

Daniel was out there. He was injured. Would I risk injury myself to get to him? Absolutely.

I took a step sideways, toward the grass.

Antone lunged forward. "No, Maya. You will hurt yourself. Badly. You know you will." He inched toward me. "Can we negotiate?"

My head jerked up at that word. He locked gazes with me again. "Yes, negotiate," he said. "I think that's a possibility. Not now. Not under these circumstances. But it is a possibility."

Across the roof, the guard just stood there, looking annoyed at the delay. Paying little attention to what Antone was saying, but still listening.

"Things need to happen for that possibility to become a reality," Antone said. "Do you understand that?"

No, but I understood he was trying to convey a message.

"I will help you," Antone said. "I know what you want and I will help you, Maya."

He'd thought he was "helping" me all along. He thought having me locked up here was helping.

I looked down again. He was right. It was too far. At the very least, I'd sprain my ankle and that would cost me any chance of escape—if I ever had a chance at all, as the yard and forest filled with shapes and flashlight beams.

"I want to negotiate," I said.

"I know you do. But you can't under the current circumstances." He sounded as if he meant "while you're standing on the roof," but he arched his brows, his look implying more. "We need to change the circumstances, and I will help you do that. Okay?"

I hesitated. Another look down, but there was nothing to be gained here except injury and trouble. Better to show that I could be reasonable.

I crouched to leap onto the roof. Antone exhaled and nodded, coming forward, hand out to help me down. I waved him off and was about to jump when the door crashed open. Two guards barreled through, rifles rising.

"No!" Antone said. "She's—"

The guards fired. The first dart hit me in the arm. The second hit me in the thigh. I froze, crouched there. Antone lifted his arms, trying to reach me, but the wall was too high.

He said something, his words fast, eyes wide with panic as he gestured for me to jump down. Now. Before—

I wobbled.

Antone shouted something. His voice thundered in my ears, words indistinguishable. I tensed to jump and—

My muscles went slack. I tried to jump, but my body wouldn't obey. Couldn't. I felt myself toppling. Falling. Then everything went dark.

TWENTY-NÎNE

WHEN I SURFACED TO feel someone sitting beside me, I cracked open my eyes enough to catch a glimpse of brown skin and dark hair and reached out to push Antone away.

"Hey," said a voice. "That's no way to treat your nurse."

I pried open my eyes enough to see Rafe sitting on the edge of my bed.

"Sorry," I said. "I thought you were . . ."

I looked past him to Antone, who was slouched in a chair across the room. He was awake, but his gaze was fixed on the wall, deep in thought.

"Mmm, yeah," Rafe murmured under his breath. "Don't blame you."

I rubbed my eyes and looked around. Daylight glowed through the frosted glass window. Kenjii walked over and nudged me. As I patted her, Antone noticed me and rose.

"How are you?" he asked.

It took a second to remember what had happened. When I did, I felt a burst of panic, until I wriggled my toes and saw them move under the sheets. I pulled my legs up and stretched my arms. Hurt like hell, but everything seemed to be functioning.

"Sore," I said.

"Yeah, you took a little tumble," Rafe said.

"Little? Ah, so I fell onto the roof, not over the wall."

"Thankfully," Antone said. "You'll have bruises, but Dr. Inglis assures me nothing is broken. Rafe's been trying to use his healing powers."

Rafe looked abashed. "I don't think I have any yet. Maybe you can try yours?"

Antone shook his head. "A skin-walker can only heal others."

He was right—I'd tried it on a few of my cuts and bumps during our adventures, and my powers had no effect.

Antone handed me a glass of water. My mouth was cotton-dry from the tranquilizers. I took it and started drinking.

"You can rest some more," Antone said. "When you're ready, though, I need to call Mr. Nast and Dr. Inglis in to talk to you about what happened last night."

"Take my statement." I glanced up around the ceiling. "I guess that means they couldn't watch the fun for themselves?"

"No, there aren't cameras in the bedrooms," he said, then mouthed, "just microphones." I knew that, from Rafe, but it was nice to have someone admit it.

"Tell them I'm ready," I said.

Antone shook his head. "Get some more rest."

"No. Let's get this over with."

Nicole was all right. I was . . . I would say I was glad to hear it, except that I was really only relieved because I didn't want to be responsible for her death, which isn't nearly as altruistic. Did that bother me? Intellectually, it did. Canada doesn't have the death penalty, and I agree with that. There was no part of me that wanted Nicole dead for killing Serena. Punished, yes. Locked up, yes. But her death wouldn't bring Serena back.

She was fine, though. Bruised and battered, but fine.

Had she been drugged? When I raised that possibility, Dr. Wiley acted like I was being paranoid. Nicole was unstable. That was all. Still, when I described how she'd behaved—the wild eyes, the inhuman strength—Dr. Inglis agreed she should be tested and promised to do it herself.

I was relieved that no one tried to say Nicole's escape was an accident. Nast had already ordered a full investigation and all security personnel on duty last night had been put on a plane to Los Angeles to face questioning there.

Near-death experience aside, I was still in trouble for trying to escape. I could have laughed at that. I think I might have. Nast did not appreciate it. Antone pointed out that, given that Nicole had almost killed me and I suspected someone in the house had engineered the attack, it made perfect sense for me to run. It was self-defense, really. And I *had* been about to turn myself in when I was shot. The other guard had confirmed that.

Nast wasn't convinced. I would spend the rest of the day in isolation. No visitors other than authorized personnel. And Dr. Wiley needed to run another complete examination, because Nast was concerned that my attack on Nicole proved I was regressing.

That really pissed Antone off. I'd been fighting for my life and they were blaming me for hurting my attacker? I said nothing, because I remembered that blind rage. I *was* regressing; I was just afraid to admit it.

If their tests discovered anything abnormal, no one told me. Dr. Wiley and Dr. Inglis didn't whisper any theories or suspicions for me to overhear. They didn't even give me hints with their expressions. Just ran the tests. Took the data. Escorted me back to my room. At least, Dr. Inglis did.

I wanted to ask what she'd found. I wanted to ask a lot of things. If I *was* regressing, would Annie's treatment work on me? If they caught it soon enough, would they be able to fix it faster, too?

If I asked, that would suggest I knew something was wrong, which would only earn me closer scrutiny. So I just walked in silence. Dr. Inglis didn't seem to notice—she was too busy chattering at me. While she'd never been cold or standoffish, I swore she said more to me in five minutes than she would have in a year at Salmon Creek. It wasn't anything important. Just talk—overly bright, overly optimistic, overly flattering talk. Under the misguided impression, I guess, that I might put in a good word with Antone. Still, I could use allies, so I nodded and feigned interest.

We seemed to take an overly complicated route back to my room. As we walked down a corridor, Dr. Inglis slowed and talked louder, and I wasn't surprised to catch a glimpse of Antone and Moreno through an open doorway, Antone sitting at a desk, Moreno perched on it, talking.

Hearing us, Antone came to the door. "All done?"

"Yes, and I was just taking Maya to the kitchen for something to eat." A conspiratorial smile my way. "And letting her avoid her room for as long as possible."

"Good plan." Antone walked out. "I'll take Maya from here and grab us coffees on my way back. We need to go over a few memos."

She hesitated, but it was clear he didn't want her accompanying us, so she reminded him she took her coffee black. When he said "I know," she glowed.

Before we left, Antone remembered something in his office and popped back in. I waited while he jotted a note on a piece of paper and dropped it into a file. As we walked, he asked how my exam went. He didn't seem to be listening, though, and when we turned the corner into another hall, he opened his hand and I saw the piece of paper that I thought he'd put in the file. He unfurled it and held it out for me to read.

Dead zone coming up.

He counted down on his other hand. Five, four, three, two . . . another couple of steps and he whispered, almost too low for me to hear. "If you want to negotiate, we need leverage. You don't have that while you're in here."

"I—"

He motioned for me to keep quiet. "I've arranged something. You'll know when it happens. You need to take advantage of it. At that point, I can't help. I need to stay clean."

"I—"

A stern look cut me off again and he counted down from three this time, then said, "Any requests for dinner? Since you're locked in your room, I'm sure we can make allowances. Takeout, maybe? Just tell me what you'd like, and . . ."

He continued talking as we headed for the kitchen.

I was going to get an opportunity to escape. To find Daniel and make sure he was all right, heal him if I could. Antone was setting it up, but once he did, he had to step back so he wasn't implicated in my escape. Or I think that's what he meant. I hoped it was. I also hoped I'd get some hints about what form this opportunity would take. An unlocked door? An ally who would break me out? And what about the others?

But that was all Antone said. In fact, it was the last time I saw him all day. So I sat in my room, waiting for . . . whatever. Nothing came. If he'd launched his "opportunity," I'd missed it. Unless he meant tomorrow. Or the day after.

Damn it. I appreciated that he thought I was clever enough to need only those few cryptic sentences, but more detail would have been appreciated.

THİRTY

I DON'T THINK I got sleeping pills in my hot chocolate. I didn't need them, considering my ordeal the night before—and the fact that I'd refused to nap all day, certain Antone's "opportunity" would come at any moment. I stayed up until nearly midnight, then drifted off, Kenjii again curled on my bed.

When I heard Kenjii growl and opened my eyes to see my door swinging open, I jumped up out of bed and sprang into fighting stance. So did Kenjii, snarling and planting herself in front of me.

Two armed guards stopped in mid-stride.

"Control your dog," one said. He waved his gun to remind me what would happen if I didn't.

"Why the hell do they let her keep the mutt?" one muttered. "Like we don't have enough to deal with."

"Calvin insists," the first said, and shared an eye roll with the second. Then he turned to me. "Grab your shoes, sweater, whatever else you need. You have five seconds."

"Need for what?" I said, still sleep-dazed.

"Grab it or leave it. Four seconds."

Antone. His opportunity. This was it.

I'd gone to sleep wearing my clothing, just in case. So I only needed shoes, a sweater, and my stash of money. They hadn't noticed the cash when they brought me in—or they didn't care—so I took it now, shoved it into my pocket, and followed the two guards into the hall.

When I stepped out, the noise hit me. Noise from everywhere—shouts and barked orders and running footfalls. The guards tried to steer me to the stairs, but I heard a voice behind me and turned to see Rafe breaking from his guards and jogging to join us.

The whole house was in an uproar. All the bedroom doors were open, as if we were all being taken out.

"What's going on?" I whispered to Rafe.

"Evacuation," he said. "No idea why."

This must be Antone's opportunity. Not just to get me out, but the others, too. That made sense. More leverage for negotiating.

Still, as they led us downstairs, I kept looking for Antone. Just a glimpse of him so he could tell me, even with only a look, that this was his scheme. But he wasn't there. Nor was Moreno. Had he launched this, then found an excuse to be elsewhere, so he couldn't be blamed? Or did this have nothing to do with him?

"Listen," Rafe whispered.

I caught snatches of conversations in other rooms. Conversations about what was happening. Most of it was out of context. Then I heard Nast's voice behind a closed door and zeroed in on that.

"—thought we had people working to prevent exactly this possibility," he was saying. "If we found out about the projects, so could the Cortezes. When they did, they'd want in and that is a problem we do not want to deal with. People were supposed to be making sure we didn't need to deal with it. So tell me why we *are* dealing with it?"

"We don't know for certain it's the Cortezes, sir," a man's voice said. "That's just the information we received—"

"So we're paying for unreliable sources?"

"No, sir, I just meant that it was a rumor. It might not be the Cortezes. It might not be anyone. Josef Nast has ordered an evacuation to be safe."

"Because he doesn't trust my judgment. Who the hell went over my head to Josef?" A pause. "His father wasn't notified, was he? I swear, if someone went all the way to Thomas on this . . ."

The voices faded as the guards hustled us through the house. So someone had told the Nasts that a rival Cabal was planning to raid the house. Had Antone planted the rumor? If so, what good did it do us?

As we were hurried out the front door, both Rafe and I scanned for an escape route, but the yard was filled with armed guards. Did Antone expect me to make a run for it? There was no chance of that. A minivan waited right at the end of the front steps. We were flanked by guards the whole ten seconds it took to get us into the van.

When I tried to lead Kenjii in, the guard stopped me. "Driver's allergic. Your dog needs to go in the second vehicle."

"Can't you switch drivers?" Rafe said. "Kenjii should stay with Maya. Or she can switch—"

"Got my orders. The girl goes here. The dog goes with the others."

Who'd given him the orders? Antone? So he'd have a hostage to secure my return? Or because it would be harder to run with a dog in tow? As much as I loved Kenjii, having her along in the city would be a problem. I whispered to her, asking her to go with the guard, then let him lead her to a second van behind ours.

As we crawled in, the others came out the front door. Nicole was first. Her hands were tied behind her and she'd been blindfolded. She held her head high, the bruises on her pale neck obvious even through the tinted glass.

Rafe took my hand as we watched her come down the steps. His grip loosened a little as they led her to the second van. Next came Sam. She was escorted to the same van. Annie and Hayley came out together. Annie seemed disoriented, blinking as if she'd been sleeping. Hayley was talking to her and she was nodding. Then they took Hayley on to the rear van and brought Annie to ours.

"Hey," Rafe said as she leaned in for a look. "Is everything okay?"

She nodded. "Emergency treatment. I'm still a little fuzzy." She looked from me to Rafe, then turned to the guard. "Actually, can I switch with Hayley? I know she hasn't had much time with Maya. I'm sure they'd like that."

Rafe snorted a laugh, but before he could say anything, Annie said, "I don't think I belong in this van."

She spoke slowly, her gaze locked with mine. Did she know something? Or was she just guessing that we'd try to escape?

"I'm better off in the other one," she said. "The doctor is there to look after me."

The guard started to say something. Then there was a commotion from the other vehicle.

"I am not riding with a killer." Hayley's voice traveled to us. "Shouldn't she have her own van? With padded walls?"

"We'll switch," the guard said quickly. "Come on."

Annie leaned in before she left. "I'll see you soon," she said to Rafe. Then to me, "Take care of him."

"I will."

It turned out we had a doctor, too. While Dr. Wiley went in the second van, we got Dr. Inglis. Other than the driver, she was our only guard. Well, the only one in the vehicle, that is. Another car swung out in front of us and I was sure it was full of big guys with guns. The second van pulled in behind, followed by another car of guards.

Rafe was studying the situation, too, and not looking very happy about it. Hayley just curled up in her seat, legs pulled under her, eyes closed. Great. She wasn't going to be any help at all. I tried prodding her awake, but she only grumbled sleepily and pushed me away.

Rafe rolled his eyes, then discreetly gestured at the cars in front and behind. Even if Hayley was awake—or had some defensive power—it didn't look as if we were going to get a chance to escape. Was this really Antone's grand opportunity? If so, he'd given me far too much credit for ingenuity.

"Are the Cortezes another Cabal?" I asked Dr. Inglis.

"Yes, they're one of the four North American Cabals. There are the St. Clouds and the Nasts, then the Cortezes and the Boyds. The Boyds are the smallest."

"But the Nasts are the biggest, right? So why the emergency evacuation?"

"While the Nasts are a larger organization, the Cortezes are widely considered—" She glanced at the driver and cleared her throat. "Some people consider them the most powerful. I wouldn't agree, but for both size and power, they come close enough to present a serious threat."

"And someone tipped off the Nasts that the Cortezes are

launching a . . . a what? An attack? A mass kidnapping?"

"We aren't sure what they have in mind, but it seemed wise to move you temporarily. While I'm sure we could handle the Cortezes, we certainly don't want you kids caught in supernatural cross fire."

"So the attack is supposed to come tonight?" I said.

"Oh, no. The information was simply that the Cortezes have discovered the existence of the project and the location of the house. It would take them at least a day to mobilize. They're based in Miami."

The driver murmured, "But they have a Seattle office."

Dr. Inglis looked over sharply. "Do they? Well, it would just be a satellite office, ill-equipped for an operation of this size, and certainly none of the staff would have the authority to lead the incursion."

"Lucas Cortez lives in Portland." The driver shot a meaningful look Dr. Inglis's way. "He *is* Benicio's heir."

She fluttered her hands. "Everyone knows that's just posturing. Benicio would never turn over the Cabal to Lucas. Not when he does all that"—another disdainful flutter—"anti-Cabal crusading nonsense."

"Maybe it's just Lucas, then," the driver said. "He's found out about this and decided to get involved. Save the kids." His tone was sharp with sarcasm.

"He doesn't have the means to pull this off. Idealism is all well and fine, but it doesn't buy proper staff and equipment." She cast a glance out the window, and in her reflection

234

I could see anxiety as she scanned the night. "No, I'm sure he couldn't do this."

Rafe looked at me and lifted his brows. He mouthed "Maybe . . ." I agreed and mentally filed the information.

I looked out my window. We were almost off the mountain now, in a densely populated neighborhood near the bottom. Lots of houses, mostly dark, the road quiet.

"Where are we being—?" I began.

The squawk of a radio cut me off. The driver answered.

"We're being followed," said the woman on the other end. "Could be nothing. I'm dispatching a backup car to handle it, but you need to follow protocol."

The driver said he'd do that. He'd barely hung up when the lead car made a sudden, unsignaled left turn, tires screeching slightly. We followed. The van behind us didn't.

"Splitting up?" Rafe said.

Neither Dr. Inglis nor the driver answered. He kept both hands on the wheel, gaze straight forward. She watched out the side window. After a minute she said, "There. The next street over. An SUV with its lights off is on a parallel course with us. I've seen them down three side streets now."

As we passed the next intersection, the driver looked. So did I. There it was—a dark, unlit SUV a short block over.

He called it in. Again, he was simply told to "follow protocol." This time, that meant he was the one hitting his brakes and making a sharp left turn. The guard car continued on without us. Our driver flicked off our headlights. At the next corner, he turned again. Same with the next.

Voices came over the radio. Conversations among the drivers. The second van hadn't noticed anything amiss and was continuing on with its escort. Our escort had gone after the SUV, which had taken off the second they appeared. They were chasing it now. We were advised to continue on, with the dispatcher giving directions that seemed to take us along every street in the neighborhood.

Finally we came out on a back road in a housing development. The homes were unfinished and unoccupied, and looked like they'd been that way for a while and would continue to be that way for a while longer—another victim of the economic crunch. It was eerie seeing them in the darkness, half-completed skeletons, stark against the—

I saw the truck at the last second. I don't know whether it came from behind a house or out of a garage. One second we were alone on that desolate road. The next I heard a motor roar and looked over to see only inky blackness. Then it seemed to appear from nothing—a huge black pickup, with its lights off, coming straight for us.

Our driver swerved. The other one did, too, our front hitting their side with a crunch that threw me against my seat belt hard enough to knock the air from my lungs. The front air bags deployed. That's all I noticed in that first post-crash moment—the huge white bags billowing.

The driver started clawing at his air bag. Hayley vaulted from the backseat and grabbed his seat belt, yanking on it with all her weight to pin him as she wedged one foot into the gap to block him from hitting the release.

As he struggled, she turned to me. "Do something! God, you guys can be useless sometimes."

Rafe threw open the door. He looked first, but the truck was gone. He scrambled out. He yanked on the driver's door, but it seemed jammed. I squeezed into the gap between seats. The driver's dart gun had been propped beside him and was now on the floor at his feet.

I glanced at Dr. Inglis. She was slumped forward as her bag deflated. I crawled to the gun, tugged it back, and managed to get out a dart. As Rafe raced around to try the passenger door, I jammed the dart into the driver's leg. I followed it with a second. Rafe got Dr. Inglis's door open as the driver stopped struggling.

"She's out cold," Rafe said. He pressed his fingers to Dr. Inglis's neck. "Or . . . worse. I can't—"

"It can't matter," I said. "We only have a few minutes before they send someone. Time to move."

THIRTY-ONE

W E'D BARELY GOTTEN BEHIND the nearest house before I caught the distant roar of a motor.

"The truck coming back?" Hayley said.

Rafe shook his head. "If whoever hit the van wanted us, they'd have stayed. Whatever's going on, it's not a kidnapping. If we're lucky, that's a random passerby. If we're not . . ."

"We haven't been too lucky so far," I muttered.

He nodded. "We should split up. It's easier for one person to hide and it triples our chance that someone will get away."

"If you do, go to Stanley Park," I said. I gave them directions to our camping spot.

"Do you really think Corey and Daniel would still be there?" Hayley said.

"No, but I hope they'll check back or leave a note."

We each picked a direction and ran.

The vehicle I'd heard never materialized. I'd barely set out when I realized the engine was moving farther away. That didn't mean I headed back, though. The goal right now was simply to put distance between myself and the wreck . . . and hope Rafe and Hayley were doing the same.

I'd chosen backyards as my escape route. Easy enough, given that there weren't fences separating them. But it was too open. And piles of debris and construction holes made it far from a fast—or safe—choice.

I raced down one street, ready to dart across when I heard the squeal of tires. I hesitated. From what I could see, the next row of houses was the last one, meaning if I could get there, I'd be out of the subdivision and . . . And what? Into an actual neighborhood, where people could spot me running through their yards? Or open ground, where I wouldn't have any shelter? I couldn't see what lay beyond the next road, which meant I couldn't take the chance. I needed to get a better look.

I backed up to the nearest two-story house. It was less than half finished, with limited hiding places, but the two flanking it weren't any better.

I picked my way through the debris to the front door—or the opening where the door would be. There weren't any front steps, either, which put the doorway a meter off the ground. I grabbed the frame, swung in, and nearly fell straight into the basement. The framework for the floor hadn't been covered yet. Same for the wall studs. It was like being inside a house built of matchsticks. Absolutely no place to hide. Wonderful.

Floorboards *had* been added to the second story, though—or part of it. I made my way up the risers that served as a temporary staircase. The interior walls weren't finished, but if I stayed on the floorboards, no one would see me from below. And I'd be gone before they brought in a full team to conduct a complete search. This was just a way station while I got a good look at the situation.

Getting that good look meant checking every window until I found one that gave me a partial view of the street where we'd crashed. There was an SUV there now, lights on, doors opening, dark-garbed figures spilling out.

I strained to listen and caught only the faintest murmur of voices, nearly drowned out by the crack and snap of tarps caught in the wind. I could see the tarps, too, ripped white flags of surrender dotting the abandoned houses. It was an eerie sight from up here—the rows of houses, the empty windows and doors like pits of darkness in blank faces.

I moved to the other side of the house and looked out the way I'd been heading. It seemed like scrub land beyond the last street. Pretty open. Too open? It was hard to tell.

When I heard a creak, I crept toward the stairwell, staying down on all fours and peering out from behind a partial wall. No one was there. I waited. Still nothing. As I turned to go back to my post, I caught what looked like a blur of motion, but when I spun, I saw nothing.

My hands started to itch. I rubbed them hard and inhaled deep breaths. This really wasn't the time to shift.

Or was it? I could move lower to the ground as a cat. I could climb and balance better, too. If someone came after me, I could disappear into one of these houses and be on the roof before they navigated across the first level.

But they didn't need to get close to me to fire a dart. Earlier today, I'd had the foresight to change into the darkest clothing they'd provided, in case Antone's "opportunity" came knocking. In cat form, I'd be easy to spot with my tawny fur.

So I needed to calm down before I shifted. Which was easy, because in contemplating which form was better, I *had* calmed down, and the process reversed.

I chuckled to myself. Good thing I hadn't decided I *wanted* to shift. I crawled back to the open window frame and was rising to look out when a floorboard creaked behind me. I whirled and saw that same strange blur, now coming straight at me. I dived to the side. Hands grabbed my ankle. I wrenched and got my foot free. I scrambled to the side and started leaping up, but something hit my side. Not "someone." Something, like an invisible force that sent me staggering.

When I caught a glimpse of my attacker, I stumbled back in surprise.

"Dr. Inglis?" I said.

"Your father entrusted me with your safety," she said. "I'm not going back and telling him you got away."

"No, he . . ." I stopped myself. If he hadn't told her he was behind this, I needed to protect him.

"He might not want me to come back," I said quickly. "After what happened with Nicole, he . . . didn't seem so convinced it was the right place for me."

A flash of guilt crossed her face. Then her eyes narrowed and I felt a chill. I wanted to brush it off. This was Dr. Inglis. I'd known her all my life. She may have played a key role in the experiment, but she'd always seemed genuine about wanting to help us.

"What did he say?" she asked.

"N-nothing. It's just . . ." I swallowed. "It wasn't safe for me there. You saw that."

"I saw that you were having trouble, Maya. Serious trouble, however much your father wants to deny it. You're reverting."

"No, I'm—"

"Stressed? Anxious?" She shook her head. "You forget how well I know you, Maya. You're strong and you're capable and you're one of the most level-headed young women I've ever met. If you haven't broken after everything that's happened, you're not going to break now. You're reverting. Deep down, you know that. If I let you leave, you could endanger your friends. What would that be like, finding Daniel, feeling relieved that he's alive . . . only to lose control and attack him."

The first heat of anger washed through me. They all knew

my weakness and they'd exploit it every chance they got.

"How about Rafe?" Dr. Inglis said. "You could hurt him. Or your brother, Ashton. Or Corey or Hayley."

"I'm not going to hurt anyone," I said, and charged her.

I didn't plan to attack her. Just knock her out of my way. She didn't move. Just started saying something I didn't understand. When I was within striking distance, I froze, just like I had in the alley.

"It's called a binding spell," she said. "Yes, I'm a witch. I tried to tell the Nasts that my sensing spell was good enough to find you, but they insisted on sending in their own witch. I *am* going to take you back to your father, Maya. He hasn't told me otherwise, so I can't be faulted for my efforts, can I? And I'm not about to let you slip away."

As she spoke, I struggled against the spell. I knew why the Nasts had called in their own witch—because Dr. Inglis wasn't good enough. We'd faced off outside Salmon Creek, and she hadn't used her spell. Or she'd tried and it hadn't worked. Now, as I fought it, I felt one of my fingers move. Then another.

Dr. Inglis continued, oblivious. "You're my best work. You and Daniel. The others may catch up eventually, but for now you two are the shining examples of everything I promised the St. Clouds when we started Project Phoenix."

As she spoke, a man appeared behind her. Just . . . appeared. Like he'd been zapped there. I'm sure I wouldn't have been able to hide my shock . . . if I'd had more control over my body. The beefy blond man looked at me and smiled, then lifted a syringe and pointed at Dr. Inglis, his other fingers going to his lips.

She tensed, as if she'd sensed something. I managed to get my mouth open.

"Nicole," I said quickly, my voice muffled, jaw barely opening. "You drugged her. That's why *you* offered to test her. To hide the fact that you drugged her and let her into my room to kill me."

The man eased forward.

"No, Maya. I was listening in. I would have interfered if she hurt you, but I knew you'd save yourself." Dr. Inglis gave a faint smile. "You always do. You'd save yourself and we'd prove Nicole was unstable, and make sure they took her far from you."

"Really? Because it sounded to me like they were planning to ship her out anyway. I think you did it to make sure they added more security to me. You knew I'd escape eventually if they didn't, so—"

The man jabbed her with the syringe. She spun. The spell broke and I toppled as she started another incantation. I leaped to my feet and raced across the floor. I was almost to the stairs when a two-by-four came sailing from nowhere and cut me off at the knees. I fell on all fours. Before I could spring up again, a hand lifted me off my feet. I twisted to see another big man—this one with brown hair—holding me in midair. Behind him, Dr. Inglis lay on the floor, unconscious. The blond man was bent over her, checking her pulse.

I took a swing at my captor. He just held me out to arm's length and laughed.

"Claws in, little cat," he said, still grinning. "Just like a cat, aren't you? Rescue you and get scratched for my trouble."

His smile was genuine, his tone light, amused. I stopped struggling.

"Who are you?" I asked.

"I'd say 'friends of your father,' but that's not exactly true. Just a couple of half-demons with special skills for hire." He set me down but kept his hand wrapped in my shirt. "You seem to have walked away from the accident all right. I hit you guys harder than I'd hoped. It's tough to plan stuff like that."

His partner walked over. "The doc's out cold. We'll just leave her here."

"So you're the ones"—I struggled to form the words— "my father hired. Now what?"

"Now nothing," said the one holding me. "This is what your daddy paid for, so now you're on your own, little cat. Except for this." He fished a wad of cash, a metal key, and a tiny voice recorder from his pocket. He slapped them into my hand. "Top-secret instructions. Listen, then eat the evidence."

"Thanks." I turned to the stairs.

The brown-haired one called, "Not even going to ask for help getting away? You are an independent little cat, aren't you?"

"No, I just don't think I could afford your fee. Even with this." I waved the bills.

Now even the blond guy chuckled. "We'll get you to the city. If we spot one of your buddies, we'll give them a lift, too, but only if we see them on the way."

The brown-haired man nodded. "Can't get caught while we're cruising looking for strays."

I tried to argue, but they were right. We left the house. The blond guy explained that he would take me in the SUV he'd used to draw off attention, while his partner got the smashed truck to safety.

On the way to the SUV, I caught the faint smell of Hayley in the breeze. The half-demons let me go after her and bring her back. There was no sign of Rafe, though, and I didn't push for them to search. He might not be as street smart as Ash, but he'd been on the road with Annie for a couple of years, so he was capable of taking care of himself out here.

THİRTY-TWO

I LET THE HALF-DEMON drive us to North Vancouver. That meant we'd have a five-kilometer hike to Stanley Park, but it was as close to our destination as I dared get. There was, I knew, always the possibility that this was a grand scheme to make me lead them to Daniel, Corey, and Ash. Given the complexity of the plan, I doubted it, but I was still being careful. The bigger risk was that these guys would decide they could make more money by turning us all over to the Nasts—or the Cortezes.

So the guy let us out in a North Vancouver strip mall, wished us well, and drove off. Hayley and I pretended to head north. Once the taillights vanished we changed course, staying hidden behind and between stores in the commercial strip along the highway.

As we walked, I explained more of what was going on.

Then I took out the voice recorder and pressed Play.

"Maya," Antone's voice began. "This is . . ." A hesitation, then "Calvin. If you're listening to this, then you've gotten away and you've met the men I hired to facilitate that. I'm sorry if you were hoping for more assistance. I don't think you were, but I'm sorry all the same. I'm treading carefully here. If you do return to negotiate, I can't help if I'm being held in the Nast jails for treason."

"Return?" Hayley said. "Negotiate? What's he talking about?"

I whispered that I'd explain later.

Antone continued. "Later on this tape, I'm going to tell you more about Project Genesis. You already know some of that—you asked me about Elizabeth Delaney the first time we spoke. You may have heard that a small group of those subjects escaped. That's not entirely true. They did, but they were found again a few months ago. The St. Clouds have been monitoring them. I've provided information on their where-abouts. You need to go to them and tell them that the St. Clouds are watching them. Then you need to convince them to turn themselves in."

"Seriously?" Hayley whispered. "Is he nuts?"

I shushed her again.

"I told you that you need leverage to negotiate, Maya. So do they. Separately, you're just two groups on the run. Join forces and you will all have enough leverage to negotiate a return on your terms." A pause. "That return will include the

Delaneys." Another pause. "Your parents. I know that's what you want and I know that's what you need."

We'd all get our families back, he promised. Then he told us everything we needed to know to get to the Project Genesis kids.

When the tape finished, I braced for Hayley's outraged protests. Instead, she was quiet for at least a half kilometer. Then she said, "Okay. So what are our other options?"

"We run."

"Run where? We'd need a goal, right? We can't just run forever."

"There's that guy they mentioned in the car. Lucas Cortez. We could go to Portland, find him, and see if he'd help."

"But his dad is CEO of another Cabal. One that's at least as powerful as the Nasts. I'm getting the impression these Cabals aren't exactly charitable organizations."

"Agreed. It's a possibility, though. Or we can find the Project Genesis group, tell them, and run *with* them."

"And then what?" She sighed and shook her head. "That's really what it comes down to, doesn't it? *And then what.* Calvin's right. We can't run forever. We don't want to. I want my mom and my dad and my sister back. And, yes, I want some kind of normal life back. I know that makes me sound like exactly what you'd expect—a spoiled cheerleader—but it's what I want."

"Me too."

She looked at me, surprised.

I shrugged. "I know that 'totally normal' is out of the question. I don't think we ever had that anyway. But I want my parents and I want a life. Plus, we have medical issues—Annie's reversion, Corey's headaches, and possibly more we haven't found out yet."

"Then this really is our only option."

"It seems so."

When we reached the park, I started getting anxious again, thinking about Daniel. Would he be here? How badly was he hurt? Had Rafe made it? Soon my hands started itching, my muscles bunching, my nails thickening.

"You know, that could get really inconvenient," Hayley said as I rubbed my hands and tried to refocus.

"Tell me about it," I muttered.

"Do you know what causes it?"

"Stress. Fear. Anger. Right now, it's door number one."

My arms started throbbing. I rubbed them. Hayley noticed and sighed.

"Okay, change of subject. Let's—" She stopped. "Um, explain to me why we don't want you changing into a big cat?"

"What?"

She gestured at my pulsing arms. "Why not let you change? You can move faster as a cougar. You can see in the dark better. You can sniff them out better."

I stopped rubbing my arms. "You're right."

"Don't sound so shocked." When I protested, she cut me off. "In the van, did you really think I was taking a nap? I was faking it so they'd relax and maybe we could escape."

"Oh."

"Yeah, oh." She rolled her eyes. "Go on and do your shape-shifting thing."

As usual, I passed out to shift. When I got to my feet, I was still groggy enough that I let out a yowling squawk when a voice behind me said, "Wow."

I twisted to see Rafe there.

He crouched to eye level. "I didn't mean to startle you. I thought I heard voices earlier, so I jogged over and Hayley said you were in here. She made me wait until she could be sure you weren't naked anymore."

I chuffed.

"Yeah, I was disappointed, too."

I rolled my eyes. He walked over and crouched again. Then he reached out and ran his fingers along the fur from my chin to my neck.

"Wow," he said. "I am trying so hard not to be envious right now."

I moved closer, rubbing against him, relieved he'd made it. Then Hayley appeared.

"Yeah, yeah," he said. "I waited. She was decent.

Although, technically, she's still naked."

"You're such a perv." She turned to me. "Okay, kitty. Lead on. We'll try to keep up."

"Yeah, good luck with that," Rafe said. "If she runs, we're history."

THİRTY-THREE

I MEANT TO KEEP at their pace, but it was infuriating. The campsite was clear across the park. I could be there in a few minutes. I could know if the guys were there in a few minutes. I could know if Daniel was okay in a few minutes. Finally, Rafe told me to go off ahead. He could see me and if they lost me, he'd shout.

We'd found the right path already. It was overgrown in parts, with downed branches in others—not a popular route—but in cat form it seemed like an open highway, as I leaped over every obstacle with barely a hitch in my speed.

Rafe had to call me once and I circled back at warp speed, heart racing with impatience until I heard him yell, "Gotcha. Go on," and I tore off again. I think he might have called again, but I pretended not to hear. I was almost there. I could easily return for them. I raced around the last bend so fast I missed seeing a rodent hole until the last second. My paw hit the edge of the hole and I stumbled.

Pain ripped through my foreleg. I forced myself up and gingerly touched my paw down. A fresh stab of pain. I gritted my teeth—which doesn't really work that well in cat form—and limped forward. I was almost there. Just through these trees and—

The clearing was empty.

I stopped and stood there, flanks heaving with panic. They weren't here. Their faint smell was at least a day old. Maybe two, meaning they hadn't come back after Daniel got hit.

I limped forward. Something rustled and I spun to see a burger wrapper caught in a bush. I went over, put my nose to it, and inhaled. It smelled like Corey. We hadn't eaten burgers before the memorial service. So he'd come back. But where was he now, and—

Another smell hit me as I backed away. Copper. Blood. I stumbled to it and found dried blood seeped into the ground. The spot smelled like Daniel. Oh, God.

Where was he? Had Corey taken him to a hospital? *Please, Corey, tell me you took him to a hospital, no matter how much he argued.*

I took off, using my sore leg and not caring as I barreled through the thick brush, branches scraping and poking me until—

"Whoa!"

I looked over to see Corey down a path, his hands raised. "Holy hell, please tell me that's you, Maya."

I hesitated, nose in the air, searching the breeze. Searching, searching . . .

I caught it. I ripped around fast enough to send Corey scrambling for cover. I barreled past him and into another clearing, where I saw a blond head bent over a fire pit, trying to get it started.

As I raced toward the fire pit, Daniel looked up. He grinned. He didn't even look to see if the big cat bearing down on him bore my birthmark. He just opened his arms and let me race to tackle him, stopping and skidding at the last moment as I remembered he was hurt, but it was too late and I skidded right into him and knocked him over, and he only hugged me and laughed and whispered, "I knew you'd come back."

"Yep, that's Maya," Corey said from behind us.

Daniel gave me a bear hug as I wriggled like a kitten, my sore paw forgotten as I rubbed against him, inhaling his scent, letting my pounding heart slow. I snuffled him, trying to find where he was hurt, but he only laughed as if it tickled. I reached up and licked his face. He let out a sputtering laugh and fell back again.

"I see you found them," a voice said.

I looked over my shoulder to see Rafe and Hayley walk out of the woods. Rafe's gaze was fixed on me, his expression cool, and I scrambled off Daniel as guilt darted through me.

"Yep, she did," Daniel said, giving me one last pat before pushing to his feet. He walked over to Rafe and grasped his hand. "Good to see you."

Rafe looked abashed, then covered it with a forced grin. I took a deep breath to still my thumping heart again.

When I relaxed, my paws started throbbing again, telling me the return shift was coming. I walked to Rafe, took the dangling leg of my jeans between my teeth and tugged him toward the woods.

"Do you want to take the clothes, or . . . ?" he began.

I let go and motioned to the forest.

"Ah," he said, grinning. "Be back, guys. Time to offer moral support, apparently."

He followed me into the forest. When we were out of sight of the others, he set my clothing on a log, then crouched in front of me.

"Okay, you do your thing. I won't look until you're decent. But if anyone asks? I totally looked."

I licked his face.

"Yow. That stings. Like being kissed with sandpaper."

He smiled, then walked to the log and sat with his back to me. I lowered myself to the ground, and almost as soon as I did I passed out, as if my body had just been waiting for its cue.

When I woke, my arm felt better, as if it had only been temporarily twisted. I crept over, took my clothing, and dressed.

Rafe stayed with his back turned until I sat down beside him.

"Fully dressed?" he said. "Damn."

"Sorry. Next time I'll leave my socks off."

He laughed and got to his feet. Before we left, he pulled me into a kiss.

"Happy now?" he murmured.

I looked up at him. "Very happy."

"Good. Now go do your healing mojo. Let's make sure he's okay."

When Rafe and I stepped onto the path, there was a guy walking ahead of us. I saw the slim figure, the dark gray T-shirt, the chestnut brown hair, and I froze.

"Ash?"

He turned, and I raced down the path and threw my arms around his neck, hugging him as his armload of sticks jabbed me.

"I thought you'd left," I whispered.

"Why would I?" he said, wriggling out of my embrace.

"Hey," Rafe said. "You must be Maya's brother. I'm—"

"I know who you are." Ash turned to me. "You okay?"

I nodded. "The Nasts aren't going to mistreat potential future employees."

He didn't ask how I got away. He knew he'd get the story eventually.

As we stood there in silence I rocked on my heels,

resisting the urge to embrace him again. I could tell that would not be welcome. "I'm really glad to see you here. I was sure you'd leave."

"Why?"

"Um, because I was taken captive. And you were nearly taken captive."

He snorted. "I don't spook that easy. And if they took you, I'm sure as hell not running away, not after you got yourself captured trying to protect me." A glare. "Which was stupid." He didn't pause to let me reply. "You needed my help, so I stayed. That's what I came here for, isn't it? Getting you out of this mess you've gotten yourself into."

"Gotten herself into?" Rafe said.

"Well, thank you." I said to Ash. "For staying." I turned to Rafe. "Although he says he knows who you are, I'm still going to annoy him by being all polite about it. Rafe, this is my brother, Ash. Ash, this is Rafe. My boyfriend."

"Yeah, I figured that when I heard he was taking your clothes to you."

"You were around earlier?" I said.

He shrugged. "Getting firewood. Didn't want to interfere with you and Daniel." A glower at Rafe. "I'm going to strongly suggest you don't go with my sister next time she shifts. Got it?"

"Yes, sir."

Rafe's words were brittle, but Ash didn't seem to notice. Or didn't care. Just waved me back to the campsite.

THIRTY-FOUR

DANIEL WAS FINE. ASH and Corey had been keeping a careful watch on him, ready to grab a taxi to the nearest hospital if he started coughing up blood or feeling sharp pains. The blood I'd found was from a nasty scrape on his arm that had opened up when Corey cleaned it. That was his worst injury. The driver had hit his brakes before impact. He'd knocked Daniel flying, but that was it. Bruises and scrapes, already scabbed over. I still used my healing on him, though. I don't know if it helped, but it made *me* feel better.

While I worked on Daniel, the guys lit a fire. It was getting cold and they'd decided it was safe enough as long as they kept it small. Once that was going, I explained what happened with us. That took a lot longer than Daniel's story.

First I told them about Sam, Annie, and Kenjii and why they weren't with us.

"And Nic?" Daniel said when I finished talking about the others. His face was drawn with worry. "Is she okay?"

I took a deep breath. "She's . . . fine, and she's not fine. I-I don't know how to tell you this . . ."

"Then I will," Hayley cut in. "Nicole—"

"No," I said sharply, then softened my tone. "Please. Let me."

Rafe stood. "Maya's right. The rest of us can find something else to do. Hayley? Can you explain to Corey?"

Ash seemed unwilling to leave on Rafe's command, but at a whisper from Corey, he followed them out of the clearing.

When they were gone, Daniel lowered his voice and said, "If Nic's been hurt, you can tell me, Maya. I know you hoped there'd be something between us, but there isn't."

And thank God for that. If you had started dating her when I pushed you to it . . .

"We're just friends," he continued. "I'm going to be upset if she was hurt, but you didn't need to send them away. Corey's just as close to her as I am."

"It's—it's not that. She's . . . the experiments . . . Or I think it was the experiments, but I don't know for sure. Maybe it's just her. I . . ."

I saw his confusion, and I tried to think of a way to word it. When no ideas came, the words did, blurted.

"Nicole killed Serena."

He didn't react. He just kept staring at me, blankly, as if processing. Then he said, "Nicole . . . ?"

"Drowned Serena. She's a xana, like we figured. She swam out under the water and pulled Serena down."

I thought of Serena, under the water, fighting for her life while I searched for her. How long had she struggled? How long had she been under there and I could have saved her if only I'd found her, if only—

Daniel put his arms around me, pulling me against him as I shook and the tears started.

I pulled back. "I'm sure."

"I didn't ask if you were."

"I know, but it sounds crazy. I started suspecting her after she was captured. Sam said some things and when I saw Nicole in the camp . . . Things happened that I didn't tell you about. I had to be sure. Then, at the house there, she admitted it. Everyone knows. There isn't any question. Nicole killed Serena."

"Why?"

I took a deep breath. "Because she was jealous that things came so easily to Serena. Nicole worked so hard on her grades and her singing and her swimming, and Serena did better than her without working at all. I know that sounds like a crazy reason to kill someone, but she's . . . well, she *is* crazy."

"Did she do this?" he asked, touching the side of my neck.

261

I reached up to feel a faint scratch there. I hadn't noticed it before. I don't think anyone had.

"We . . . had a fight," I said.

"She attacked you." He stopped my protest. "I wouldn't blame you for going after her when she admitted to drowning Serena, but that's not like you. She attacked you. She tried to kill you." His hand tightened on my knee, mouth tightening, too. "Again."

"She's not stable. She—"

"I know. And I should care. Legally insane, that's what the verdict would be, and someone who plans to be a lawyer should understand that. But I don't care. She killed Serena. Her friend. Probably her *best* friend. After she tried to drown you, she mourned Serena with you and she pretended to be your friend. Then she tried to drown you again, crossing the channel. I don't care how crazy she is. I don't care if they fix her." His grip on my knee tightened even more. "She had better never, ever come near you again, or . . ."

I must have winced as pain shot through my knee. He looked down and yanked his hand away, then swallowed, flexing his hand.

"I wouldn't hurt her," he said finally. "Not if I didn't need to. But that doesn't mean I wouldn't want to. I don't care what that makes me. I just—"

I put my arms around his neck and buried my face against his shoulder. "I know."

۞   ۞   ۞

When the others came back, I told them about Antone. That was tough. How to explain that the guy we'd been running from had helped us escape? That he wanted to help us solve our problem?

I focused on the role he'd played in our escape and how he'd championed us against the Nasts, to help Daniel and the others understand why I came to see him—however reluctantly—as an ally.

I kept glancing over at Ash. He sat so far back that if he didn't have skin-walker hearing, I'd have thought he was ignoring the conversation. But he wasn't. I knew that.

I wondered what he was thinking. What he was feeling. Abandoned by our mother. Sent away by the couple who'd taken him in. Repeatedly rejected by foster families. After that, you'd want to flip a middle finger to the world and say, "I don't need anyone." But he'd still feel the longing, the bitterness at missing out on what should be a normal part of any kid's life—family. Then he discovers he has a father who seems to want him—really want him. Only he's playing for the bad guys, and even if he was on our side, could Ash ever trust anyone again? Wasn't it better—safer—not to?

When I finished, everyone went quiet. Then Daniel said, "Antone wants you to go back, doesn't he? Voluntarily."

I looked over at him.

Daniel continued, "I know he wasn't going to let you just walk away. If he cares about you—which he seems to—he knows we can't make a go of it out here. We could find our parents, but that only endangers them. You seem resigned to letting him have Kenjii, which tells me it's temporary. As does the fact that Rafe doesn't seem too anxious about Annie."

"Believe me, I didn't leave her behind by choice," Rafe said. "She figured out we were going to try escaping and . . . and they're helping her. I hate to admit that, but it's true. I'm not sure I would have chosen to leave if . . ." A sidelong glance at me.

"It's okay," I murmured. "You didn't have any choice, either."

I knew what he was saying—that given the option, he might have stayed behind with Annie. Did that sting? Choosing his sister over me? No. I knew where his priorities lay.

"The point is that you're okay leaving her there for now," Daniel said. "She needs their help. Corey needs it, too. Maybe we're all going to have side effects—serious ones." There must have been a look on my face, because he glanced at me sharply. "Maya? Are you—?"

Ash came out of the shadows, cutting him off. "Go back? Did I hear that right?"

"Not go back," I said. "Negotiate a settlement."

"With a Cabal? Are you all crazy?"

"That's what I thought," Hayley said. "When you break it down, though, Daniel's right—it's our only real choice."

I played the recording. Silence followed. Ash broke it.

"You get what he's doing here, don't you, Maya? He's using you to bring in these other subjects. You turn them in, like some kind of bounty hunter." He met my gaze, his eyes shuttered. "I can't believe you'd do that."

"She's not," Hayley said. "Did you even listen to the tape? Calvin is telling us exactly where the Genesis subjects are because the St. Clouds *already* know."

"So he's 'Calvin' now?"

She met his glare with one of her own. "That's his name, isn't it?"

"Hayley's right," Daniel said, his voice taking on his calming tone. "By talking to them, we'll be warning them. Then we'd try to persuade them to join us in going back and negotiating."

"With the *wrong* Cabal," Ash said. "The St. Clouds sold you guys to the Nasts. The St. Clouds have your parents. The St. Clouds own these Genesis kids, and the St. Clouds are the ones who know where they are."

"You heard the tape," I said. "Antone says the St. Clouds don't want our parents—they're just stuck with them. They can't exactly fob *them* off on the Nasts. As for the Genesis kids, their medical team is gone. Died in a fire at the lab. All except one doctor, who's with the kids now—an aunt. The St. Clouds don't really want them back. For the right price, they'd let the Nasts take the Genesis kids and our parents off their hands."

"And then what?"

"Then we prepare," Daniel said. "We take their training. We take their medical care. We take their protection. We pretend we're going to grow up to work for them and we use that to learn everything we can about them."

"Then we fight back," I said.

Ash sputtered a laugh. "Against a Cabal? The *biggest* Cabal?"

"Yes. It won't be easy. It won't be soon. But we'll take our time. We'll grow into our powers. Then, one day, we get free of them. For good."

The debate continued. It really was Ash against everyone else, which felt completely unfair. Finally he threw up his hands, muttered under his breath, and stalked off.

"Damn," Hayley murmured to me when he was gone. "Figures, doesn't it? The hotter the guy, the bigger the jerk."

"I'm not really seeing the first part," I said.

"Which is good." She grinned. "All things considered."

"True. But, while Ash *can* be a jerk, I see his point on this one. Going back feels like throwing up a white flag."

"But it's negotiation, not surrender. And it's not permanent. It's like a covert operation. Using our heads."

"That's the plan," Daniel murmured. "But I agree with Maya. I'd be more shocked if Ash agreed."

"I'll go talk to him."

THIRTY-FIVE

I FOUND ASH BACK by the old camp. He was sitting on the ground, legs pulled up, just staring into the forest. I approached slowly, making enough noise so I wouldn't startle him.

When he looked over I said, "Getting used to it, huh?"

He lifted his brows.

I waved around us. "The forest."

"Right. Yeah." He gazed out again. "Never really been in one this big. I know this isn't big for a forest, just . . . It's different." He paused. "No people. I can see why you like it. It feels like . . ."

"Home."

He shrugged that off, making a face. Another moment of silence. "If you've come to talk to me about this negotiating crap—"

"I haven't." I sat down beside him. "I just want to . . . check in with you. I know this isn't the resolution you want, and I'm hoping you don't decide to cut out."

He glanced over. "Cut out?"

"Take off. Leave. We're not at the point yet of making an absolute decision. So I'm hoping you'll stick around until we are. And then I'm hoping you'll give it more thought."

"Have I bolted yet?"

"No, I'm just—"

"Well, don't."

He studied me for a moment, then said, voice lowered, "I'm not our mother."

I nodded. Another minute of silence. Then I said, "He . . . Calvin . . . Antone." I sighed. "I don't know what to call him."

"Just not *Dad*, I bet."

I shook my head. "No, never. Calvin, I guess. He told me what happened to you. What our mother did."

He snorted. "Yeah, I can just imagine his version."

I told him what Antone said. He listened, then shrugged. "Close enough, I guess. So what's he been doing? Sitting back and watching me?"

"Looking for you. He'd get updates from one of the parents you were in contact with, one working both sides—trading information between the St. Clouds and your contacts."

He cursed at that. Really cursed. For a while.

"But that contact wouldn't tell Calvin where you were. I think he was trying to protect you."

He met my gaze. "He was protecting himself and his kid. Don't sugarcoat things for me, Maya. Ever."

"I'm sorry." I paused. "Do you know anything about a guy named Lucas Cortez?"

"Huh?"

"He's the son—"

"Oh, I know who he is. I'm just really hoping you aren't asking because the Cortezes are getting involved in this. Because if they are, we might as well throw in the towel now. One Cabal is tough to outrun. Two? Damned near impossible, as you've noticed. Three?" He shook his head.

"They aren't involved. But someone mentioned Lucas Cortez as a crusader against Cabals. That might be a backup plan, if you know anything about him."

"I know he's the son of a Cabal CEO. I know he's the supposed heir to the Cortez Cabal. I know he used to be a crusader, until his brothers got murdered and he had to step up in the family business."

"Oh."

Ash shrugged. "Some say he's still helping supernaturals. Some say it's a front and he's luring them into the Cabal. Cyril Mitchell believed he was still helping, but there's a reason he never went to him for help. Or to the interracial council that's supposed to help supernaturals. Because they can't fight the Cabals on big things like this. If the Cabals want us, they'll get us. That's the way it works in the world, Maya. The good guys have ideals; the bad guys have cash and firepower. You can guess which one wins in a real battle."

I could tell he'd worked this through long before now, probably some cold and hungry night when he just couldn't take it anymore. He'd come to the conclusion that this Lucas guy and the council couldn't help. I agreed. The Cabals had massive corporate and supernatural resources. Which was why we had to deal with them or spend our lives running.

"We need to get going," Ash said, standing. "Can't take a chance they'll find a way to track you."

We started to walk.

"So, this Rafe," Ash said. "He's really your boyfriend?"

I looked over sharply. "What does that mean?"

"Nothing. Lot of guys. It gets confusing. Especially when you seem to hug all of them."

I made a face at him.

A few more steps. Then, "He's a skin-walker, right?"

I nodded.

"That makes sense, I guess."

This time, I didn't ask what he meant by that, just kept walking.

"Like I said, though, I don't want him following you off to shift. You need to be careful or he'll take advantage. Which he'd better not do while I'm around."

I could say that I'd been successfully dating so far without a brother to watch out for me. But it was kind of sweet, in a misguided "girls need a guy to look after them" kind of way.

"He doesn't take advantage," I said. "If he did, I wouldn't

have let him come with me. Hell, if he did, I wouldn't be dating him."

"Good," Ash grunted. A few more steps. "Is he shifting yet?"

"Nope. Developmentally, the guys are all lagging behind." I shot him a grin. "As usual."

He rolled his eyes and muttered under his breath, and we continued on to the campsite.

THIRTY-SIX

THE KEY THE HALF-DEMONS had given me was for a gym locker. We were at the gym when it opened that morning, Daniel and Ash sneaking in to retrieve the contents—fake IDs, real passports, tickets, and everything else we needed. Then we were off.

One long plane ride took us across the country. A bus carried us over the border. A second bus deposited us, the next morning, in the small Pennsylvania town near where the Project Genesis subjects were hiding. According to Antone's message, we had a ten-mile walk. That didn't sound too bad to all the Canadian kids, who heard "kilometers" instead. The extra six kilometers were a lot when you were running on junk food and a few hours of sleep.

Daniel suggested we try to get better food from a corner store before we left. When he asked for fruit, the clerk pointed to dusty cans of peaches.

"We're not on the West Coast anymore," I murmured.

"Thank God," Ash said, grabbing two chocolate bars in one hand and a Coke in the other.

"There are protein and energy bars over here," Daniel said. "We'll get that, milk, and some juice."

Ash stared at him, then at the rest of us as we headed for the milk and juice.

"You guys aren't really teens, are you?" Ash said. "They've brainwashed you into miniature adults, full of responsibility and good eating habits. I'm surprised you haven't bought a—" He noticed the toothbrush in my hand. "Seriously?"

"Haven't used one of those in a while, huh?" Hayley said. "Let me guess. You haven't been dating in a while, either. News-flash: the two are not unconnected."

He scowled at her. "I have one in my pack." He pointed to Rafe's toothbrush. "Have they infected you, too?"

"Your sister gave it to me. I think it's a hint. Use it or keep my distance."

Another scowl. "Better keep your distance anyway. We don't have time for that crap."

Rafe was about to shoot something back when Daniel waved us to the register. "We're losing daylight, guys. Time to move."

We were careful on the walk, though Antone had said not to worry about being spotted by the St. Clouds. They were only

273

doing periodic spot checks on their wayward subjects.

As for how they found them, a werewolf bounty hunter had tracked down the group a few months ago. That's when the St. Clouds had decided to let them stay "on the run" for a while. Wear them down until they were tired of hiding. It's not like they were going anywhere. Sure, after a few months in one place, they'd hit the road again, but they kept the same van . . . which now had a tracking device on it.

"What types have we got again?" Ash asked as we hid in the forest behind the Genesis subjects' farmhouse.

"For the kids—werewolf, necromancer, witch, and sorcerer," I said. "For the adults, a sorcerer and a doctor with necromancer blood, but apparently no powers. I'm guessing the werewolf explains the conveniently located forest."

Daniel nodded. "He's also the biggest threat."

Ash snorted. "Your average wolf is about seventy-five pounds. Even Maya could take him on in her cat form."

"Um, thanks," I said. "But you weren't paying attention to Antone's message, were you?"

"Considering how long it was, I don't think anyone was. The guy just goes on and on. I see where you get it from."

I made a face at him. "He said that werewolves in human form have the same extra-sharp senses as skin-walkers, but they get super strength, too."

Ash shrugged. "And we get agility. Ever seen a boxing match? Speed and agility win over brute strength."

Daniel cut in, "How about we just avoid spooking them into a confrontation?"

"Where's the fun in that?" Corey said.

Daniel ignored him. "Okay, guys, let's get this rolling. It'll be less threatening if we show up in daylight. Corey, Rafe, and Ash are staying behind. Hayley? You're coming with Maya and me. We could use your help."

"Oh?" Hayley perked up. "What do you need me to do?"

"Smile and look blond," Ash said. "Which you're good at."

She scowled at him.

"Except the smiling part," he continued. "You have some trouble with that. They want you because you're window dressing. Blond, perky, and completely nonthreatening."

Daniel shook his head. "Let's go."

The place was a two-story old farmhouse on a dirt road with no neighbors in sight. It was bordered on either side by fields and backed onto a forest. We went straight to the front door. I knocked. No one answered. I tried again and put my ear to the door, but it was quiet.

Daniel walked out to the barn, which seemed to be used as a garage. "Empty," he said after peering through the window.

"Seriously?" Hayley said. "What'd they do, go out for pizza?"

"They've been on the run for months," I said. "They'll be

trying to live as normally as possible."

"Great. Now what?"

"We wait in the forest," I said.

We didn't dare leave a trail heading straight to the woods. Antone's note warned that the werewolf would be able to track us by smell, so he'd likely know strangers had visited his house. Better to lay a trail heading back to the road, as if we'd been just salespeople at the door.

I'd found a tree earlier with a good sight line to the house. Rafe volunteered to watch with me. Ash insisted on joining us.

When it was almost dark, I climbed down and conferred with Daniel at our temporary campsite. He wanted to give it another hour. We did. Still no sign of anyone.

"It's too late now," I said when I returned to Daniel. "I say we wait until morning."

"Agreed. Though it may take all of my special persuasive powers to keep the troops from mutinying." He tried for a smile, but it was strained.

"Are you getting any sleep at all?" I asked.

"I'm fine." He caught my look and some of the steel went out of his shoulders. "Yeah, I'm tired. But I can rest soon."

"Tonight?"

He shrugged and gazed out at the forest.

"How are you doing otherwise?" I asked. "We haven't had much time to talk."

"We haven't had *any* time to talk." He paused and

managed another wan smile. "Sorry. Obviously we can't expect time alone right now. It's just . . ."

He rolled his shoulders and looked away. He was right, of course. It wasn't the time. But I didn't care. I wanted to be with him. Alone. We hadn't really had that since I'd escaped the Nasts, and I longed for it. Just a few minutes alone with him to talk, to relax. I felt guilty about it. Felt insufferably selfish. But it's what I wanted.

"Let's go talk now," I said. "Rafe and Ash are standing watch. Corey and Hayley are dozing." I looked around. "I saw a stream that way. I say we be completely irresponsible and sneak off duty. At least for a few minutes."

A more genuine smile. "Sounds like a plan."

We got about five steps when brush crackled behind us. Rafe stepped through.

"Hey," he said. "Ash is getting antsy. Have we got a plan?"

"Actually, Daniel and I were just . . ."

I trailed off. When I glanced at Rafe, I couldn't think up a good excuse to take off with Daniel, and I felt like we needed one.

"Call Ash down," I said. "It's conference time."

THIRTY-SEVEN

N O ONE WAS HAPPY about spending another night in the woods. We were on the run, Ash said, so why the hell *wouldn't* we come knocking in the middle of the night? He had a point, but my gut told me it was better to wait for daylight, and Daniel agreed.

We found a place deep in the forest patch and settled in for the night. Before we did, I suggested we take turns patrolling and standing watch—in hopes that that would let Daniel get some rest. Even Hayley agreed. We could see the toll this was taking on Daniel, when he was still recovering from his accident, and we really needed him in top shape for the next step of persuading these people to listen to us.

Part of my plan, too, was to take first round, and that way, if Daniel still wanted to talk, he could slip out with me.

Except Rafe offered to share my shift and I couldn't say much about that.

We headed out to patrol so we wouldn't disturb the others. After we'd circled the campsite a few times, Rafe caught my hand and tugged me behind some bushes.

"I think we're supposed to be standing guard," I said.

"Mmm, maybe, but that sounds like a token protest."

His hands circled my waist. I hesitated, about to say it wasn't a token protest, that we had to be on guard in case the werewolf—or anyone else—came out here and found strangers sleeping in the forest.

Even as I thought that, though, I felt silly. Paranoid. The forest was silent. There was nothing wrong with a brief break. God knows, a few days ago, I wouldn't even have thought of protesting—just one look in Rafe's eyes and caution be damned. Another sign I was stressed and anxious, I guess.

I kissed him and it only took a moment for me to lose that hesitation. His fingers moved against my bare skin where my shirt had lifted from my jeans. I eased back and looked up at him, smiling lazily, my eyes half-closed, feeling drowsy and happy as his scent washed over me.

"This is when it's perfect," he murmured. "When we're alone like this, when you kiss me like that, when you look at me this way. I see that and I don't have any doubts that this will work."

I smiled wryly. "Oh, I have some doubts our plan will

work. It's just a lot easier to forget them right now."

"I don't mean—" He cut himself off and nodded. "I think it's the best we can do. Doubts are expected."

He bent and kissed me again and it was a strange kiss, one that kept picking up, then slowing down, like running uphill. I'd feel that heat, then he'd pull back a little. Kiss me harder, deeper. Pull back. Finally he broke it off and stepped away so abruptly that my hands fell from his neck.

"I didn't mean the plan, Maya. I meant us."

"Us?" My heart picked up speed. "Doubts? What's wrong?"

He took another step, and I wanted to pull him back, just say, *Whatever it is, forget it*. But I just stood there, heart thumping.

"I don't want to be that guy. I really don't."

"What guy?" I said. But I knew. I knew and I braced myself.

"The guy who has a problem with his girlfriend hanging out with another boy. I'm not like that, Maya. I don't get jealous unless there's a reason."

"Is this about what Sam said? That story she told? She made that up to—"

"I know she did."

"Then why . . . ? Is it because I was worried about Daniel?"

"No. Yes. No." A sharp shake of his head. "Getting jealous because you're worried about a friend who was hit by a car? What kind of jerk does that? I knew you'd be worried. Hell, I'd be concerned if you *weren't* worried. But when I'd see *how* worried you were, I'd feel . . ." He let out a soft snarl and kicked the ground as he turned away. "I'd feel like a jerk. I want to be okay with your friendship. I really do. But little things keep piling up and I keep thinking about what Corey said, and . . . and I'm not okay with it."

"What did Corey say?" I asked, my voice low, a spark of anger igniting in my gut. "If he implied there was ever anything between me and Daniel—"

"It's not you. It's Daniel."

"What?"

He hesitated and seemed ready to brush it off, then backed up, putting more distance between us, cracking his knuckles. "You and Serena drew straws to see who would ask Daniel to a dance a couple of years ago, right?"

"Yes, but— Wait, who told you that?" Only Serena and I had known about the game.

"She told Daniel."

"What? No. Why—?"

"You drew straws and you let her win."

"Whoa, wait. No. I never told her that I let—"

"But you did, right?"

I paused. "Yes, because she was crazy about him."

"And you weren't. He was just a friend."

"Exactly."

Rafe nodded, as if it was what he expected. So why were

we even having this conversation?

"Wait a second. Serena *told* Daniel that I let her win?"

He nodded.

"Why would she do that?"

"Because she knew he'd only go to the dance with her if he knew you weren't asking him and that you weren't asking because you didn't want to."

"I . . . I don't understand."

"Don't you?" Rafe's voice softened. "Daniel wanted you to ask him to the dance. I don't know why he agreed to go with Serena. The obvious answer is that he hoped to make you jealous, but that doesn't sound like him. I think he agreed because they were friends and it would be rude not to. That sounds more like Daniel."

"No." My heart beat so fast my words came out breathy. "It wasn't like that."

"Yeah, it was. He went to the dance with her because he felt he should. And maybe, a little bit, because you broke his heart."

I looked up sharply. "No. I never—"

Rafe held up his hands. "Not on purpose. Corey said it wasn't like that. Daniel didn't go out with Serena because he was mad at you. He just . . . I don't know. Corey figures he was killing time, maybe trying to show you he'd be a good boyfriend, maybe even hoping you'd realize you did have feelings for him. Only you didn't."

I thought of what Daniel had told me a few days ago,

about his relationship with Serena. *We were doing fine. But it wasn't . . . going anywhere. When she first asked me to that dance, I didn't feel right saying no. She was a friend, and—*

And . . .

He'd stopped there. Just stopped and looked away.

And you didn't want to ask me.

No, it wasn't like that. Rafe was wrong. Corey was—

"Corey told you this?" I said. "When did he tell you? *Why* would he tell you?"

"It was at Salmon Creek, after you and I started getting together. He was trying to scare me off. If you dated summer guys, that was fine. But this didn't look like a summer thing and he wanted me to know, in no uncertain terms, that you were taken. I ignored him. Sure, I could tell Daniel liked you, but if he hadn't made a move, that was his problem. You snooze, you lose. I thought he couldn't have been serious about it or he'd do something. But then, when we were hanging outside that helicopter, and I saw his face—he was going to hold on to you even if it meant he fell out that door with us. . . ."

Rafe shook his head, turned away, and took a few steps before stopping, his back still to me. "I realized I hadn't seen things right. Daniel wasn't sitting on the sidelines because he wasn't sure how he felt about you. He was waiting. Waiting for a sign from you, because he was afraid to make a move and risk losing you as a friend. I felt bad for him because I was sure you didn't feel the same way. And then . . ."

He turned now, slowly. "When I got back to Salmon Creek, it was just . . . this whirlwind of stuff. You were so happy to see me that I couldn't doubt what you felt for me, especially after I confessed about being wired and it didn't make a difference. You wanted me. No doubt. When you insisted on telling Daniel about the wire, I told myself that was the right thing to do, as a friend. Nothing more. But it was like turning on a switch. A little tickling doubt, and now every time his name is mentioned or I see you two together, I'm watching for signs. And I'm seeing them. Something changed after that helicopter crash. I notice you two looking at each other, whispering together, and maybe whatever I'm seeing was always there, but I don't think it was like this."

He took a deep breath and walked back toward me. I stood rooted, unable to move, much less speak. Rafe stopped right in front of me, then rested one hand on my waist.

"I need you to tell me I'm imagining things, Maya."

"Wh-what?" I managed.

He leaned in and a strand of hair fell forward on his cheek. I stared at that strand. I wanted to reach out and tuck it back, laugh, and tell him he was crazy. But I couldn't. Underneath the panic swirling through me was something harder. A tiny core of anger. Not just anger. Hurt. Confusion. Betrayal.

"Tell me I'm wrong, Maya. Tell me you feel absolutely nothing for Daniel except friendship."

"Or what?"

He blinked at my tone. "I—"

"We are getting ready for what could be the most important meeting of our lives," I said, brittle words snapping as I forced them out. "I have spent the last few hours struggling not to run behind the nearest tree and puke. We have to pull this off or I might never see my parents again. And you decide we need to do this now? No, you decide *I* need to do this now. Forget everything else. My boyfriend is feeling jealous so I need to reassure him?"

His eyes widened then. Sparks of panic. He said something, but I didn't catch it. Blood pounded in my ears.

"—right," Rafe was saying. "It can wait. I never meant to talk about this now." He paused, then squared his shoulders. "But at some point we do need to talk about it. He's in love with you, Maya—"

"No, he's not."

"Yes, he is, and everyone knows it. Not just Corey. That's why Sam hates me. She thinks Daniel deserves what he wants, and what he wants is—"

"No, it is not!"

The words came out as a roar that had Rafe stumbling back. Tears filled my eyes, the forest shimmering through them. My chest tightened until I had to pant to breathe. Slowly I lifted my gaze to look at him.

"Why would you tell me this? He's my friend. My best friend. And now every time I look at him, I'm going to know he wants more, and . . ." Quick breaths, gasping for air. "And it'll never be the same. That's what you wanted, isn't it? To make sure that even if it is just friendship, it will end."

A scent wafted past on the breeze. When I tried to catch it, it was already gone, but somehow it lingered in my brain and swirled with the anger and the hurt and I felt my hands start to throb. I clenched them into fists.

"That's not what I want, Maya. I would never come between—"

"You just did!" I said. "I have been through hell this past week. I thought I saw you die. I watched my parents at my funeral. I found out my entire life is a lie and I might never get any kind of normal one back. And do you know who got me through? The one person I can count on—always count on. Maybe you're jealous because that's not you, but as crazy as I am about you, there's someone who's been there a hell of a lot longer and that's who I needed. But you couldn't handle that, so you took it away. When I need it most, you yanked it away."

I took off his bracelet and set it on a tree stump. He stared at it, then at me, and I saw the panic in his face. I saw regret, too, and shock, and I wanted to seize on that. *He's sorry. He didn't mean it. He made a mistake.* But all I could think about was Daniel, and what this meant and how I felt about it and, oh God, how did I feel?

And that smell. That tendril of scent that I couldn't catch, that made something in my gut throb and made my hands throb and—

Rafe reached for me. I stumbled back, wheeled, and took

one step away and when I did, I took another, then another, starting to run, crashing through the forest, branches whipping me, running faster and faster, feeling my body shifting, screaming at me to stop, just stop, let it finish, but I kept going, Rafe behind me, yelling my name, spurring me on, until finally I tripped and blacked out before I even hit the ground.

THIRTY-EIGHT

WHEN I WOKE AS a cat, it was as if I hadn't done more than stumbled and fallen. I sprang up and kept running, pushed by the distant sound of Rafe's voice and pulled by that smell, that damned smell. Danger, that's what my gut said. It smelled like danger and I had to focus on this. Find the source of the threat before it found us.

I tore through the woods, following that teasing scent. Running here was different. The forest was different. Not my rainforest, but thick deciduous woods, the ground heavy with vines and undergrowth. After I tripped a few times, I forced myself to slow down and find a path. Then I flew along it until the ground blurred beneath me.

"Maya!"

The voice came from in front of me and I skidded to a stop, panic rising.

"Maya?"

It came clearer now, accompanied by running footsteps and I recognized those steps, just as I recognized the scent. My heart gave a little thud. A good thud. A relieved thud. Until Daniel stepped onto the path and everything Rafe said flooded back.

"I thought I saw you. Yes, I know, I'm supposed to be resting, but Ash snores even louder than you." He grinned. "I had to take a walk."

I looked at that grin and I heard Rafe's words. *He's in love with you.* But I didn't see love. Not the kind Rafe meant. I just saw Daniel with his open, infectious, happy-to-see-you grin. Nothing else. Not in his smile. Not in his face. Not in his eyes.

That was good. Corey was mistaken. Maybe there'd been a time when Daniel thought we could be more than friends, but then he got together with Serena and that changed. He might not have fallen in love with her, but he'd realized he didn't feel that way about me, either.

Relief. That's what I should feel, looking into Daniel's face and seeing nothing more than friendship. So why didn't I?

My stomach clenched. I turned to leap into the forest.

"Hey!" Daniel said, jogging toward me. "What's up?" He

paused, then scanned the woods. "You're playing with Rafe? Is that it? I'm interfering."

He tried for a smile, but there was something about— No. There wasn't. It was just a smile.

He stopped about a meter away. "You guys out blowing off steam?"

I shook my head.

The grin returned. Brighter? *God, stop analyzing.*

But that's how it was going to be now, wasn't it? Analyzing. His feelings. My reactions.

"Maya?" He hunkered down. "Is everything okay?"

The scent wafted past again and I seized on that. I made a show of lifting my nose and sniffing.

"You smell something?" He pushed to his feet, shoulders tightening as he scanned the forest. "Someone's out there. Okay, let's deal with this. You lead . . ."

He said something more, but all I caught was that scent, wafting around me now, filling my head.

"Maya? What's—"

I bolted.

As I raced through the forest, I told myself I was just following the scent. But the fact that it happened to lead me away from Daniel helped. *Focus on this. This is real. This is important.*

The scent grew stronger. Dog? Human? No, it wasn't dog and it wasn't human. It was something in between—

The answer hit me as the scent did, a full blast of it, as if my target was right in front. . . .

But all I saw was darkness. I'd plunged into a thick copse and I could make out the faint glow of a birch tree, but that was it. The rest was black—

Two eyes swung my way. Bright green eyes. Peering at me from the darkness. Then that darkness erupted. A massive form flew at me, black as midnight, green eyes glowing. And fangs. Huge white fangs, bearing down on me.

I turned to run, but the beast was too close. It hit me in the side and knocked me down. Before I could scramble up, before I could even see what it was, the beast sprang. Teeth clenched my throat and pinned me to the ground.

"Derek!"

A girl's voice. The beast stiffened. Not a beast. A werewolf.

He kept me pinned. He didn't clamp down harder, though—just held me there.

"What is that?" the girl asked.

Those green eyes shifted to her, his grip on my throat relaxing a fraction. I unsheathed my claws and swatted at his chest. It wasn't a hard swipe. Just enough to scratch him and just enough to startle him. He let go. I flew to my feet and twisted, backing up, showing him a hissing mouthful of my own sharp teeth.

"T-that's—" the girl stammered. "I guess they aren't extinct around here after all."

The clouds blew from the moon and light streamed down, and I finally saw what I was facing. It looked like a wolf . . . if wolves grew to two hundred pounds. A massive black wolf with green eyes fixed on me, assessing, considering.

"Okay," the girl said. "It's backing away. Everything's o—"

I glanced over and she stopped short. She was a little younger than me. Tiny, with reddish-blond hair and blue eyes. I swore I could smell fear waft off her. The wolf smelled it, too, and bristled, growling at me.

"No," she said, then again, firmer. "No. It's okay. Everything's okay. We'll just let it leave."

The wolf growled again.

The girl's voice rose. "I said we'll let it leave, Derek. It's not attacking us and I don't want it getting hurt if we can help it. You, either."

The werewolf—Derek—snorted and gave me a look that said he considered personal injury highly unlikely. My hackles rose and I drew back my lips. He seemed to take that as a challenge, shifting forward, almost swaggering, like a schoolyard bully, certain his smaller target will back down. I considered it. For the sake of making nice, I should retreat. Surrender. Submit. But that was weakness and everything in me rebelled at the thought. So I held my ground.

"Derek."

The girl's voice was low, annoyed now, and it was almost comical when he shot her a sheepish look. He turned back to me. Considered. Took another slow step—

"No!"

The familiar shout hit with an equally familiar sonic boom of force. It knocked the werewolf off his feet. The girl let out a shriek and ran forward. Daniel raced through the trees. The wolf scrambled up and swung around on him.

I sprang between them. I lowered my forequarters and let out a snarl, fur standing on end. That made the wolf stop. He stared at me. Then his gaze lifted to Daniel behind me. I snarled again.

"The cat—" the girl said.

"Is not a cat," Daniel said. "Like that's not a wolf."

"Y-yes. I mean, no, he's a hybrid. Part-wolf, part-dog. I—"

"He's a werewolf," Daniel cut in. "And she's a skin-walker, another kind of shape-shifter."

"She . . . ?"

"A friend of mine. Like he's a friend of yours. And I'm going to ask you to back him off. Can you do that, Chloe?"

The wolf's head shot up at the name.

Chloe. The necromancer. That made sense. The other girl was a witch and would have tried a spell by now.

"So you understand me. Derek, right?" Daniel moved up beside me as his voice took on that special tone. "I'm going to ask you to take a step back. Maya will do the same. I'm sure she hasn't attacked you or tried to attack Chloe, so there's no threat here, right?"

The wolf snorted and looked at me.

"Don't even think about it," Daniel said, an edge creeping into his voice. "You attack her? You attack both of us."

The wolf snarled. They locked gazes. When it was clear neither was backing down, Chloe came forward and grabbed Derek by the scruff of the neck.

"Come on," she said. "Please. Just step away." She looked at Daniel. "You're on his territory, which is never good with a werewolf. Your friend—Maya—startled him, even if she didn't mean to. Plus he really doesn't like you knowing our names."

"Well, I do know them, which shouldn't come as that big a surprise. Do you really think a couple of kids with supernatural powers are going to accidentally stumble on you? We were at the house earlier. I'm sure Derek smelled us. We were waiting in the forest until morning to make contact, so we wouldn't spook you."

I chuffed.

Daniel shot a smile over at me. "Yeah, that one didn't work out so well."

"All right," Chloe said. "We're backing up. Right, Derek?"

He snorted, but took a step back. So did I. We both retreated a few more, until I was at the clearing's edge.

"I don't suppose you remember where you left your clothing," Daniel murmured to me.

Chloe gave a soft laugh. "That's always a problem, isn't

it? Okay then. You two go find that. We'll meet you here. Hopefully everyone will be in human form." A wry smile. "Though I'll warn you, he's not a whole lot more pleasant that way. At least as a wolf, he can't talk."

The wolf growled, but she only laughed and gave him a pat, then tugged him away as we went to retrieve my clothing.

THİRTY-NİNE

AS HAD HAPPENED BEFORE, after I'd passed out, I'd seemed to sleep-undress, which was handy. So my clothing was where I'd left it, still intact.

When I stepped out from my hiding spot, Daniel rose and came over to me. "You didn't get bitten or anything, did you?"

I shook my head.

He exhaled. "Good. I was worried. I don't know if that's how you really do become a werewolf." He paused. "It could be kind of cool, though. A werewolf and skin-walker hybrid. Time to shift? You pick your form."

He grinned and I managed a soft laugh. "My luck, it'd be a mix of the two. A shaggy, brown monster with retractable claws and an irresistible urge to chase sticks."

"As long as it's not an irresistible urge to hump legs and sniff crotches."

I laughed again, a real one now. "This is why I'll stick with feline, thank you."

"I'm glad you're okay. Seeing you facing off with that monster was scary enough. I can't imagine what it was like to *be* the one facing off with him." He shook his head. "We need to have a little chat with your brother about werewolves before he decides to challenge one."

"Nah. I say we let him try. Take his ego down a notch or two."

We both laughed and I looked at him, and I felt . . . okay. I looked at his expression and listened to his laugh and I saw nothing more than I'd always seen. My friend. My best friend.

"Everything all right?" Daniel asked.

I smiled up at him. "We should hurry back and talk to them, and hope the others stay sleeping for a while."

"Rafe's looking after that."

I looked up.

"I saw him while you were shifting back. We talked. He agreed to make sure the others stay put if they wake up. You and I will handle this first encounter. He seemed cool with that."

No, he probably wasn't cool with it at all. I didn't care. Well, yes, I did, but I didn't want to. Even if Rafe hadn't ruined my friendship with Daniel, he'd sure as hell tried. He was supposed to care about me. That wasn't something you did to someone you cared about.

"You guys had a fight?" Daniel asked.

I nodded. "Lousy timing, I know. Sorry."

"I'm sure the timing has a lot to do with it. Everyone's on edge. Whatever it was, he seemed sorry."

"He always is," I muttered before I could stop myself. I shook my head. "We'll deal with it. At a much more suitable time."

"He really does like you, Maya. He fell from a helicopter for you." His voice dropped, his tone almost . . . wistful. I looked up to see his expression, then quickly yanked my gaze away. *Don't analyze. Do not analyze. I won't do this. Damn you, Rafe.*

"We'd better go," I said. "Before they get tired of waiting."

I instinctively knew where we'd left Chloe and Derek. When we drew close, I could hear Chloe talking just above a whisper.

"How many?" she asked.

She paused, as if waiting for a reply. I didn't hear Derek's response, but then she said, "And they're all teens? No adults?"

Still no answer, but again she responded as if there'd been one. We stepped past a clump of bushes and I saw them ahead, sitting at the foot of a huge oak. Chloe had her knees pulled up, one arm wrapped around them. Her other hand was entwined with Derek's. He leaned back against the tree. Slumping, as if it was holding him up. His face glowed with sweat and his eyes were closed.

When I'd seen Derek in wolf form, I figured werewolves

grew when they shifted, like the ones in movies. They didn't. He was really that big. Even slumped, he was more than a head taller than Chloe. A huge football player of a guy.

Beside me, Daniel whispered, "I was going to tell him off for bullying you. But I'm having second thoughts."

I smiled at him. "I don't blame you."

Despite his size, Derek was obviously no older than us. His cheeks were dotted with mild acne and I could see the ghosts of fading pocks, as if it had been much worse not too long ago. Dark hair tumbled into his eyes as he rested with his head bent forward.

"Anything else?" Chloe whispered.

I realized she wasn't talking to Derek. She was looking up. But there was no one there.

"Ghost," Daniel murmured.

I tried not to shiver. I cleared my throat so we wouldn't surprise them. Chloe still jumped a little, but Derek's head only lifted, eyes snapping open, hand tightening around Chloe's. He got to his feet, inadvertently tugging her up with him. She murmured something and he let go of her hand but stepped in front of her. She sighed, pushed him aside, and came forward with her hand extended. When she saw me step into the moonlit clearing, she hesitated, but found her smile quickly and reached for my hand.

"Maya, is it?" she said.

I shook it. "It is. And this is Daniel."

Daniel shook her hand. Derek just stood there, until

Chloe prodded him and he shook our hands—not without a grumble, though, a low one, almost like a growl.

"I'm sorry I startled you," I said. The startling had definitely gone both ways, but from the look on Derek's face, I figured the apology was a good idea. "Like Daniel said, we went to the house earlier, and when you weren't there, we decided to wait out here until morning."

"It's not just you two," Derek said. "There are others. We know that."

"A ghost told Chloe, right?" I said.

She hesitated, then nodded. "A friend of ours. Liz."

"Liz?" Cold fingers touched the back of my neck, as if I was feeling the ghost herself. "Elizabeth Delaney?" Derek stiffened and I hurried on. "I saw her name in some papers the Edison Group had. I noticed because we have the same last name. I'm Maya Delaney."

Chloe looked sharply to the side, as if the ghost was still there and had said something.

"There's no relation," I said. "I'm adopted, for one thing, and it seemed to just be a coincidence, but I noticed the name and they said she was dead, so . . ."

I trailed off. Chloe was still looking to the side. Looking at her friend. Her dead friend. The Edison Group had murdered this girl and now I was going to suggest everyone just try to get along? Negotiate with the Cabals? My gut sank.

Daniel took over. "There are four more of us. We're all Project Phoenix subjects. They're in a clearing over there."

300

He pointed. "Three of them are sleeping and don't know what's going on, but the fourth—Rafe—is standing guard to make sure they don't interrupt while we're talking. Is that okay?"

Chloe seemed ready to say it was fine, but Derek cut in, "What are their powers?"

"A lot of skin-walkers," Daniel said. "Maya's brother is one and so is Rafe. Neither has shifted yet. Corey's a seleni. Hayley's a xana. I'm a benandanti."

Derek shook his head. "None of that means anything to me."

"Not surprising, considering we're resurrected extinct supernatural types. That's what Project Phoenix is. But if you're uncomfortable talking here, we could go inside, where you guys have the advantage of numbers."

Derek bristled, as if Daniel had just announced plans for an invasion. "No. We talk here. Chloe—"

"Don't even suggest *I* go inside," she said, lowering herself to the ground. "Everyone sit. Let's talk."

We told them about Salmon Creek and how we'd been raised. Then I explained about Serena and how that led to the whole cover-up unraveling.

"But they didn't kill her," I said. "I know that happened in your experiment, but it didn't in ours."

"Yet," Derek said. "Just wait until things start going wrong."

"They *have* gone wrong. But I think whatever happened to you guys was different. Different people were involved, for one thing."

Derek snorted—he wasn't buying that—but I was relieved to see that Chloe seemed to be considering it.

"Do you know who the Nasts are?" I asked.

"It's a Cabal," Chloe said. "Like the St. Clouds, only bigger. And, well, nastier." A small smile at the play on words.

"They kidnapped my dad," Derek said. "Held him captive for months, leaving my brother and me on our own, which is how our problems started."

So they hated the Nasts. With very good reason. Great.

I continued with our story—the fire, the kidnapping, the long trip home, our "deaths." The more I talked, the more I really understood how ridiculous our solution was going to seem. Negotiate with the people who'd done all this to us? How could we even consider it? Yet given the alternative, how could we not consider it?

When I faltered, Daniel would reach over and squeeze my hand. Just a reassuring gesture. But Chloe and Derek noticed and it was as if I could hear them mentally processing the information, drawing the same conclusion that Ash had, that Daniel was my boyfriend. Did it really look that way?

I mentally cursed Rafe some more before pushing on with my story.

"So my biological father helped us escape and sent us here, to you guys," I said as I concluded.

Derek peered at me, brow furrowed. "How the hell did he know we were here?"

"That's what we came to warn you about. He got the information from someone who works for the St. Clouds. They know exactly where you are."

Derek scrambled up so fast his legs tangled and he nearly went down again. "What?"

Chloe was on her feet, too, eyes bright with alarm. "They know?"

We rose and Daniel put out his hands. "It's okay. Well, not really okay, obviously, but it's nothing new. They've known for a few months."

"And you sat there, chatting away, without saying anything?" Derek stepped toward Daniel, looming over him.

Daniel stood his ground. "Like I said, it's not an emergency. If you run in the middle of the night, it might be . . . considering they've got a tracking device on your van."

Derek didn't seem to hear him, just peered into the forest, braced for attack.

"Where are your friends?" he said.

"Over—" Daniel began, pointing.

"Take us to them. Now."

We ran to the others—it was clear Derek wasn't accepting a leisurely stroll. I took the lead so this huge guy wouldn't come barreling down on them. That wasn't the way anyone needed to wake up. It was still chaos. Derek barked orders. Chloe tried to calm him. When he didn't listen, I snapped that he wasn't helping matters. He snapped back. Ash jumped to my defense, snarling like an alley cat. Daniel intervened to mediate. Derek turned on him. Corey rushed to Daniel's side, fists ready. Rafe braced to join in if a fight broke out.

It was fun.

Eventually Chloe, Daniel, and I got everyone calmed down enough to grab our stuff and head to the house.

FORTY

DEREK BANGED THROUGH THE side door, leaving us on the porch.

"Dad!" he shouted, loud enough to make my ears ring. "Dad! You need to get down here!"

Chloe held open the door and whispered to me, "I could say he's not always like this, but I'd be lying."

She ushered us all in. I heard footsteps on the stairs and looked up to see a man in jeans, pulling on a T-shirt as he hurried down. He was about my dad's age, Daniel's height, and slender. Kit Bae, Derek's adoptive father. Kit's son was coming down behind him. He looked like his father, except for his light brown hair. Simon Bae.

"Hey, bro," Simon called sleepily. "What's—?"

He stopped. His gaze traveled over the kids crowding into his hall and he gave a sharp shake of his head.

"Apparently, we have visitors," he said. "I gotta hear this one."

A woman appeared at the top of the stairs. A petite blonde, pulling her robe tight. Lauren Fellows. Chloe's aunt. The doctor who'd worked with the Edison Group.

A girl pushed past her. Taller than Dr. Fellows, with short dark hair and piercing dark eyes. Kit's daughter. Simon's half sister. Victoria Enright. Antone's message said she was related to the Nasts' witch, but distantly, which explained the different spelling of the surname. I was just really glad Antone had given us all the details—and that I'd listened to his message about a half-dozen times on our trip—or I'd never keep all the relationships straight. I suppose they were about to have the same problem with us.

"We need to go," Derek said. "Everyone, back upstairs, pack your things."

"Wh-what?" Simon said.

"Slow down," Kit said as he reached the landing.

Derek towered over him, but moved back so he wasn't looming. "They know where we are. The St. Clouds. They've found us."

Kit's gaze swung to us, and I stepped forward to explain, but his gaze moved to Chloe and she took over.

"These kids are from Project Phoenix. They escaped. Maya and her brother"—she pointed at me and Ash—"their father told them to come here."

"Doesn't matter," Derek cut in. "The St. Clouds know

where we are. Which means we need to leave. Now."

"Hold on," Kit said, raising his hand.

"Didn't you hear me?"

"Yes, Derek, I did, but—"

"Derek?" Dr. Fellows called as she descended the stairs. "Why don't you go upstairs while we talk. I think that would be best for everyone."

From her tone, you'd think she was talking to a misbehaving puppy.

Chloe shot her a look. "That isn't necessary. We all just need to give Maya and Daniel a minute to explain." She glanced at Derek. "Please."

Derek looked from Chloe to his father, then nodded. Simon brushed past Kit. He gave us a smile, friendly but cautious, and went to stand by his brother and Chloe.

"You *are* explaining, right?" a voice said.

I looked up. It was Victoria, still on the steps, staring at me.

"Waiting for that explanation," she said.

I lifted my brows and turned to Kit. "The St. Clouds know where you are. They've known for months. They're just wearing you down, waiting until something goes wrong or you get tired of running, then they'll pounce."

"How did they find—?" Kit began.

"Not important right now," Derek cut in. "She's explained it to us; we'll explain it on the road. The point is that our cover has been blown."

Kit moved quickly to the window. "They're watching us now?"

I shook my head. "They have someone doing spot checks, but since you've only got one means of escape—your van—that's what they're monitoring. With a tracking device."

"So now can we leave?" Derek said.

"How?" Victoria said, walking down the rest of the steps. "Set off on a midnight hike to town? Like that's not going to be noticed."

"Tori's right," Kit said. "If they've been monitoring us for months, there's no need to rush off in a panic. Tomorrow we'll look for the tracking device. If we can't find it, I'll get to town and rent us another van. Then we'll leave."

Derek clearly did not like this idea. Neither did Ash—his scowl had deepened more than usual. Daniel looked uncomfortable, which is pretty much how I felt. I might not have been in Derek's mad rush to leave, but I didn't think we should hang around. I looked at Daniel. He glanced at Kit, then shrugged, leaned over, and murmured to me, "It'll be morning soon enough."

"Let's go into the living room," Kit said. "I'm sure we have a lot to talk about."

I let Daniel tell the story this time. I was too anxious, as I realized how foolish our mission was. These people were never going to negotiate with a Cabal. They might even think we were using them to get what we wanted. *Were* we doing that? We needed Dr. Fellows and, more importantly, Kit Bae to handle negotiations. They'd both worked for the Edison Group and Mr. Bae was a lawyer. But it was true that our position was stronger if we brought the Genesis subjects along to sweeten the deal.

Daniel didn't mention any of that. Not yet. Instead he stressed that we'd come here for help. We were on our own, separated from our parents. Not helpless—Ash was quick to make that clear—but not naive enough to think we could handle the Cabals on our own. That was what he said—"handle" them. For now, everyone could interpret that as they liked.

After that, Kit said we should get some sleep. Anyone who was hungry could help themselves to the kitchen. Otherwise, grab a couch or bunk up with the other kids, and we'd reconvene in the morning.

As the others went to look around, I ducked away and waited in the back hall until the last figure left the living room.

"Mr. Bae?" I said, stepping out.

He turned, saw me, and smiled. "It's Kit."

"Can I talk to you for a minute? Outside?"

He followed me out the back door to the stoop. I held out the mini recorder.

"Calvin Antone gave me this. He's my . . . Well, Daniel explained that. Anyway, this is what he gave me when we escaped. It was instructions and information and . . . a

309

suggestion. A really detailed suggestion, actually. About how we might all get out of this mess. I added my own ideas at the end." I swallowed. "I don't think you're going to like any of it, and obviously it's totally up to you, but I'm hoping even if you don't agree with what he suggests, you'll help us do it."

He looked at the recorder. "We could just talk about it."

I shook my head. "Just listen tonight. Please, we can talk in the morning."

"All right." He took the recorder. When I turned to leave, he stopped me. "We will help you, Maya. However we can. Lauren and I were part of all this. The experiments. We take responsibility for that. We'll make sure you're safe now."

I thanked him and went back inside.

They'd put Chloe in Victoria's room, and Hayley and I were supposed to sleep there, too, leaving Chloe's bedroom for the guys. Chloe wasn't in Victoria's room, though. She was off with Derek, I guessed.

That left me with Hayley and Victoria—Tori, as everyone called her. She sat cross-legged on her bed, watching us like we were stray cats someone had stuck in her room—strays that were liable to pee on her ankle boots and shed all over her designer jeans. Hayley was anxious, and when I tried to calm her down she snapped at me, and Tori made some snarky comment and I decided they'd do just fine if I left them together. I couldn't possibly sleep anyway.

When I went downstairs, I'll admit I was looking for Daniel. I shouldn't feel guilty about that. But after what

310

Rafe had said, now even something so simple felt electric with subtext. But all I heard was Kit and Dr. Fellows, talking in lowered voices in the living room.

I went into the dining room, opened the curtains, and peered out. I dimly heard the back door open and shut, then soft footsteps, but I paid little attention until a voice said, "Do you see something?"

I turned to find Chloe hesitating in the doorway.

"Just thinking," I said.

"Worried?"

"Just thinking of my parents. Home." I thought of a segue from there. Broaching the topic that would eventually need to be broached. "Is this your home now? On the run, I mean."

"I hope not."

"Where do you plan to go from here?" I paused, then hurried on. "I don't mean your next destination. I'm not fishing. I just mean . . . what do you do? Keep running?"

She walked in, voice low. "I don't know. I spent most of my life moving around. My dad and I had just settled in one place when all this happened. I . . ." She shrugged. "I guess I'm hoping it doesn't last much longer. I want a home." She glanced over her shoulder. "I know you do, too, even if you don't like to admit it."

I thought she was talking to me. Then Derek stepped into the doorway.

"He wasn't eavesdropping," she said to me. "He just doesn't like me being alone with strangers in the house." She

311

aimed a pointed look his way. "Even if I end up rescuing him from danger as often as he rescues me."

Chloe waved him over. As she did, someone else poked his head in. Rafe.

"Maya?" He looked at the other two, then me. "Can we talk?"

"Rather not."

He lowered his voice. "Please?"

"Later," I said. "Just not tonight. Okay?"

He nodded and retreated.

"Sorry about that," I said when he was gone. "Inconveniently timed relationship angst."

"Relationship?" Chloe looked from me to the now-empty doorway. "You and Rafe? Oh, I thought . . ." She trailed off and shook her head. "Never mind. So you were saying—"

"I thought you were with Daniel," Derek cut in.

Chloe gave him a look as I inwardly flinched.

"We're just really good friends," I said. "We all grew up together. Well, the Salmon Creek subjects, anyway."

"That must have been nice," Chloe said, a touch of wistfulness in her voice. "Not the experiment part, of course, but . . ."

"We didn't know about the experiment. It was just a really good life. They made it that way—we know that now. But even without all the extras, it was a great way to grow up." I turned back to the window as my eyes prickled with tears. "It could drive you nuts, being with the same kids all the time, but I wouldn't have traded it for anything. Except . . ." I shrugged, still looking out. "They made a mistake not telling us. If we'd grown up with it, things might have been different."

"Us, too," Chloe murmured. "I'm not sure it would have fixed all our problems, but I wish I'd known. So all you guys grew up together, then. Well, except Rafe and Ash."

I nodded. "Speaking of my brother, I should probably check on him. Have either of you seen him?"

They shook their heads. I said I should go find him and I'd see them in the morning.

FORTY-ONE

A S I PASSED THE kitchen, I heard someone. I poked my head in. Corey was opening a can of pop with one hand and balancing a slice of cold pizza on the other.

"Hey," he said. "Just in time to keep me from eating alone."

"No, I'm not hungry," I said, and started to withdraw.

He came over before I could disappear. "Did you find Daniel? He was looking for you."

I muttered that I hadn't seen him and, again, tried to leave. This time Corey swung into my path.

"Okay, what'd I do?" he asked.

"Nothing. I'm just tired."

"Uh-uh. I suspected I was getting the cold shoulder earlier, but with everything going on, I wasn't sure. Now

I'm sure. You're giving me the look."

"What look?"

"The Maya's-pissed-with-Corey look. Fifty percent disappointment, thirty percent disapproval, twenty percent exasperation. I've done something you're not happy about."

I hesitated, then blurted, "Rafe told me what you said about Daniel."

He frowned. "You're going to need to be a little more specific."

"In Salmon Creek, when Rafe and I started getting together. You told him to back off because Daniel . . ." I glanced at the open door and lowered my voice. "Because Daniel likes me."

He swore, then dropped his pizza on the counter and started for the door. "I'm going to kill him."

I caught the back of his shirt, reached past him, and closed the door.

Corey turned. "Rafe should *not* have told you that. He had no right. What the hell was he thinking?"

"So it's true? What you said?"

His face went still for a moment, then he looked down at me. "Do you need to ask that? Really, Maya?"

I opened my mouth to answer, but it felt like someone was sitting on my chest and I gasped for air. Corey swore, grabbed my arm, and steered me to a chair. Then he pushed me down into it and crouched, face lowering to mine.

"Breathe, Maya," he said. "Just breathe."

I scowled as I found my voice. "I'm not—"

"Oh, yes you are. You look ready to pass out. Apparently it *is* a surprise." He swore some more, then shook his head. "What a mess. Of all the crappy timing . . . I'm going to kill him."

"He didn't mean it. He's just stressed and anxious and he wasn't thinking." Was I defending Rafe? I took a deep breath, then looked at Corey. "You shouldn't have said anything to him."

"Why?"

I met his gaze. "Why? You have to ask?"

He pulled over a chair and sat down. "Yeah, I do. Daniel's my friend, Maya. I've watched him go through hell over this for two years now. Liking you but dating Serena, which was a stupid idea, which I told him many times. Then him finally realizing it was a stupid idea, and torturing himself about dumping her. Which was nothing compared to the torture of having her die, then being trapped between grieving for her and wanting to be with you and knowing there was no way in hell that was happening anytime soon. A year goes by, and I'm pushing him to make his move and I finally convince him to give you a hint, and in strolls Rafael Martinez. Daniel's this close to actually doing something and you decide you're going to date a town boy? After all these years? There was no way in hell I wasn't going to tell Rafe to back off."

When he finished, he glanced at me and swore under his breath, reaching over to grasp my shoulder.

316

"Breathe, Maya."

I shook off his hand. "I'm fine."

"No, you're not. You look like someone hit you in the gut with a sandbag." He sighed. "I kept telling myself you knew. You had to know."

I looked at him. "And what? I was just being a heartless bitch, ignoring it?"

"'Course not. I just figured you weren't ready. After Serena and everything. You were playing it cool until you got enough distance. . . ." He trailed off. "I'm sorry. You shouldn't have found out like this. Not now. Not from Rafe. Not from me. I blame Rafe and I kinda blame Daniel. You know how he is. So damned worried about doing the right thing. But it's out now and you know, so I sure as hell hope you're going to do something about it."

I looked up at him.

"Don't look at me like you don't know what I mean. Maybe you aren't as obvious about it as Daniel is, but you can't tell me you don't—"

The kitchen door opened.

Daniel walked in, saw us, and stopped. "You guys having a party and forgot to invite me?" He went to the counter where the pizza box sat. "You better have left some."

Corey's gaze swung from me to Daniel. Then he stood. "Maya and I were just talking. There's something—"

I grabbed the back of his shirt and wrenched hard enough for him to stumble. Daniel looked over and frowned.

"What's up?" he asked.

"We were talking about Hayley," I said. "Something she said to me in confidence. Can I have a minute with Corey?"

"Sure. Holler when you're done."

Daniel left. Still holding Corey's shirt, I stood and moved closer to him.

"You are not going to tell him," I whispered.

He twisted to look at me. "Why not? I'm sick of this. It's like being twelve again, dealing with all that damned drama. *I like her. Does she like me? What if she doesn't like me?*"

"Except when we were twelve, it was us dealing with your drama." I moved closer and lowered my voice even more. "Don't do this, Corey."

"He likes you. You like him. You know you do."

"Yes, I like him. As a friend. Beyond that?" I steeled myself and met Corey's gaze. "When I let Serena ask him to the dance, I wasn't ready to date. Anyone. I just wasn't at the stage. By the time I was, Daniel was off-limits. In my mind, he's been off-limits ever since. I have no idea how I feel about Daniel. I'm not being coy. I really, really don't. I'm freaked out and I'm confused, and I'm dealing with so much other crap that there's no way you can expect me to figure out anything right now. Hell, at this point I couldn't decide whether I want the Hawaiian pizza or the veggie."

"Veggie. Trust me, you always pick veggie."

I shook my head. "Even if I did feel something, I wouldn't do anything about it now, would I? Under the circumstances?

318

Kinda more worried about the rest of my life."

When he said nothing, I headed for the door. "I'll call him back in."

Corey shot forward and grabbed my arm. "I'll keep my mouth shut on one condition."

I looked back at him.

"Don't punish Daniel over this," he said.

"Punish . . . ?"

"Maybe that's not the right word, but you know what I mean. Don't shut him out. Don't run away from him. Don't make things weird."

"They are weird."

"But they've been that way for years. Daniel's felt like this forever and he hasn't let it change your friendship. He hasn't interfered with you and other guys. He's been cool about it. You need to be cool about it. He didn't do anything wrong."

"I know that."

"Then act like it, okay?"

I nodded. I opened the door and leaned out.

"Daniel?"

He stepped from a room at the end of the hall. "All clear?"

I said yes and started to withdraw, but he motioned me into the hall. I hesitated, then came out. He walked over.

"Everything okay?" he whispered.

"Sure." I started backing up, but he stopped me.

He moved closer and as he did, I stiffened. *Exactly what*

Corey asked me not to do. Damn you, Rafe. Damn you, too, Corey, for starting this.

"What's wrong?" he whispered.

I looked up at him and when I did, I saw worry. Worry and concern. Corey was right—if Daniel did feel something for me, then it wasn't new. It was just this—Daniel, as he always had been.

I leaned against his shoulder, resting my cheek on it. His arms went around me in a hug. Nothing weird. Nothing new. Just a reassuring squeeze.

"Rough day, huh?" he whispered.

I nodded as I pulled back. "Can we grab pizza and talk about it?"

"Sure. I don't think anyone's getting much sleep tonight."

We went into the kitchen. At first it seemed empty and I frowned as I looked at the half-eaten slice on the table.

"Corey was right here—"

At a noise to my left, I turned to see Corey on the floor.

FORTY-TWO

DANIEL AND I RACED over as Corey rose, rubbing his shoulder and wincing. "Okay," he said. "How did I end up—?"

He convulsed and retched, spewing the cupboards with half-digested pizza.

"Really not a cool power," he mumbled as he tried to push up.

He went down again, crouching, hands to his head. We took him, one at each arm, and moved him to a cleaner spot in front of the fridge. He sat with his back against it, heaving deep breaths as he winced in pain.

"Where are your pills?" Daniel asked.

"Hell if I know," Corey said. "My bag. Maybe." He swore and doubled over. "Just hold on. I'll remember as soon as I can think—"

He let out a yowl, hands to his head.

"Breathe," I said. "Just breathe."

He scowled at me for echoing his words from before, but took deep breaths, chest heaving. When the door banged open, we all jumped. It was Derek, with Chloe right behind him.

Derek's gaze shot to Corey, sitting on the floor, us crouched on either side. "What—?" His nose wrinkled and he looked over at the vomit.

"He's having a vision," I said. "That's what happens."

"Attractive, I know," Corey said between gritted teeth. "And now I get new witnesses to my humiliation. Wonderful."

"We're used to it," Chloe said. "Derek used to do that when he Changed. Only worse."

"Thank you for sharing," Derek muttered.

She grinned. "You're welcome."

Chloe grabbed paper towels from the counter. When I realized she was going to clean up, I hurried over, saying, "No, I'll get that."

"You look after your friend," she said as Derek went to help her.

I was going to protest again, but Corey doubled over, groaning, and I returned to him.

He had his eyes squeezed shut. "Trees," he said. "I'm seeing trees. Which better not mean we're going to end up in another forest, because I am so damned sick—" He gasped as if hit by another wave of pain. "Yep, it's a forest.

Trees, trees, and more trees."

"Deciduous or coniferous?" I asked.

He opened one eye. "English?"

"Leaves or needles?"

He closed his eyes but didn't flinch or gasp this time, just leaned back against the fridge, as if he was seeing the vision play out behind his eyelids.

"Mostly leaves. Changing color, like they are here." A pause. "I think it is here. I see a mark on one of the big trees. Blue paint. I saw some with that."

Chloe nodded, walking back with Derek. "It's a woodlot behind us. The owner marked trees for cutting."

Corey winced and jerked forward again, eyes squeezed shut. "People," he gasped. "I see people. In black and camo. There are two women. They're doing something. Casting spells, I think."

I described the two witches we'd seen—the St. Cloud one and the Nasts'. Corey was seeing both. When I realized that, my stomach plummeted.

"You led the *Nasts* here?" Derek said.

"No," Daniel said. "Obviously the St. Clouds did. Somehow they knew we were coming here—"

"Somehow?" Derek turned on me. "Your father told them. He set this whole thing up."

"What for?" I said. "If he wanted the Nasts to know, he'd have told them without sending us here."

"Let's not do this," Chloe said. "If Corey's telling us these

323

people are in our back woods, we can't sit around flinging blame."

"No, he's saying they *will* be there," I said. "It's a vision."

"We don't know that for sure," Daniel murmured. "When you were taken, he had a vision of that and, according to Ash, the timing was pretty much dead-on. It was happening simultaneously."

"So there *could* be people in our backwoods?" Derek grabbed Corey's shoulder. "What else do you see?"

"Hold on." He closed his eyes.

"We don't have time to 'hold on.' Tell me what you—"

"Oww!" Corey shoved Derek's hand off his shoulder. "That hurt, asshole. I'm doing my best here."

"I didn't mean—"

Corey silenced him with an angry wave, then rubbed his shoulder with one hand and his temples with the other.

I took Corey's elbow, leading him to a chair. "Daniel? Can you check his bag? See if you find his meds?" I crouched as Corey sat. "Did you see anything else?"

He glowered at Derek. "I'm sure I would have if Teen Wolf hadn't tried to dislocate my shoulder. The vision's gone now and once it's gone, it doesn't come back."

Derek mumbled an apology, then went to the window and peered out. Chloe walked up behind him.

"If anyone *is* out there, let's not give them a target, okay?" she said. "We should tell your dad."

"Right." He paused. "Is Liz around?"

"I've been trying to contact her." She turned to us. "That's not easy if she isn't here."

I wasn't sure exactly what that meant. I guess just that we didn't have ghostly help for scouting the situation.

Derek strode out the door without so much as a glance our way. Chloe paused to ask if we wanted to come, but I said no, Corey still wasn't feeling well. If Kit wanted to talk to him, we'd be here.

"Are you sure about that?" Corey muttered once they were gone. "Chloe is nice enough, but that Derek? Real charmer. If anyone busts through that door, he's liable to throw us to them as cannon fodder."

I wasn't sure I disagreed.

"Their dad seems okay," he said, "but I'm not convinced he takes us seriously. The aunt definitely doesn't. I can't get a read on the brother, but the sister?" He rolled his eyes. "A bigger diva than Hayley."

"I know," I murmured. "As soon as Daniel brings your meds, we'll get Hayley, Rafe, and Ash, and if these guys don't decide to run, we will. It's not exactly shaping up to be the partnership I hoped for."

"Let's focus on the others, not my meds, okay?" Corey said. "Daniel's right. My last vision seemed to be a glimpse of the present, not the future. I don't want to hang around here hoping this one's different."

I agreed and we went to gather our group.

We found Ash first. He was in the front foyer, sitting on

the floor, as if guarding the door. I wouldn't have noticed him if he hadn't seen me passing and asked if something was up.

When I told him what had happened, I think he was almost happy. Relieved, at least. He hadn't wanted to stick around and this gave him the excuse he needed. He said he'd head outside and scout. I tried to stop him, but he ignored me, so I settled for telling him to be careful, which only earned me a disdainful glower.

Up to Chloe's room next. We met Daniel in the hall. He had the meds and passed them to Corey, who dry-swallowed one as we kept moving to the bedroom.

When we walked in, Tori squawked.

"Um, I don't know how you do things," she said, "but around here, the guys knock before they walk into a girl's room."

"The door was open," Corey said. "Wide open."

"No excuse," Hayley said. She was now sitting on Tori's bed, where they must have been chatting away, as if this was a sleepover party.

I told them about Corey's vision.

"And what do you want us to do?" Tori said.

"You? Nothing. Hayley? If Mr. Bae doesn't decide to go, we're leaving."

"If Kit doesn't decide to go, why would anyone go?" Tori said. So she called her father by his first name? I wasn't surprised.

Hayley glanced at Tori. "She's right. He's the grown-up

and the Cabal expert. That's why we came here. If he doesn't want to leave, I don't see the point."

"Then I guess you're staying," Corey said.

"What's going on in here?" said a voice from the doorway.

It was Dr. Fellows. As I repeated my explanation, Simon appeared behind her. When I got to the "we may be surrounded by Cabal hit men" part, Simon took off, thundering down the stairs.

When I finished, Dr. Fellows said, "And this was a vision you had, Corey?"

"Right."

"Are you sure?"

"Huh?"

She lowered her voice. "Is it possible that Derek . . . influenced this vision of yours?"

"What? No."

"Absolutely not," I said. "Derek's the one who cut it short. Accidentally, but still. And if by influence, you mean 'talked us into telling a lie to get everyone out tonight,' then I don't appreciate the insinuation, Dr. Fellows."

Her brows shot up to meet her hairline. Tori smirked and leaned back onto her pillow.

"Well, Maya, I don't know you yet, so you'll forgive me if I question you."

"I don't blame you. You don't know us. But you do know Derek and, sorry, but persuasion doesn't seem to be the guy's strong suit."

"She has a point, Lauren," Tori said.

Dr. Fellows shot her a look, which Tori met with a cool gaze.

"Also," Tori said, "I really think you'd know your niece better than that. I wouldn't put it past Derek to lie to get us out of here, but no way would Chloe let him pull others into the scheme." Before Dr. Fellows could answer, Tori turned to me. "I don't doubt tall, dark, and seriously cute had a vision, but I'm still going to wait for Kit's call on this one."

"Did she just call me cute?" Corey said.

Hayley turned on Tori. "Did you just flirt with my boyfriend?"

"Boyfriend?" Corey said.

"Are you coming?" I asked Corey. "Or staying to flirt back?"

"Bossy, isn't she?" Tori said.

"Yeah, I think it's hot," Corey said with a grin.

Daniel prodded me along before I could retort. Corey fell in beside us and we were at the bedroom door when Ash came running in.

He stopped in front of me. "There's definitely someone out there."

Tori stood. "Um, don't you think you should tell the person in charge here?"

Ash gave her a cold look, then stepped to the left, so he was addressing both me and Daniel. "There's definitely someone out there."

"Not really what I meant," Tori said.

"Don't really care," Ash said. He caught my sleeve and tugged. "Forget them. We're going. Now." He looked over at Hayley. "You coming, blondie?"

She hesitated.

"Whatever," he said, waving her off as he herded me out the door.

"Hold up," Hayley said, and hurried after us.

"I really don't think—" Dr. Fellows called.

"Really don't care," Ash called back.

"You guys are definitely related," Corey said as we jogged down the hall. "The only difference is that Maya is polite when she's getting in your face."

Ash snorted and started to reply.

"Wait!" I skidded to a halt halfway down the steps. "Where's Rafe?"

"Already outside," Ash said. "I took him scouting. He's standing guard on the porch. Now stop talking and move!"

FORTY-THREE

I TURNED LEFT AT the bottom of the stairs and headed for the living room.

Ash caught the back of my shirt. "The exit is this way."

Daniel brushed past us. "Yes, but we're going to take the extra minute to tell Kit and the others that we're leaving."

"Fine, go," Ash said. "Maya, stay with me."

I followed Daniel into the living room.

"Hey!" Ash said. "Both of you don't need—"

The back door banged open. Shoes pounded down the hall as Rafe raced in.

"They're coming," Rafe said. "I saw someone around the side of the garage. They shot out the lights on it."

Daniel was now in the living room doorway, hands braced

on either side as he leaned in, talking fast. Then he jogged back to us.

"Daniel!" Kit shouted. Daniel didn't stop. Kit swung out the door. "Hold on. They'll have the house surrounded. There's no place you can run."

"We're sure as hell not surrendering," Ash said.

"No," Chloe said. "There's an escape route in the basement."

"You guys take them down." Kit pushed Derek, Simon, and Chloe toward us. "I'll get Tori and Lauren."

When Chloe and the guys caught up, they started waving us down the hall. Ash didn't move.

"Come on," I said. "There's a way out."

"You really think so?" He tugged me aside, out of Derek's path. "A secret escape in the basement? Like hell. It's a trap."

"Why would they—?" I began.

"They're going to use us. Lock us in the basement and negotiate with the Cabals."

"We wouldn't do that," Chloe said.

"Why not?" Derek said. "It'd work."

"Really not helping, bro," Simon muttered.

"I'm being honest," Derek said. "It's a good plan. It isn't what we have in mind, but they don't know that. They don't know us. I don't blame them." He looked at Daniel, then me, his gaze shifting between us. "It's not a trick. I don't know how to convince you of that, but we can't stand here and argue."

"Split up," I said quickly. "Ash, if you have another idea, you do that with . . ." I hesitated and looked from Rafe to Daniel to Corey. "Take me. Guys—"

The back-door window shattered. Something dropped, hissing, on the floor, spinning, smoke swirling out.

"Gas!" Ash yelled. "Everyone down!"

We all dropped. I told them to pull their shirts up over their mouths, and a second canister crashed through a front window, then a third someplace else, only the explosion of glass reaching us. Smoke from the first canister filled the hall.

"Stairs," I said. "Where are the—?"

Fingers clasped my upper arm. It was Chloe, mouth covered, her slitted eyes already tearing up. Daniel reached over and grabbed a handful of my shirt hem.

"Everyone grab somebody," he called. "We're moving."

And so we did, a slow, awkward, blind snake crawling along the hallway. Someone bashed into a wall. I told them to move slowly and hold on—and to make sure whoever had them was still holding on. My words came out slurred, and I could feel myself blinking hard, not just against the smoke, but against a numb, floating feeling.

"It's a sedative!" I yelled. "Try not to breathe it and try to stay awake. We're almost there."

I had no idea if we were really "almost there" until I felt a rush of cool, clean air . . . and nearly toppled headfirst down the stairs. Chloe released my arm and I reached back for Daniel, guiding him onto the steps. We crawled down backward. When Corey tried to stand and walk, he lost his balance, woozy from the gas, and fell onto Daniel. Daniel and I managed to get him downstairs with Hayley's help.

We ended up in almost a heap at the bottom, everyone hunkered down together, sputtering and wheezing. Gas filtered through the open doorway until Derek—bringing up the rear—closed it and stumbled down the stairs.

I lifted my head and peered around. "Rafe? Where's Rafe?"

Derek stepped over us. "And where's Simon?"

No one answered either of us. I sprang up. Derek wheeled toward the stairs. Chloe shot up and grabbed him.

"Simon was beside me when the gas hit," she said. "He said someone should warn your dad. Rafe said he'd go with him. I said no, your dad would be fine, we just needed to get to the basement. Then I couldn't see and I thought he was right there."

"He went for your father," I said. "And Rafe went to help."

"And neither of you can go after them," Chloe said, jumping into our path when we started for the stairs. She turned to Daniel, arm shooting out as he tried to get around her. "None of us can go back. You know you can't. They're fine. Simon can take care of himself and he has Rafe. They'll watch out for each other."

I looked at Daniel. He rocked there, gaze on mine, ready to go after Rafe if I gave any sign that that's what I wanted him to do.

I took a deep breath. "Chloe's right."

When Derek hesitated, Chloe said, "If you leave, either I go with you and take the same risk or I stay here, with strangers. Without you."

He scowled at her.

"Yes, it's a low blow," she said. "But I'll use whatever works right now." She got to her feet, wiped her eyes again, and looked around. "Okay, I'm going to suggest we don't wait for Kit and the others. We get out of here before the bad guys break in. I'm guessing that's the plan—knock everyone out with gas, then come in and scoop them up."

"It's an old Nast trick," Ash said. "They won't wait long to swoop in, either."

As if in reply, booted footsteps thundered across the hardwood overhead.

"So where's this escape tunnel?" Corey asked.

"It's not really a tunnel," Chloe said as she waved for us to follow. "Beyond the basement is a cold cellar for storing vegetables and preserves. There's a chute from the barn."

"Which is now the garage," I said.

She nodded. "Kit installed a fire-escape ladder. That's why we rented this place."

She pulled open a door on the far side of the basement, then reached in and pulled a string. A bare bulb lit a corridor with cement walls and a dirt floor. She waved us in.

"Yeah, right." Ash caught my arm before I could walk in, then pointed at Chloe. "You first."

Derek muttered something and shoved past. He headed

into the dimly lit hall. We followed. The hallway passed a couple of rooms that must have been for storage at one time, the wooden shelves now rotting and dotted with dusty jars filled with gray preserves.

The hall ended at a rope ladder. Derek gave it a tug, then went up first. When I tried to follow, Ash elbowed me aside and cautiously ascended, peering through at the top before waving us up.

We came out in the barn/garage, as Chloe had said. Derek motioned for silence. I peered around. It was nearly pitch black—the only light coming through a break in the roof. But after being in the cold cellar, my eyes had adjusted. When I could make out a ladder leading to the hayloft, I tapped Derek's arm—figuring he'd have better night vision than Chloe. I pointed to the ladder and mouthed "safe?" He nodded and led us over to it. We went up.

At the top, mouldering straw covered the floor. I could smell feces. Cat or rat, I wasn't sure. I just kept my ears attuned for squeaks or hisses as we cleared spots and hunkered down.

Outside, all was silent. Or so it seemed, until we quieted down and I could pick up the distant murmur of voices. Then one grew louder.

"I want to speak to Dr. Inglis." It was Dr. Fellows. "Are you listening—?"

An outraged squawk, then muffled cries, as if someone had gagged her.

Derek winced. He shot a glance toward Chloe, but she didn't seem to have heard. He cast a glower at me, as if warning me not to tell her that her aunt had been taken. I wasn't about to.

A minute later, when I caught a noise below, I shot up, but Derek waved me down and went to the stairs. He leaned out. Then he climbed down a few stairs. A moment later he returned. Kit followed him. As Kit surveyed our faces, Derek headed back down a few steps to look around below. Then, almost simultaneously, they whispered, "Where's Simon?"

The next few minutes were a flurry of whispers and worries as they each realized Simon wasn't with the other one. Then I caught his voice in the distance. Derek heard it, too. He told Kit. They whispered together, but there was nothing anyone could do. The Cabals had Dr. Fellows, Tori, Rafe, and Simon.

"They aren't going to hurt your son," Hayley said. "Rafe left his sister with them."

Kit looked ill, but managed to nod. "Yes. They won't hurt him. Not if they hope to convince us to rejoin the fold."

Derek snorted. "Like that would ever happen."

Kit said nothing. But Derek's head whipped around to face his father.

"Dad?" he said.

"Simon will be fine," he said. "But if we hope to end this on our terms, we need to get everyone else out of here."

FORTY-FOUR

"THEY'VE GOT THE HOUSE surrounded," Ash said.

I looked over to see him perched on a rafter near Hayley.

"*House*, but not barn," he said. "But that still means they're very close."

"Which means we need to revert to our favorite ploy," Daniel murmured. "Divert their attention away from the barn so we can get out. Is there a back door?"

"There is," I said. "I saw it when we came in. But I vote for the aerial route if we can. The trees come up to the roofline, right?"

"They do," Ash said. "And there's a busted-out window back there. A decent branch comes close enough to grab. That was gonna be my suggestion."

I looked over at the others. "Anyone have tree-climbing issues?"

Obviously Ash and I didn't. Daniel, Hayley, and Corey said they'd be fine. Chloe hoped she would—she had gymnastics training. Mr. Bae joked that it would be his first time in a couple of decades. Derek said nothing.

"Derek?"

"It looks like I'll be the guy doing the distracting. I'm not trusting a tree branch to hold me."

"You're not playing decoy," Chloe said. She turned to us. "I'm sorry. I know that sounds like a cop-out, but he really can't. The last time we were in a fight against the St. Clouds, the orders were to tranq all of us except Derek. For him, it was shoot to kill. They don't trust werewolves."

"I think they've calmed down," Derek said. "They've been watching us for months and haven't tried to assassinate me yet."

Chloe put her hands on her hips. "And that's your definition of acceptance? Not going out of their way to kill you?"

"You're both right," Kit said. "I do believe they've realized Derek isn't the threat they expected, but I also don't trust them not to use excessive force."

"He's not going out there," Daniel said. "When I suggested that, I meant I'd do it."

"What?" I said.

"That's commendable, Daniel," Mr. Bae said. "But we do need to maintain our strongest negotiating position.

338

According to what Antone says, you and Maya are the most valuable subjects. You're both clearly successes."

"Negotiating position?" Derek said.

"I'll play decoy," Corey said. "Done it before. Got away, too. That's a good sign."

Kit shook his head. "We need you, too. The Cabals may not realize it, but you're also a success, if you're seeing visions. I'll go."

"You can't, either," I said. "You're the lawyer. We need you to negotiate."

"There's that word again," Derek muttered.

Ash dropped from the rafters. "Can we all stop falling on our swords and actually do something? Another couple minutes and those witches will cast their sensing spell and figure out where we're hiding."

"So you're volunteering to do it?" Corey asked.

Ash met his gaze. "No, I'm not. Anyone has a problem with that? Too bad."

"Well, I guess blondie is playing decoy," Hayley said, trying for a smile.

Daniel stepped forward. "No. You've already done that once."

"And I was pretty damned good at it, wasn't I? Face it, I'm an excellent actor."

"No," Daniel said. "There's enough bargaining power here. This is my turn."

"You stay. Help Maya. Fight the good fight. Blah-blah.

Personally, I didn't mind being captured. Hot food. Hot showers. I'm not really cut out for this running around stuff."

Hayley headed toward the ladder. When Daniel went after her, Derek caught his arm and yanked so hard that Daniel flew off his feet.

"Hey!" Daniel said, twisting in Derek's grip.

Derek just stood there, impassive. As Daniel struggled, Corey stepped in front of him. "Uh-huh. Time to let someone else be the big damn hero. We need you here."

"Hayley's gone," Ash said. "So how about we go, too. Before she distracts everyone for no reason."

Ash led the way and we crawled out across the rafters. Behind me Derek balked, but Chloe urged him on and his dad told him to just take another rafter if he was worried. He did.

I don't think Derek's weight would have made much difference. There were six of us, putting about eight hundred pounds of weight on a very old piece of wood. When it creaked, I swung over to the one Derek was using. Ash picked up speed and got to the window first. Daniel helped him clear the glass. Then Ash leaned out, peering into the night. When he gave the all clear, we started through. Ash went first, with me right behind. Daniel stood watch and made sure we waited our turn so we didn't overburden the branch.

As we crawled out, I could hear a commotion to the left—Hayley running through the woods, making enough racket to be a half dozen of us. Somewhere below, a shadow tore after her.

As Hayley crashed through the trees, we continued along. Ash and I swung to the next tree. Daniel followed. So did Chloe. Corey almost missed, but made it. Mr. Bae didn't try—just whispered for us to go ahead, spread out, and he and Derek would get on the ground as soon as they could, and travel that way.

At the next tree, I decided we should split up, Chloe and Corey taking the easy route. Daniel, Ash, and I crossed another tree, then another.

"Okay," Ash whispered. "We're spread out enough. Time to go—"

His gaze shot to the side. Before I could look, he knocked me so hard that I'd have fallen if Daniel hadn't grabbed me. Something hit Ash in the shoulder. He toppled. We tried to grab him, but he was a dead weight, and he fell from our hands, tumbling down, striking one branch before hitting the ground.

When I tried to go after him, Daniel caught me. I swiped at him, but he held me firm.

"It's a tranq dart, Maya," he said.

"I don't care. He—"

Daniel clapped a hand to my mouth as a dark-suited figure slipped from the trees and crouched beside Ash's sprawled body. The figure pressed a hand to his neck and nodded.

Daniel tugged me up and motioned to the branch above. I hesitated. Then another figure joined the first below, both armed, and I realized any rescue would turn into a group capture. So, after one last look down, I steeled myself and escaped with Daniel.

FORTY-FİVE

ANIEL AND I MOVED carefully, crossing to the next tree then waiting there until they finished scanning the treetops and decided Ash had been alone. They carried him away and we continued on.

Now and then I'd hear a tree limb creak, but that was it. Then I caught the faint sound of footfalls on the ground. When I peered over I could make out the pale shape of faces moving in the forest. Two of them. I squinted.

"Derek and Kit," I whispered.

Daniel nodded. We were about to head away from them when I heard the crackle of undergrowth. Derek froze, then yanked Kit down. Their faces vanished, their dark clothing blending into the night.

Daniel and I watched as two figures stepped through a cluster of trees. Men dressed in camouflage gear, carrying rifles. Tranquilizer rifles, I hoped. They were heading straight for where Derek and Kit were hiding.

I tensed, but they just kept looking around, not calling for backup, unaware of how close Derek and Kit were.

Daniel had tensed, too. His jaw worked, as if he instinctively wanted to use his shout. Of course he couldn't. Invoke his power and every Cabal guy within a kilometer radius would come running.

I laid my hand on his. "It's okay. Derek knows they're there."

Daniel nodded and rubbed my thumb. I looked down at my hand on his. There was a time, not long ago, when I wouldn't have done that. Rafe was right. Something had changed, and I don't think either Daniel or I had even realized that. It was the little things, like this, reaching out to reassure each other, the chaos giving us an excuse.

I leaned down to focus on the men below. If they walked under us, we could have leaped on them. They didn't. But they were still heading straight for—

Derek pounced, slamming one guy to the ground before his partner had time to react. I heard a sizzle, and a bolt like lightning flew from Kit's fingers. The other guy stumbled back. Kit took him down with a right hook. Beside him, Derek let out a hiss of pain. I didn't see what had happened—presumably his opponent used his supernatural powers.

Derek flipped his target onto his stomach and pinned him there as Kit fought with his. At a thump from below, I glanced over to see that the spot beside me was empty. Daniel was on the ground, running toward them. He grabbed the guns and threw them aside, then helped Kit subdue his target.

As the fight ended, I crawled closer. I stayed in the tree, though, where I had a better vantage point if anyone else came. They had just gotten both men secured when Corey tore from the woods.

"I missed the fight?" he whispered. "Damn."

Derek wheeled on him. "Where's Chloe? You were supposed to be—"

"I'm right here," whispered Chloe as she stepped through.

I inched along until I was nearly over them. Daniel noticed me first and nodded. Kit crouched to take a radio from one man. I realized they were unconscious. Knocked out or tranquilized. Daniel bent to take the other radio.

"Guns?" Corey asked.

"Just take the darts," Kit whispered.

"Is it okay if I stay grounded?" Corey asked. "The monkey route really isn't my thing."

Kit said it seemed safe enough now, and asked Daniel if he'd stay down, too, keeping the fighters on the ground. Daniel glanced up at me, just a quick check. I nodded.

"I'm staying here," I whispered down. "I'll keep an aerial eye out for trouble."

"I'll come with you," Chloe said.

Derek tried to stop her. She said it made sense for her to be in the trees with me in case of a ground attack, and that convinced him. Not that it mattered, I think—she'd have done what she wanted. She obviously didn't take his crap. Still, it would drive me crazy, constantly needing to remind my boyfriend that I could handle myself just fine. My brother was bad enough.

Chloe climbed up and we set off. The guys broke into pairs to get a little distance from one another, so there weren't four of them tromping together. They stayed close enough to keep an ear on the others in case they needed help. Chloe and I followed from the trees.

As we moved, I could hear the distant noise of the searchers, but none got close again. I kept an ear out for Hayley, hoping she might have avoided capture, but there was no sound or sign of her, and I knew she'd been taken.

Finally, Derek led us to a spot he'd picked on the edge of the woodlot. There was a house just past the tree line. It was dark—everyone gone or asleep.

Chloe and I climbed down and found Kit easing open the door on a pickup.

"We'll take this," he said. "Boys? Get up front and push when I give the signal. We're going to roll it out of the drive, then I'll get it started. Everyone can pile in the back while I do that."

Corey looked over sharply. Kit was stealing the truck? I guess I shouldn't be surprised. He'd been on the run for years; he'd do whatever it took to get his kids out of here. Daniel didn't seem shocked at all. He's all for law and order—unless it interferes with common sense and necessity.

When Kit released the brake, the guys rolled the pickup out of the drive. With Derek's super strength it was easily done, and Kit decided to have them keep pushing—from the rear now—down to the first side road. He got around the corner, then we crawled into the truck bed and lay down while he hot-wired it. Within minutes we were off, leaving the Cabals behind.

We drove for two hours, then ditched the truck a couple of kilometers from a roadside motel and walked back to that motel.

Mr. Bae checked in while we hid. Then we made our way in twos to the room. Mr. Bae left to make a call on the prepaid cell he'd picked up in the first major town. He was calling Calvin Antone to begin the process of negotiation.

On the car ride, he'd told Derek and Chloe about Antone's suggestion. To my surprise, it was Chloe who'd protested, while Derek just sat there, processing. Chloe was worried about how the Cabal treated werewolves. Beyond that, though, she wasn't personally averse to the idea. They'd been running for months and had all come to realize there was no foreseeable end to that running. They'd talked about moving to Australia, but no one was particularly keen on that. Even if they made it there, it would involve more hiding and more lying.

It wasn't hard for Kit to convince Chloe that he'd never take any step that would endanger Derek. He'd uprooted his life a decade ago and spent the intervening years on the road to protect him. Now Derek had come fully into his powers and he was, by any standard, a success. Chloe's own powers had apparently gotten off to a rough start, but she was also a Project Genesis success. Same went for Tori. They'd all learned to control any side effects and were super-powered supernaturals, which made them valuable. Simon wasn't showing the same power boost, but he hadn't displayed any negative issues, either—just a smooth transition into a supernatural.

Still, the Nasts *had* been the ones to kidnap Kit and hold him captive for months. He seemed remarkably unconcerned about that. It was business, he said. He'd been part of a top-secret science group and the Nasts wanted to know more about it. His imprisonment had been more like house arrest. The worst part of it had been worrying about his boys, but he couldn't ask the Nasts to check on them without, in effect, handing them over, so he'd had to trust they were safe while he worked on getting free.

When he was released, it was actually Mattias Nast who'd helped. The same Mattias Nast now heading the work in Vancouver. Not a nice guy, Kit admitted, but Nast was a businessman, inclined to be reasonable if it helped him climb the corporate ladder. Bringing us all to the fold would certainly do that.

No one was forgetting what the Edison Group did to Liz Delaney and a couple of other subjects. Not forgetting. Not forgiving. But the people who'd done that—Dr. Davidoff and others—were dead. That knee-jerk reaction to problems seemed to have died with them. And it wasn't the St. Clouds we hoped to deal with anyway. As "nasty" as the Nasts were, Kit felt he could work with them . . . at least for a few years, long enough for us to grow up into the kind of powerful supernaturals they wanted, and use those very skills to fight back.

Is fighting back what Antone expected? He'd never said it, but he'd hinted that he didn't expect us to grow up to be Cabal wage slaves. Just let the Cabal take care of us until we were old enough to take care of ourselves. Maybe that meant fighting back. Maybe it just meant breaking away safely. Either way, it was freedom, something we had no shot at otherwise.

All this wasn't to say we could trust the Cabals. We couldn't. But Antone had provided a detailed proposal for negotiations, and Kit thought it was workable.

First, though, Kit needed to speak to Antone.

So he did that. When he came back almost an hour later, he said only that he needed to wait for a call. That came twenty minutes later. He took it outside and returned to say a preliminary negotiation meeting had been arranged. It would be tomorrow in Buffalo, where their ordeal had begun, and he would attend alone while we stayed here in Pennsylvania.

While Kit had been doing all that, Chloe had managed to make contact with Liz again, and she was outside, patrolling. That let us relax a little—you can't beat an invisible guard. Though we'd napped in the truck, everyone was exhausted. Kit said he'd stay awake and "make a few calls" while we got some sleep.

349

FORTY-SIX

I WOKE TO A rap on the door. Kit had left the lights off with the drapes pulled, so it took a moment to get my bearings. When the knock came again, I shot up and looked wildly around. Kit was walking to the door.

"Don't—!" I began.

Corey cut me off. "The bad guys aren't going to knock, Maya."

Kit looked out the peephole. Then he spun to us.

"Don't think of going out the bathroom window," called a vaguely familiar, but muffled voice. "It's covered."

"We're just here to talk, Kit," said a woman's voice. "That's what you want, isn't it? To talk."

Something flickered on our side of the door. Moreno appeared. *Inside* our hotel room. I fell back in surprise. Daniel was on his feet. Derek was already barreling toward

Moreno, who reached out and quickly undid the chain, then vanished. The door flew open before Kit could leap forward and relock it.

In walked Dr. Inglis, flanked by two men with guns. Real guns.

I turned to look toward the bathroom.

"Uh-uh," Moreno said. "Already warned you about that, Miss Maya. But you can go check if you like."

Beside me, Chloe was whispering. To Liz, it seemed. From the way Chloe was reassuring her, Liz had been around back when they arrived. An invisible guard is helpful, but not perfect.

"Can she scout now?" I whispered.

Chloe nodded and told Liz to see what we were up against. Moreno and the others didn't seem to notice—they were too busy convincing everyone not to bother resisting. We knew better than to try as soon as we saw the other two armed men blocking the door. These two had tranquilizer guns. Four armed guys here and more out back. Plus two supernaturals—a witch and a teleporting half-demon. Not odds we could take on.

"It's been a long time, Kit," Dr. Inglis said. "You've been busy."

"So have you."

"But I've been more successful in my endeavors. I told you Project Genesis was doomed. The real money was in Phoenix. Genetic tinkering with existing types will never be as valuable as reintroducing extinct types." She pulled a chair from a tiny dinette, sat, and waved for him to take the other one. "So let's talk."

"This wasn't the plan."

"Because it *isn't* the plan. Right now, executives from both Cabals are hopping onto their jets and flying to Buffalo. I'm beating them to the punch. I had the advantage of knowing exactly where you were. Thanks to Maya."

"Wh-what?" I scrambled up. "No. If you're saying I betrayed—"

"We know you didn't," Daniel said, pulling me down.

Corey seconded that and said, "She's lying to divide the ranks."

"No, Maya did tell me . . . unintentionally. When she was at the Vancouver house, I implanted a tracking device. The St. Clouds have been working on an undetectable one ever since last spring, when the Genesis subjects escaped. I used the latest prototype. Apparently, it worked. When I realized you'd joined Kit, I knew I couldn't hold this meeting at the farmhouse—the St. Clouds might notice. So I had an associate tell the Nasts he'd overheard Maya and Rafe talking about finding Kit. I dutifully informed the Nasts that the St. Clouds knew where Kit was. A joint raid was born. I managed to divert attention enough for some of you to escape. Now you're here, out of sight of the Cabals, and we can talk."

"What do you want?" Kit asked.

"Not Simon or Derek or Tori or Chloe. That's your main concern, isn't it?"

"I'm concerned about all—"

"Very noble. But your focus is on your own children and Chloe. You can have them. In return, I want the Phoenix subjects."

"Why?"

She laughed. "Didn't I just mention how valuable they are? I can have a dozen buyers lined up in a week. International Cabals, independent brokers . . ."

"Sell us?" I said. "We're not commodities."

"Oh, yes, dear. You are."

"But . . . Calvin Antone. You . . ."

"Your father is desperate. Desperate men are easily fooled, particularly by middle-aged women who play the love-struck fool. He thought he was using me. It was the other way around."

I turned on Moreno. "And you. He trusted you."

Moreno shrugged. "I was happy to be his wingman while it seemed to my advantage. Then I got a better offer. It happens."

"If it's an outside deal, how will I get my kids back?" Kit asked. "The Cabals have them."

Chloe's and Derek's heads both whipped Kit's way.

"You're considering this?" Chloe said.

"I can get them," Dr. Inglis said. "We'll take Corey now, as a gesture of good faith from you. Then I will take Daniel for your son and Maya for your daughter."

"Dad?" Derek said.

Kit didn't answer him. He didn't even look over.

Chloe looked from us to Kit, her blue eyes wide. "Y-you c-can't—"

Derek leaped to his feet. "I won't let you do this, Dad. These kids came to you for help."

I gaped at Derek. Even Chloe looked confused. I might have known the guy for less than twenty-four hours, but short of demonic possession, I couldn't imagine him saying that. Derek was a wolf and I knew enough about pack canines to know—as he'd shown already—that his priority was his family. The welfare of strangers came a very distant second.

As he argued, though, Kit looked . . . relieved.

Daniel looked at both of them, then jumped up beside Derek. "You are not going to trade us for your kids. After everything we've been through? I won't let that happen."

Kit stood and faced the two, his back to the intruders. He lifted his hands. "Stay calm, boys. Just stay calm. We need to make a deal, but I promise no one will get hurt."

"No way," Derek said. "I cannot believe you would . . ."

As he ranted, Kit mouthed something to Daniel. Daniel hesitated, but Derek glanced over with a nod.

"Just relax, boys," Kit said. "Look at Maya and Corey. They're being reasonable. I need you two to follow—"

"No!" Daniel shouted—his sonic boom shout was so loud, my ears rang.

The shout sent Kit and the guards flying. Everyone who'd been behind Daniel only wobbled, only those in front of him fell. It took a split second for most of us to realize what had happened, and that the guards were on the floor, stunned by that sonic shout.

Derek hadn't hesitated. As soon as Daniel shouted, he charged. He grabbed the gun from the nearest guard and threw it aside as Daniel tackled the next one. Corey went after the third and I pounced on the fourth. I got the gun easily—my target was still on the floor, stunned. I kicked it over to Chloe, who was gathering them up.

Beside me, Corey was struggling with his guard, who'd snapped out of it and was on his feet again. Daniel raced over to help. The gun fired. Daniel staggered back.

The other guards were up now, fighting back, but I saw none of that. Just Daniel stumbling, Daniel falling. Daniel with blood blossoming on his chest. Daniel shot.

I screamed. I barely heard it in the din around me. Everyone was shouting. Everyone was fighting. No one had noticed Daniel fall. Just me. No one was running to help him. Just me.

I raced over as Corey continued struggling with his guard, oblivious. Out of the corner of my eye, I saw Corey get the guy in a headlock. Saw him look over. Saw him notice Daniel. His eyes rounded and the blood drained from his face. As I ran to Daniel's side, Corey began to release his grip on his target, as if he'd forgotten he was still holding him.

"No!" I said.

He snapped out of it, then hauled his guy out of the way as I dropped to the floor. Daniel was blinking to stay conscious, his breathing shallow.

"It's okay," I said as I tugged his shirt off to get a better look. "You're okay."

He wasn't. I could tell that by his breathing and his face, ghostly white, his lips trembling.

Someone knocked into me. I twisted, ready to shove, claw, whatever I had to do. I felt a faint twitch in my hands, and terror shot through me. I couldn't shift. Not now. But it was only Derek bumping me as he grappled with a guard. They toppled the other way, and that first lick of rage subsided, letting me thankfully focus on Daniel.

The bullet had gone into his side. The right side, away from his heart. Were there any vital organs there? I should know, but my panicked brain kept throwing up images of animal anatomy instead. My hands shook as I pressed the wadded-up shirt to his wound to stanch the blood.

"I liked them better when they were using tranq darts," Daniel whispered, managing a weak smile.

"Don't talk."

He reached to touch my hand and I looked at his face. There was a smattering of freckles across his nose, usually invisible unless he'd been out in the sun, but I could see them now, his skin so pale, I stared at them, then lifted my gaze to his eyes and felt my heart squeeze so hard my eyes filled with tears.

I love you. I'm not sure if it's the way you want me to. I think it might be. But I know that I love you. I absolutely love you.

"Maya?" He wiped tears from my cheek. "It's bad, huh?"

"No," I said, snapping out of it. "No, it's not. You'll be fine."

Someone grabbed my arm and yanked me to my feet, and there was a moment where I had no idea where I was, why someone was with us. Then the room snapped back into focus, and I heard the grunts and the smacks, saw the blur of fists and bodies.

One of the guards had me. He whipped me around, arm going to my neck. I bit him. Didn't think about it. Just saw that bare arm coming toward my face and chomped down. He yowled. I started to let go. Then I saw Daniel on the floor, and I bit down harder, kicking back at my captor as my mouth filled with blood.

Let me go or I'll kill you. I swear I'll kill you if you keep me from him.

The guard continued to yowl, but didn't release his grip. Then someone grabbed him from behind. His arm loosened. I stopped biting and jammed my thumb into the wound, grinding it. He let go then, screaming, as Corey whipped him off me.

357

I scrambled down beside Daniel again. I pressed my fingers to the shirt wadded against his wound, closed my eyes, and focused on helping him. On healing him. I imagined the bullet in his chest and imagined the tissues around it sealing off, blood vessels closing, keeping him safe.

When I opened my eyes, he was even paler, his pupils starting to dilate.

"No!" I said. "Do you feel that? It's shock. Don't go into shock."

He nodded and swallowed.

I clasped his hand with my free one. "Stay with me, okay? Please. Just stay with me."

He looked up at me and smiled. "You know I will. Always."

His eyelids fluttered, then closed.

"No!"

I grabbed his shoulders and his eyes opened.

"Okay," he mumbled. "I'm okay. Just give me a sec."

He rubbed his face with both hands, and some of the color started to return. Then a hand touched my shoulder.

I looked to see Chloe kneeling beside me. "Can he move, Maya?"

I looked around. Three of the guards were unconscious, two with tranquilizer darts sticking out of them. One sat in the corner, cradling his arm, bone sticking from it, his eyes wide with shock. There were two more—presumably the ones who'd been outside, including the one I'd bitten. Corey, Kit, and Derek were subduing them. Dr. Inglis was unconscious on the floor. And Moreno? He was nowhere to be seen.

"Can he move?" Chloe repeated.

"He shouldn't—" I began.

"I can," Daniel said. "I'll just need a little help."

Across the room, Derek slammed his opponent's head against the wall. Kit hit the other with a spell like a lightning bolt and Corey jumped him with a dart.

Kit looked over. "Can he—?"

Chloe nodded.

"I'm not sure he should . . ." I began.

"I have to," Daniel said.

"It won't be far," Kit said as he hurried over to help Daniel.

"I've got him," Derek said. "You'll need to clear the way with spells."

"Liz says we're clear," Chloe said. "The parking lot's empty, but we should go out the back if we can."

"And fast," Corey said. "This guy over here's starting to stir."

We got into the bathroom. The window was big enough for Derek to get through, so we'd all make it. They broke the glass and cleared it. Chloe went out. Derek next, to help lower Daniel, but as soon as we tried to boost him up to the window, blood gushed from his wound.

"We have to go out the front," I said. "Everyone else can go out here. Derek? Can you help me take him?"

Derek nodded. "Dad? Take Chloe and Cor—"

Chloe cut him off, talking fast, "Liz said reinforcements just arrived. A big black SUV full of big guys in black suits. We need to go this way."

"I can do it," Daniel said. "Just hand me that towel. It'll stop the bleeding long enough . . ."

He trailed off as Kit edged past us, through the bathroom door, back into the bedroom. Derek strode after him. One of the guards was stirring. So was Dr. Inglis, groggily pushing her way up.

"Dad?"

Kit pulled back a corner of the drape. He peered out, then turned to us. "It's not reinforcements. Not theirs, anyway. Do you still want to cut a deal?" He looked at me. "I can get us out of here, then we can work on getting my children and your friends back. We can fight. Or we can follow the plan."

Fight or surrender. The answer seemed so obvious, didn't it? If we had an ounce of guts, of inner strength, of pride, we should go down fighting. Never stop. Never surrender.

Fighting could mean freedom. That had been our goal all along. For the Genesis kids, who'd taken down the Edison Group for their freedom. For us, who'd escaped a fire, helicopter crash, and kidnappings for our freedom. We'd lost friends for that freedom. Friends who were now waiting for us to come back and save them. How could we even consider giving up?

Because sometimes fighting wasn't the strong choice or

the smart choice. It was just the stubborn, proud choice. We'd decided to negotiate. Just because we'd beaten Dr. Inglis and her goons didn't change the situation. Kit and his group had done a lot more than that, and they'd still admitted that it hadn't really gotten them anywhere, hadn't even gotten them freedom—just the illusion of it, hiding, terrified of capture, all the while being monitored by the St. Clouds.

Out in the world, we were mice, not just fleeing the cats on our tails, but hawks and owls and weasels and a host of other predators that were just waiting for the opportunity to swoop in and steal us. We weren't ready to fight back and we weren't ready to keep ourselves free and enjoy any kind of decent life. We needed to take what the Cabals offered, until they made us ready, in spite of themselves.

"Negotiate," I said.

The others agreed. Kit nodded and pulled open the door, said, "Sir," and stepped back.

The man didn't look like a "sir." He was probably in his late twenties. His blond hair was pulled back in a small ponytail. His brilliant blue eyes reminded me of Mattias Nast's but there was no chill in them, just calm. He was dressed in casual pants and a pullover. Guards flanked him, hulking guys bigger than Derek, both wearing shades.

Someone strolled past them. A familiar figure. Moreno, just sauntering in, smiling, as if quite pleased with himself.

"Looks like your timing was a little off," the young man said to Moreno.

Moreno shrugged. "Close enough. They handled it."

"Mr. Nast," Kit said to the young man, his chin dipping in a respectful nod.

"Sean, please," the young man murmured as he walked into the room, surveying everything. His gaze went straight to Daniel as Derek helped him back into the room. He spun to his guards. "Get a medic in here. Now."

Sean Nast. I remembered Antone had been told this would be the man in charge of the operation, not Mattias. Antone had wanted Sean.

"Sean," Dr. Inglis said as she pushed to her feet. "This isn't what it looks like."

"You will call me Mr. Nast." Sean's eyes chilled as they swung her way. "You've attempted to sabotage an operation organized by your employer. That's treason."

She staggered forward, bleating excuses. Sean waved for the remaining guard to take her and called others into the room.

"Clean this up," he said, waving at the guards on the floor, as if they were pieces of litter.

Two medics came in then and rushed to Daniel. They got him onto a stretcher and took him out. When I tried to follow, the female medic stopped me.

"Let her go with you," Sean said. He turned to me with a faint smile. "Maya, isn't it?"

"Yes, sir."

He nodded and waved for me to follow the medics. Outside,

two state police cars blocked the motel room entrance. Between them was an ambulance. That startled me . . . until I realized the people in them had to be Cabal employees, pretending to be real emergency personnel, as they waved away onlookers. Commandeering police cars and ambulances? Now I realized why Antone said we couldn't fight the Cabals.

I followed the medics to the ambulance and stayed out of their way as they checked Daniel. As I'd hoped, the bullet hadn't done any serious damage, but they did need to get him to a hospital for a better look and possible surgery. They had a clinic in Philadelphia—a special medical clinic for supernaturals, staffed by supernaturals. He'd go there by private jet. I'd accompany him and the others would follow.

FORTY-SEVEN

MORENO WAS ASSIGNED AS our security detail. Sean Nast came in the jet with us, so he could arrive in advance of the others. On the way he explained what had happened. Part of Antone's plan had been contacting Sean and getting him involved. At the same time, Moreno had gained Dr. Inglis's trust enough for her to tell him of her plan after the farmhouse raid. He'd then told Antone, who'd gone straight to Sean.

They hadn't been able to arrive before Dr. Inglis launched her attack, but they'd been on their way.

"It would have been nice if you found a way to tell us rescue was coming," I said to Moreno when Sean paused to take a call. "Or helped out during the fight."

He only arched his brows, as if the suggestion was preposterous.

"After all we've been through, you should have trusted me," he said.

I snorted a laugh at that. "Yeah, because you're such a trustworthy guy."

"Oh, I am, for the right people, under the right circumstances. It's a flexible concept."

"Don't expect me to forget you tried to shoot me, with a real gun."

"Because you looked like a mountain lion, attacking your daddy, who is one of those 'right people.' I'm a damned fine shot. I wouldn't have hit you if I didn't need to, and if I did I'd have only winged you. If you're hoping for an apology, Miss Maya, you won't get it. Pull that stunt again, and I'll pull my gun again. And maybe this time, I'll hit you."

I glowered at him. He smiled.

We got to the clinic and Daniel went in for surgery. He was stable and there was no risk . . . or no more than the usual risk that comes with any surgery, but I tried not to think of that.

There was a Cabal satellite office next door to the clinic. That's where Sean took me after Daniel had been prepped for surgery. They'd cleared out the employees for our negotiation meeting, and when we walked in it was eerily silent. Then I heard the quick march of footsteps. Antone rounded a corner. He saw me, picked up his pace, and caught me up in an embrace. I didn't return the hug, but didn't push him away, either.

When I heard more footsteps, I looked up to see Rafe, stepping from a room. He was grinning, with Ash and Corey behind him. Antone waved them back. When I drew closer, I spotted Kit, Sam, Hayley, Chloe, Derek, Tori, and Simon inside what looked like a boardroom.

"Everyone's here except Kenjii and Annie, and only because we didn't want to stress them out with a long plane ride." Antone patted my back, leaned down to my ear and whispered. "It's almost over, Maya. Just hang in there."

As we walked into the room, there were murmured hellos and a few hugs, but attention quickly shifted to the guy who was with us—for most of them, a stranger.

Sean introduced himself, then Kit introduced everyone else. When he got to Tori, Sean's smile widened.

"Ah, yes," he said. "The other witch-sorcerer."

She frowned. "There's another one?"

"Savannah, my little sister." He paused. "Well, not so little. She turned twenty last month. If everything here works out, you'll have to meet her someday. Not anytime soon, I'm afraid—too many people know about the experiments already."

Kit introduced Derek, and Chloe stiffened, her gaze fixed on Sean's face, waiting for his reaction. He just smiled and shook Derek's hand.

"He's a werewolf," Tori said.

He looked at Derek. "I hear you're Changing already. How is that going?" A small laugh. "Hellishly painful, I've heard, meaning it's a dumb question. But otherwise? Everything's all right?"

Derek nodded.

Tori moved closer. "I thought Cabals had a problem with werewolves."

"They do. An old prejudice. But that sister I mentioned? She grew up spending summers with the werewolf Pack."

"The one near Syracuse?" Chloe asked.

He smiled. "Heard some stories? I can imagine. I certainly wouldn't want them as enemies, but the Alpha is a good man. Again, I'm in no rush to introduce you all to the rest of the supernatural world. Not until you're older. But if Derek has werewolf issues, I can get answers from the best source."

"So what happens now?" Tori asked.

"We talk about what comes next. Now that I've learned this project exists, I've convinced my grandfather—the CEO—to put me in charge. Since most people expect me to succeed him, they tend to listen to me." He sobered. "I know what you guys really want is freedom. Just reunite you with your parents, let you go and leave you alone. But even if I could convince the Cabals to do that—which I can't—it wouldn't take long for you to land on someone else's radar, as you've already seen. What we're going to try to do today is come up with a compromise. We give you as much freedom as we can and as much support as you need and we hope that in doing so, we'll eventually convince you that working for a Cabal someday isn't quite the worst-case scenario you expect."

"So this is about grooming future employees," Tori said.

Sean nodded. "Very valuable future employees. It's not charity or civic duty—I'll be clear about that up front. It's like any other investment—we're willing to take the financial risk in hopes of a very nice payoff. But for now, our focus is on reaching a compromise everyone can live with."

There were representatives from both Cabals waiting to negotiate. Antone and Kit would speak for us.

Corey stepped forward. "We'd like Maya to represent Project Phoenix." He turned to Antone. "You seem to be on our side, but after running from you for a week, I'm not taking that chance." He looked over at Kit. "And you seem to be on our side, too, but you've got your own kids in this. I want Maya to speak for me."

Do I sound like a coward if I say I wished Daniel could join me? There was a time when I'd have leaped at the chance to speak for my friends. But now, after all we'd been through, I'd learned a little humility. I won't say my confidence was shaken, but it was, perhaps, tamped down to a more manageable level. I had doubts. I had worries. As uncomfortable as that felt, I think it made me better suited to step into those negotiations than I would have been. My actions and my decisions had consequences for all of us and if I wanted to be a leader, I could never forget that. So I agreed, with trepidation.

As Antone said, it was almost over. No more running. No more hiding. No more fighting. Just talking. But of everything I'd gone through in the last few weeks, nothing was harder—or more terrifying—than those negotiations. I was bargaining for my future and for the futures of my friends. If they agreed to my deal, and things went wrong later, it would be my fault. If they didn't agree because of some concession I failed to win, it would be my fault.

The plan Kit and Antone proposed wasn't much different than what I had in mind. It was better, actually—Kit had the legal experience to push harder, even if we were unlikely to win those concessions.

Partway through the meeting, the clinic called to say Daniel was out of surgery and awake. That made it easier for me to focus.

Finally, we came to an agreement. Was it perfect? No. Did I completely trust the Cabals to abide by it? No. But Kit seemed satisfied and I knew he had his children's best interests at heart, which meant I had to trust his judgment.

The next step was to tell the others. Did they pat me on the back and say I'd done an amazing job? Of course not. I had to explain why we'd made certain concessions and what we'd tried—and failed—to win. Corey was most wholeheartedly behind the plan. Rafe knew I'd done my best and seemed satisfied. Hayley and Sam grudgingly agreed it seemed the best solution. The biggest surprise, though, came from Ash, who muttered that he wasn't promising anything, but he'd stick around and see how it played out. And so, with the most lukewarm response to my endeavors, I got the most satisfying response, the one that truly told me I hadn't totally screwed up. My brother would stay.

They took me to Daniel next. He was up already, trying to use his persuasive powers to convince the doctors to let him join us next door. As soon as I heard his voice, my heart jumped and I wanted to break into a run, like I had in the park when I'd seen him by the fire. I'd told myself then that I was just so happy and relieved to see he was okay, and of course that was part of it, but there was more. I always felt something when I saw him, whether we'd been apart for days or hours. My heart jumped and my pulse quickened and I felt myself grinning, the very sound of his voice making me happy and relaxed and centered in a way nothing else did. It was like the universe clicked into place when Daniel was there. It always had.

I stood there, outside the door where he couldn't see me, and I tried to look at him. I could see him just fine, but I didn't mean that. I meant look at him. As a guy. As soon as I tried, though, it was like my brain threw up a barrier. Off-limits. Taboo. I wasn't supposed to look at him that way, because he was Serena's and even now, a year after her death, I'd kept thinking that, kept feeling that. It had made things easier. *Do not look at him like that, because if you do, you'll have to face things you're not ready to face, things you've been feeling since he really was Serena's.*

I've said that I let Serena win that game two years ago because I didn't feel that way about Daniel. That wasn't true. I let her win because I'd been starting to feel that way about Daniel, starting to watch him in the boxing ring, watch him stripping off his shirt and pants to swim with us, and I'd been feeling things I wasn't ready to feel. It was all too confusing. And embarrassing. So I let Serena win, and then he was hers and I would never look at my best friend's guy that way, so the problem was solved. Except it wasn't. Not really. I just took what I was feeling and relabeled it as simple friendship. A really close friendship that no one was allowed to interfere with, not even a guy I genuinely liked.

So where did that leave me? The same place I was two years ago. Confused. Because now there was Rafe and he wasn't just a substitute or a distraction.

Daniel noticed me then, and when he did, he broke into a grin. I froze there a second, before he called, "You coming in?" and I did. I went in and told him about the deal I'd brokered with the Cabals.

When I finished, he caught my hand and pulled me closer. "You okay?"

"I'm not the one who got shot."

"Yes, but I think you might have had the harder ordeal. I know that wasn't easy and I wish I could have been there, but obviously I didn't need to be. You did great. Better than great." He pulled me into a hug. "You did perfect."

$$\text{\textasciitilde} \qquad \text{\textasciitilde} \qquad \text{\textasciitilde}$$

"This looks familiar," I said as I looked around the helicopter, seated behind the pilot, Daniel beside me.

"Except this time, I'm not unconscious on the floor," Rafe said from my other side.

"Just keep your seat belt on," Daniel said. "Until this bullet wound heals, I'm in no shape to hang outside helicopter doors."

"How many times are you planning to mention that bullet wound?" Corey called from the seat behind us.

"Um, I think this is the first time I brought it up."

"Well, stop." He shook his head. "Big damn hero." He looked around. "Does anyone else think that putting us on a helicopter really doesn't send the right message of peace?"

"Which is why they said we could wait for the private jet to come back from Vancouver."

It was true—they'd fully understood that we might not want to climb into a helicopter after that fateful flight from Salmon Creek. But everyone was tired of waiting. So we'd agreed to the helicopters—two of them.

We tried to stay calm during the flight, but everyone was anxious. Excited and not sure we dared to be excited. The flight landed on schedule, at the airport they'd promised. Then we had to go through Customs.

"Canada?" Ash said. "You didn't say it was in Canada."

"I said Ontario."

"I thought you meant Ontario, California."

"Seriously?" Tori said, rolling her eyes. "A helicopter to California? You may be hot, but your sister clearly inherited all the brains in the family."

"Did she call me hot?" Ash whispered to me, looking more annoyed than he ever did when someone called him a jerk.

"She hasn't been on a date in six months," Derek rumbled behind us. "No offense, but as long as you aren't related to her, you're fair game. Hell, even—"

Tori spun on him. "I didn't know."

"Um, wait a sec," Corey said. "So Ash is hot and I'm seriously cute? Is there a difference?"

"Yes," Hayley said, and propelled him through the line.

FORTY-EİGHT

THE VANS TOOK US deep into the wilderness outside of
Algonquin Park. As I stared out at the forest I started
to relax and started to think maybe, just maybe, this
would all be okay.

We'd been getting updates through Sean on the fallout
from everything. Dr. Inglis was in Cabal custody. Annie was
still being treated, but they were bringing her out to join us
tomorrow. Nicole was also undergoing treatment, but we had
been assured that no matter how much progress she made,
she'd never rejoin our group. As for my own regression issues,
Antone said we could look at those right away.

Before Annie arrived with Kenjii, there were others coming. Very important others. Our families.

When I'd won this concession from the Cabals, there had
been strings attached. Our parents could never know that

the people who'd arranged this happy reunion were actually the ones responsible for the separation. There was no way to explain that, especially to my parents, still reeling at the news that not only did supernaturals exist, but their daughter was one of them.

Which parents had always known their kids were part of an experiment? The Morrises and the Tillsons. That's why the Tillsons got custody of Sam—the St. Clouds had asked them to take her in with the false story that she was their niece. Chief Carling hadn't known; her husband was the one who'd agreed to take part in the experiment and moved them to Salmon Creek. She had, however, known that supernaturals exist—her family were sileni, like her husband's. So she'd understood that the St. Clouds were a Cabal, but had been told they were developing medicine for supernaturals, which explained all the secrecy. Daniel's father had found out when his wife left.

Now all the parents knew about Project Phoenix and their children's role in it. Those who hadn't known were furious, of course. But that anger was mitigated by the lie that the Cabals had "found" their children and returned them. The fire, they said, had been set by a rival group, who'd stolen us and faked the crash, complete with DNA. But the Nasts figured it out, tracked them down, and rescued us. So they were the heroes in this story and now, to make up for everything we'd been through, they were going to give us a new town and everything we needed to be happy, healthy teen supernaturals. Did it make sense? I don't know. I think our parents were just too happy right now to question it.

Was *I* happy with a version of reality where the Cabals were the good guys? Of course not. Would I always be able to keep the truth from my parents? Probably not. But as much as the lies hurt, I knew this was best, for now.

The van continued through the forest. We went from a two-lane highway to a narrow paved road to a dirt lane to something that was little more than tracks heading into the brush. Then, without warning, it opened up into what looked like an overgrown parking lot. A half dozen trucks and vans were already there. Cleaning and repair crews, Sean said. Making the place ready for our arrival. "The place" seemed to be a two-story wood building, but when we got out, Sean led us around it and we found ourselves at the edge of a lake circled by wooden cabins.

Everyone spread out, walking to the lake or perching on the picnic tables.

"For now, you'll live in the cabins," Sean explained. "We'll get them cleaned up, of course, but we'll have construction crews here tomorrow. They'll tear down some cabins and begin building houses. Ontario winters aren't as kind as British Columbia's, but we're hoping to get the homes done before Christmas."

While the Cabals envisioned a new Salmon Creek here, they were starting with just us. If other kids came into their powers, they'd be moved here, and the necessary facilities—shops, clinic, school—would grow.

"Was it a camp?" Daniel asked.

Sean nodded. "A naturist camp."

"Maya will feel right at home," Corey said from his spot on a wooden lawn chair.

Daniel sputtered a laugh and Sean tried to hide his.

"Naturist, not naturalist," I said. "It means nudist."

Corey leaped up and spun. "You mean old, naked butts sat on these chairs?"

"It's been a few years," Sean said. "There's not nearly as much call for those camps these days, which is why we got this one at a reasonable price. The naturists liked privacy, so it's not easy to get here, as you saw."

So the Nasts bought it. Just like that. I remembered Dr. Inglis saying they'd already been planning a new Salmon Creek, which was probably this place, but still I was stunned by how fast they'd moved. We agree to their terms, and less than a day later we're seeing the genesis of our new town.

"What do you think?" Rafe asked as I wandered toward the woods. "It's not quite like your forest, but see those trees? Deciduous. You know what that means."

I grinned over at him. "Easier climbing. Custom-made for big cats."

He returned my grin and when I looked into his eyes, my heart fluttered. I cared about him. I really did. I'd forgiven him for telling me about Daniel. He'd been under a lot of stress and I'd been too quick to blame him. To judge him. It was a lesson I was learning, but change came slowly.

When I looked at him, grinning at me, amber eyes dancing, my own stress evaporated for a moment and I wanted to grab his hand and run into the woods. And kiss him. Yes, I wanted to kiss him. Whatever I'd felt before, I still felt. And yet . . .

I didn't look over at Daniel, standing by the water's edge. I wouldn't do that to Rafe. But I was still thinking about him. Still confused.

Rafe leaned in and whispered "It's okay," and I was transported back to that horrible moment when he'd fallen from the helicopter, those same words the last ones he said to me. *It's okay.* The same tone. The same wistful look. I wanted to throw my arms around his neck. Instead I stood there, feeling a tear creep down my cheek.

"None of that today," he said, reaching out to wipe it away. "Today we rest. Put everything else aside and rest."

He took my hand and tugged me toward the forest. I ran with him. We'd only gone a few steps when tires crunched on the parking lot gravel and I stopped. Rafe leaned in again and whispered, "I think you'll want to go see who that is."

I did throw my arms around his neck then. I hugged him and gave him a quick kiss, then I raced off toward the parking lot. Corey was running, too. And Hayley. Sam kept her pace to a walk, but only because she was still limping.

Only Daniel hung back. When I stopped, he looked over and mouthed, "Go on."

We ran to the lot. There was one van there, half hidden behind trees. The doors were all closed, the windows dark. A face pressed against the glass. It was Corey's brother, Travis. As Corey raced forward, Travis threw open the door and practically fell out, his mother catching him, making sure he had his balance, then running with him to Corey.

The Morrises piled out next—Mr. and Mrs. Morris and fifteen-year-old Brooke. They ran to meet Hayley. When Mrs. Tillson came out, she stood there a moment, peering toward the building. Sam was beside me, hidden by the trees. She took a tentative step forward. Mrs. Tillson saw her. Her hands flew to her mouth and she staggered forward as Sam broke into a hobbling jog.

I stayed where I was. I could see the dim shadows of my parents behind the van's tinted glass, as if they were looking for me, unwilling to come out until they were sure. I wanted to race to them like the others had, but I couldn't. I'd waited so long and I'd hurt so much and this was so public—too public. I wanted it to be us. Just us.

I turned and found Daniel there.

"Your dad . . ." I said.

"He's not coming. Sean just told me. They couldn't get a message through to warn me sooner. So . . ." Daniel shrugged. "He decided not to come."

"Oh."

I looked up and felt my heart breaking for him. If Mr. Bianchi was around, I'd have wanted to strangle him. Except, I guess, if he was here, I wouldn't have needed to. We'd heard he might not come. That he'd asked whether he had to. They hadn't meant for us to overhear that, but we had. I wished Daniel hadn't. I'd give anything to have spared him that. Just like I'd give anything to spare him this, standing here, watching the other parents and knowing his wasn't coming. Had decided not to come. Had abandoned him.

"I am so sorry," I said, throwing my arms around his neck and hugging him.

"Don't be," he murmured. Then he tugged me back and held me in front of him, gaze meeting mine. "I mean it, Maya. Don't be. I know I shouldn't say this, but I was hoping that's what he'd decide. As much as I want to go back to what we had, I don't want to go back to *that*. My brothers will find out soon. They'll come, at least for a visit."

I nodded. "I just . . ."

"I know." A quick hug. "Now go on. This is what you've been waiting for."

FORTY-NİNE

CREPT AROUND THE parking lot, moving through the trees. I saw my parents get out of the van. They hovered there, holding hands, looking around tentatively, as if they almost didn't dare admit they were expecting to see me. I snuck around the van, ran, and launched myself at my dad's back, nearly toppling him over. Then, still on his back, arms around his neck, I grinned at Mom.

"Hello," I said.

She stared up at me, her eyes filling with tears, her arms going out. I jumped down and into them and hugged her as hard as I could, Dad hugging me from behind, the three of us together again. What I wanted. The thing I'd fought for the hardest in those negotiations. Give me back my family. And I'd won. Whatever else happened, I had this, so I'd won.

We walked around the van to talk privately for a while. It wasn't really much of a talk. More like long periods of silent hugging and crying, interspersed with rapid-fire questions.

When we finished hugging and crying our hearts out, I dried my eyes and said, "There's someone I'd like you to meet." And I took them to Ash.

The next step for settling in was figuring out who'd live where. Obviously I'd stay with my parents, Corey with his mom, Hayley with her family. But what about the rest? The teens were given options pending any changes when the houses were complete. There were some obvious choices and some surprises.

Annie and Rafe were getting their own cabin. Sam decided to stay with Mrs. Tillson, even if she now knew she wasn't really her aunt. Tori opted out of staying with Kit, Simon, and Derek and instead wanted to stick with Lauren and Chloe. Both my parents and Chief Carling were quick to offer Daniel a new home. He considered, then took me aside and said, "I'm going with Corey. I think that's best."

"Okay," I said, heart hammering. "Is something wrong? You've stayed with us plenty of times and you know my parents would love to have you. I would, too."

"Would you really? Me there, day in, day out? It sounds cool, but . . ." He met my gaze. "I want to be your friend, Maya. Not your brother." His eyes bore into mine, as if searching for something. "Is that what you want? A brother?"

"No." The answer came automatically. I didn't want that. Had never thought of him like that. He was right, in ways he didn't even know—if I was still working through what I felt for him, living together wouldn't be the right move.

"I already have a brother," I said, managing a smile. "And he's quite enough to deal with."

Speaking of Ash, that was the next matter of discussion. Antone was staying on-site as our Cabal liaison and he wanted Ash to come live with him. My parents knew who Antone really was, and I'm not sure how they felt about that. Mom said it would be good to have my biological father in my life, but I still think they would have been happier if that meant "visiting every other weekend," not "living a few doors down." Moreno was staying, too—as head of a new security detail. Yes, Chief Carling was no longer enough for us. While she'd be involved, we were now getting full-time guards, though the Cabal promised they were there for our protection, not prison guards. We'd see about that.

As for Ash, though, Antone wasn't his only option. My parents had also offered. I don't think Antone was pleased about that. But Ash was their daughter's brother and they'd be thrilled to have him if that was what he wanted.

Again, I got pulled away for a side discussion.

"What do you want me to do?" Ash asked when we were out of earshot.

"Dumb question," I said. "You're my brother. I want you to be with me."

That seemed to catch him off guard and he scowled, as if I was mocking him.

"What?" I said. "Yes, you're a pain in the ass, but they tell me that's what to expect from a brother." I touched his arm lightly. "Seriously. I know Calvin really wants you and I feel bad for him, losing us, but if you're asking my honest opinion, I'm going to be selfish and say stay with us."

"You think they mean it? Your parents? Or are they just being nice?"

"Oh, they're never nice. You'll figure that out if you come live with us." I paused, sobering as I let him think it over. "You can always change your mind if it doesn't work out. Calvin would be happy to take you at any point."

He met my gaze. "You can change your mind, too. None of that polite Canadian crap. If it doesn't work, say so. I'll respect you more for that than if you grit your teeth and put up with me."

"Understood. So you'll stay with us?"

He nodded. I reached over and hugged him, whether he wanted it or not.

By evening I was feeling a little overwhelmed, and told my parents I was taking a walk. I hadn't gone very far before I heard footsteps behind me and caught a familiar scent. I turned, smiling, to see Rafe.

"Hey, you," I said. "Getting away from it all, too."

"Coming to talk to you, actually."

I kept smiling, hoping he'd smile back, but he just kept walking toward me, face unreadable.

He was going to ask for answers. Had I thought about everything? Did I know what I felt for Daniel? Was I still "with" him or was that over now? It wasn't over. I only had to look at him to know it wasn't over. But how did I say "We're still good," when I couldn't answer those other questions?

"I never did thank you," I said, desperately trying to deflect the coming questions, "for playing decoy back in Salmon Creek."

He shrugged. "It was the right move. Until I start shifting, Daniel's got better defensive powers. And I know, no matter what happens, he'll watch out for you."

I moved toward him. "He's not the only one. I seem to recall you dropped from a helicopter for me."

"True. But the difference?" He closed the gap between us. "Daniel would have *jumped* from the helicopter for you. And you'd jump for him."

"I—"

He put his fingers to my lips. "I'm not asking you to deny it or say you'd do the same for me. You've known him all your life. I'm still the rookie here. Which is why I'm going to make this decision for you." He moved his fingers down. "I think we could have something. Really have something. But I also think, now that you know about Daniel, you're going to wonder, and you can't wonder if you're supposed to be with me. You're not that kind of girl. So I'm ending it."

"No. Please. I—"

His fingers moved back to my lips. "Let me reword that. I'm stepping back. I'm still going to try to convince you I'm the guy you want. But I'm not going to do it by luring you into the woods for a make-out session. No more of that. Not until you've decided. From now on, I'm your friend, same as Daniel." He paused, then lowered his gaze to mine. "And I hope—really hope—that no matter what you decide, I'll keep on being your friend. Whatever happens, I don't want to lose you, Maya."

I put my arms around him. "You won't."

Once again, Rafe had done the right thing. The noble thing. Just as he'd let go of my hands to keep from pulling me out of the helicopter with him. Just like he had given himself up so we could get away.

A few weeks ago, I'd accused Rafe of a complete lack of regard for others, when he'd chased the girls of Salmon Creek to find out who was the skin-walker. I'd been wrong. Big surprise. He wasn't afraid to make the hard choices— even the life-threatening choices—for others. Breaking up with me wasn't exactly on the same scale, but it was still a tough choice, and I wasn't sure I could have made it.

So, if I knew it was right, why did it hurt so much? Because I cared for him. Maybe even loved him. If it was love, why was it so complicated? Shouldn't I just be able to look at Rafe and Daniel, turn to one, and say, "It's you. I want you." Was I being fickle? Or was I being selfish?

I wouldn't be selfish. I wouldn't string them along. Until I got my brain—and my heart—straightened out, it would be as Rafe said. Friendship. With both. And if they both found someone else while I was making up my mind? Well, that was the chance I took. Rafe was right—I couldn't be with one of them if I was still looking at the other, thinking "Maybe . . ."

"Maya?"

Daniel's voice drifted through the trees. I got up quickly from the stump where I'd been sitting and wiped my eyes as he appeared.

"Are you crying?" He stepped closer. "What's wrong?"

"Nothing." I paused. "Yes, something. Rafe and I . . . We ended it. He ended it, I mean." I took a deep breath. "He decided this wasn't really a good time, with everything going on. It's stressing us out and we're arguing and . . . we just need to step back."

"I'm sorry."

He sounded like he meant it. When I looked into his eyes, I saw that he did. Fresh tears welled up and I brushed them away.

"He's right," I said. "It hurts, but he is right. It happened so fast. Too fast. It just . . . got complicated. We need to slow down and get to know each other better."

He nodded. "Okay, well . . . I'd leave you alone, but I suspect you'd rather be distracted."

I managed a smile. "You know me well."

He looked around. "We have a whole forest to explore."

My smile widened a little. "We do."

"I overheard your dad saying they need to stake out a place for your house. Away from the town, since he'll be in charge of the forest again. You guys will pick a place and your mom will design the house again. Kenjii will come tomorrow and . . . Did I hear Fitz is coming, too?"

I nodded. "The people at the wildlife rehab center think that's best. Apparently, although he treats us like his personal servants, he's lonely there, and they don't see any hope of reintroducing him to the wild."

"He's used to you guys. This might not be his forest, but he'll make it his. And so will you."

I looked around. It was nothing like the temperate rain forest at home. It looked different. Smelled different. Even sounded different. But when I closed my eyes, I could feel the draw of it, just like in Salmon Creek. Daniel was right. It would be my forest someday.

"What do you say we start looking for a building spot?" he said.

"Dad will want to pick one."

"Right. And do you really think if you say 'I want my home here,' he'll ignore you? Face it, Maya—you're spoiled."

I smiled.

"So come on," he said, backing up. "Lets go find the perfect spot."

"We aren't supposed to go out of shouting distance."

"So if we did, that would be wrong. Irresponsible. Immature."

"It would."

"Well, I think we've earned it." He started backing up. "Race you?"

"To where?"

His smile broke into a grin, blue eyes glittering in the twilight. "Anywhere."

He turned and ran. I laughed and ran after him.

EPİLOGUE

Eight Months Later

WHEN ASH ENTERED THE kitchen, I noticed. He didn't make a sound as he crept in. Maybe I caught his scent, but I still wasn't good at distinguishing that. I just knew he was there. And I knew why he was there. I continued cutting sandwiches until his hand slipped around me, heading for the pile. A flash of the knife and the hand vanished in a volley of curses.

"Watch the language," I said. "You know house rules. That particular word is not permitted, on pain of laundry duty."

"It's the pain of having my hand sliced open that I'm worried about."

He eased around the island, still eyeing the sandwich pile. I waved the knife at him.

"Wait two minutes and you can make your own. I'll even

leave everything out . . . for you to put away."

"I want half a sandwich. We've got a million kids coming to the party. No one's going to notice one half missing."

"Still working on your math, huh? It's twelve kids, plus Annie."

"Feels like a million," he grumbled as he settled onto a stool.

"Then don't come." I handed him one of the sandwich halves. It was slightly mangled, from a poor cutting job.

"How would that look? Me skipping Daniel's birthday? It's an insult."

"He'd understand."

Ash only grumbled some more. He wasn't big on crowds—and to him, a dozen was a crowd—but he'd go, for Daniel's sake. When he reached for another half sandwich, I threatened him with the knife again.

"No one's going to miss—"

"They aren't for the party. Daniel and I are releasing the rabbits later, and I'm bringing food."

"So it's a picnic?"

"Right," I said, packing the sandwiches into the box.

"Just the two of you?"

I gave him a look. "We're releasing the rabbits."

"With a picnic. For two." He leaned over and lowered his voice. "I've got a couple of beers in my room if you want—"

Dad walked in. Ash sat up fast and took another bite of the sandwich.

"What's up?" Dad said, looking from me to my brother.

"Ash has beer in his room. He was offering me some."

Ash's eyes narrowed.

"What kind?" Dad said as he opened the fridge and took out a pop can. "If it's Labatt's, I'll buy one off you. I'm all out and I'm not going to town until Tuesday."

Ash mumbled under his breath. He hadn't quite figured my parents out yet. If they didn't complain about the beer, he thought they were just accommodating him, treading carefully until they were comfortable enough laying down stricter rules. Which was true, in a way, but only that, when the time came, Dad would insist that if Ash wanted beer in the house, he had to keep it in the fridge, not hide it in his room. And if they caught him with anything stronger before he was nineteen, there would be trouble.

I started cutting up brownies. When Dad reached for one, Ash said, "Watch it. She's quick with that knife. Those are for her picnic with Daniel."

"Daniel?" Dad said.

I put the brownies into the box. "About five-ten? Blond? I think you've met him."

Dad and Ash exchanged a look.

"Been spending a lot of time with Daniel lately," Dad said.

"I've been spending a lot of time with Daniel since I was five. Stop. Now."

"I'm just saying. You know how I feel. Daniel—"

I brandished the knife. "If you say he takes care of me again, I'm going to have the Nasts open a time portal and send you back to the nineteenth century, where I'm sure you'll be much happier."

"What's wrong with saying he takes care of you?" Ash said. "Are we supposed to want you dating a guy who doesn't?"

"Not answering that," I said as I headed for the stairs. "I need to get ready. Ash? Touch the food and I won't take you for a driving lesson tomorrow. Dad? Touch it and I'll make *you* take him for a driving lesson tomorrow."

Dad backed away from the counter. Ash scowled. I laughed and continued upstairs.

Ash, Kenjii, and I walked into our "town." Badger Lake was the name of it, imaginatively named after, well, the lake in the middle, which was really more the size of a large pond, but no one was getting technical.

It was a Saturday, but construction crews were hard at work, as they had been since the frost broke. Everyone who'd come to Badger Lake with us had a house now, and several of the community buildings were done. More houses were going up, for families who'd moved into trailers or were coming soon—town support personnel, mainly. They were Cabal families, those with special skills that the Nasts deemed worth the security risk.

While most of them performed regular town duties— nurses, teachers, security, even a shopkeeper—they all had special skills, too. Skills that would help us grow into . . . well, I'm not sure. Deadly assassins? Super spies? Crack mercenaries? Or just really good, multi-talented Cabal employees. They weren't saying, of course, but from the type of instructors we were getting, it seemed to be leaning toward the first three. We had three experts in fighting skills alone. I was starting fencing lessons Monday, a skill they deemed suitable for a cat's fast reflexes. Somehow I doubted they were training me for the Olympic team.

Did we balk at any of that? No. If they wanted to make us super soldiers, we were happy to take their training. And, someday, use it to get free.

A couple of the new houses were for new kids. One was a Project Genesis subject they'd tracked down, with her mother. Rachelle Rodgers was a fire half-demon that Chloe and the others had known. The other house was for someone from Salmon Creek who seemed to be showing signs of powers. They weren't telling us who it was yet, in case they were wrong. They were in talks to bring in Chloe's father, too. Her aunt had been in contact with him, mostly to stop him from looking for her. Now that we were with the Cabals, there was no need to worry about that, so Chloe had seen him for the first time in six months and they were talking about bringing him to Badger Creek.

Ash, Kenjii, and I walked along the main street, dirt now, though they'd already paved the road into the town. Daniel and Corey lived on the edge of the lake nearest that paved road, next to the main community building, where Chief Carling had her office.

As we walked, someone hailed us. It was Antone. He came around his house, hammer in hand, Moreno trailing behind, beer in hand.

"Ah, Daniel's party," Antone said, waving at the picnic basket and wrapped gift. "Say happy birthday to him for me." He shifted the hammer to his other hand. "So, we're still on for Sunday dinner?"

He looked anxious, as if he expected us to back out. We'd been doing Sunday dinner every other week for six months now, but I think he kept expecting us to make excuses. We didn't. It wasn't an easy relationship. Maybe it never would be. But Ash and I understood how important this was to him, and even if we'd never be a family in the way he'd dreamed of, we'd be something.

I assured him we were coming.

"If it's still warm, we'll eat on my new back deck," he said. "Which I hope to have done . . . if someone exchanges his beer for a hammer."

"Hey, I have two hands," Moreno said. "So, kiddies, are we still on for *our* dysfunctional family moment? Lessons at the range next week?"

"Wednesday after school," I said. "We'll be there."

"What?" Antone looked at Moreno sharply. "Guns? You are not teaching them—"

"They asked. Well, Ash did, and God forbid Miss Maya

should miss out on anything."

"I just want to be ready in case you ever pull a gun on me again," I said as we resumed walking, leaving them to argue it out.

Climbing a cliff side. After a birthday party. Zooming up alongside Rafe as our friends cheered us on. It all felt very familiar. How much changes . . . and how little changes.

When we mentioned we wanted to rebuild our climbing wall, Antone said they'd get a construction team on it right away, recreating exactly the one we had in Salmon Creek. Which was more than a little creepy, really. So we insisted on doing it ourselves. I'd noticed footprints in the soft earth between our building sessions, telling me they were coming out to check our work and make sure it was safe, but they said nothing, just left us to it. Which was, so far, Sean's approach to us in general. He'd supply whatever we needed and he'd happily do things for us, but he seemed even more pleased if we did them ourselves. They wanted independent-minded, self-directed, capable young adults. And that's what we planned to be.

So now I was throwing a seventeenth birthday party for Daniel, just like he'd thrown my sixteenth one for me. And we were in another forest, climbing another wall. Rafe was beside me, for the final race, and as we climbed, it was just like the first time, me looking over, seeing his grin, feeling him there, swearing I could hear the pounding of his heart, spurring me on.

The same. Yet not the same.

Something had changed between us in the last eight months. I'm not sure when it started. There seemed to be no start. Just a gradual . . . change. I looked over and I saw him and his grin made my heart beat faster, but it was a different kind of beating. It was adrenaline and excitement and happiness. Nothing more. Maybe that's all it had ever been. Maybe I'd misinterpreted. Sometimes I wonder if Sam was actually right, and what Rafe and I felt—that crazy whirlwind of emotion—really had been just animal attraction. Like calling to like. The thrill of meeting another skinwalker, hormones twisting it into something else, something my brain mistook for love.

Or maybe it had been something, and with nothing to feed the flames, they just cooled and, eventually, extinguished altogether. We'd decided to back off and be friends, and there'd been a time, in the first few months, when I'd be with him and I'd want more, and I could tell he wanted more. But then those times came more rarely, until I could look at him now and see a friend. Just a friend. And I could tell he felt the same when he looked at me.

How did I feel about that? A little sad, I think. Part of me mourned what we'd had. It had been so new and so raw and so thrilling. And then, when it faded, it left me feeling . . . a little frightened, I guess. How can something that strong disappear so easily? No, not disappear. Mellow. Morph. Change into something good and real, but still, not the same, never again the same. I'm happy with what we have, but I do grieve a little, for what we had.

"Maya! Come on! He's gaining on you!"

I looked up and the sun hit me square in the eye, setting me blinking. Then a head moved in front of it. My spotter. The guy making sure I didn't fall. The guy who would always make sure I didn't fall.

Daniel grinned and it was like that sunlight hit me again, and I faltered.

"Hey! No! Keep going! You've gotta show him who's still top cat around here."

Rafe yelled something up. I didn't quite catch it, just kept staring at Daniel's grin, feeling tiny firecrackers igniting in my gut.

This had changed, too. My feelings for Daniel. Or not so much changed, as slid from the darkness and into the light.

I loved Daniel, and it wasn't a BFF kind of love or a brotherly kind of love. It was real and it was wonderful and it was absolutely terrifying, because the more I accepted it, the more I started to wonder what he really felt for me. Was it anything even approaching my feelings? I had no idea.

When I looked up at Daniel, I didn't feel what I'd felt for Rafe. It wasn't that consuming, blind, must-be-with-him-now need. It was a different need, more grounded, just as intense, stronger even, in its way. I wanted to get to him. Just get up there, feel his arms around me, inhale his scent, hear his laughter, and be with him. I wanted to grab my picnic basket, say good-bye to all our lovely-but-temporarily-inconvenient friends, and take Daniel for myself, someplace quiet, where we could be alone and . . .

And . . . Well, that was the obstacle I hadn't quite overcome yet. While I was happy to just be with him and talk to him and goof around with him, I could think of more I'd like to do. Enough to make me very glad no one could tell I was blushing. I settled for averting my eyes and focusing on the climb.

"Almost there!" Daniel called. "Pick it up a little! You can do it. You already beat Ash."

"My hand slipped," Ash muttered from somewhere above.

I looked up at Daniel again, caught his grin, and felt an extra jolt of adrenaline zip through me. Get to him. Just focus on that. Getting to him. Two more handholds. One more. Now reach—

"We have a winner!" Daniel shouted, and pulled me up for my victory hug.

We had our little party after that. I'd had pizza delivered by one of Moreno's security guys. They're very useful for that sort of thing. The Nasts aren't keen on announcing our presence to the outside world, so we can't order anything in, and the nearest village of any size is a thirty-minute drive down crappy roads, meaning our parents aren't eager to just "run into town" for us. That's what the security guys are for, apparently. It's not like we require much actual security.

We're more isolated than we were in Salmon Creek, but we're dealing with it. Monthly helicopter trips into Toronto help. They give us the Friday off so we can make a three-day weekend of it. They aren't yet letting us go without our parents—and Moreno's men—but we're working on that.

So we had our pizza-and-beer party. Derek and Chloe slipped out as soon as he got his pizza, Chloe saying they'd be back for the cake and gifts. Like Ash, Derek wasn't good with crowds. Or parties. Simon had no such reservations. He'd made himself a part of our group from the start. I had wondered if that would bother Derek, but it didn't seem to. He was happy to relinquish his brother to us and hang out with him other times.

Tori wasn't exactly a core part of our group. Neither was Hayley. They'd become fast friends, and tended to keep to themselves, though they'd join us for group events like this. I'd found a friend in the Genesis group, too. Or we were working in that direction. Chloe was still quiet, a little unsure of herself, most comfortable with Derek and her "tribe," but we hung out together more and more, which was nice. She didn't quite take Serena's place but was filling that void.

Of the Phoenix kids, the one Derek got along best with was Daniel. In him, Daniel had found a good sparring partner. And a plotting partner, too. Derek wasn't just the biggest and strongest in our group. He was also the smartest. Scary, off-the-charts smart. That intimidated Daniel a little at first—he's bright, but he needs to work for his grades. But

Derek wasn't a show-off or a know-it-all, so they got past that and we would hang out together, the two guys, Chloe, and I planning and plotting our future, bouncing ideas off one another.

As for romance among the others, there was little of that so far. Corey and Hayley had taken another run at it, but I think Corey just felt bad about how he'd treated her before and when they tried again, they realized it wasn't really a good match. Ash and Tori snarled and snapped at each other enough that I thought there might be something there . . . if they didn't kill each other first. And Sam? Well, there was no one for Sam, which was one of the problems with our isolation. Even for the heterosexual kids, you couldn't expect everyone to just pair up out of necessity. A bigger dating pool was needed. I'd told Sean that. He understood and was working on ways to get us involved with our larger community, maybe lessons of some sort in a nearby city.

So life in Badger Lake wasn't perfect. But as much as we might hate to admit it, it was good. Really good. It wasn't a forever kind of life, but when I chafed at the boundaries, I had only to look at the kids who'd grown up on the run—Ash, Derek, Simon, Rafe, Annie, and Sam—and see them relaxing and flourishing, and I'd know we'd made the right choice.

"Okay," Daniel said as we picked our way along the boggy path. "You stay right there while I find a place to release these guys. And no peeking. I don't want you knowing where

I'm hiding potential snacks for cougar-time."

"Ha, ha," I said as I hopped over a wet patch. "I keep myself well fed before I shift. Fixing animals up only to hunt them down would be kind of pointless."

"Or diabolically clever. They'd smell you, think food was coming, run over to greet you, and . . . chomp."

I made a face at him. "It's Ash we need to worry about. Ever since he started shifting, I've noticed him gazing longingly at the animal shed. I've told Dad we need pick-proof locks."

Daniel laughed and waved me off the path. We'd left Kenjii behind. Fitz was out here, somewhere, but he knew to keep away when I had prey animals or he'd find himself locked in the shed. We continued to a drier spot, over by the cliff. I found a deadfall and we opened the box. The rabbits—orphaned by a mama-bunny-killing hawk—made their way out. They sniffed around, then zoomed off, some making a break for freedom, some zipping under the deadfall to safety.

"You're welcome!" I called after them, then muttered, "Ingrates."

Daniel laughed. "Good prep for having kids, I bet." He glanced over. "Back to the subject of snacks, did I hear that there's food in that basket?"

"Yes. For those of us who didn't eat five slices of pizza and two pieces of cake."

"I'm in training."

"You're always in training."

"That's why I'm always eating."

We kept talking as we continued on a little, closer to the cliff, looking until we found just the right picnic spot. Then I set out the blanket and we ate. We talked more, mostly about issues we were working on with our powers. Dr. Fellows—Lauren—had been monitoring me over the winter and concluded, after consultation with others doctors, that my "rage attacks" were indeed a form of regression. She'd been treating me, like they'd treated Annie, but I'd asked for fewer drugs and more training to learn to control it. That seemed to be working.

Daniel was dealing with some anger-management side effects of his own. In his case, it wasn't misplaced rage, but a disproportional reaction to a threat. Like a bull seeing red. Sam was experiencing the same side effect, and probably had been for longer. Daniel was dealing with his in the same way I was—some drugs, lots of training, and talk, the two of us hashing it out, what caused it, how we dealt with it. Mutual support and kicks-in-the-ass when needed.

As we finished, we compared schedules for the week. Life was busier now than it had been in Salmon Creek. Busier and more complex. Not just the added complications of dealing with and working on our powers, but personal stuff, too. I had Ash and Antone to factor into my life. Daniel was dealing with his brothers, one of whom wanted to come live in Badger Lake for the summer. He was pre-med and the Cabal had offered him work here, then wanted him to go to medical school in Toronto. Daniel was happy to have his brother around, but not really sure how he felt about him joining a Cabal. He was coming tomorrow for a birthday visit . . . and a recruitment chat. So, yes, complications.

"Is your Wednesday still free?" I asked. "I can slot you in for Wednesday."

A short laugh. "Yeah, it's starting to feel like that, isn't it? Yes, keep Wednesday night free and we'll hang out. Also, don't forget we're driving into the city Saturday. Just the two of us. Not a word of it to the others until we're five kilometers away."

"Trust me, I know better. Mention 'field trip' and we'll be stacking them into your truck like cordwood."

Yes, Daniel had a truck. No, it wasn't his old, falling-apart one. It wasn't brand-new, but the Nasts diligently rewarded responsibility. Daniel could be trusted not to take off at midnight and go partying in the next town, so Daniel got his own truck. Corey had a bicycle.

"Do we have plans for this trip to town?" I asked.

"Lunch and a movie, I thought. Maybe dinner, too, if your folks are okay with you coming back late."

"Oooh, that almost sounds like a date."

Spots of color flushed his cheeks and he forced a laugh. "Yeah."

I reached for a brownie and asked, as nonchalantly as I could manage, "And what if I wanted it to be a date?"

"What?"

I steeled myself, struggling to calm my racing heart, and forced my gaze to his. "What if I wanted it to be a date?"

He tried for a laugh, but didn't quite find it, then rubbed at his mouth, his gaze dipping from mine. He cleared his throat and unfolded his legs, shifting position. Then he looked at me again, his gaze wary, guarded.

"Is that a no?" I said.

"No. I mean . . ." He struggled for the smile again. "I'm just waiting for the punch line. Something about making it a date so I need to pay. Or you expecting flowers. Or . . ." He trailed off.

"There isn't a punch line," I said.

I rose onto my knees and inched over, in front of him. Then I stopped about a foot away.

"No punch line, Daniel," I said. "I'm asking if you'll go out with me."

He didn't answer. Just reached out, his hand sliding between my hair and face, pulling me toward him and . . .

And he kissed me.

His lips touched mine, tentatively, still unsure, and I eased closer, my arms going around his neck. He kissed me for real then, a long kiss that I felt in the bottom of my soul, a click, a connection, some deep part of me saying, "Yes, this is it."

Even when the kiss broke off, it didn't end. It was like coming to the surface for a quick gasp of air, then plunging back down again, finding that sweet spot again, and holding onto it for as long as we could. Finally it tapered off, and we were lying on the picnic blanket, side by side, his hand on my hip, kissing slower now, with more breaks for air, until I said, "We should have done that sooner."

He smiled, a lazy half smile, and he just looked at me for a moment, our gazes locked, lying there in drowsy happiness, before he said, "I think now's just fine." And he kissed me again, slower and softer now, as we rested there, eyes half closed.

"So, about Saturday, did you ask me?" he said after a minute. "Because I'm pretty sure that means you're paying."

"Nope. You were imagining it. Considering how you eat, the meal bill is all yours. But I will spring for the movie. And bring you flowers."

He chuckled. "Will you?"

"Yep, a dozen pink roses, which you'll have to carry all night or risk offending me."

"And what happens if I offend you?"

"You don't get any more of this."

I leaned in and kissed him again. And we stayed out there, on the blanket, as the sun fell, talking and kissing, mostly, just being together. We had a long road ahead of us, and I knew it wasn't going to be easy. But I had everything I wanted—everything I needed—and I'd get through it just fine. We all would.

ACKNOWLEDGMENTS

FIRST, A HUGE THANK-YOU to my agent, Sarah Heller, for taking my dream of writing YA and making it a reality. And an equally huge thanks to the editors who took a chance on this new direction of mine—Rosemary Brosnan at HarperCollins US, Antonia Hodgson of Atom UK, and Anne Collins and Kristin Cochrane at Doubleday Canada.

A special thanks goes out to my beta readers for this series. Stephanie Drum, Terri Giesbrecht, Matt Sievers, Nicole Tom, and Sharon Young all read early copies of most of the books and helped keep me from making some humiliating mistakes. Thanks, guys!

ABOUT THE AUTHOR

Kelley Armstrong lives in rural Ontario, Canada, with her husband, three children and far too many pets. She is the author of the bestselling Women of the Otherworld series, the highly acclaimed Darkest Powers young adult series and two adventure novels about a hit woman, *Exit Strategy* and *Made to be Broken*. For further information visit www.kelleyarmstrong.com and www.darkestpowers.com